THE REST IS DEATH

James Oswald

WILDFIRE

First published in 2025 by Wildfire
An imprint of Headline Publishing Group Limited

1

Cataloguing in Publication Data is available from the British Library

Hardback ISBN 978 1 4722 9888 1
Trade Paperback ISBN 978 1 4722 9889 8

Typeset in 12.76/16.24pt Aldine401 BT by Jouve (UK), Milton Keynes

Printed and bound in Great Britain by Clays Ltd, Elcograf S.p.A.

Headline's policy is to use papers that are natural, renewable and recyclable
products and made from wood grown in well-managed forests and other
controlled sources. The logging and manufacturing processes are expected
to conform to the environmental regulations of the country of origin.

HEADLINE PUBLISHING GROUP
An Hachette UK Company
Carmelite House
50 Victoria Embankment
London EC4Y 0DZ

The authorised representative in the EEA is Hachette Ireland,
8 Castlecourt Centre, Dublin 15, D15 XTP3, Ireland (email: info@hbgi.ie)

www.headline.co.uk
www.hachette.co.uk

THE REST IS DEATH

For the Highland coos, who stop me
getting ideas above my station.

1

They are fools, all of them.

She stands at the edge of the trees, looks out across the rough ground of the clearing. It's been a hard trail to get here; these lands are not easy for a woman travelling alone, however well she might conceal herself. It was a necessary journey though, to see this act completed, this sorrowful chapter of history brought to a close.

And the fools are going to ruin it all.

Is it her fault, for assuming they understood what they were dealing with? Perhaps, although this isn't her domain and shouldn't be her problem.

They have prepared a tomb, that is their first mistake. Far from the world of men, it is highly unlikely anyone will ever stumble upon it. No doubt in years to come these deep forests will earn a reputation for haunting. People will enter and never be seen again. Superstitious folk will shun the darkness under the trees and they will be wise to do so. For most that might even be enough.

She watches the procession, figures swathed in heavy cloaks against the chill. At their head, the high priest carries his prize like it's the word of God himself. A small wooden box, even at her safe distance she can see the intricate inlays that have gone into its construction. She can feel the power they represent too, a shield around the dark malevolence that is trapped within. It's a fine piece of work, she can't fault them that. She would have constructed something similar, were it her task to constrain this evil. But she would not do with it what they are now doing.

She doesn't need to enter the tomb to know what it will look like inside. A cavern, deep in the earth, its walls carved with warding sigils, a massive guardian statue at each of the four points of power. The floor will be paved with stones brought from far away. Perhaps India, or Thule to the north. No easy connection to the land all around. They will place the box at the perfect centre, upon an altar cut from granite, and weigh it down with heavy silver chains. They will chant binding spells as they do this, layer upon layer as they retreat from what they believe will be the final resting place of the creature they all fear.

It won't be enough.

An hour passes, two, and finally the procession leaves the tomb. Four fewer now than went in, so they have performed that needless act as well. Poor souls, their sacrifice might be noble but it is unnecessary, and quite likely in vain.

She feels the tension building in the air, a prickling on the skin of her face and a deep, uncomfortable ache in her bones. The high priest and his retinue stand before the entrance to the tomb, and at a command, the rest of the party spread out across the clearing. She shrinks back into the trees, unwilling to witness what will come next, although she knows that she must. She can scarce believe they are doing this one, final, foolish act. But then, they have done everything else wrong, so why not this?

The blast is not an explosion as men would understand it. The earth doesn't move, and neither is the lid blown off the tomb they have so meticulously prepared. Instead, the shock moves through the gathered priests and workers like a swift pestilence. One by one they gasp their last, then crumple to the ground where they stood. Crashing in the branches nearby, the bodies of birds fall lifeless from the sky. She is not sure, huddled and shielded from the blast as only she knows how, but it's possible the circle of death spreads for a mile from this point. Such tragedy, such waste.

The bodies lie dead where they fell as she picks a path towards the centre and the tomb. It is sealed shut, beyond even her power to open. Well, that is for the good, but how long will such protections last, even paid for with so much life? A few centuries perhaps. Not long enough for the evil trapped inside to finally wither and die.

With a shrug, she pulls her coat tighter, looks up at a sky that promises snow. Nothing to do but make the long, perilous journey home now, and hope no one strays upon this place for many lifetimes yet.

2

A light dusting of what looked like snow clung to the very tops of the Pentland Hills as Detective Chief Inspector Tony McLean crossed the bridge over the bypass at Fairmilehead, southward bound. No obvious sign of activity at the Hillend artificial ski slope, but that could have had as much to do with the early hour as inclement weather. And weren't skiers supposed to like snow, anyway?

Beside him in the driver's seat, Detective Sergeant Jay Stringer concentrated on the traffic. How long had he been working with Stringer now? Years, for sure. Certainly long enough to know that the detective sergeant was anxious about something. Fair enough. He wasn't exactly overjoyed with this assignment either.

'Technology park, right?' he asked, as much to engage the detective sergeant as through any need to know.

'Aye, sir. Drake Biotech.' Stringer reached for the satnav screen and tapped at it once. 'Think it's away past the big house.'

'I know the place. New lab they're building, right?' McLean reached for the grab handle above the door as they turned in through the old estate gates, past the oddly phallic stone carving that was supposed to represent a pine tree or something. It had been years now since the rolling parkland had been earmarked as a suitable site for pharmaceutical and biotech start-ups. Something to do with Edinburgh University spinning out research into profitable companies. Or judging by the prominent 'For Let' and 'Office/Lab Space Available' signs, maybe not so profitable. Like so much else these days, a victim of choices made by politicians many hundreds of miles away.

Drake Biotech bucked the trend, clearly. Still very much under construction, its frontage at least had been completed. A squat two-storey structure of smoked glass and black steel, it sat in the landscape like some crashed alien spaceship, surrounded by cranes and heavy machinery, Portakabins and piles of building materials. To the front, neatly landscaped banks and escarpments hid the full extent of the works from view, the architect clearly at pains not to spoil the rolling parkland that surrounded the nearby mansion house.

The parking area had space for only a dozen cars, most of which appeared to be taken up by forensics vans. Stringer parked at the far end, on a patch of bare earth that was going to make a mess of shoes and trousers.

'Who's CSM?' McLean asked as he hauled himself out of the car and stretched. Something in his spine made a pop audible even over the noise of construction work, but he managed to keep his reaction to a grimace.

'Not sure. Guess there'll be someone inside, right?' Stringer pointed to the entrance, the two of them reflected in the dark glass. Someone could be looking out at them right now and they'd not know. As if on cue, the doors slid open and a white-boiler-suited forensic technician came out, closely followed by a grey-haired man. As she pulled down her face mask and tugged away the hood, McLean recognised Amanda Parsons, senior forensic technician. The man he didn't recognise, although his ill-fitting suit, thinning grey hair like an explosion in a candy-floss factory and general air of scarcely contained anger gave McLean a hint.

'Ah, Tony. You're here. Good. I wonder if you could have a word with—' Manda Parsons was about to introduce him, but the grey-haired man interrupted.

'Are you the one in charge?' he asked in a voice dripping with sarcasm.

'Detective Chief Inspector McLean. And no, the crime scene manager is in charge. You are . . .?'

From the sneer on the man's lips, McLean figured he wouldn't have been impressed if the chief superintendent herself had turned up to supervise the investigation.

'Magnus Caine,' he said. 'Professor Magnus Caine. I run all of Drake Biotech's advanced research, and there's very expensive and sensitive equipment in these labs. Commercially sensitive information.'

McLean looked from the professor to the cranes and scaffolding behind the shiny facade. 'I wasn't aware this facility was up and running,' he said.

'It isn't. Not fully. But we're installing state-of-the-art machinery. This isn't off-the-shelf stuff you can just bolt to a wall and plug in. It has to be assembled by skilled technicians, calibrated and double-checked. Bad enough the bloody animal rights lot making a mess of it, but these . . .' He paused as if searching for words, waved one hand at Parsons in the manner of dismissing a tardy servant. '. . . people are almost worse. Poking their noses in everywhere, taking photographs of everything. It's . . .'

The irate little man gave up with a slump of the shoulders. McLean tried not to let his own irritation colour his impression of the professor. No doubt he was under stress, as they all were.

'Professor Caine. I can assure you that the forensic team know their way around a laboratory better than most. They're professionals. You've no need to worry about your equipment. Any photographs taken will be used only for the investigation. We're here because you asked us to investigate a break-in. I assumed burglary, but you said something about animal rights? Is this just vandalism we're looking at here?'

The professor stared at him with a strange expression on his face, holding his gaze for just a little longer than was both comfortable and polite. It might have worked on a boorish undergrad, or even a bolshy PhD student, but McLean had faced worse across the table in many an interview room. Eventually the man looked away, motioned towards the now-closed doors.

'Why don't you come inside and I'll tell you everything. It's been a difficult morning for all of us, so my apologies if I'm a little abrupt. It doesn't help that Nathaniel is flying in this afternoon either. Could do without him breathing down my neck all the time.'

'Nathaniel?'

'Drake. As in Drake Biotech. He's the one pays for all this.'

'Ah. Him.' McLean knew of the man, it was impossible not to. Drake was the reason a detective chief inspector had been assigned what really should have been a job for a uniform sergeant. He turned his attention to Manda Parsons, still standing beside him.

'How are you getting on in there?'

'Done most of what we can, given the place is pretty much still a building site. The fingerprint team's finished, although they'll need to get comparables from everyone with access to the lab before we can do much analysis on that. There's some interesting boot prints I need to deal with, and then they can get on with cleaning up the mess.' Parsons shrugged. 'Half an hour, maybe. An hour?'

'OK. Let me know when you're finished. Jay can go talk to the security team.' He turned back to Professor Caine. 'And maybe you can bring me up to speed on what you do here and what happened last night.'

'Really not sure what they thought they'd achieve, Inspector. We're not even operational here yet. And even if we were, there'd be no animal experiments.'

McLean's initial dislike of Professor Caine had not eased in the

7

half-hour or so he'd been following the man around the building site. It wasn't that he was arrogant and clearly disdainful of anyone he considered less than his intellectual equal, although there was plenty of that about the man. It wasn't even that he insisted on calling McLean 'Inspector' despite knowing that his full title was detective chief inspector. He'd been insulted in more creative ways by much better men before, and the full handle was an unwieldy mouthful at the best of times. No, the thing that most irritated McLean about the professor was that the man was lying to him.

'What sort of research is it that you do here then?' he asked. He knew both that Caine would not tell him the details, and that whatever the professor did say, he'd probably understand at best half. But the whole point of being given this tour of the unfinished facility and irritated by the man was so that the forensic team could get on with their work undisturbed. Sometimes you just had to take one for the team.

'Well now, where to start? At the moment, we don't do any research. Building site, remember? But when we're up and running? Well, perhaps we could have a coffee and I'll try to explain it all.'

The professor used his keycard to swipe open a security door at the end of the bare corridor along which they had been walking. At his gesture, McLean stepped through into another world. A vast, round room, it was much warmer than the work in progress outside, quite clearly finished and ready for occupation. The domed ceiling was entirely made of glass, triangular panes arranged into a geodesic pattern that would have made Buckminster Fuller weep. A wide space ran the full circumference of the room, five doors identical to the one he and Caine had come through at regular intervals along it. These presumably led to the other wings of the complex still under construction, but it was the space in the middle that took McLean's breath away.

They were at ground level where they stood, but the room dropped away from them, its centre dominated by a large pond. Steps led down to it, repeated for each of the five other doors, and the gaps between them had been planted with what looked like a jungle. A narrow arched bridge, like something from a Japanese etching, spanned the centre of the pond, and gave access to an area on the far side with small cafe tables and chairs. Beyond that, built into a section of the wall, stood an array of shiny modern vending machines.

As they crossed the bridge, McLean looked down to see fat carp swaying against an invisible current. The sound of splashing water filled the space and lent the air a humid feel.

'This is a bit posh for a research lab, isn't it?' he asked as Caine gestured towards a table and chairs. The professor didn't answer, but went over to the vending machines and swiped at a pad with his pass again. Buttons pressed and gurgling sounds done with, he returned bearing two mugs.

'It's only a machine, but it does make damn fine coffee.' Caine handed one of the mugs to McLean, then took a seat. 'Once the place is fully up and running, there'll be a staffed canteen here. Doesn't make sense while it's still mostly a building site though.'

McLean took a sip, had to agree that it was indeed damn fine coffee. The mug bore the Drake Biotech logo around its side, and had a heft to it that suggested few expenses had been spared in kitting everything out. It was all very impressive, he had to admit, but he still had little idea as to what it was all for.

'You asked me what it was we did here,' Caine said, as if reading his thoughts. 'Well, Inspector. At the moment we don't do much at all, as you can see. But when this place is finished, our research will be the very stuff of life itself.'

McLean took another sip of his coffee. 'Still none the wiser.'

Caine sighed as if he were a lecturer dealing with a particularly slow student, then appeared to remember where he was and to whom he was talking. 'How would you like to live to a hundred and fifty? Two hundred? More, even.'

McLean leaned back in his seat, winced a little at the pain that shot through his hip. The downside of a room dominated by an indoor carp pond was the dampness of the air, even if it was pleasantly warm.

'Sounds miserable to me. Endless decades in a wheelchair, watching daytime television and waiting for the next meal.'

The smile Caine gave him was almost identical to an old lecturer McLean recalled from his university days. That man had been insufferable too.

'But what if you could live those years in your prime, eh? No aches and pains, no debilitating disease. Fit and strong and young. For ever.'

That sounded even worse, but McLean kept it to himself. Best to let the professor get on with it. That had been the only way to deal with his old lecturer, too.

'What we will be doing here at Drake Biotech is re-engineering human DNA. We can already extend life significantly, but like you say, what's the point? Length of life is nothing if quality of life is diminished. So we're addressing both. Our therapies have proved successful in reversing senescence in several key biomarkers already. We can, genuinely, turn back time. Make people younger.'

McLean took another sip of his coffee and suppressed the urge to glance at his watch.

'And you can do that without carrying out experiments on animals?'

Caine shook his head, a look of disappointment on his features.

'Animal studies are so twentieth-century, Inspector. They're a very poor analogue for the human system anyway, but we've moved past the need for them. We're not so far from Roslin here, you know? The birthplace of Dolly the Sheep, if "birthplace" is even the right term.'

'She was born, though. She was cloned, but the embryo was then implanted in a ewe.'

'True, true. But my point is, that opened the door on cloning. Cell line research, sample cultures. We don't need to test on an animal when we can use cloned human flesh.'

There was something deeply unsettling about the way the professor said 'flesh'. His enthusiasm for his work was clearly evident, but he seemed to almost shudder at that one word.

'So. If you're not using animal testing, then why would a bunch of animal rights activists break into your lab? What were they hoping to find?'

The professor shrugged. 'Perhaps they were merely misinformed. These people aren't exactly operating from a full deck, if you get my meaning. They're cultists, really. Ideologues. And Luddites, of course. Anything to stop the march of progress, no matter how damaging to society as a whole that might be.'

McLean opened his mouth to explain that the Luddites hadn't been particularly anti-progress so much as anti technology being used to diminish the value of their work and force them into poverty. It was probably for the best that the door on the far side of the room clicked open at that moment, distracting them both. One of the security guards entered, followed by DS Stringer, whose reaction to the great glasshouse was much the same as McLean's had been when he'd first seen it.

'That's forensics done in the lab, sir,' the detective sergeant said once he'd arrived at their table. McLean nodded his acknowledgement, but not before he noticed a scowl flit across the professor's face as he stared at the security guard. As if he felt that he alone should be able to grant access to this sanctuary.

'Thanks, Jay. I'd best go have a look for myself then.' He took a last swig from his mug, savouring the taste. 'I'm sure the professor here will get you a coffee if you ask nicely.'

3

A part from the obvious vandalism, the lab looked like a thousand and one others, at least to McLean's eyes. A wide and long room, it had smoked-glass windows along one wall, the bulk of the light from them obscured by expensive-looking machines arranged along a workbench. Each corner housed a fume cupboard far more sophisticated than the ones he remembered from chemistry practicals at school, and a series of heavy-duty industrial fridge units hummed gently to themselves, green LEDs indicating all was well in their world. More benches were spaced regularly across the centre with wide gaps to avoid research scientists bumping into each other. Empty of people, it still managed to look cluttered and slightly chaotic, not helped by the dayglo-orange graffiti sprayed everywhere. A few hackneyed slogans like 'Stop Killing Animals' and 'Meat Is Murder' alongside various logos that McLean only half recognised.

'I'm surprised you've got a lab up and running at all,' he said. 'What with the rest of the site being still under construction. Can't be easy running controlled experiments in these conditions.'

'We don't. This lab's the first to be fitted out, but nobody's done any research in here yet.' Professor Caine shoved irritable hands into his pockets, no doubt still smarting at being asked to fetch coffee for a mere detective sergeant. Luckily Stringer had declined and they had all come back to the lab now vacated by forensics.

'This whole complex was supposed to be finished a year ago,' he continued. 'But the pandemic threw a spanner in the works. We're at least eighteen months behind schedule. Place was going to be opened by the Queen, you know. Don't know if the King will do us the honour yet. Way things are going, I don't even know which king.'

It was probably meant as a joke, but humour was something Professor Caine hadn't mastered. Along with normal human interaction, as far as McLean could tell.

'We know how they got in?' he asked, pitching the question more at the detective sergeant than the professor.

'Looks like the fire escape across the corridor. Somehow managed to bypass the security and open it from the outside.' DS Stringer stood at the propped-open double doors that gave access to the lab from a wide, airy corridor. Almost directly opposite, a fire escape door was liberally peppered with fingerprint powder.

'And this was the only room they went into?' McLean asked.

'Apparently so. There's not much in any of the others, mind. This should have been locked too, but when the security guards arrived after the alarm went off it was open. They almost caught one of them, and he was seen coming out of here.'

McLean stepped further into the room, taking in as much as he could. It was the sort of place where it would be hard to tell if anything had been moved unless it was lying broken on the floor.

'What about the researchers who work here? Have they been allowed back in yet?'

'No one's working here yet,' Stringer said. 'There's a few technicians and the installation crew for the machinery. The professor's getting me a list of names. Said it won't be a long one.'

McLean looked back to the open door, where Professor Caine

stood with his back to them both. He held one hand to an ear, busy talking on his phone. Probably bringing his boss up to speed.

'And the security guards. You've spoken to them?'

'Just the one so far. He was on the front security station watching the monitors. Didn't see anything until the one guy came out of the lab and walked straight for the front door. If they'd gone back the way they came, chances are nobody would've known until, well . . .'

McLean pinched the bridge of his nose in the hope that it might make the pressure building in his head go away. It never worked.

'So what you're saying is there was one security guard on duty, guarding a building site where no actual research is taking place. A bunch of animal rights activists broke in through a fire escape that should have been wired to an alarm but wasn't, and nobody noticed anything until one of them tried to walk out the front door?'

'Succeeded too. Anyone coming in needs their own security pass or someone inside to open the door for them, but going out it just automatically opens. By the time the guard realised what was going on, the man had legged it.'

'Why go out the front door though? Presumably they'd found a way to override the alarm on the fire door, so why not go back that way?'

Stringer shrugged, which more or less summed up how McLean felt about the whole thing. He didn't really want to be here, knew the whole investigation was politically motivated. There was no other reason it would have been assigned to him and not just the detective sergeant on his own. Even a uniform sergeant would have been overkill, really.

'Are we nearly done here, Inspector? Only, I'd like to start auditing what's been damaged. We'd hoped to start using this lab in the next couple of weeks. This could set us back months now.'

McLean considered the lab. There really wasn't much he could glean from the place, no obvious sign of theft, just a bit of mindless vandalism. That set his internal alarms ringing, but only half-heartedly. This was strange, no doubt, but hardly a major incident. He turned slowly on the spot, taking it all in one last time, already writing the dismissive report in his head. And that was when he noticed the door set into the wall opposite the entrance. Understandable that he might have missed it before, it sat flush with the wall, sandwiched between two ceiling-height cabinets. The benches obscured it further, so that it looked like somebody's workspace. Only the warning sticker gave it away, that and the small security keypad beside it that McLean could see now that he was looking. He could ignore it, turn his back, head to the station and write the whole thing off as a wasted morning. But there was that niggling sense of something bigger going on here. A puzzle he'd not be able to put aside unless he was sure he'd been thorough.

'What's through there?' He pointed a finger.

Professor Caine paused a moment too long before answering. 'Through there?' His nonchalance was well acted, but false all the same. 'Nothing at the moment. It's a temperature-controlled storeroom. Nothing more.'

'Can we have a look?' McLean studied the professor's face as he asked, and sure enough, there was a twitch. The lightest drop of the shoulders in disappointment that might simply have been because he wanted the police out of his thinning hair, or it might have been something else entirely. It was swiftly suppressed, replaced by that bland smile.

'Of course. Let me open it for you.'

The door slid open onto almost utter blackness, only the light from behind him painting an angular shape on a smooth, grey floor. Before McLean could say anything, the professor tapped at the same control pad he had used to open it, and overhead LED spotlamps popped into life. They cast a blue-white glow over a small, square room, empty save for a stainless-steel trolley table in the middle.

'We'll store samples in here when the lab is properly up and running. It's temperature and humidity controlled, hence the lock and seal on the door.'

McLean ignored the professor and took a step inside. The air changed as if crossing that threshold were more than a simple movement between rooms. It felt older somehow, stagnant like a long-abandoned basement. Like a dungeon. There was a smell to the place he couldn't immediately identify until his arm started to ache. Reflexively, he reached up and massaged the muscles around the bone that had broken. Recalled how that had happened and what had been done to him afterwards, or at least what little he remembered. They had been going to bury him alive, cast into a pit deep below the Christian burials of the Leith Parish Kirkyard.

It was that same scent which filled his nostrils now. Or not exactly that scent, more the memory of how it had felt. Earthy, with just a hint of decay in the mix. A corruption of the flesh.

'As you can see, there's nothing in here yet. No evidence to suggest they got past the door. It's pretty secure.'

McLean turned to face Caine, unsure exactly how he knew that the man was lying or indeed what he was lying about. Of one thing he was certain though, this lab had been in use before it was broken into, whether the rest of the complex was a building site or not. Perhaps it wasn't licensed for use yet, and that could prove an embarrassment should it come out. And yet it wasn't just that. Had they been doing something here that wasn't strictly legal? If so, he could understand why they'd want to keep it from the police, but then why call them in at all? Who had actually called it in, and how had it ended up being assigned to him?

'Have you any idea why someone would want to break into your lab, Professor?' McLean noticed that the man hadn't joined him in the room, still stood in the doorway as if he were some kind of vampire awaiting an invitation. There was something cadaverous about the man, now McLean thought about it. His flesh clung tightly to his bones in a manner that suggested disease as much as lack of nutrition.

'Who knows what goes through the minds of these people, Inspector? Like I said before, they probably thought we were conducting animal experiments. Or it might just have been a protest against Mr Drake. He's not universally loved, I'll be the first to admit it. Visionary men seldom are.'

McLean nodded his head as if agreeing, although he was barely listening to the professor now. He paced slowly around the room, keeping close to the wall, fingers brushing against the smooth painted surface. There were no windows, no shelves, not even power sockets low down. The ceiling lights were sealed units, the only break in the wall a vent at the far end. Approaching the steel table, he crouched down to inspect the floor underneath it, expecting to find a drainage grate, but it was only smooth polished concrete, curved up at the edges to meet the walls.

'You think him a visionary?' he said as he reached down and ran fingertips over the area where the table legs met the floor. They came away almost clean, but in the harsh white light he could just make out a few grains of dark grit on his skin. When he sniffed, that earthy tone was there again, fleeting and ephemeral.

'He wants to defy death, Inspector. I'd call that visionary, wouldn't you?'

'That depends.' McLean straightened up, suppressing the groan that usually accompanied the movement these days. He brushed the dirt off on his trouser leg as he walked back to the open door. The professor had still not entered. 'If he only wants to defy it himself, then that's more megalomaniacal than visionary, I'd say.'

A flicker of something marred Caine's face for a moment, swiftly suppressed into a bland smile. 'Drake Biotech is developing therapies for the masses, Inspector. It's not Nathaniel Drake's personal plaything. If it were, I certainly wouldn't be heading up his research efforts.'

Looking past the professor at the state-of-the-art lab facilities, through the smoked glass window to the parkland beyond, McLean wasn't so sure. The money that paid for this kind of facility could buy off a lot of ethical objections too. He stepped out of the room and the door swished closed behind him without any obvious intervention from anyone in the lab. Something in the lock whirred as it sealed once more.

'I'm glad to hear it.'

'Is there anything else you'd like to see?' Caine asked. He didn't quite lead McLean back towards the lab entrance, but he telegraphed that desire so strongly it was hard to ignore.

'No, I think we're done here. You can start cleaning up. I'd appreciate an update on anything you find missing or interfered with. It would help us to build a better picture of why someone might want to break in.'

'I'll have a report sent to you as soon as we've done a full audit.' The professor seemed to relax with each step away from the secure storage room, each step closer to getting the policeman out of his lab.

'DS Stringer will liaise with your security team. We've people going over the CCTV footage from the whole science park, too. Should help us build up a picture of where they came from and hopefully where they went. We'll do our best to catch them, Professor.'

Caine smiled again. 'Thank you, Inspector. Be sure I'll tell Mr Drake how helpful you've been.'

McLean left the man at the front door, crossed the short distance to the pool car and the waiting detective sergeant. A brief glance back at the frontage of the building as he unlocked the door and climbed in only hardened his suspicion that there was more going on here than met the eye. A break-in by some animal rights activists would have been nice and simple to deal with. Somehow he knew he wasn't going to be so lucky this time.

4

Detective Inspector Janie Harrison sat at her desk in the tiny office they'd given her at the back of the station and stared at the blur of lines on her computer screen. She knew if she shifted her focus one way or the other she'd either be able to see the over-time figures she was meant to be processing, or the dirty golden sandstone of the wall a few metres beyond the grimy window. And yet either movement was too much effort right now.

It had seemed a good idea at the time, accepting the promotion that had been thrust upon her. The exams had been easy enough, and there was no denying the pay rise helped. Having an office of her own that she could retreat to when the station grew busy was an added bonus, even if this tiny room hardly warranted so grand a title. It had been Inspector McLean's office when he'd first moved out of the CID room too, a few words in his cursive script still half readable on the whiteboard where it hadn't been cleaned properly in years. There were boxes of old case files piled under the win-dowsill, but most of them were from a generation earlier even than McLean. Not so much an office as an oubliette. A place things went to be forgotten.

With an almost inaudible sigh, she pulled her wandering thoughts back into line and reached for the next sheet on the never-dwindling pile. At the same moment she placed it in front of her keyboard, the phone on the other side of her computer gave out a tinny electronic chirp. Reception desk or working through the fiction that was Constable Petrie's overtime claim? It wasn't a hard decision.

'DS—DI Harrison.' Janie kicked herself both for the stupid error she still kept on making even months since it had been changed on her warrant card, and for sounding like a secretary in a bad eighties sitcom.

'Hey Janie.' Police Sergeant Don Gatford's gruff voice came over the handset. How the old man hadn't retired yet was anyone's guess, but he did a good job manning the front desk.

'What's up, Don? Not just a social call, I take it.'

'Aye, no. I've a young lass here says she knows you and would like a word. If you're no' busy.'

'Young lass?' Janie fought back the retort she wanted to use now that she was the sergeant's senior officer. 'Does she have a name?'

A moment's rasping noise as the sergeant put his hand over the receiver at his end. Janie couldn't be sure why, since there was no reason he would have called up to her without asking the name of the 'young lass' first.

'Shauna Lennox. Says she was at school with you.'

Janie scrunched up her face trying to remember the name, even though there was nobody else in her tiny office to see. It rang a bell, but only very quietly. There'd been a Bobby Lennox in the year above her, she remembered. Brute of a fellow who hit on all her friends but somehow seemed to be scared of Janie. No great loss, but he'd not been a Shauna. People change though. Maybe he'd become a she.

'Did she say what it was about?' she began to ask, then stopped herself. On her desk was a pile of overtime forms that wouldn't get any smaller but also didn't need to be done right away. Any excuse was a good one. 'Put her in interview room one, can you, Don? I'll be down in five minutes.'

It was more like ten minutes before Janie pushed open the door to interview room one and stepped inside. Any thought that this might have been a transformed Bobby Lennox vanished when the woman looked up from where she sat at the chipped Formica table. She was plain, there was no better way of describing her. Overlarge glasses hid most of her face, along with a curtain of dark hair that came down to her shoulders. She wore a neat business suit of the kind you might see on a bank teller if there were any branches left open these days, and she held herself in an almost hunched position, as if cowed by life. Or maybe it was just being in an interview room in a police station, although at least this one had a window and comfortable furniture.

'Ms Lennox?' Janie held out a hand. The woman's every movement was timid as she stood up, took the hand in a feeble grip for the shortest possible time.

'Thank you. For seeing me. You must be very busy.' Her accent was familiar at least. Janie pictured the stack of overtime sheets waiting in her office upstairs and shook her head.

'Sure I can spare a few minutes for someone from the old school.' She indicated the seat that Lennox had been sitting in and the woman sat down again.

'You don't remember me, do you.' It was a statement, not a question.

'It's been a while since I left, and I've no' kept up with many of the folk I knew back then.' Janie pulled out another chair and sat down. 'You'd be a couple of years below me though, wouldn't you?'

That brought the beginnings of a smile to Lennox's face. 'Aye, that's right. You'll ken Bobby, right enough. He's my half-brother.'

Janie nodded, still unsure if she remembered. 'This about him then? He in some kind of trouble?'

'Bobby? No.' Lennox looked almost terrified for a moment. 'Least, I don't think so. I've no' spoken to him in a while now. He's away over in Glasgow working for the cooncil.'

'So what is it about then?' Janie started to look at her watch, stopped herself before Lennox noticed. She'd give the woman time enough to settle. There had to be a good reason why she would make the effort to track down a police officer she had only a tenuous link to.

'I . . . Well. It's a wee bit complicated, see? There's this man I know. He's gone missing. I think he might be in trouble.'

'OK.' Janie leaned back in her seat, took her notebook from her pocket and opened it up on the table in front of her. This was beginning to sound like something a uniform constable should be dealing with, but she was here now. 'Why don't we start at the beginning. This man, what's his name?'

A short pause, and Janie could almost hear the gulp before Lennox spoke again. 'Mihailovic. Vaclav Mihailovic. You want me to spell that?'

Janie nodded, then wrote out the name in capital letters as Lennox enunciated each one with the clear diction of a seasoned call centre operative.

'Everyone just calls him Vash. Makes things easier, aye?'

'Not from Broxburn though, with a name like that.'

Lennox let out a little nervous laugh. 'No, no. He's Serbian. Been in Edinburgh about ten years now working on building sites and stuff.'

'And how do you know him?'

'Is that . . .?' Lennox pulled in on herself again for a moment, then rallied. 'I guess he's my boyfriend? I mean, that sounds a bit weird when you reach our age, aye? But it's no' like we live together or anything. Just hook up when we're feeling lonely, right?'

'But you've not seen him in a while?'

'Aye, no. Couple of months since we last . . . Well. But we chat on the phone when we can. Last time would've been a couple of weeks back? Maybe three? I can . . .' Lennox shoved a hand in her pocket and pulled out her phone, swiped the screen a few times. 'Aye, I spoke to him end of last month an' he said he'd a job on and he'd no' be able to phone for a while. But there'd be some extra money coming in, like. He texted me week past to say he was back and he'd gie me a call so's we could meet up, but then nuthin'. I called him a couple of times since then but it's just voicemail, an' he's no' answering texts either.'

'Is that unlike him?'

Lennox waved her head from side to side. 'Aye an' no. He can be moody sometimes, ken? But it wasn't like we argued or anything. An' I went round his place too, but nobody'd seen him for days. Least, that's what they told me.'

'You think they might have been lying? Covering up for him?'

'I don't know. Can't think why, only I got that vibe, ken? An' it was the same at his work. He never told anyone he wasn't showing up, just didnae. An' that's no' like him.'

Janie looked down at the page, concerned to find she'd started taking notes, questions to follow up after the interview, even though this was something that she really should be passing on to missing persons. Well below a detective inspector's grade, that was for sure. On the other hand, an hour spent making a few enquiries would be more satisfying than an hour spent wading through the overtime sheets. Or she could find one of the detective sergeants and palm it off on them. But then they hadn't been at school with Shauna Lennox, even if her big brother – half-brother – had been a dick.

'OK. I'll take all the details you can give me, have a look into it. But I can't promise anything. A missing person's hardly a major incident.'

'Major?' A look of confusion spread across Lennox's face.

'Aye, that's me. Head of one of Edinburgh's major incident teams. MITs, we call them. Policing's all acronyms. We're the ones get called in for all the serious stuff. The things you see on the news.'

The confusion faded away as Janie spoke, replaced by a downbeat expression like a scolded puppy. 'You think he's no' worth looking for?'

'That's not what I meant at all, no. Look, Shauna. I'll no' lie to you, people go missing the whole time and that's usually because they don't want to be found. Could be that's the story with your man here. But I'll do what I can, aye?'

The woman nodded once, wiped at her nose with the back of her hand. 'Thank you.'

Janie tried her best reassuring smile as she took up her pen once more and started to write down the details. Not her case, she knew. Not even a case, really, just something brought to the attention of the police. And yet as she filled the page with address, phone number, workplace and everything else, she had a horrible feeling Vaclav Mihailovic was going to be a thorn in her side for a while to come.

5

'You know how much I hate it when it's political, Jayne. Couldn't you have given this to someone else?'

McLean sat at the conference table in Chief Superintendent McIntyre's office, a cup of coffee in front of him, half-eaten chocolate Hobnob on the saucer. He'd sent DS Stringer off to the CID room to start putting together a strategy for the investigation before heading up a floor to report to the boss. There was no need for an incident room for what amounted to little more than a glorified act of vandalism, but McIntyre needed to be kept in the loop. She'd insisted he get involved, after all.

'It's precisely because it's political that it had to be you, Tony. Nathaniel Drake has sunk a lot of money into the city. He has a lot of influential friends.' McIntyre paused as if considering her words. 'Well, maybe "friends" isn't quite right. Men like him don't really do friendship.'

'All the same, it's a break-in at a lab. Not even a secure lab, given that the whole place is still a building site. Nothing appears to have been stolen, according to the man in charge. It's a simple enough case of interviewing the security staff, collating the forensic evidence and reviewing all the CCTV footage we can get our hands on. A detective sergeant could coordinate all that.'

'And I'm sure DS Stringer is on the case, Tony. But he can't go and reassure a man worth the wrong side of ten billion dollars that everything's fine and under control. That's got to come from someone with a bit more clout.'

'So send the chief constable. She's surely senior enough for him. Or you could get Kirsty to do it if she's busy. Superintendent's got to sound more impressive than Inspector, surely?'

'I'd do it myself, believe me. Last thing I really want to be doing is sending you to schmooze the rich and powerful. That's like . . . I don't know. Something deeply inappropriate for the situation anyway. But you have previous. You're a known quantity. You're—'

'Male?'

McIntyre laughed without much mirth. 'That as well, but mostly it's your history with a certain Jane Louise Dee that counts in your favour.'

McLean tensed at the name, and the insinuation that came with it. McIntyre must have seen the hurt written on his face.

'You ran her out of town, Tony. That's how people like Drake see it, anyway. It's all about posturing, about showing who's boss.' The chief superintendent leaned back in her chair again. 'And you're a man.'

McLean took a bite out of his Hobnob and washed it down with some coffee. Ever since getting the early morning call that sent him out to the science park he'd known this was going to be a complicated case. Perhaps not the solving of it, given what he'd seen of the crime scene, but a ball-ache dealing with the public side of things.

'I've never been a big fan of the whole boys' club thing,' he said. 'It's narrow-minded, apart from everything else, and that leads to overlooking important details. Same as letting the high heidyins push an investigation in the direction most expedient to their own interests. You know how well I react to that sort of thing.'

'I do.' McIntyre nodded her head once, focus stretching away to who knew how many memories of his ignoring the dictates of his seniors, as often as not her. The pause lasted a few seconds, so it could have been quite a few. 'And I'm not going to tell you how to conduct this investigation, Tony. I know better than that. But if it takes you in directions that might be uncomfortable to Drake Biotech, or even if it takes you in no direction at all, you'll be better placed to tell the boss man that. He'll listen to you where he'll just smile at me and then go over my head. Same even with the chief constable.'

'I didn't much like the idea of him before. Really don't like him now.'

'Ah now. Don't you go getting narrow-minded on me. Treat him fairly, same as you would anyone else.'

McLean dipped his head in acknowledgement. McIntyre was right. He'd already let his judgement be clouded by the way this investigation had been handed to him. He owed it to himself, and the team under him, to work the case properly. And if that meant embarrassing a few politicians and rich businessmen, well, so be it.

'I'll do my best,' he said.

'Can't ask more of you than that. But if you felt like keeping me up to speed, that'd be great too. This will come up in pretty much every strategy meeting until it's done.'

'Of course. Hopefully it won't take too long. Forensics might come up with something, but if they don't there's lots of CCTV at the research centre, and good coverage over the whole science park. We know exactly when they left, so that makes searching easier. If the high heidyins want more, then we can do a deep dive into the security staff, but it feels like overkill. This isn't exactly a major crime.'

'You think it might have been an inside job?' McIntyre asked.

'I don't know. Part of me thinks it's just a bunch of opportunist eco-warriors making a nuisance of themselves. The state of the building's security, they probably didn't need much help getting in.'

'Why do I sense a "but" coming next?'

McLean paused a moment before answering, aware that he was digging a hole for himself and yet unable to stop.

'If that was all it was, then I doubt anyone would even have bothered reporting it in the first place. Maybe get themselves a crime report number for the insurance claim, I suppose. But this whole thing smells wrong, and I don't just mean assigning the DCI in charge of major incidents in Edinburgh to investigate a break-in where nobody got hurt.'

McIntyre did a good job of suppressing her sigh, but McLean heard it all the same. Well, if she'd not wanted the crime investigated thoroughly, she should have given it to someone else.

'They had to have had help,' he added, warming to his theme. 'Sure, it's a building site mostly, but the main block is finished. The fire escapes are all alarmed and linked into the central security system. But that one closest to that lab had been bypassed. The group went straight to it, and on into the only lab in the whole complex that's kitted out and functional, even if Professor Caine says it's not being used yet. These people, whoever they are, they knew what they wanted and where to find it. Someone must have told them.'

'But I thought you said nothing had been taken.'

It was McLean's turn to lean back in his chair, the last of his Hobnob chewed and swallowed before he answered.

'Aye, and that's the other thing bothering me about it all. The professor told me nothing had been taken, right enough. He might be lying about that. He was certainly lying about something. But you don't always break into a place to steal something. Sometimes you might break in to leave something behind.'

What would always be the CID room to him hadn't changed all that much in the far too many years since McLean had first entered it as a newly minted detective constable. There were fewer desks, perhaps, and the computers on them hadn't been there when he'd started. But the whiteboards around the walls were the same, the old clock above the door still ticking along the hours until shift end. Perhaps the most noticeable change was the lack of cigarette smoke, although it had been decades since smoking in the office had been banned. Now the room smelled of cheap deodorant, sweat and stale coffee. It was still a huge improvement.

'All squared with Jayne?' DS Stringer asked as he approached from the far side of the room. That was another change McLean found more difficult to cope with, the first name informality. He'd never have dared refer to the station chief as Keith when he'd been Stringer's rank. It was *sir*, or *Chief Superintendent, sir*, depending on the man's changeable mood.

'For a given definition of "squared", yes. How are we doing for spare detectives?' He looked around the CID room noticing another thing that had changed. There were far fewer people than when he'd started.

'Depends what you mean by spare. The sort of things we're going to have to do with this one are time consuming. There's likely hundreds of hours of CCTV footage if we get all the cameras in the science park. Let alone what they give us from the building itself. And we'll need to talk to all the people who have access. Drake employees and builders. It's a long list.' Stringer ran a hand through his hair. 'Is this really a good use of our time?'

'The short answer to that is no. It's a bloody stupid use of our time. I've no doubt there's plenty of other far more pressing investigations we should be prioritising. But Nathaniel Drake is very rich and has the ear of half the cabinet. Probably the first minister. So we run it like it was a murder investigation, right? No stone unturned, and no worries about drafting in a few uniforms to help.'

As if on cue, the door swung open. The newest recruit to the team, Detective Constable Connor Fairley, saw McLean and immediately went bright red. The young lad showed promise, especially when it came to being thorough with repetitive tasks, but he needed to lose his fear of authority figures. Or maybe that was being unfair. McLean had probably been just as nervous around the boss at Fairley's age.

'Sir,' he said, unsettled. 'Just popped down to the canteen for a coffee. I didn't think—'

'Don't worry about it, Connor. Nobody's clock-watching here. I've got a job for you though.'

A look of panic widened the young constable's eyes for a moment. He visibly gathered himself before speaking again. 'Of course.'

'Jay will bring you up to speed. We need to review a lot of camera footage as quickly as possible. You can grab a couple of uniforms if the duty sergeant will spare them.' McLean paused a moment, aware that he'd missed the morning briefing going out to the science park, and wasn't sure what everyone else was up to. 'Unless, that is, you've already got your hands full with something else?'

'I . . . No, sir. That is . . . DI Harrison did ask me to look into something, but it's no' high priority. I'll get this done first, shall I?'

'That depends on what Janie wanted you to do,' McLean said.

'Oh, just some initial enquiries with immigration services about a missing person. She did say it wasn't important.'

'Then I'll pull rank on this one, but don't worry, I'll square it up with the DI next time I see her.'

Fairley bobbed his head by way of acknowledgement, but didn't actually move away to begin his newly assigned task.

'Was there something else?' McLean asked, but the young detective constable shook his head.

'Right. Well. I'll see if I can't rustle up a few more bodies and we can get started on the CCTV,' Stringer said. 'I've a list of security staff and other folk with access to the building. We'll work our way through interviews with them too.'

'You going back to the lab to do that or bringing them here?' McLean asked.

'Probably easiest to do it there. I'll get Connor set up and then head out after lunch.'

McLean glanced at the clock, half the working day already gone and it had started early. 'OK, Jay. Give me a shout when you're ready to go. We can split the interviews and get them done in half the time.'

'You think that's . . .' Stringer didn't finish the sentence, his brain catching up with his mouth before he said something stupid.

'Overkill? A DCI interviewing security staff about a spot of vandalism? Aye, it probably is. But someone's going to have to speak to Professor Caine again, and he'll be straight on the phone to his boss. Nathaniel Drake, in case I need to remind you both. So if it's me doing the questioning, at least the first minister's new friend will think we're taking this seriously.'

And if that meant another chance to find out what it was Caine was hiding, then McLean could live with that.

6

Vaclav Mihailovic lived, or perhaps no longer lived, in a flat in a tired-looking concrete tower block in the south-east of the city. Janie knew it by reputation as a place where migrant workers stayed either until they earned enough to find better accommodation or they moved on to another job in a different city, perhaps another country. Three-bedroom ex-council flats often lived in by upwards of twenty people, day-shift workers vacating beds just in time for the night shift to fall into them. Totally illegal, of course, but like so many other things, overlooked by an underfunded and understaffed council.

She'd been part of a police-backed council housing department raid some years ago. Not to this particular block, but something similar, so she more or less knew what to expect when she turned up. That was why she'd bullied Detective Sergeant Lofty Blane into accompanying her, even though he barely fitted in the little Nissan Leaf pool car despite pushing the passenger seat all the way back. He wasn't by nature a violent man, but at six foot seven, he was good at looming.

'You reckon that'll be safe there?' he asked as they walked from the parked car to the tower block entrance. Janie cast a glance back at it. True, it was newer by a decade than any of the other cars parked nearby, but it was dirty with road grime and didn't look expensive.

'For a half-hour or so, maybe. Let's get this over and done with, eh?'

The ground-floor entrance hall to the block was surprisingly clean, although no amount of careful scrubbing could hide the fact that the tiles were cracked and occasionally missing entirely. Lights above it suggested that the lift was working, but Janie opted for the stairs instead. Four flights up brought them to a narrow corridor with windows at either end. Again, the floor was clean, although a pile of cardboard boxes outside one door leaned into the passageway, the contents of the top one spilling out. As they approached, Janie saw a few items of men's clothing, and she wasn't at all surprised to find that the door was the one she was looking for.

'This one?' Lofty asked before rapping hard against the flimsy veneer.

There was no answer, so Janie tried the door handle. It was locked, but as she rattled it a quiet voice called out something from beyond. The noise of locks clacking and bolts being slid back, and then the door opened a crack wide enough only to make out an eye under a shaggy mop of unkempt dirty blond hair.

'What?'

'I'm looking for Vaclav Mihailovic.' Janie held up her warrant card a little too far away from the gap in the door to be easily seen. The eye stared at her, then rolled upwards to where she knew DS Blane stood behind her.

'Is not here.'

'But you know him, right?'

The eye dropped down to her level again. 'Is not here.'

'Do you know where he is? Maybe you've got a phone number for him?' Janie pulled out her own mobile and waved it around, just in case the eye didn't know what one was.

'Is not—'

'Here, I know. Look, maybe we could come in? We're not here to arrest anyone. I'm only trying to find Vaclav.' It was hard to tell from the voice and the eye whether she was talking to a child or a grown woman. Either way, Janie could see she was getting nowhere. There was one last thing she could try.

'Look, I'm a friend of Shauna's. You know, Shauna Lennox? Vaclav's girlfriend?'

The door closed, and for a moment Janie thought she'd blown it. But then the sound came of a chain being unhitched. The door opened wider to reveal a short young woman in baggy clothes chosen more for warmth than fashion. She raised a hand to her lips, one finger stretched out in the universal sign of quiet.

'The men are sleeping. No noise, please.'

Janie nodded, then followed as the young woman led them down a narrow corridor and into a tiny kitchen. She closed the door behind them, went to lean against the wall where a single window let grubby light in. When she spoke, her voice was low and quiet.

'Vaclav, he go home.' She shook her head slowly as she said the words, as if she didn't really believe them herself.

'When was this?' Janie asked, then added 'sorry' in a quieter voice when the young woman flinched.

'A week. Ten days maybe. That was last time I see him.'

'And you think he's gone home? To Serbia?'

The young woman shrugged, but said nothing more.

'What was he like?' Janie asked. She knew what he looked like, Shauna had shown her some photos on her phone. What she didn't know was what kind of man he was and whether he might up sticks and walk out on everything without even leaving a message.

'He OK, I guess. Better than some of men here. They treat me like property, no? Cook and clean and washing and never a thank you. Is expected, and if I complain is slap or punch. Or sometimes worse.'

Janie had no idea who this young woman was, but she knew

34

enough about the kind of life lived by these migrant workers to understand how precarious her situation must be. Would a quiet call to social services be a blessing or a curse? Hard to know.

'But Vaclav wasn't like that?' she asked.

'He never hurt me.' Again that slight shake of the head as if the young woman knew what she said was a lie. Or a half-truth at best. 'But he talk. All the time he talk. Nadia, he say. You should leave here. Find better life. Better job. Like it is easy, no?'

So Nadia was her name, that was something. Janie took out her phone again, swiped at the screen until she found the best of Shauna's photographs of Vaclav. A selfie, the two of them sitting in a pub somewhere, cheeks squeezed together. Mihailovic held a half-drunk pint of lager aloft, a cheesy grin on his face. Good times, by the look of things.

'This is him, right?' She held out the phone for the young woman to see. Nadia's eyes filmed with tears and she nodded once.

'That was just a month past. Do you really think he'd just leave without saying goodbye to her?'

'He had plan, Vash. Would not say what it was. Just that he was going to make money. Enough he could get out of this *sranje*'. Nadia spat out the word so that Janie felt no need for a translation. 'I not know what he do. Maybe this is plan. Maybe he come back soon. Maybe not. The others . . .' She nodded her head in the direction of the rest of the flat, where who knew how many people were sleeping before their night shift. 'They say he go home. He not come back. They put his stuff out for others might need.'

For a moment, Janie didn't understand the young woman's words. Then she remembered the pile of boxes at the front door. It made sense that there would be an informal sharing network in a place like this, the closest thing to charity these exploited people could manage. But they wouldn't give a man's possessions away unless they knew he wasn't coming back for them, would they? And what connection was there between this woman's situation and Mihailovic's disappearance? Was there any connection at all? So many questions unanswered here, but she was all too aware that it was an unsanctioned investigation that had brought her to the flat in the first place. Pick up any rock in the city and you'd likely find something unpleasant squirming underneath.

She put away her phone and brought out a card, handed it to the young woman. 'Thank you for speaking to us, Nadia. If you think of anything else, or just want to talk, give me a call, aye?'

Edinburgh seemed to be in a constant state of demolition and reconstruction these days. Janie couldn't recall a time when there hadn't been giant cranes reaching into the sky like the talons of some vast, dead bird. Every day brought a new temporary road closure and complicated traffic diversion as old frontages were shored up while the buildings behind them were gutted and repurposed. Some developments younger even than her had been deemed unsuitable, left to the cruel mercies of the wrecking ball. The futuristic constructions of glass and steel that rose up from the destruction looked out of place amongst the soot-stained sandstone grandeur of an earlier century, but who was she to deny such progress?

The building site where Vaclav Mihailovic had been working was at the mud and concrete stage of the process. Janie wasn't sure what had been there before – an old factory perhaps – but now modern housing blocks were budding from the ground like mushrooms after rain. She guided the electric Nissan towards a set of stacked Portakabins surrounded by a sea of muddy gravel, parked in a space between a battered Transit van and a gleaming new JCB telehandler.

A chill wind chased her and DS Blane across the short distance to the site office, the warmth inside welcome if laden with the smell of drying mud, body odour and fried food. A middle-aged woman sat behind a desk, mostly hidden by a pair of computer screens and a stack of folders that made Janie's collection back at the station look amateur. All around the tiny room, the expensive tools of the building trade leaned against walls or were piled high in their cases.

'Help you?' the woman asked. Not enough words for Janie to place her accent.

'Detective Inspector Harrison. This is my colleague, Detective Sergeant Blane.' She pulled out her warrant card, surprised when the woman reached forward, plucked it from her fingers and then peered closely at the details before handing it back.

'So?'

'I'm looking into the disappearance of a man, Vaclav Mihailovic. He was working on this building site until a few days ago.'

Janie watched the woman's face as she spoke the name, but there was no flicker of recognition or any other obvious tell. She reached for a mouse that was half buried under what looked very much like the overtime sheets Janie herself had to authorise across the other side of the city, and only then looked up.

'Mihailovic, you say?' Swift fingers clattered over the keyboard without needing to be asked how to spell the name. Maybe a lot of Eastern Europeans worked on this site. That would explain it. Aye, right.

'I've a Mihailovic V as part of the first fix joinery team. Permits are all checked and in order, but he's not down as active on site at the moment.' Another swipe of the mouse, tap of the keys. 'No time sheet submitted last week, an' that's no' like that lot.'

Janie raised an eyebrow at 'that lot', but let the casual xeno- phobia slide. 'You know when he last clocked off?' she asked instead.

'I shouldn't really be giving out this information, you know.' The woman shook her head, but carried on digging through what- ever it was she had on the computer.

'If it makes you happier, I already know his address, phone

number, date of birth. Just trying to trace where he's been and when, aye?'

The woman shook her head almost imperceptibly, her face impossible to read. Janie let her get on with whatever she was doing.

'Clocked in Friday last at half seven in the morning. Knocked off at a quarter to five. That tallies with his worksheet, and he was paid into his bank account the following Tuesday.' The woman pushed the mouse aside and leaned back in her office chair with an alarming creak of springs. 'I'd no idea he'd left, but then they're all just names to me here anyways. Always some coming and some going. It's the nature of the work.'

'Do you know who he was working with? A gang boss, maybe?'

That got Janie an appraising stare. A hardening of the features, perhaps. She'd not meant the term as anything other than descriptive, but it was loaded all the same.

'Aye, an' I suppose you'll be wanting to talk to them too. Pull a man off his work.' With another slight shake of her head, the woman reached for a mobile lying face down amongst all her paperwork. She swiped it on and hit a speed dial icon, paused for a couple of seconds while the call was connected.

'Kevin. It's Babs. Is Sasha about?' Another pause, then 'Aye, send him over will youse?' For a moment Janie thought the woman, Babs, was going to say what it was about, and spoil any element of surprise. But she thumbed off the call and put the phone down before pushing her seat back with a sigh.

'He's away the other side of the site. Be ten minutes maybe before he gets here. I suppose youse two'll be wanting a cup of tea.'

7

S asha turned out to be a blond man built like the proverbial brick shithouse. He wasn't quite as tall as Lofty, but there wasn't a lot in it, and he carried maybe half as much weight again as the detective sergeant. Janie wouldn't have liked the odds should the two of them get into a fight either, even without knowing that DS Blane was naturally mild-mannered and slow to anger. They'd enjoyed a surprisingly good mug of tea in a small meeting room off the main Portakabin, courtesy of Babs the site manager, as the middle-aged woman had turned out to be. More information about her than that Janie hadn't managed to glean, but it wasn't important.

'Vash was good worker. Skilled. Not like some of these cowboys, no?'

The small meeting room would have comfortably sat a half-dozen normal-sized men around a cheap Formica-topped table. With Lofty and Sasha filling the space, Janie felt a little claustrophobic. A situation not helped by the one narrow window being both glazed with frosted wire-reinforced glass and covered up with a metal shutter on the outside. In the hope of a little privacy, she had closed the door through to the reception area when the gang boss had arrived, and was now regretting that.

'I know what you mean,' she said. 'I've brothers in the trade.

Seems pretty much anyone can lease a van, write "Joiner" on the side and charge fifty quid an hour to bodge some repairs. No one takes pride in a job any more.'

Sasha beamed a wide smile at her. His eyes were a startling blue colour that seemed to glow under the single bare fluorescent tube fixed to the ceiling. 'You understand.' He raised hands the size of dinner plates upwards in a gesture of amazement. 'Is hard to find good men. Skilled men. Is why I am sad to say goodbye to Vash.'

'Do you know why he left?' DS Blane asked.

'Something about family back home, he said. Not one for much small talk, you know? Was urgent, he say.'

'And did he say how long he'd be away? Was he planning on coming back here?' Janie waved at the room with one hand.

Sasha's shrug was answer enough. 'He not say. I not know if Babs would welcome him back either. Plenty others like him to fill the gap, no? How you say it? Cowboys with "Joiner" painted on the side of their vans?'

Janie suppressed a smile at the way the big man said 'Babs'. She doubted the site manager would appreciate the informality. And she could see that Sasha had done it deliberately, too. He wasn't quite so good at hiding his unintentional facial tics, and she was trained to seek them out when interviewing people. The twitch of a smile at the casual use of his boss's nickname suggested to her that it was a calculated move, and the more she looked, the more evidence she found of the man's hidden unease. Well, nobody liked being asked questions by the police, least of all a migrant worker from a country where the law was often a violent tool of a repressive state.

'So, you're the gang boss for the first fix joinery team, right?' This time Janie let an innocent smile grow.

'Is better word. Foreman, no? "Gang boss" sounds so ugly.'

'Nevertheless, you're in charge of the team. I take it you collect them all from their homes? Like the block of flats where Mihailovic lives? Lived, I should say.'

Something like a frown passed briefly over Sasha's face as Janie corrected herself. He affected a thick Slavic accent, but she could tell his understanding of English was near perfect. He knew what she implied by the change of tense.

'Some have their own cars. Vans with "Joiner" written on the side, yes? But others . . .' The big man waggled his head and shoulders in a manner that might have been a shrug. 'And is not always this building site. Some days the work is in other places. Maybe Glasgow, maybe Dundee. Makes sense to all go in one van.'

'And the last day he was here. You took Mihailovic home?'

'He was in bus, yes. Lots of workers live there.'

'And that was the last time you saw him?' This time Janie closed her notebook and set her pen down, knowing it would put the big man at ease to think the interview was over.

'Yes. I wish him good weekend. When I come for him on Monday, he is gone.'

'Gone? So you didn't speak to him before he left? He didn't tell you himself where he was going?'

Janie was glad that Lofty Blane had asked the question, as it allowed her to study the gang boss's reaction more closely. There might have been a perfectly good reason for the discrepancy between what he had said at first and how the story had then played out, but the momentary pause, the subtlest of flickers around his eye, the tensing of the muscles in his neck and shoulders all telegraphed the lie perfectly.

'I . . . He call me. Late on Sunday. Say he going home, right? I think maybe one day, two day later, but six o'clock on Monday morning. He not there.'

'And the other people in his flat. They knew where he'd gone too?'

Sasha shrugged. 'I not speak to them.'

Janie looked once more at the big man. He had recovered his composure almost as swiftly as he'd lost it. There was little point

41

in continuing to question him now that he had settled on his version of events. This wasn't even a case, and she knew full well how much trouble she'd be in if it got back to the wrong senior officers. Except that she was a senior officer now, wasn't she? She had some leeway when it came to this sort of thing.

'Well, thank you for your time.' She pushed back her chair and stood up, getting surprised looks from both the gang boss and DS Blane. The latter struggled to extricate himself from his chair in the small room, and only caught up with Janie as she pulled open the door to leave.

Babs the site manager wasn't quite caught leaning with her ear pressed to the door, but it wasn't far off. Janie heard the protesting squeak of springs as the older woman sank into the chair behind her desk, one hand reaching for the mouse. It might have been convincing, had the blank screen of her computer monitor not been clearly reflected in her spectacles for a moment before it flickered into life again.

'All done?' she asked with perhaps a little breathlessness.

'Aye, we're good.' Janie fished around in her jacket pocket as she crossed the small room, pulled out a business card and offered it to the site manager. 'See if he gets in touch, aye? Maybe you could let us know. Or if anything else comes up.'

Babs eyed her suspiciously, but took the card anyway. 'They're all legit, you know,' she said.

'Legit?' Janie asked.

'Aye, the workers. Even your lad Mihailovic.' The site manager gestured towards her computer screen. 'They've all got papers, an' they're checked properly. Immigration services comes round, they won't find anything suspicious.'

For a moment Janie couldn't quite understand why the woman had brought it up, but it made perfect sense of course when seen from her perspective. A sudden and unannounced visit from the police with questions about a foreign worker. No doubt Babs was fully expecting a full Home Office raid team to be knocking on her door within the hour.

'I'm just trying to track down a man who's gone missing, nothing more,' she said. It felt like the kind of thing McLean would have said in similar circumstances, although she wasn't sure she'd quite yet mastered his knack of putting even the most hostile people at ease.

'We're no' some fly by night operation here, you know. We've Scottish Government contracts, running sites all over the country. Can't afford to hire the wrong people, ken?'

'I believe you. I know the trade. Reputation's worse than the reality most of the time. Like I said, just trying to find this man. If he's gone home, then that's fine.'

Babs looked at her with narrowed eyes, not quite unfriendly but certainly suspicious. Janie realised the big gang boss, Sasha, hadn't come out of the tiny conference room yet. Presumably he was sitting there waiting for the police to go. Well, they'd done enough here.

'Thanks for your time,' she said. DS Blane already had a hand on the door, opened it for her and together they headed back out into the cold.

8

The text came through as he was taking a break for coffee, otherwise McLean would have ignored it. Most of the time he viewed his phone with a mixture of dread and resentment. It was a useful tool, for sure, but it had a nasty habit of interrupting his train of thought, like a demanding and badly behaved toddler. Not like the old days when he'd first started in plain clothes, hefting around clunky radios or trying to find a call box that hadn't been vandalised beyond use. Even compared to the airwave sets of a few years back, a modern smartphone was a technological miracle. But it came with a cost, and that was never being able to escape from the unreasonable demands of his superior officers.

Slipping the sleek metal and glass handset from his pocket, he stared myopically at the screen until it recognised him and unlocked itself, showing a single notification of a text not from Chief Superintendent McIntyre or even Detective Superintendent Ritchie, but from Emma. A single line that made him feel both guilty at his forgetfulness and relieved at the excuse the message gave him.

Hattie and Megan for supper tonight, remember. Don't be late home.

McLean glanced up at the glass that stretched the entire length of one wall. He'd been given an unoccupied office in the mostly completed administration block of the Drake Biotech complex to work from, although the few interviews he'd carried out had been in the conference room along the corridor. Outside, the light was failing already as the afternoon gave way to evening. It wouldn't be long now before darkness fell by teatime and the city put on its winter clothes. He tapped out what he hoped was a reassuring reply, sent it and slipped the phone away. He'd barely had time to sip the lukewarm coffee he'd forgotten about before a sharp knock at the open door distracted him again. DS Stringer stepped into the room, Detective Constable Mitchell close behind him.

'That's statements taken from all the security and janitorial staff, sir,' Stringer said. 'We've made a start with the builders, but nobody really has access to this part of the site without signing in at the front door. There's only a couple of research staff to do, but we thought you'd maybe want to talk to them yourself.'

'Oh aye?' McLean peered into his cup, not quite sure if the need for coffee outweighed the disappointment of it having gone cold. 'Any particular reason you don't want to talk to the eggheads?'

It was perhaps an ill-judged comment given Cass Mitchell's smooth-shaved scalp, but the detective constable showed no sign of having taken offence.

'Happy enough interviewing all of them, sir.' Mitchell had a slim tablet computer with her, which she placed on the desk, swivelled around and pushed towards him as she spoke. 'Only, I think you know one of them?'

McLean picked up the tablet, pleased to see that it didn't want to scan his face. The screen showed a list Professor Caine had drawn up, or most likely had a secretary draw up for him. Admin, security, janitorial were all there, along with the names of a couple of electrical contractors and specialist laboratory equipment installers. There were only two names in the column marked *Research Staff*.

Caine himself at the top, of course, and another name beneath it that came as something of a surprise. Dr Caroline Wheeler was a senior consultant neurologist working out of the Royal Infirmary. She'd treated Emma over the years, and himself too.

'I do indeed. Surprised you'd know that.' He put the tablet back down on the table and picked up his mug again. The omens had not changed.

'I remember speaking to her when you were in the hospital a couple of years back. Didn't know she was in medical research.'

'I didn't either. Is she here, then?'

'Aye, she's waiting in the conference room.'

'And Professor Caine?' McLean found himself tapping at the screen with one finger. He'd not seen the man since arriving at the lab complex after lunch.

'Aye, he's no' here, sir,' Stringer said. 'Something about going to meet Mr Drake at the airport.'

Mr Drake. Of course. The whole reason why there were three detectives of increasing seniority here doing a job that a uniform sergeant with a fresh-faced constable helping could have done.

'OK. I already spoke to him this morning, so a follow-up interview can wait, I suppose.' McLean picked up his mug once more, looked into it and then put it back down again unfinished. 'Better go speak to Dr Wheeler then.'

Like everything else at Drake Biotech's new research centre, the conference room was shiny, modern and not quite finished. No expense appeared to have been spared on the furniture, even if much of it was still wrapped in plastic. The room was dominated by a round table big enough to seat perhaps twenty people. More, if they pulled up the shiny chrome steel and padded leather seats stacked neatly in one corner, waiting to be unbagged. The ceiling felt low, but only because the room itself was so large. When he entered, McLean thought for a moment that it was empty, a slim

46

stack of papers indicating where someone had been sitting. Movement to one side turned out to be a person helping themselves to coffee from a Thermos flask on a polished mahogany sideboard. She turned too swiftly to face him, spilling hot liquid onto her hand, and let out a curse that would have made a sailor blush.

'You OK?' McLean hurried over, pulling out a clean handkerchief to offer. Dr Caroline Wheeler looked at him with a worried smile, and helped herself to a couple of paper towels from a dispenser on the sideboard.

'Clumsy, that's all. Good to see you, Tony. Even if the circumstances are a bit . . .' She didn't bother to finish the sentence.

'Good to see you too, Caroline. I must say I was a little surprised to find your name on the list. I didn't realise you were involved in this kind of thing.'

That got him an arched eyebrow. McLean couldn't quite remember how long he'd known Caroline Wheeler for now. She'd been one of the consultants in the coma ward when he'd been visiting his grandmother in the eighteen months between her stroke and eventual death. That had been well over a decade ago, and their paths had continued to cross ever since.

'How's Emma?' she asked, reminding him of the main reason their paths had continued to cross. Without thinking, he checked his watch. Still plenty of time before he needed to be getting home.

'Much better, thanks. The physiotherapy worked wonders, although she still gets the occasional spasm and she'll never be a hundred per cent on her right side. Her speech is near enough perfect now, though. And her mind's as sharp as it ever was.'

'I'm very glad to hear it. Poor Em's been through the wringer enough, hasn't she.' Dr Wheeler dabbed at her hand with a paper napkin, took a sip of her coffee and then put cup and saucer down on the sideboard. 'But that's not what you're here to talk to me about, is it.'

'Not really, no.' McLean indicated the table, two chairs already pulled out in front of the papers. 'Shall we?'

They both sat down, Dr Wheeler taking a moment to compose herself. McLean pulled out his notebook and a pen, found a clean page.

'I spoke to Dr Caine this morning, first thing.'

'Professor Caine,' Dr Wheeler interrupted.

'Professor?'

'He gets very annoyed if you call him Doctor. Magnus is . . .' Dr Wheeler looked around the room for a moment, as if she thought there might be hidden cameras and microphones. McLean wouldn't have been surprised if there were. 'Well, he's a bit of a stickler for formalities. Let's just put it that way.'

'You know him well?'

'I wouldn't say well, no. I've known of him for most of my working life. He's been pursuing his somewhat unorthodox line of research since the eighties, and the rest of the scientific world's only just beginning to catch up with him now.'

'Unorthodox? Should I be worried about what's been going on here?'

Dr Wheeler smiled at some joke only she understood. 'Nothing's going on here, Tony. Not yet, at least. It can't start until Drake Biotech's fully licensed by the Home Office. That'll happen soon, but not as soon as we hoped.'

'I heard about the delays, right enough.'

'And this break-in doesn't help. Probably set us back another month. Not that it affects me all that much. My work's mostly still at the hospital, overseeing clinical trials. It's Magnus who's most frustrated by the setbacks. He's itching to get started on his new anti-senescence therapy work. Pretty much built the whole facility just for it.'

'This would be the unorthodox line of research you mentioned?' McLean persisted.

Dr Wheeler gave him that pained smile of hers he recalled from many a hospital bedside chat. 'Professor Caine's approach to increasing human lifespan is a little different to how other labs have been doing things. Most research has taken a bottom up approach, you might say. Looking at individual systems within animal and human biology. Telomeres, apoptosis, stem cells, all that sort of thing. Magnus started with the organism as a whole and looked at the way all of these various systems interact. The connections are often the place where breakdown begins, you see?'

McLean wasn't sure that he did, but it was clear Dr Wheeler was enthusiastic.

'So why would anyone want to break into the lab? As I understand it, Drake Biotech doesn't do experiments on animals, right?'

Dr Wheeler shook her head. She'd laid her hands in her lap, but now she brought them back up again in an expression of bewilderment.

'We use bio-assays. Cloned tissue in petri dishes and the like. The few whole organism tests we carry out are on human volunteers, and like I said before, they're all Home Office licensed.'

McLean had been half-heartedly jotting down a few notes, but his pen stopped mid word.

'Human trials?'

'That's what I was brought in to oversee, actually. Seeing as I'm a medical doctor as well as a PhD. It's all very early-stage stuff, you understand. All carried out at the hospital too. Volunteers mostly, but a few last resort therapy cases that have shown some very promising results.'

McLean leaned back in his chair, notebook forgotten. 'I didn't realise the work was so far advanced,' he said after Dr Wheeler had outlined the half-dozen different therapies undergoing early human trials.

'Drake has lab facilities all around the world, three at universities in England already. This place is meant to bring all of that together, along with a plant nearby for manufacturing any drugs we produce here. All told, Nathaniel is investing over a billion pounds in the UK, most of it here in Edinburgh. Of course, if even ten per cent of what we're researching comes to market, that'll have been a very good investment.'

'Might that be what was behind the break-in? Someone looking for information on what you've been up to? Steal a march on you?'

'It's possible. Far as I can tell, they didn't take anything from the lab, just broke some things and sprayed graffiti all over the place. From what I've seen, most of it can be fixed fairly easily, and a coat of paint will cover up the mess. You've seen what they wrote, though. It looks like anti-vivisectionists or some other fringe group, except as you know, we don't experiment on animals at all.'

'So why do you think they did it? Break in, that is.'

'Well, they might have been acting on bad intelligence and thought we were doing things we weren't.' Dr Wheeler put one hand to her face, stroked her upper lip with the edge of a thumb whose nail was chewed down to the quick. 'But then if that was the case, how did they know how to get in so easily? That had to have been an inside job. And if it was an inside job, then they'd have known we didn't have animals here. Makes no sense.'

'In my experience these things rarely do. Could be something as simple as a grievance against billionaires, could be something much more sinister. We'll get to the bottom of it either way.'

'Really? I'd have thought Police Scotland had far better things to do with their time, surely.' Dr Wheeler cocked her head to one side, as if only now seeing McLean. 'Come to that, it seems a little over the top someone of your seniority overseeing the investigation.'

'Believe me, Caroline. It's been mentioned once or twice. But you said it yourself. Mr Drake is investing a lot of money in this place, bringing a lot of jobs to Scotland. That gets the attention of the politicians, and if he says jump, they'll ask how high. Then they tell me to do it. That's why we're here and not a couple of uniforms, and that's why we'll keep looking until we find the people who did this and why.'

'Best of luck to you there. I just hope nothing important comes up while you're at it.' Dr Wheeler fidgeted with her coffee cup, clearly impatient to be getting on with other things herself. 'We're going over the lab equipment tomorrow, and checking whoever did this didn't gain access to anywhere else on the site.'

'Well, be sure to let me know what you find, can you?' McLean glanced at his watch. There were other things he needed to be doing too, not least of which was getting home before his guests arrived.

'Is that us done then?' Dr Wheeler put on a winsome smile, held up her hands with the wrists pressed together. 'You're not going to arrest me and lock me up?'

'Not today, no.' McLean closed his notebook and shoved it back in his pocket. He pulled out a card, was about to hand it over when he realised what he was doing. Dr Wheeler already had his number and Emma's both. 'But if you think of anything, let me know?'

9

'See if you can't get in touch with the Serbian consulate, Lofty. Run Mihailovic's name past them. Reckon there's not much else we can do apart from that.'

'On it, boss.' DS Blane nodded and set off towards the CID room, leaving Janie at the top of the stairs. As he approached the open door, she couldn't help but notice how he seemed to shrink in on himself, shoulders hunching and back slightly bent to shave a few inches off his height. Partly it was done to avoid braining himself on the frame, she knew, but it was also a self-defence mechanism so ingrained as to be unconscious now. A lifetime of being the tallest in his group, the natural centre of attention, even if he only ever wanted to be left alone.

She checked her watch, surprised at how late it was. Lofty would be clocking off soon, and Janie probably ought to head home herself, even if as a DI she no longer worked shifts. The downside of a day spent chasing around after a missing immigrant worker was that her desk would be piled high with paperwork though. Might as well make a start on it.

Tucked away at the back of the station, Janie's office had the advantage of not being on the way to anywhere else. Passing traffic didn't tend to drop in for a chat, which was why she was surprised to see the door open and the light on as she approached. She tended to close the door behind her when she left, leaving it ajar only when she was in there. A cue she'd picked up from DCI McLean now she thought about it. As she came closer, she could see the movement of someone inside.

'Hello?' It felt a little strange, announcing herself that way, but the last thing she wanted to do was surprise someone and have them knock all the carefully organised piles on her desk onto the floor.

'Oh, Janie. You're back.' Retired Detective Sergeant Grumpy Bob Laird emerged from one corner of the room, a large archive box file in his arms. There had been a pile of them lurking there when Janie had taken over the office, and she'd not been bold enough, or foolish, to open them and see what was inside. By the thick layer of dust on the top one, they pre-dated the office's former occupant too.

'Hey, Bob. Wasn't expecting to see anyone in here. You after anything in particular?'

'Just moving the last of these old files down to the basement. Grace wants everything checked over before it all gets shipped out to the new archive centre at Bilston.'

With anyone else, Janie might have suspected some ulterior motive, some reason to snoop around her office while she wasn't there. She'd known Grumpy Bob all her working life, had been a part of his team when she first moved to plain clothes. He wasn't one to skulk around behind a person's back when asking them to their face was simpler. Even so, it seemed a little strange that he'd be up here doing the heavy lifting when he could have bullied any passing young constable to do it for him.

'Everything OK downstairs?' she asked, and there was the slightest of tells about the old detective sergeant's eyes to suggest that whatever he said in reply, the answer was most likely no.

'Ach, it's no' so bad really.' Grumpy Bob belied his words by lowering the box to a point where it rested on the edge of Janie's desk. 'Dagwood can be a bit much when he's in one of his moods, right enough, but I've been dealing with him near thirty years.

Best thing with him is to smile and let it go. Grace . . .' He let out a weary sigh. 'Well, let's just say she can be hard work. And you know how I feel about that.'

Janie smiled at the little joke, even though she could hear the tiredness in her old friend's voice. Grumpy Bob was legendary for being able to find himself a quiet spot for a kip of an afternoon. She'd have been less surprised if she'd found him with his feet up on her desk and an open report file draped over his face. But he was also reliable, good at getting the job done properly and on time, which was why none of his superior officers had ever complained about the feet up on the desk thing. Retired and working on a consultancy basis for the Cold Case Unit, he shouldn't have been under any great stress, though.

'You working on anything in particular? Or is it just sorting through old forgotten case files?' She gestured at the dusty box.

'A lot of missing persons cases being reviewed at the moment. Mostly just double-checking the dates before putting them to bed. It's unlikely we'll turn up any new clues for folk who went walkabouts in the eighties. Makes me feel very old to think that was forty years ago now.'

To Janie, still a few months shy of her thirtieth birthday, it might as well have been another country. Still, she could recognise the anxiety in Grumpy Bob's words, and it was likely down to a bit more than being made to work harder than he was used to by ex-Detective Chief Superintendent Ramsay.

'As it happens, I've spent most of the day trying to track down a missing person myself.' Janie leaned against her desk and outlined the basics to the detective sergeant, marshalling the facts the way she had been taught to. The more she spoke, the more the feeling grew in her that she'd wasted a great deal of police time on a fool's errand. Everything pointed to Vaclav Mihailovic having simply hopped on a plane or a train and gone home to Serbia, for reasons he had no interest in sharing with anyone else. Least of all his part-time girlfriend.

Grumpy Bob waited patiently until she had finished, saying nothing as she spoke, not even nodding. Finally, when she was done, he picked up the box and grinned at her.

'Looks like I'm not the only one finding ways to avoid the dull work, aye?' And with a nod and a wink, he walked out of the office. As Janie pulled out her chair, settled in behind her desk and clicked her computer into life, she couldn't help thinking that maybe he'd got the right of it.

Two hours later, she scribbled her signature on the bottom of the last overtime sheet, closed the folder and shoved it into the out tray on her desk. One of the admins would pick it up in the morning, no doubt replacing it with a new folder at the same time. Rubbing at her eyes, Janie dragged the next sheaf of papers from the pile towards her. Performance appraisals for the detective sergeants and detective constables on her team were yet another of the tasks she would have happily delegated, but it was as true in the police as in any other organisation that the higher up the pole you clambered, the more your job became one of managing those doing the actual work beneath you.

Staring at the top form on the pile, it took her far too long to register that it was for Lofty Blane. As with all things, there was a set process for appraising an officer's performance, but as she tried in vain to focus on the questions, Janie realised that she wasn't going to get any of it started that evening. A glance at the clock in the top corner of her computer screen suggested a reason why. It was well past time to go home.

Light off and door firmly closed, she made her way through a quiet station, signed out at the back door and stepped into the night-dark car park. This late, she'd have to walk up to Nicholson Street to get a bus, a route that took her past the pub where she'd first learned of her promotion to detective inspector. The same pub outside which the same boss who had promoted her then tried to sexually assault her.

Janie shuddered at the memory. It had all worked out OK in the end, but she could still recall the sharp pain of Detective Superintendent Pete Nelson's too-tight grip on her arms, smell the mixture of whisky breath and rotting teeth as he tried to force himself on her. There was some small satisfaction in the memory of her knee colliding with his private parts, the look of surprise and the 'oof' noise that had exploded out of him when she fought him off, but as she walked past the entrance to the dark alley she still found herself shaking.

Another image rose in her mind then, of Nelson on his side, hands shoved together into his crotch, knees pulled up towards his chest. And Cerys Powell planting one of her heavy Doc Martens in his side with a viciousness born of personal trauma. Janie had gained a new friend that day, and the memory reminded her that she'd not seen the mortuary assistant in a while. As she hurried away from the scene of the crime, she pulled out her phone and tapped out a quick text. Wine and pizza in their near future, if she could just get on top of the endless paperwork. And maybe spend a little less time chasing wild Serbian geese.

A thumbs up emoji response arrived on Janie's phone as she sat on the bus and stared at the trees on the Meadows. They were starting to lose their leaves now, but the one where they found the dead body, high up in the canopy and naked as the day, had been cut down a few years earlier. She wasn't quite sure how she felt about that. It had been her first case in plain clothes, plucked from the ranks of uniform by DCI McLean. Had he been DCI then, or busted back down to DI? Janie smiled at the thought. Tony McLean was another one who would much rather be doing the work of a detective than the mundane processing of time sheets and performance appraisals. Unlike her, he could afford to be demoted, or even give up the job entirely. And yet he hadn't stayed away long in the end.

Lost in thought, Janie almost missed her stop. Not that it would have mattered, as the next one was only a few hundred yards further up Lothian Road. It had rained earlier, but now the sky was clearing, a few pinprick stars showing through gaps in the orange-hued clouds. A bit more of a walk might have done her good, but the climb up three flights of stone steps to her top-floor tenement was exercise enough. There was wine in the fridge, if her flatmate hadn't finished it already, and Janie reckoned she'd earned a glass.

The lights were on in the living room when she pushed through the front door into the hall and shucked off her boots. Janie would have expected to hear the television through the open doorway, but there was no sound at all. No flickering light either.

'You in, Manda?' she asked the silence, walking through to find her flatmate before waiting for an answer. Manda Parsons sat on the old armchair they'd found in a skip a few years earlier and wrestled up the stairs together. Bare feet, legs crossed, she had balanced a glass of wine on the arm in what was surely an accident waiting to happen. She sat so still that for a moment Janie thought she might have fallen asleep. Except that her eyes were open and staring at the coffee table in front of her. A sheet of A4 paper lay there, two creases in it where it had been folded for an envelope. Blank, so whatever it said was on the other side, out of sight.

'What's up?' Janie asked, a whole gamut of possibilities running through her mind. For a moment it was as if Manda hadn't even registered her coming in. And then her flatmate's eyes regained focus, her gaze moving to Janie's face. With a slow hand, she waved towards the paper. Janie took two steps forward and scooped it up. Flipped around, she saw the address and logo of a letting agency. Their letting agency. A date. A subject line in bold just below the words 'Dear Dr Parsons and Miss Harrison'. Part of her bridled at that. Her proper title was Detective Inspector, surely? But it was the rest of the letter that stirred a coldness deep in her guts.

'Landlord's son wants the place back to live in,' Manda said. 'They need us out by the end of next month.'

10

There was, McLean had to admit, a lot to be said for an evening of good food, fine wine and interesting conversation with friends. A tension he hadn't known was building up in him had ebbed away as he and Emma had chatted with Hattie and Meg Turner about all manner of things that had nothing whatsoever to do with his work. The meal had been simple, a hearty stew with chunky vegetables, followed by baked apples that were merely an excuse to eat cream. Emma still struggled with fine motor control and tired easily, but she wouldn't countenance help or even buying pre-made meals. Simple fare suited McLean fine, and if either the professor of forensic archaeology or her much more sophisticated sculptor wife felt hard done by, their clean plates suggested they hid their disappointment well.

'So, Em. When are you going to start up your studies again? We're all very keen to see you back.'

They had moved from the somewhat chilly dining room through to the library, Meg still cradling her half-full wine glass in one hand. Professor Turner had not been drinking, and neither had Emma, both sticking to sparkling water even though only one was the evening's designated driver. McLean was fairly sure that Emma hadn't touched a drop of alcohol since the night of her stroke, when she had let slip the wine glass that was twin to Meg's and he had watched it shatter on the carpet not three feet from where he now sat. He suppressed the urge to look at the spot, see if he could still make out the stain on the ancient Persian rug.

'Start up . . . Again?' The tremble in her voice and the quietness with which she spoke drew McLean's attention far more strongly than if Emma had shouted. The look on her face was one of puzzled surprise more than anything, as if the thought of returning to her studies had never occurred to her. It was on balance a fair point. She'd been recuperating from her stroke for the best part of two years now, after all.

'Of course. You didn't think we'd let you bunk off for ever, did you?' Hattie Turner's tone was playful, but there was a seriousness to her expression.

'I . . . I don't know.' Emma raised one spindly arm. The shake was always more noticeable at the end of the day, and she'd done more work than usual. 'Don't think I'd be all that good on a dig site.'

'There's more to the job than grubbing around in the dirt, Em. You know that as well as I do.'

'It's the fun bit though, isn't it, Hattie,' Megan said, her words slightly slurred. 'Getting yourself covered in mud and other questionable things. We all know that's why you really do it, right?'

The professor looked at her wife with a mixture of annoyance and good humour. McLean enjoyed watching the easy familiarity of their relationship, the utter lack of pretence or need to protect each other's feelings. It was rare these days that he could find that level of relaxation. Emma could be fine one moment, and the next he'd be treading on eggshells. It wasn't her fault, particularly, same as it wasn't really his. It was how it was and he had to deal with it. An evening with company seemed to be doing them all good, and Em had been planning it for weeks now.

'Could I really come back?' she asked in a voice so quiet McLean wondered that Hattie and Meg would hear her.

'Of course you could, Em.' With much effort, the professor leaned forward from the nest of cushions on the sofa that were trying to eat her, patted Emma on the knee. 'Maybe lab work first, see how you feel about getting back out into the field later.'

'I . . . I'll have to think about it. There's the whole travel thing, for a start. I can't drive at the moment.' Emma lifted up her weaker arm, the hand drooping at the wrist. 'Not sure if I'll ever be able to again.'

'Ach, that's just an engineering problem. Sure we can come up with a solution to it. Thing is, do you want to come back? No point my bullying you if your heart's not in it.'

The professor flopped back down into the cushions. Emma said nothing in reply, but McLean could see by the way she sat a little more upright, the sparkle in her eyes, that the answer would be yes. Eventually. She'd need a little time though.

He stood up, went to the hidden cupboard in the bookcase and clicked it open. In the dark recess behind, a neat row of crystal tumblers reflected sparkles of light, and behind them a small collection of bottles held varying quantities of fine amber liquid.

'Dram, Meg?' He held up a single cask Ardbeg so peaty he could smell it before even opening the bottle.

'Actually, no. Thank you, Tony.' Meg waved her not quite empty wine glass in a gesture of dismissal. 'I've a meeting with a new gallery manager at ungodly o'clock tomorrow morning. Should probably quit while I'm ahead. Tempted though I am. You have such an interesting collection of very expensive whiskies.'

'Probably wise. I've an early start tomorrow too.'

McLean popped the cork out, took a sniff, then slid it back into the bottle, returned it to where it had come from and lined the two empty glasses up with the others. He clicked the heavy door closed, ran a finger down the spine of one of the fake books.

'Oh lord. Your idea of an early start and mine aren't even in the same time zone. You out on a crime scene? Not that you'd be able to tell us anything about it, I suppose.'

'It's hardly an operational secret. Not like you're going to spill all to the tabloids or anything. I've the dubious pleasure of paying a visit to a "Very Important Person" on behalf of Police Scotland.' McLean couldn't help himself from making little bunny ear air quotes as he spoke. 'You've probably heard of him, actually. Nathaniel Drake, the biotech entrepreneur?'

An odd silence fell on the room at that, the sort of thing that would have had Mrs Dawson the old housekeeper looking at the nearest clock and saying that an angel must have passed overhead. Professor Turner hauled herself out of the cushions again, leaned her elbows on her knees as she fixed McLean with an intense stare.

'Nathaniel Drake, you say? Now there's someone I've not thought about in a while.'

'You know him?' McLean asked.

'Oh, aye. She knows him.' Meg drained the last of her wine and placed the glass somewhat haphazardly on the floor. Too close to her foot for McLean's comfort, given the only marginal control she seemed to have over her limbs. 'What was that expedition he paid for? Searching for the tomb of Vlad the Impaler or something, wasn't it?'

'No, Meg. It wasn't him. Nobody knows where Vlad Dracul was buried. But you're in the right part of the world and the right century. Ancient Walachia, modern-day Romania. And it was all very odd.'

'Odd?' McLean asked in the pause that the professor left for that very purpose. 'How so?'

'Well, on the face of it, I was supposed to be identifying and cataloguing bones. Only a lot of the bodies were surprisingly well preserved, given how long they'd been in the ground. Something in the soil, we thought. Anaerobic conditions like you'd find in a peat bog. Unusual to find so many in one place, though.'

'So many? How many?'

'I think the final tally was about a hundred and eighty. Mostly men, but some women and children too. Consensus was they'd all gathered for some kind of ceremony and got caught by an unexpected landslide.' Professor Turner puffed her cheeks and then blew the air out in a long, sceptical breath. 'Seemed a little far-fetched to me, given the terrain. Nowhere for the land to slide from, least not so swiftly they'd be caught by it. Mind you, something would have had to cover them up, I suppose.'

'What do you think caused it?' McLean might have been a little biased, but he'd trust Hattie's hypothesis over that of any other forensic archaeologist.

'Now you're asking. We did think it might have been plague of some form. Even had some of Drake Biotech's researchers come and take samples for analysis, but nothing came of it. Certainly not Black Death or bubonic plague, and they didn't find any viral fragments they could identify. Just a lot of people who all dropped dead at the same time and whose bodies ended up being preserved.'

'And that was how Nathaniel Drake got involved?' McLean asked. 'Because of the potential plague angle?'

'Oh no. He paid for the whole dig. Well, his foundation did. They support a lot of archaeological work around the world. Apparently he's quite the fan of ancient history.'

'Did you meet him, then?'

'Briefly, yes. Not at all what I was expecting, which just goes to show.'

'How do you mean?'

'Well, you'd think from the way the media treat him and his weird eternal-life obsession he'd be like Howard Hughes, all reclusive and germaphobic, but actually he didn't seem to mind getting his hands dirty. Never stayed on site long though. Always flying off to some meeting or another.'

'So he's all right then? For a billionaire? I'm going to be talking to him tomorrow, so any pointers would be useful.'

The Aga gurgled gently as McLean stacked plates into the dishwasher and lined up the wine glasses for washing by hand. The two black circles that were Mrs McCutcheon's and Cecily Slater's cats curled tight up to the enamelled cast-iron front of the stove, greedily soaking up its waste heat. He wasn't fooled. They'd be out in the garden hunting as soon as he was done in here. A night spent terrorising the local wildlife before slinking in just before dawn to spend the day asleep. He envied them sometimes, although both had come through trauma to end up sleeping on his kitchen floor.

'You don't have to do that now, Tony. It can wait until morning.'

He turned to see Emma leaning against the open door. She hadn't been using her wheelchair as much recently, but his trained detective's eye couldn't help but notice how she navigated the house by points of support. A coping mechanism, and a sign of how determined she was not to show any weakness. He loved her for it, even as he saw too well how much it cost her sometimes.

'Just thought I'd get things tidy so it's not a tip come breakfast time. I wasn't lying to Meg when I said I'd have to get started early tomorrow. I need to be at the station for a briefing before coming all the way back across town to see this Drake fellow.'

Emma smiled at that. She took a few unsteady steps, using a hand to stop herself when she reached the kitchen table. She didn't so much sit as fall into the chair, her wince at the impact impossible not to see. Even so, there was a glint in her eye as she spoke, a trace of laughter in her voice.

'Only you could refer to one of the richest men in the world as "this Drake fellow", Tony.' She, too, made little rabbit ears with her fingers to emphasise the point. 'Honestly, I'd have thought someone with a job like yours would read a newspaper every now and then.'

'Famous, is he?' McLean had meant it as a joke, but clearly Emma was too tired to get it. Her earlier smile faded as if it were too heavy to hold on to for long.

'He owns the company that developed the drug that I take every day, for one thing. You know, the one that stops me from having another stroke, hopefully. The one that helps my brain recover from the damage done to it.'

'I know, Em.' McLean pulled out another chair and sat down with a touch more grace than Emma had managed. 'And I do follow the news. I know who Drake is and what he's done. It just bothers me that we have to go the extra mile for him because he's rich and influential. You know how I feel about people like that. His research facility got broken into and now I have to treat it like a murder investigation. There's better things I could be doing than stroking someone's ego just because they've got the first minister on speed dial.'

'There's more to it than that though, isn't there.' Emma leaned forward, reached out and tapped McLean lightly on the forehead with her good hand. 'I know you. Something else is bothering you about this than having to do what the politicians say, right?'

'Aye, you're right. There's more to it than that. Don't get me wrong, that would be enough to make me dislike Drake even before I've met him. But he's bought the old Spenser place just up the road. He's almost a neighbour.'

'Spenser . . .' Emma's brow furrowed for a moment before understanding dawned. 'Oh, yes. The big house on the corner. Why's that such a problem? It's been empty for a while now.'

Put like that, McLean couldn't easily come up with an answer that would satisfy anyone. Not even himself, if he was being honest.

'I don't know. It's just the history of the place, I suppose. Gavin

Spenser was an old friend of my grandmother. Knew her when they were both students. He was another one who went off and made obscene amounts of money. Not that it did him much good. He was murdered in that house.'

'I know. I was part of the forensics team, remember?'

McLean did then, although he'd forgotten. It was around that time he'd first met Emma, now he thought about it. How much she had changed since then. How much both of them had.

'After he died, the place was rented out for a while. Jane Louise Dee lived there until she'd finished renovating that mansion out near Dalkeith.'

Something must have shown on his face as McLean said the name, as Emma reached out again, this time taking his hand in hers. 'That why you don't want to go? Because she used to live there?'

'Who said I . . .' McLean started, then shook his head to stop the words. 'Aye, probably. It's stupid, I know.'

'Not really, Tony. Well, not your reaction. Stupid sending you there, yes. Stupid bending over backwards to keep someone like Drake happy, just on the off chance he'll bring a few jobs to the city. There's far better ways to do that, but politicians, eh?' Emma shrugged, took her hand back, and McLean found he didn't much like that. A quick glance at the clock told him there were far too few hours left before he had to get up and go to work. He pushed back his chair and stood up again. The washing-up could wait. Now it was time for bed.

11

The thing that struck McLean most, when he and Janie Harrison arrived at the Edinburgh residence of Nathaniel Drake, was how little the house had changed. How long had it been since last he'd visited? Ten years? More? Even the furniture looked the same, as if Mrs Saifre had walked out and closed the doors, and then a decade later Nathaniel Drake had walked right on in. It wouldn't have surprised him to find rooms upstairs with everything draped in dust sheets. Certainly the house didn't feel much like a home.

On arrival, the two detectives had been greeted by a nameless assistant, taken through the house to a room at the rear that had been turned into a gym. Drake had been partway through a rigorous workout, aided by two impossibly muscled trainers, but he'd at least been polite enough to break off as soon as he saw them. Coffee had been served as the introductions were made, although shockingly no offer of biscuits. Drake drank something that looked a little like the engine oil that had come out of McLean's old Alfa the last time he had tried to service it himself. Judging by his expression as he swallowed it down, it must have tasted like it too.

'It's really very good of you to come and see me, Detective Chief Inspector. The chief constable said she'd put her best man on the case, but you never know with politicians. Promises are easy, it's the delivery that matters.'

McLean wasn't quite sure what to make of Nathaniel Drake. According to the newspapers, the celebrated biotech engineer, billionaire wunderkind and searcher for the fountain of eternal youth was either thirty-five or thirty-seven years old. That he went to great lengths to hide his true age was strange enough, but Drake could easily have been mistaken for a man much older than he claimed. McLean would have comfortably aged him a decade, and a hard one at that.

He didn't look old particularly, so much as haggard. There wasn't an ounce of fat on him, his face like a skull wrapped in rubber skin. In photographs it looked odd, but up close and in person it was almost unsettling.

'Our senior police officers aren't quite the same as yours, I think,' he said after Drake had taken another reluctant swig of the foul dark brown sludge and swallowed it with a heavy bob of his prominent Adam's apple.

'That's right, that's right.' Drake wiped his lips with the back of his hand and then thumped his chest gently as if the engine oil had given him bad acid reflux. 'Y'all don't have elected commissioners and the like. Don't carry guns neither.'

'We have armed response units, but generally speaking we try not to solve every problem by shooting at it.'

Drake narrowed his eyes as he stared directly at McLean. 'Why do I get the impression you don't much like me, Detective Chief Inspector?'

'We've only just met, Mr Drake. I've not had time to form an opinion.'

That got him something of a wry smile. 'Nate, please.' Drake picked up his engine oil again, looked at it and then put it back down. 'Horrible stuff, but Prof Caine insists. You didn't come here to talk guns and dietary regimes though. So tell me, how is the investigation going?'

McLean looked to Harrison to do the honours, but she was

staring in the opposite direction with an expression of extreme concentration on her face, distracted by something, although he couldn't tell what.

'It's very early days, of course. But we've interviewed all the staff and workers with access to the building already. Forensics have done what they can and are processing their samples. Should have results soon, but I don't hold up much hope given how contaminated the scene was.'

'Contaminated? I thought those labs were sterile.'

'When they're in operation maybe, but there's been a stream of workmen in and out of them over the past couple of weeks. Every contact leaves a trace, or so the saying goes, and there's been a lot of contacts.'

'What about CCTV?' Drake asked.

'I've a team reviewing everything your security people gave us. We've picked up feeds from the rest of the science park. We know exactly what time they left, since one of them decided to go out the front door, so ANPR might give us a lead.'

'ANPR?'

'Automatic Number Plate Recognition,' Harrison explained, her previous distraction apparently over. 'Licence plate, as you might say. If we find a vehicle of interest, we can track where it goes as long as it keeps passing the cameras. Well, up to a point.'

'Sweet. And I thought we were a surveillance state. You any idea why one of them went out the front door anyway? Seemed odd to me when Magnus took me through what had happened.'

'Magnus?' Harrison asked.

'Professor Caine,' McLean and Drake both said at the same time. McLean waited a moment for the tech billionaire to go on, but he didn't seem inclined to add any more detail.

'As to your question, no, we've no idea why one of them went out the front door. Chances are they could have come and gone without being noticed if he hadn't.'

'He?' Drake asked.

'The security guard was fairly certain it was a man, even though his face was covered. He had a backpack on, but didn't appear to be carrying anything. Professor Caine didn't think anything was stolen anyway. They were there to vandalise, not steal. A protest, although it's not exactly clear what they were protesting against.'

'Do people need a reason these days?' Drake picked up his engine oil again, gulped down a mouthful with a grimace and then motioned for his assistant to take the rest of it away. As she did so, McLean noticed that Harrison was staring at the woman, a frown of concentration creasing her brow. With an almost imperceptible shake of her head, she dragged her attention back to the reason they were there.

'I suppose you get that sort of unwanted attention the whole time,' she said.

'You're not wrong.' Drake laughed, an odd sound coming from a face that lacked much in the way of animation. 'Not as bad as some of the Silicon Valley techbros I know. I keep away from social media best I can. Try not to court too much publicity.'

'Very wise. And I think it would be helpful to us both if we could keep this incident away from the news, at least for now. We will of course keep you informed about any developments, but I'll not waste any more of your time just now.' McLean pushed back his seat and stood up. Beside him, Harrison took a moment to register what was happening and follow. Drake stayed in his seat.

'Thank you, both,' he said with a tiny nod towards each of them in turn. 'I'm sure I can count on Police Scotland to do a good job.'

'Everything OK, Janie? Only you seemed a little distracted back there.'

McLean tilted his head towards the rear of the car and the rapidly receding house. As the distance grew, a tension he'd not known he was feeling, or at least hadn't been prepared to acknowledge, began to ease. Too much history with that place, he'd have been happy never to return.

'Sorry. A lot on my mind.' Harrison shifted slightly in her seat.

'It's a big step up from sergeant to inspector,' he said, knowing full well that wasn't her problem.

'Aye, tell me about it. Who knew there was so much paperwork?'

McLean didn't bother answering that, and they drove on in silence for a while. As they dropped down the hill through Bruntsfield and past the tenement flat Harrison shared with Manda Parsons, the detective inspector let out a slow sigh, but still said nothing. A domestic problem then. Well, if she wanted to share then he'd listen and give what support he could, but he wouldn't press.

'What did you make of him?' he asked.

'To be honest, I thought he was OK, really. Nothing special, apart from looking like he's trying too hard. It was that snooty assistant of his who wound me up, whispering away like that the whole time. Just rude, you know? If she'd had to make a call couldn't she have gone to another room?'

'Whispering?' McLean asked.

'Aye, could you no' hear it? Thought she must have had one of those earpieces in. Probably keeping tabs on his security or something. Didn't see any bodyguards unless those two trainers were it.'

'Didn't hear anything.' McLean reached up and tugged at his earlobe without thinking. 'You were sitting closer, mind. And these old lugs aren't what they used to be.'

Harrison didn't say anything, which probably meant she didn't disagree. It would explain how she might have been distracted during their conversation with Drake though. McLean hoped it hadn't annoyed the billionaire. The last thing he needed was a stern lecture from the chief constable.

'How's your schedule looking?' he asked as they crossed the Meadows towards Sciennes and Newington. 'Only I reckon we're going to have to throw everything we can at keeping Mr Nathaniel

Bloody Drake happy. Unless something more obviously important comes up.'

'Careful what you wish for,' Harrison said. 'But right now it's not too hectic, for a change. If Jayne's happy signing the overtime sheets, I've plenty of detectives who can waste time chasing eco warriors.'

'You reckon that's what this is? Some protest group with an axe to grind? I didn't think Drake Biotech's research was that controversial. From what they've told me they don't even do animal experiments.'

The look Harrison gave him was fleeting; McLean only glanced briefly as he negotiated the traffic lights across South Clerk Street. Even so, he could tell she thought him a fool.

'What?' he asked.

'Animal experiments are, I don't know, a bit last century? I mean, sure, scientists still do them, particularly on mice and fruit flies and wee worms and stuff, but there's not many folk protesting that. Least, not by breaking into labs and hardly touching anything.'

'So what kind of eco warrior are you talking about then?'

'The sort who'd like to see Nathaniel Drake and all the other billionaires lined up against a wall, I guess. Or at the very least made to pay more tax rather than raking in subsidies from governments around the world. Drake Biotech's only the latest of his ventures, you know? He made his billions in cloud computing services and home delivery apps. Things that don't much help the environment or lead to secure and well-paid jobs for the masses. If I had to make a guess, I'd say someone thought the lab would be an easier target than a well-guarded server farm in the middle of nowhere. The graffiti was kind of generic, mind you. Going by the photos I've seen. Surprised they didn't break more stuff and steal anything they could flog. Seems a lot of effort to go to just to have a wee look around and then bugger off.'

'Aye, I know what you mean.' McLean negotiated the turn

across the oncoming traffic and into the side street that led to the back of the station. A uniform constable who had clearly done something to piss off his sergeant raised the barrier, and they drove into the car park.

'Of course, we've only their word for it nothing was stolen,' Harrison said as the car came to a silent halt in front of the electric vehicle charging point. McLean hit the off button, but made no other move to get out.

'Go on,' he said.

'Well, I don't get why there's all this fuss if it's over nothing. They had a break-in. Happens all the time, aye? So hire a few more security guards and get the locks upgraded. That's what'd happen anywhere else. But someone makes a big deal of it and we're suddenly being told to jump through all the hoops. Overtime no problem, as long as we can find out who did it and arrest them.'

McLean leaned back into his car seat, felt its support. The interior of the car was warm after the drive across town, but that heat would seep out soon enough. He stared at nothing through the rain-spattered windscreen, his mind on the day before and his visit to the research facility.

'So you think they've had something taken that they don't want us to know about. They just want us to find the people who took it in the hope they can get it back and no one will be the wiser?'

Harrison shook her head once. 'Aye, put like that it sounds daft, right enough.'

'Everything about this sounds daft. Or suspicious. Don't discount your theory, Janie. It's as good as any other right now.' McLean reached down and unclipped his seat belt with one hand, pulling the door release with the other at the same time. 'Let's go see if the security camera footage is any help before we start chasing shadows though.'

12

The morning had not started well, Janie had to admit. She'd woken with a sore head anyway, the direct result of an evening spent getting too pally with a bottle of wine as she and Manda trawled the listings for a flat they could move to. Nothing was as nice or as convenient or as familiar as the flat they were already living in, and everything was way more expensive than she'd been expecting. So much for the increase in salary her promotion to detective inspector had brought. It would be wiped out in increased rent easily.

Accompanying DCI McLean on their visit to Nathaniel Drake should have been a simple task and a chance to get her head together before the real work of the day began. Instead, she'd been annoyed by the constant whispering of Drake's assistant, surprised that neither McLean nor the tech billionaire himself had noticed. It had put her on edge, and the drive back to the station past what was soon to be no longer her home had not helped things.

She probably should have told McLean, but the DCI had enough troubles of his own. She and Manda would sort this out themselves, if either of them ever had some spare time. Not today though. She'd barely sat down in her office when the call from control had come in. Now she was heading out beyond the bypass, onto the A1 and east towards Haddington, DC Bryant driving the electric Nissan pool car.

'What's the story again, Jessica?' Janie carefully popped the lid off her waxed cardboard cup and sipped the scalding hot coffee she'd managed to grab on her way out. Not as good as the cup served at Drake's house, but she had a feeling she was going to need all the caffeine she could get if she was going to make it through the day.

'All I heard was a body in the woods south of a place called Ormiston.' The detective constable tapped the satnav screen in the dashboard as if that might help. 'Something about it being part buried. Grisly, Don Gatford said.'

'And how would Don know? He's not been out there, has he? Meant to be running the front desk, I thought.'

'Aye, he is. You know what he's like though. Talks to everyone. The only person I know who's better clued-up about what's going on is Grumpy Bob.'

Mentioning the retired detective sergeant's name reminded Janie of her brief encounter with the man himself, snooping about her office the previous evening. Missing persons cases, that was what he'd said he was catching up on. Well, maybe they'd just found one.

'I'll be sure and let him know what we find out here, then. Wouldn't want his reputation being ruined.' She took another sip of coffee, blew on the surface to cool it, then almost spilled the lot on her trousers as the car hit a pothole.

'Sorry, boss.' Bryant hunched herself over the steering wheel as if that would make things any better. 'Roads are a bit shit round here.'

'So I see.' Janie clipped the lid back on the cup and placed it in a holder designed for something twice as big. Well, if it spilled it wouldn't be the worst thing that had soaked into the floor carpet in the pool car, judging by the smell that wafted up every time she scuffed it with her boots.

'Almost there anyway.' Bryant pointed ahead to a band of trees marking a turn in the road. Janie caught the yellow fluorescence of a Police Scotland safety tabard. Soon they were at a narrow turning into scrappy woodland and being waved down by a couple of uniform officers. From the way they stood, and the way they leaned heads together to exchange some unheard words, she could tell that they were jumping to conclusions they would come to regret.

'Detective Constable Bryant and DI Harrison,' Bryant said through the open window before either of the officers could tell them they were in the wrong place. She already had her warrant card out, and held it up just long enough for them to see without registering any of the details. The closest of the two had already bent down, his expression of authority ebbing away to one of disbelief as he saw the two young women control had seen fit to send out to his serious crime scene. He had an old face, much weathered by walking a beat rather than sitting in front of a desk. A greying moustache drooped from his nose like sooty snot, not helped by the general dampness around.

'Constable, Inspector.' He nodded his head once, sending a spray of raindrops against the lower half of the window. 'There's a parking area that way. Crime scene manager's set up there. Forensics are here already.'

'Thank you, Sergeant Handley,' Bryant said, and Janie enjoyed the little flinch of surprise on the old man's face that she would know who he was. Before he could say anything to it, she inched the car forward and the two men moved out of the way.

'Know him well?' Janie asked as they bumped through potholes on the way deeper into the woods.

'Couldn't say I know him at all. We were both on a training course a couple of years back though. I'm good with names.' Bryant smiled widely, then concentrated on directing the pool car into a space in a wide parking area. Two squad cars sat on the far side of the clearing, a white and mud-coloured forensic services van close by with its back doors open to the trees beyond. One other car alongside it was the only one that looked at home this deep into the countryside, although Janie knew the dark green Land Rover belonged to the city pathologist, Tom MacPhail.

'Looks like the doc's here already,' Bryant said as she unclipped her seat belt and clambered out of the car. By the time Janie had followed suit, she was stretching as if they'd driven for half the morning, rather than the forty minutes it had actually been.

'Good.' She pulled up the zip on her fleece jacket all the way to her chin, shoved her hands in her pockets and tried not to shiver against the damp cold that hung about the trees. 'Let's go see what he's got to say for himself.'

It took longer than that, of course. First they had to find the crime scene manager and sign in, then they had to wait while one of the forensic technicians found them white paper overalls. At least the extra layer gave Janie a bit more insulation. Bryant didn't seem to notice the cold at all.

They followed a marked path through trees that looked both spindly and old. Janie was no expert, but she thought they might have been oak, or maybe ash. Whatever they were, they'd dropped most of their leaves but kept a hold of just enough to soak her through every time she brushed past an overhanging branch. How forensics thought they could get anything from such a hostile environment was anyone's guess. No doubt Manda would tell her if she asked.

The narrow path meant they had to walk in single file, and the twisty nature of it as it wound around the trees blocked the actual crime scene from view until they were almost upon it. Janie slowed up when she heard low murmuring voices. She ducked carefully past a branch that had drooped across the track, which meant that when she emerged into the small clearing she was crouching like a child doing a monkey impression. Fortunately no one was looking, all eyes on something lying in the dirt.

'Who's in charge?' she asked, trying to pitch her voice so as not to surprise anyone. Perhaps she and Bryant should have made more noise as they approached.

'That'd be me.' A white-suited figure stood up from where it had been crouching at the far side of the huddle. 'Detective Inspector Harrison, I presume?'

Before she could say anything, another of the figures had turned around, pulling down her hood to reveal short-cropped dyed pink hair and a nose piercing. Cerys Powell, the pathologist's assistant, greeted her with a wide, friendly smile.

'We really have to stop meeting like this, you know?'

It had become something of an in-joke between the two of them, and Janie felt a little warmth chase away the chill of the damp woods for a moment. She was about to launch into the standard response when her gaze drifted past the small group and she saw what they had all been huddled around. Behind her, DC Bryant let out a small yelp of shock, and Janie couldn't have agreed more.

The naked body of a man lay half in, half out of the ground. Dead leaves clung to his pale flesh and partially covered the black soil around him. From where she stood, she could see most of his back down to the start of his buttock cleft, but his head was turned away. One arm reached out towards a tree a metre or so beyond, the other arm half buried. His legs were still in the ground, she assumed. Same as she assumed he had been buried alive and tried to climb out of his grave. That was what it looked like, however horrific it sounded. She'd have shivered even without the cold.

'It's quite the sight, isn't it?' The white-suited figure who had first spoken now approached Janie, pulling down the hood of their overalls to reveal short grey hair and a round, weathered face. 'Sergeant Wemyss,' she said. 'I was first on scene after the body was discovered. Used to work plain clothes a long time ago, so I more or less knew what needed to be done.'

'Who discovered the body?' Janie asked, without looking back to see it again.

'Local lad out at first light after pigeons. Charlie Johnson. Well, technically his dog, but it amounts to the same thing.'

'Where's he now?'

Sergeant Wemyss pointed back the way Janie had come. 'He lives in the farmhouse about a half-mile down the road. These woods are part of his dad's farm. I told him to go home, we'd be in touch. Didn't seem much point keeping him here.'

'Fair enough. I'll need to speak to him once I've finished up here.' Reluctantly, Janie approached the group around the body. Cerys had gone back to helping her boss, who was leaning in close to study the dead man's exposed arm. Crouched down the other side of the body, a forensic technician held a professional camera, clicking off shots like this was some bizarre fashion show.

'What's the prognosis, doc?'

Dr MacPhail leaned back with a groan and a flex of his shoulders as Cerys shuffled to make a gap for Janie to kneel beside him. The damp ground had already soaked through her paper boiler suit and trousers, chilling her knees, before she noticed the two of them had lightweight foam plastic boards like old people used when gardening.

'Don't think I can save this one, Janie,' the pathologist said.

'He been out here long, you reckon?'

Another shrug turned into a rolling of his neck, accompanied by a horrible popping sound as vertebrae shifted back into place. Dr MacPhail grimaced a little, raised one gloved hand as if to massage the sore spot, then remembered he was wearing dirty latex gloves.

'It's hard to tell. Not more than a day or two, for sure. Weather's been cold enough to stop him putrefying, but there's no obvious damage to his fingers either. They'd be the first thing a fox or badger would have a go at.'

'And the situation?' Janie asked, waving one hand to take in the way the body appeared to be clawing itself out of the ground. 'Tell me something started digging him up and was disturbed before it had finished. Please.'

'Wish I could, J. But that would leave marks on the body. Something big enough to pull him out of the ground would have bitten an arm, or here on the shoulder.' The pathologist reached forward and grabbed the man's clavicle gently in one hand. 'But there's no sign of damage anywhere on his body that I can see so far. Might be different once we've got him out and back to the mortuary, but either this has been staged to look horrifying or it actually is.'

Janie stared at the naked, dirt-smeared back of the man, his dark, wet, wavy hair clinging to his scalp in heavy locks. The bare arm bore the faded marks of an old tattoo around the wrist, which a calculating part of her mind reckoned would make identification easier. She didn't want to, but she was going to have to ask.

'Have you moved him at all yet? Is it possible to get a look at his face?'

'Funnily enough, we were just getting to that. Not going to be easy given how half of his body's still in the ground, but if you can give us a bit of space.'

Janie took the hint, easing herself to her feet with a bit less drama than the pathologist. She wiped at the twin dark splotches on the knees of her paper overalls as she stepped back, then looked up to see the crime scene photographer point the camera straight at her. A click and that was one more for next year's office calendar. Ah well, she'd had worse.

'Is this not creeping you out, boss?' DC Bryant asked from the spot where the marked path entered the clearing. Not usually squeamish around dead bodies, she nonetheless seemed unwilling to come any closer to this one.

'I'm trying not to let it show, Jessica. DI, remember? I need to be professional.'

Bryant made the briefest of glances down to Janie's muddy knees, but kept a straight face all the same. She might have said something, but at that moment Dr MacPhail and his assistant managed to roll the body onto its side. The pathologist supported the dead man's head with one hand, the better for the photographer to click off a dozen or more rapid snaps. Janie took a step forward for a better look and couldn't help the gasp that escaped from her lips.

His eyes were open, long lashes encrusted with dirt. Mud smeared his cheeks like bad camouflage paint, and his hair had plastered itself to his forehead. His skin had the dull, waxy death sheen she more associated with cadavers in the mortuary than bodies half buried in the woods. But it was the shock of recognition that had unsettled her.

'I . . . I think I know this man.'

13

B ogside Farm was a mixture of old stone buildings and modern steel-sided sheds arranged around a well-kept yard a half-mile down the road from the woods where they had found the body, just as PS Brenda Wemyss had said. As DC Bryant piloted the car in past a tractor the size of a starter home and negotiated a sudden horde of barking sheepdogs, Janie couldn't help thinking it would have been better to bring the old sergeant along with them, since she probably knew the farmer and could have made introductions.

Behind the tractor and an elderly Land Rover, the yard opened onto a narrow driveway and a substantial stone farmhouse. Bryant pulled up as close to what looked like the back door as possible, but there was still a perilous gap filled with baying hounds to cover.

'You reckon they're just excited to see us, or actually feral?' the detective constable asked as she hesitantly unclipped her seat belt and made no other move to exit the car.

'Only one way to find out,' Janie said and pushed open her door. Immediately the barking stopped and a hundred wet and muddy noses pressed themselves in through the gap with heavy breaths and lolling tongues. She had never been particularly frightened of dogs, and this pack, while noisy, didn't give off an aggressive vibe. She'd still probably need a clean pair of trousers when she got home, but then the mud and damp of the crime scene had already made that a necessity.

'Hoy, you lot. Leave 'em alone.' The shout came from the open doorway to the house, where a middle-aged woman stood. She whistled once and all the dogs flowed away like a river. They raced off to a corner of the old stone steadings and disappeared through an arch into darkness. Sensing the moment was right, DC Bryant clambered out of the car. Janie followed from the other side, and they both made it to the house without being savaged.

'You'll be the polis,' the woman said as they arrived at the door.

'Detective Inspector Harrison, aye. And this is my colleague, Detective Constable Bryant.'

The woman considered them for a moment, then said, 'Aren't you a little young for an inspector?' before dismissing the question with a shake of her head. 'Alice Johnson. Come in, why don't you. I've got the kettle on.'

They followed her through a ramshackle room piled high with old rubber boots and shepherds' crooks, waxed cotton jackets and abandoned farm overalls. A Sheila Maid drying frame hung from the high ceiling, draped with heavy woollen socks, and as they passed it, Janie saw a washing machine gently tumbling suds back and forth. The air smelled of damp dog and old coats, but as they stepped into the kitchen beyond, the scent was replaced by one of fresh baking. The temperature rose ten degrees too, bringing a prickling sweat to Janie's scalp for a moment.

'Grab a seat if you can find one. I'll give Charlie a shout.' Mrs Johnson walked to the door on the far side of the room and did just that. Something that might have been a grunt of acknowledgement filtered into the kitchen, but by then she had crossed to the huge range cooker and hefted a kettle onto one of the hotplates.

'So. A body in Priory Wood. Not one of the old monks come back to haunt us, is it?'

Mrs Johnson had a friendly face, weather-beaten and lined,

with a ready smile. Her hair was as much grey as not and she busied herself about the kitchen like a woman used to doing things. Something in the expression on Janie's face, and DC Bryant's too, must have registered though, as she stopped busying herself with teapot and mugs, pulled out a chair and sat down.

'Is that what it's called then, Priory Wood?' Janie asked.

'Has been as long as I've lived here, certainly. I'm told there was a nunnery there hundreds of years back. I don't know if there's any history about the place. Can't say I've seen much in the way of ruins either. It does have a lot of pigeons in it though, and they make a good pie.' Her gaze darted to the door again and she stood up swiftly. 'Ah, here we are. Come in, Charlie. It's the polis. They won't bite.'

Janie turned in her seat to see a young man standing in the doorway. Taller than his mother by almost a head, he was gangly thin, his hair messy as if he'd been asleep, his face bearing the scars of teenage acne. Despite that, it was easy enough to see the mother in the son.

'Mr Johnson.' She stood up, offered a hand to shake. 'Detective Inspector Harrison. I wonder if I might ask you a few questions about what you saw in the woods.'

Charlie Johnson looked at her as if she had two heads, his eyes widening as he noticed DC Bryant as well. He almost took a step back, but then seemed to gather himself and came into the room.

'Detective Inspector?' he asked, the emphasis on the second word, the disbelief in both. 'Are you no—'

'Don't be rude, Charlie. Sit yourself down and I'll get you a cup of tea. There's shortbread in the tin if you're hungry.' Mrs Johnson turned her attention back to the cooker. The young man pulled out the chair she had been sitting in and lowered himself into it.

'Do I need a lawyer?' he asked. Janie found it impossible to tell whether he was being serious or not.

'Not at all. You're no' in any trouble, haven't done anything wrong. I just want to know in your own words what happened. If we need a formal statement we can get that later. Right now it's just helping us put together a picture, aye?'

Charlie shuddered slightly, either from the temperature change as he adjusted to the warmth of the kitchen or because he was putting together a picture in his mind much like the one Janie had in hers.

'Is like I said to Brenda, right?' He hunched his shoulders as behind him his mother tutted. 'Sergeant Wemyss, y'know.'

'We've spoken to her, yes,' Janie said. Beside her, Bryant had her notebook out and was scribbling industriously.

'What time did you head out this morning? You were after pigeons, wasn't it?'

'Aye. Me an' Basil. He's my Patterdale, right. Guess I was up about half four, out by the back of five.'

'That's early,' Bryant observed.

'Need to be there for first light, see? Get myself set up.'

'Are the woods the best place to go?' Janie asked.

'This time of year, aye. They roost in the trees, then fly out to the winter barley when it starts to get light. Have a wee feed.'

'PS Wemyss said it was your dog that found . . .' Janie tailed off, not wanting to think too hard about the body.

'Aye, Basil.'

As if hearing his name, a wiry-haired black terrier came bustling into the room. He trotted up to Janie, sniffed her, then scuttled under the kitchen table. A moment later he appeared on Charlie's lap and stared at her from a distance. The young man scratched his dog between the ears.

'He was a wee bit skittish when we got to the woods, but I thought that was just because of the . . .' He stopped, his face turning red, acne scars even darker.

'Because of the what?' Janie asked.

'It's . . . Ah. I don't . . .'

84

'Doggers?' Bryant asked, then pointed at Basil, whose ears had pricked up at the word. 'And I don't mean that kind, aye? Folk coming out in their cars at night. Getting up to, well, don't need to say, do we.'

Charlie's shoulders slumped in relief, although his embarrassment was still evident. 'Aye.' He looked briefly around at where his mother was standing, but she just shrugged as if she'd seen it all before.

'Does that happen often?' Janie asked. 'People in those woods?'

'Don't really know,' Charlie said. 'Just see lights there after dark sometimes. And then the next day there'll be . . . stuff left lying about the car park.'

'And there were lights last night?'

'No' last night, no. But I saw them maybe two, three nights ago. I've no' had time to go out after pigeons since then. An' I didn't notice any rubbish this time, but like I said, it'd been a couple of days.'

'But Basil was acting up all the same,' Janie said, earning herself a gruff little bark and a wag of the tail.

'Aye. He was whining, see? And he's usually off hunting for mice an' stuff. There's hardly any rabbits since the myxie got them all, but that doesn't stop him trying. But this time he was round my feet. Clingy, like. An' then he took off through the undergrowth and started barking his wee head off. Well, that set the pigeons flying, so we weren't going to get anything. I called him back, but he wouldn't come. Just kept on barking like I don't know. I had to go in after him. It was still dark in the trees, mind, so I used my head torch. An' that's when I saw it.'

Exhausted by his story, and by the memory of what he had seen, Charlie fell silent. Basil turned around in his lap, reached up and licked him on the chin. Mrs Johnson stepped up behind her son and put a gentle hand on his shoulder for a moment. The kitchen fell to almost total silence.

And then the kettle boiled over onto the hotplate.

They managed to avoid being mauled by a pack of sheepdogs as they left Bogside Farm a cup of tea and a couple of home-made biscuits later. Janie let Bryant drive again, and spent the first twenty minutes on her phone getting on top of what looked like it would be a tricky investigation. Not the least of which would be explaining to her superiors how she was able to identify the body.

'Just how is it you know this Mihailovic bloke?' Bryant asked as Janie hung up after a detailed conversation with Sandy Gregg. So she was going to be explaining it to her juniors too.

'His girlfriend, partner, I don't know. She came to see me a few days back. Said he'd gone missing and was there anything I could do.'

'Straight to a DI? That's pushy.'

Janie didn't so much laugh as breathe out heavily through her nose. 'Aye, well. We were at school together. Reminds me, I'll have to give her a call.' She held up her phone again.

'We not trying to keep this quiet for now?' It was a fair question. They'd asked the Johnsons not to tell anyone about what had happened, although Janie didn't hold up much hope of the young lad keeping quiet. He'd paled when she had asked him if he'd taken any photographs, sworn blind he hadn't even thought of it. On balance, Janie was prepared to believe him, so hopefully the internet would take a while to catch up. If the press got a hold of the story, a buried man clawing his way out of the ground, then all bets were off.

'I'll need to tell her he's dead, aye. But I was thinking more of asking her to formally ID the body. We'll keep the details of where he was found and how to ourselves for now, mind.'

'So that's what you and Lofty were up to when you went out for most of a day, right?' Bryant asked.

'Aye. We spoke to one of his flatmates, then went to his work.

Guess we'll have to do that all over again, only a bit more formal this time.' Janie tried not to let the heavy sigh escape, but failed miserably. She didn't much fancy facing down Babs the site manager, or Sasha the gang boss. Perhaps a chat with Nadia at Mihailovic's grubby digs would be better.

'Who do we know in the modern slavery investigation team these days?' she asked, even though chances were Bryant wouldn't have much more of a clue than she did.

'Isn't that something Kirsty was working on with the NCA over at Gartcosh?'

'Aye, you're right.' Janie took up her phone again and swiped through the favourites, looking for the detective superintendent's number. 'Cross border stuff's going to involve them anyways, so we might as well get them in at the start.'

She lifted the handset to her ear, heard the all too familiar sound of Detective Superintendent Ritchie's voicemail.

'Not answering?' Bryant asked.

'I'll send her a text.' Janie started doing just that, half concentrating on the road ahead. The detective constable drove with a slightly nervous energy that made it hard to anticipate what she was going to do next. Not as comfortable behind the wheel as some, although she had happily taken the keys when offered them. As they approached the roundabout at Cameron Toll, indicating the turn-off up Dalkeith Road towards Newington and the station, Janie had a change of mind.

'Next turning on, Jessica,' she said. 'I think we'd better go see Mihailovic's flat again before word gets out he's dead. Or perhaps that he's been found.'

Bryant did as she was told, earning a sharp toot of the horn from the car behind. 'Thought they said he'd left weeks back.'

'Aye, they did. Doesn't mean I believe them though.'

14

It might have been Janie's imagination, but the apartment block where Vaclav Mihailovic had lived seemed a lot quieter than the last time she had visited. Fewer people hung around in the lobby, and as she and DC Bryant made their way along the corridor towards the flat, she saw several piles of boxes outside other doors.

'What's all that about?' Bryant asked as she stepped around a neatly tied bundle of clothes.

'Apparently anyone going home leaves stuff they don't want to take with them for charity. Or to be shared out among the other people in the block.'

'There's a lot of it though.'

'Aye. It's almost as if something's scared these folk enough to leave. Can't imagine what that might be.'

When they reached the apartment door, Janie knocked lightly, ear as close to the grubby surface as she dared so that she could listen for movement within. The silence echoed, and when she tried the handle she found the door unlocked.

'That's not good,' Bryant said.

'Not good at all.' Janie edged the door open onto the small hallway she'd seen before. Where that time there had been coats hanging from a rack on the wall, now there were only empty hooks. The boots had gone too, and someone had taken the trouble to sweep the floor.

'Hello?' She took a step inside, Bryant waiting in the corridor. No one answered, so she carried on through to what would have been the living room when the apartment was first planned. Now it was decked out with four bunk beds, bare, stained mattresses and thin pillows showing that nobody was sleeping here any more. It was the same in the two actual bedrooms, pressed to accommodate far more than the architect had ever envisioned.

Whoever had swept the floor had also cleaned the bathroom, but no amount of bleach and scrubbing could hide the fact that it had been heavily used. Black mould crept around the edges of the bath and up the tiles of the separate shower. The linoleum floor was cracked and worn, warping upwards around the edge of the toilet and suspiciously discoloured. At least the last person had left a half-roll of toilet paper, but there was no towel to dry your hands on if you washed after you'd wiped. No soap either.

'Heard you were looking for somewhere to stay,' Bryant said as she peered in over Janie's shoulder. 'Could be your lucky day.'

'There's ten bunk beds in this flat, Jessica. Twenty people sharing this space. Maybe more. They were almost certainly doubling up with shift work. How could people live like that?' Janie crossed the hall to the kitchen, as empty as all the other rooms. 'And how could they all up sticks and disappear?'

'I guess where they come from the police knocking on your door unannounced is not always a welcome thing.' Bryant opened a few cupboards and bent down to peer into the oven. When she stood up again she shook her head, even though Janie had already seen there was nothing. 'So what next? Knock on the neighbours' doors? Only, if what you say about the boxes is true, I don't reckon there's many left on this floor at all.'

'Aye, I know. We'll still have to do door to doors on the whole block anyway.' Janie already had her phone out, ready to put in a call to the station. 'We'll need a lot more bodies if we're going to do that. Probably ought to find out if there's a local community organisation. Speak to someone who knows these people. That and find out who owns this flat so we can have a word with them about multiple-occupancy rental.'

'All that today?' Bryant asked, her gaze turning towards the window. Janie followed it, saw what the detective constable was talking about. A quick glance at her phone confirmed that they were fast running out of hours. They'd need to plan carefully how they dealt with a place like this tower block. Come in too heavy-handed and they'd do more harm than good. And it wasn't as if they were going to find anything in this flat to tell them what had happened to Mihailovic.

She put her phone away, wandered over to the window and stared out over the tops of the nearby buildings. The view took in Craigmillar Castle Park and Liberton golf course, the distant Pentland Hills and Hillend Ski Centre. It could have been a great place to live were it not for the run-down facilities, the overcrowding and quite illegal multiple occupancy, and the transient nature of most of the people living there.

Movement below caught Janie's attention. She looked down to see the small, litter-strewn communal area. Despite the lowering clouds and threat of rain, someone was boldly hanging out washing. Someone familiar-looking even at this distance. She turned from the window and set off for the door.

'Stay here can you, Jessica? There's someone I think I should go and talk to alone.'

A couple of teenage boys tried to get in her way as she clattered down the stairs, but Janie had grown up with older brothers and knew how to deal with their nonsense. Their angry shouts and lewd suggestions bounced off her back as she left them far behind, confident their bravado was not strong enough for them to bother following her.

When she reached the ground floor, it took a moment to locate the corridor that would take her to the back of the tower block and the scruffy drying green-cum-playground that she'd seen from the kitchen window up above. A couple more women were hanging clothes from one of the lines despite the ominous rain clouds. Three more teenagers kicked a soggy football back and forth between them, which was an improvement on the loiterers up the stairs. And there at the far end of the green, the sight that had prompted her to hurry down here. Janie attempted a casual nonchalance as she approached, while scoping the ground for potential exits. Doubtless the fences that surrounded the area had holes in them, but she reckoned the teenagers were more likely to use them than the woman busy with her washing basket.

'It's Nadia, isn't it?'

The effect of hearing her name spoken was perhaps much the same as if she had put her finger in a live electrical socket. The young woman stiffened, jerking upright so sharply that she dropped the pair of dungarees she had been about to peg to the line. Janie almost took a step back when she saw the pure anger and hatred that flashed across her face, but then it was replaced in an instant with fear and alarm.

'You.' It was all the young woman could manage. Her gaze darted from Janie to the other two women using another washing line, to the fence, to the reinforced glass door that led into the tower block, back to Janie. She looked like a cornered animal desperately searching for a way out.

'I'm not here to cause any trouble.' Janie raised both hands, palms out in what she hoped was a calming gesture.

'Is too late for that,' Nadia spat. And then the fight went out of her, almost as swiftly as it had come. She stooped, grabbed the dungarees from the dirty grass and gave them a hefty shake before pegging them to the line.

'We found Vaclav,' Janie said.

'Is too late for him too.'

'You knew?' Janie wasn't surprised. 'When?'

Nadia pulled out more washing from her basket and pegged it up to dry before answering. 'I suspect. When you first come round. When he go, Vash, it was sudden, you know? I see him in morning, he seem fine. Tired, maybe, but who of us not tired, no?'

Another stoop, a handful of men's underpants in varying shades of grey and stain. Janie watched as Nadia's swift, skilled fingers juggled pegs and clothing into a neat row.

'You saw him the morning before he left?'

A shrug. 'I think. Was some time ago. He not come for breakfast next day.'

Janie waved a hand back in the direction of the tower block. 'Looks like everyone's left now.'

'They come, they go. Is happens all time. Work in other city maybe. Or go home. Who know?'

'But you stayed?'

The woman picked up another T-shirt, shook angry creases from it before pegging it to the line like a torture victim. 'Nadia cook and clean and do washing. Is all Nadia good for, no?'

Something about her tone put Janie on edge. That and the way the young woman glanced up at the building as she spoke.

'You still have my card? My phone number?' she asked. The young woman snapped another T-shirt into shape, the noise of it echoing off the building like a gunshot, but she nodded at the same time.

'Well, use it, aye?' Janie said. 'If you're being forced to stay here against your will, I can help you get out. All you need to do is give me the word.'

Nadia almost laughed. 'Help from police? I think is unlikely, no?' She shook her head. 'And I no have phone I can use for this.'

Janie almost scoffed at that. Everyone had a phone, surely? But then Nadia's full meaning sank in – 'I can use for this' might simply have been her slightly broken English, or more likely it meant that Nadia's access to a phone was tightly controlled. She wasn't locked away, but whoever gave her the occasional use of a phone had enough of a hold on her that she couldn't simply run. No one was supervising her out here on the drying green, after all. But modern-day slavery didn't always mean shackles and chains. Not physical ones, anyway.

'OK. I understand.' Janie shoved her hands in her pockets, aware that soon a lot more police officers would be arriving at this tower block. Perhaps not that evening, but tomorrow morning for sure. And what were the chances Nadia would disappear the moment they did? What were the chances she was going to disappear the moment Janie left? It was tempting to arrest her on the spot, bring her in for questioning, but she knew that would yield nothing and lose whatever scant cooperation with the local immigrant community there might be. No, this needed to be played gently. Slowly, for all that there was a suspicious death at play.

The young woman kept one eye on her while she continued to hang out the washing. All men's clothes, a mixture of styles and sizes, if there was one unifying theme to them all it would be 'well worn'. Workmen's clothes, with the emphasis on 'men'.

'You do laundry for all the workers?' she asked. 'Only, the flat you were in before is empty, right?'

Nadia hung the last pair of underpants on the line, stooped for the basket and tucked it under one arm. 'Is always workers needing clean clothes, no?' She waved her free hand at the other two women, one of whom was staring back at Janie with a thunderous scowl on her face. 'Nadia do washing. Nadia make beds and clean rooms and cook meals. Sometimes maybe Nadia do more.'

Janie didn't bother asking what more Nadia might do for the men whose beds she made and clothes she washed. It wasn't hard to guess, and it was clear the young woman was becoming increasingly agitated. The other two women had wandered over to see what was going on, open hostility on their old, lined faces. Only laundry and perhaps cooking for these two, although there was no accounting for taste.

'Is problem?' one of them asked, her accent thicker even than Nadia's.

'Just looking for someone. Seems he's not here, so I'll let you all get on, aye?' Janie held Nadia's gaze for a second, trying to convey to the young woman that she wasn't the enemy here. None of them said anything, so she turned and walked away. It was only a couple of steps before the chatter started up in some language she had no hope of understanding.

15

L ow, grey clouds scudded across the sky, the occasional flurry of rain spattering the glass as McLean stared out of the long window wall of his office. Better to be inside on a day like this than out there walking the beat, and yet part of him would have been happy doing just that. Or maybe walking across town to visit a crime scene, interview a witness, talk to a victim. Anything other than the headache in front of him right now.

He had formed an almost immediate dislike of Nathaniel Drake. It wasn't hard, of course. McLean had disliked the idea of Drake before ever meeting the man. But that morning's chat, with Janie Harrison along to show the biotech entrepreneur the seriousness with which Police Scotland were taking his grievance, had only deepened the enmity. It wasn't so much the man's wealth; McLean wasn't exactly on the breadline himself. No, it was the way the billionaire simply expected the world to be at his beck and call. And perhaps the way it so often was.

At least, that was what McLean had managed to persuade himself so far. The part of him that would have been happy treading a path along the city's damp pavements reckoned he was trying to duck a more difficult question, and that part was sadly right.

A gentle knock at the doorframe dragged his attention away from the morose. Looking around he saw Detective Sergeant

Lofty Blane leaning half into the room, as if uncertain his great size would fit all the way.

'Please tell me you come bearing good news, Detective Sergeant.' McLean tried to inject some levity into his voice, but the way Blane's brow furrowed in response suggested he'd missed the mark.

'Ah, I'm not sure, sir. We may have found something on the camera footage. Thought I'd run it past you before we chase it any further.'

'Is it on the system, or would I be better coming down to the viewing room?'

DS Blane's gaze shifted briefly from McLean to the tiny screen of his laptop computer and then back again. 'Easier to see on the big screen, sir. Resolution's not as good as it might be.'

McLean levered himself out of his seat to a chorus of squeaks and groans, some of which might have come from him, then followed the detective sergeant along the corridor and down the stairs. The CCTV viewing room had come on a long way since his early days in plain clothes. Back then video had been mostly on tape, and you watched it in what was a repurposed store cupboard, presumably chosen for its lack of windows. Now a whole room had been taken over, with large wall screens and a row of smaller monitors. Feed could be piped in from much of the city's many hundreds of council-run cameras, images of relevance to any ongoing investigation stored on racks of networked hard drives that whirred away in one corner and meant the room was always that little bit warmer than the rest of the station.

Two other officers were already in the room, which wouldn't have been physically possible back in the store-cupboard days. Detective Constable Cass Mitchell sat at a long desk, peering at a couple of the smaller screens as she flicked at the wheel on the top of her computer mouse. Beside her, the new boy, DC Connor Fairley, snapped to attention as he saw who had entered the room.

'At ease, Detective Constable,' McLean said before the young man could salute. The latest recruit to the team, Fairley was hard-working and conscientious, if a little too eager to please. McLean was reliably informed he was twenty-two, although he looked about fifteen. What was that old saying about policemen getting younger?

'You got everything lined up, Cass?' DS Blane asked. Mitchell answered with a gracious movement that involved pushing her seat back, rising to her feet and gesturing for McLean to take her place.

'What am I looking at?' he asked as he fumbled in his jacket pocket for his reading spectacles. Fortunately the spare pair were still in there, otherwise he'd have been sending DC Fairley up to the third floor to fetch them for him.

'White Transit van at the Straiton lights, sir.' Mitchell leaned over him and clicked the mouse. Both screens came to life, the image one of traffic waiting. After a few seconds, they started moving, the cars leaping forward swiftly, heavier vehicles taking a little longer to gather momentum. McLean picked out the white van easily enough as it belched black smoke into the air for a moment, and then it was past the camera and gone.

'Any particular reason why it's of interest?' he asked, although he knew well enough there would be. Mitchell did something with the mouse again, and the images jumped.

'We see it going past the Park and Ride, but not into Loanhead or Roslin. This is about an hour before the break-in was discovered, and this . . .' Mitchell leaned again, her closeness perhaps a little too familiar, although trapped in his seat there was nothing McLean could do about it. He distracted himself by concentrating on the image that came up after she had clicked and scrolled a couple of times. '. . . is it heading back to town less than twenty minutes *after* the break-in was discovered.'

McLean saw the battered white Transit van turned a yellowy-orange by the street lamps. The scene was darker now, full night compared to the earlier video. Rain speckled the camera lens, making the image look like the start of a migraine.

'Definitely the same van?' he asked.

'Aye, we managed to get most of the number plate on that camera, and the earlier image showed the whole thing clear enough after IT worked their magic on it.'

'So why aren't we out there arresting anyone?'

'Ran the number and it belongs to a Renault Megane registered to a retired teacher in Inverness,' Blane said. 'We've spoken to Highlands and that car's parked outside the owner's house. Plate's a clone.'

McLean reached for the mouse, tried to remember how the system worked. He must have got it right, as the image started to go backwards slowly. There wasn't much to see in either direction, the resolution of the video too low to make out anyone inside.

'So how is this useful to us then?' he asked, then worried that his tone sounded too dismissive.

'Well, the plate's no use to us, and white Transit vans aren't exactly few and far between, but . . .' Mitchell left a dramatic pause, then reclaimed the mouse from him. In a moment the first image came up again, and this time it was blown up on the big screen.

'There's a distinctive dent in the front of the van here, and a shape that's either flaked-off paint or rust on the roof just above the passenger seat, see?'

McLean stood up and leaned forward to get a better look, but that only increased the size of the pixels making up the image. There were signs of wear and tear on the van though.

'You reckon we can positively identify this van from that damage?' he asked.

'I'd say yes,' Blane answered. Then had the decency to look a little sorrowful. 'All we need to do is find it first.'

★ ★ ★

The sound of urgent conversation disturbed McLean a while later as he finished drafting an initial report for the chief constable and first minister. He'd already put in a request for the details of the white van to be circulated to all patrol cars, although how far they'd get with that was anyone's guess. It was the sort of desperate lead they might chase in a murder investigation or perhaps a child abduction, but it was the best the team could come up with. And who knew? Maybe it would keep Drake happy for a few days more.

Already out of his seat to see what the commotion was about, he twisted badly and slumped back down as DI Harrison and DC Bryant appeared in his open doorway. A sharp jab of pain ran up his leg into his hip where he had broken it years before. Something of the grimace must have shown on his face as Harrison's expression changed from excitement to concern.

'You OK, sir—Tony?' she asked. The old mistake brought a smile to his face. She'd more or less got the hang of using his first name now, but reverted to 'sir' whenever she was flustered.

'Just stood up too quickly.' He started to massage the pain away, then stopped when he realised how suggestive it might look. 'Something come up? Last I heard you were heading out Haddington way.'

'Aye, we were. We did. Dead body half buried in the woods.'

McLean stood up more slowly this time, easing the pain from his leg, and gestured towards the conference table. By the time he'd sorted out coffee for the three of them, Harrison had told him most of the details about the grisly find, as well as the fact that she'd been unofficially looking for the man whose body she reckoned it was.

'Have you spoken to Border Control about this Mihailovic?' he asked, skirting over the fact that she had probably committed half a dozen breaches of procedure in looking for the Serbian before. He'd long since lost count of the number of times he'd done similar, although perhaps a quiet word later might be in order.

'Not about him being dead, no. Lofty was talking to them about him possibly having gone home. Guess that wasn't the case after all.'

'How're you going to play this, then?'

'First off, I'll have to speak with Jayne about how I knew who he was.' Harrison winced slightly as if imagining the trouble she'd be in. 'We've not had a formal identification yet, mind you. I was going to get back in touch with his girlfriend about that. He's no family here, far as I know.'

'You've set up an incident room?' McLean asked.

'Sandy Gregg's on it at the moment. We'll need to get a move on assigning roles, too. I'll need more manpower if we're going to do door to doors at the tower block where he lived. Not sure how much that'll turn up given the flat's empty right now, but we can try and track some of his flatmates. If nothing else we can get the coonncil on to the landlord about illegal multiple occupancy leasing.' The detective inspector paused a moment as if ticking off a to-do list in her head. 'An' I need to talk to Kirsty about a possible modern-slavery case there too, only that's going to need careful handling if we want any chance of finding out what happened to Mihailovic.'

'You want me to speak to Jayne so you can get on with prepping a briefing?' McLean checked his watch, noticed he'd missed lunch again, and tea. 'Say six o'clock and I'll see if Kirsty's about too.'

The detective inspector's relief showed in the sagging of her shoulders. Even DC Bryant let out a gentle sigh. Harrison finally took a sip from her mug and then grimaced at the bitterness of it. Fair enough, it had been sitting in the glass jug on the hotplate far too long.

'Thank you,' she said, and placed the mug on the table far enough away from her to make it clear she wanted no more. 'I'd better go see how Sandy's getting on then.'

16

A heavy darkness hung over the city as McLean plugged Emma's little Renault Zoe into the charging point by the old coach house many hours later. He'd let her know he was going to be late, of course. The discovery of a dead body and the subsequent organised chaos of setting up a major incident investigation could have meant nothing else, even if newly promoted Detective Inspectors Harrison and Gregg were doing all the heavy lifting. By way of a peace offering, he had stopped off at the pizza restaurant on his way home, and now the smell of melted cheese and toasted bread was making McLean's stomach grumble in anticipation. Lunch had been a long time ago, and he'd missed it anyway. He reckoned he'd probably earned a beer to wash it down, too.

The two cats stared up at him as he entered the kitchen and placed the slim cardboard box on the table. It was getting so that he could hardly tell the difference between them, so it could have been either Mrs McCutcheon's or Cecily Slater's that raised its head and sniffed the air.

'Later.' He opened the door to the Aga's warming oven and slid the box in, out of the reach of thieving fangs. 'If you're lucky and I'm not too hungry.'

Through the far kitchen door, the corridor leading to the main hall was dark. As he walked along it with the confidence of someone who has lived there his entire life, McLean began to make out the sound of voices. For a moment he thought Emma must be watching television, and then a familiar deep laugh assured him she was not. With a mixture of annoyance that he'd not be getting his pizza soon, and guilt that he might feel that annoyance when a friend dropped by to visit unannounced, he pushed open the library door and stepped inside.

'Tony, you're back.' Emma didn't exactly spring from her seat on the sofa; her days of springing were in the past now. She did, however, climb to her feet with a grace he hadn't seen in a while. Beside her, Madame Rose lounged as if it were her library and her house, they the guests. With anyone else it would have been annoying, but McLean found he really didn't mind the old medium treating his house as a home. He stepped forward and gave Emma a hug, and couldn't help noticing that for all her reclaimed agility, she was still thin and frail.

'I brought pizza. Didn't know we had guests.'

'Oh, Tony. You know better than to call me a guest now, surely?' Madame Rose hauled her not inconsiderable bulk out of the sofa with rather less athleticism than Emma. 'And besides, we've both eaten already. Emma didn't know what time you'd be back, so I cooked us up an omelette.'

As she said the words, so McLean noticed the tray with stacked plates, the bottle of wine now half empty. There had been no car outside, so Rose hadn't driven here. No doubt a taxi would arrive without any sign of her having ordered it, at exactly the right time for her to leave.

'So what brings you to this neck of the woods then?' He went to the hidden drinks cabinet in the bookcase, pulled it open and found himself a glass. Wine would go with his pizza just as well as beer, and it looked like the cats were in luck too.

'Can I not just drop by to say hello?' Madame Rose hammed up her Morningside accent to let him know that she wasn't serious.

'Actually, I wanted to see how Emma's been getting on these past few months. We've not been having our regular speech therapy sessions since she doesn't really need them.'

It was true she was much improved, although McLean could still hear the slur in Emma's voice, especially when she was tired or stressed. He could also tell when Madame Rose was telling only half the truth; he was a detective, after all. Of course she would have wanted to check in, but there was always more to her visits.

'And what is the prognosis then, Doctor?'

'Oh, I think a full recovery is on the cards.' Rose accepted a top-up, indicating for McLean to stop when the glass was not quite half full. 'That is if she ever eats a proper meal. Honestly, Tony. I might have to come round more often just to cook. Especially if you're going to be off chasing murderers at all hours.'

McLean felt a little twinge of unease at the word 'murderers'. There was no way Rose could know anything other than that they had a major incident to investigate, could she? Before he could raise even an eyebrow at it he was distracted by Emma hefting the tray with the plates on it.

'If you two are going to talk about me, at least have the good grace to wait until I'm out of earshot?'

'Here, let me get that . . .' McLean began, but the look on Emma's face shut him up. This was one of those simple tasks that had become hard since her stroke, and she was tenacious to do it herself. Well, if the price of her stubborn refusal to give in was a few broken plates, it was a cheap one. He still opened the door for her, and kept an ear out as her shuffling footsteps disappeared in the direction of the kitchen.

'She's determined, that one. You've got to give her that,' Madame Rose said. Wine glass refilled, she had slumped back down into the sofa as if it were magnetic.

'She certainly is. And you're not wrong about her eating too little. The psychology student in me suspects it's because she's worried her lack of physical activity will lead to her getting fat. But then he graduated too many decades ago to think about now, so he's probably wrong.'

'Well, he's probably only half wrong, but you really must try to get her to eat more regularly. Of course, it would help if you did that yourself, Tony.' Madame Rose glanced past him to where the old carriage clock sat on the mantelpiece. 'Coming home late with pizza mustn't become a habit again, eh?'

McLean took a sip of his wine, picked up the bottle again and studied the label. Two Paddocks Picnic Pinot Noir, from New Zealand. It was very good, but he had no recollection of buying it. He savoured the mouthful before turning his attention back to Rose.

'Duly noted. And I promise this won't become a habit. We're setting things up today. Tomorrow it's for Janie Harrison and Sandy Gregg to deal with, OK?'

Rose said nothing, but the look on her ancient face gave McLean hope that she might have accepted his assurance. He meant what he said, too, although good intentions hadn't always worked out. Time to find out what she had really dropped around for.

'So. How are you keeping then?' McLean asked. 'Like you said before, it's been a while.'

'Am I that easily read?' Rose crossed her arms across her ample bosom and leaned back in her seat.

'When you want to be.'

'Well, there is that.' The medium paused for a moment, head tilted slightly as if she was looking for the right words. When she finally spoke again, all sense of jollity was gone from her voice.

'I don't know what you're working on right now, Tony. I don't particularly want to know, and you wouldn't tell me if I asked. There is something going on in this city though. Something I can't quite put my finger on. If you know what I mean.'

McLean suspected that he did, although he would never acknowledge as much. Not directly, anyway.

'A threat to the city?' he asked.

That brought a smile to the old medium's face, albeit only a brief one. 'A threat? For certain. To the city? That's what I'm not sure about. Call it . . . I don't know. A change in the air? A bad feeling? Whatever it is, I've no doubt it will make itself known soon enough. Maybe it already has.'

'And you came by to warn me, I suppose.'

'Would it do any good?' Again that little smile crinkling the edges of Rose's eyes. 'No, it's more to be on the lookout for strange things. Stuff that doesn't immediately make sense. I know you always get sent those cases anyway, but just . . . be aware.'

McLean studied his glass and the red liquid within for a moment. Then he held it aloft in a mock toast. 'To everything strange, then,' he said. Madame Rose raised her own glass, too far away to clink them together.

'Aye, to everything strange.'

The taxi arrived about five minutes later, and soon Madame Rose was gone. McLean watched the twin red pinpricks of brake lights down the drive and away before closing up the front door and heading to the kitchen, via the library to rescue his wine glass and the almost-empty bottle. He found Emma sitting at the table, the tray in front of her still bearing everything it had been piled up with. Carrying it down the corridor without dropping anything might have been a small victory, but it had left her too exhausted to do much else.

'Rose said to say goodbye. She didn't come through as she reckoned you'd maybe had enough of her.'

That raised a weary smile, and Emma rubbed at her eyes as if they were gummed up with sleep.

'She makes a fine omelette, and she means well. But too much social interaction leaves me exhausted for days.' She let out a long, slow sigh that made McLean feel tired just to listen to it. 'Still not really recovered from Hattie and Meg coming for supper.'

'It takes time. And I know you're sick of hearing that, but it's true. You're better this month than you were last, and you were better then than the month before that. There's no way you'd have even tried lifting that tray a year ago, let alone carrying it all the way here.'

McLean did just that himself, taking it over to the counter above the dishwasher.

'Aye, and a year before that I'd not have thought twice. Sorry, Tony. Just feeling a bit low is all.'

Tired though she might have been, Emma still managed to twist around in her chair and watch while McLean loaded dishes and cutlery, somehow managing to convey that he was doing it all wrong just by the way she said nothing at all. It wasn't until he went to scrape the last remnants of omelette into the cat bowl that he remembered his pizza in the warming oven. Half a glass of wine had somehow managed to quash his appetite almost completely.

He pulled the now warm cardboard box out and laid it on the table. A waft of delicious melted-cheese smell filled the air and two pairs of shiny yellow eyes suddenly opened in the blackness at floor level.

'So what were you and Rose gabbing about behind my back? She looked like she wanted a word with you as much as to check in on me.'

McLean drew out a chair and settled himself in, flipped the lid of the box. Pizza had seemed like such a good idea an hour earlier. Now he wasn't sure he had the energy to eat.

'You know what she's like. Vague prognostications are her stock in trade. She seems to think something strange is going to happen, or might already have happened. Thing is, much as I'd like to just dismiss her woowoo as nonsense, she's almost always right.'

'Well, something has happened, hasn't it?' Emma reached out and pulled a hunk of half-burnt topping from the pizza, held it up to the light as if it were a diamond freshly liberated from the ground rather than a crispy half of cherry tomato. 'I mean, you're setting up a major incident investigation, so I'm guessing a body's been found somewhere? Suspicious circumstances?'

'I can't really go into detail, Em. You know that as well as I do. But you're not wrong. It's Janie's case though. I'm just the DCI overseeing things.'

The look Emma gave him at that was all-knowing. Her revenge, perhaps, for his telling her it would take time for her to recover. At least she ate the nugget of tomato, as he would have hated seeing it go to waste.

'And the case you're in charge of,' she said between licks to the tips of her fingers. 'Is that not strange?'

'Not so much strange as annoying. It's political, and you know how much I dislike that sort of thing. Same as dealing with rich people who think the world somehow owes them.'

Emma glanced at the window beyond the kitchen sink. It looked out mostly onto the garden, but if you craned your neck you could see the wall that separated it from the next property, half hidden behind rhododendron bushes. You couldn't see all the way to Nathaniel Drake's new Edinburgh residence, but it was in that direction.

'You never said anything about him after your visit this morning. I take it you'll not be adding him to the dinner-party list any time soon then?'

McLean remembered the used sump oil that Drake had been drinking after his early morning workout and couldn't help a smile spreading across his face. 'Only if he brings his own food.'

Emma leaned back in her chair and yawned like a cat, arms half raised as she stretched. McLean tried not to be too alarmed by the popping and cracking noises from her neck and spine, or by how thin and spindly her fingers were as she flexed them.

'Well, if he pops round to borrow some sugar, I'll be sure to let him know we have standards in this neighbourhood.'

17

The morning had started far too early, tiptoeing through the darkened hallway so as not to upset the snores coming from her flatmate's bedroom. The briefing had been a quiet affair, everyone too tired to do much more than accept their tasks and start work on them. Now Janie was tucked away in her tiny office at the back of the station, poring over the information that had been collated so far about Vaclav Mihailovic. Not much, but then it was only twenty-four hours since his body had turned up half buried in the woods. This had the feel of an investigation that was going to be long, complicated and drawn out.

There was still plenty to do, all the same. The body would need to be formally identified, which would be tricky given Mihailovic had no family in the country. His immigrant status meant even more bureaucratic hurdles than if he'd been native born. She'd have to keep an eye on the performance of all the officers assigned to the case too. Most of the detectives she worked with day to day, Janie could trust to be as thorough investigating this suspicious death regardless of the nationality of the victim. She couldn't say the same for all of her colleagues in Police Scotland though, loath as she was to admit to any institutional racism. It would be all too easy to view this as someone else's problem, write up a simple report for the Serbian consulate and hope the whole thing went away. And the sad truth was it probably would.

But it was a suspicious death and someone had tried to cover it up. Janie couldn't let that lie even if she had wanted to. That she had the loosest of personal connections to the case didn't help either. It wasn't the sort of thing that might exclude her from the investigation, but it gave her more impetus and bolstered her determination to see justice done.

A tap at the open door turned out to be DC Fairley, looking far too bright-eyed for such an ungodly hour. The young detective waited patiently for Janie to close the window on her laptop, not saying anything.

'Was there something you wanted, Connor?' she asked once it became clear that he wasn't going to speak until given permission. It was endearing in some ways, his shyness, but he was going to have to grow a pair if he wanted to make a career in plain clothes.

'Aye, ma'am. That's Miss Lennox arrived. I've put her in interview room two for now.'

It took Janie longer to understand than she might have liked, and she almost asked who Miss Lennox was before it clicked. She logged out of her computer, grabbed her notebook and stood in one swift movement.

'Thanks. I'll go talk to her now.' She was at the door, the detective constable hurrying to make room before she thought of something else. 'And you couldn't rustle us up a couple of coffees, could you?'

Shauna Lennox was standing when Janie let herself into the interview room a few minutes later. She had been staring at the safety posters on the wall, but turned at the sound of the door, an almost guilty expression on her face. It eased away as she recognised who had disturbed her.

'Janie,' she started, then looked a little worried. 'Or should I call you Detective Inspector Harrison?'

'Janie's fine, Shauna. Please, take a seat. DC Fairley's just sorting us out some coffee.' Janie waved a hand at the chair on the far side of the table, pulled out the one nearest to her and sat down. She had brought a folder along with her notebook, but it contained only a couple of close-up photographs of the dead man's face. The rest were too disturbing for someone unprepared, and at least for now they were trying to keep as many details about the incident secret as possible.

'I . . . What's this about?' Lennox took a long time to sit, as if not trusting herself to the chair. 'Is it Vaclav? Have you found him?'

Before Janie could answer, there was a knock at the door and a moment later it opened. Fairley edged in backwards, a tray held precariously in one hand.

'Two coffees as requested, ma'am,' the detective constable said as he placed the tray carefully down beside Janie's folder. 'I wasnae sure how you took it so there's a wee jug and some sugar there.'

Looking down at the tray, Janie saw that there was indeed a small bowl and a couple of teaspoons, as well as a jug of milk and a plate of chocolate Hobnobs. The young lad showed promise if he could sweet talk all that out of the ladies who ran the canteen.

'That's great. Thanks, Connor. You can leave it here.'

The briefest flicker of disappointment scurried across the detective's face. Perhaps he had been hoping to be asked to sit in on the interview. Or maybe Janie was reading too much into it. Either way, in moments he was gone, the door pulled gently closed behind him.

Janie picked up one of the mugs and passed it across the table to Lennox, followed by the plate of biscuits. Waited until she had taken a sip and a bite before starting.

'It is about Vaclav,' she said. 'And it's not good news, I'm afraid.'

Lennox stared at her, face a picture of horror. 'Is he . . .?'

'We found a body. Can't give you too many details, but I think it's him from the photos you showed me.'

'A . . . A body? Where? How?' Lennox had gone very still, and now she started to shake. 'Are you sure it's him?'

Janie stood up, took the folder with her as she walked around the table to where the other woman sat. She half crouched, and put a gentle hand on Lennox's shoulder.

'I've a photograph I'd like to show you, Shauna. It's just a face, but it will probably be a shock all the same. You OK with that?'

A sniff, a nod of the head. 'Aye.'

Janie opened the folder, extracted the first photograph and laid it on the table. She knew by Lennox's reaction that they had the right identity. She stiffened, reached one hand towards the pale, dead face, then curled her fingers and snatched the hand away.

'He . . . He looks like he's sleeping.'

An image of the scene came to Janie's mind then, a naked body half out of the ground, twisted as if desperately flailing to release itself from the earth's cold embrace. These two photographs had been taken after the dead man had been freed, laid out in a body-bag, his eyes closed by the pathologist.

'Aye, he does,' Janie lied. Now came the hard part. 'We've spoken to the Serbian consulate, and the people he shared a flat with. Seems Vaclav had no family over here, and we've not tracked down anyone back home either.'

'That's right.' Lennox sniffed again, produced a crumple of paper tissues and blew her nose noisily. Never once taking her eyes off the picture laid out in front of her. 'He told me his parents were both dead. He had a brother, but they lost contact years ago. There's a grandmother in a care home, but she's got Alzheimer's or something.'

Janie slowly slid the photograph away, flipped open the folder and put it in with the other one. They were similar enough that Lennox didn't need to see both. And if she played this right, they'd be unnecessary anyway. Taking a deep breath, she jumped straight in.

'In which case, it's possible you can do me a big favour.'

The city mortuary was only a few minutes' walk from the police station, tucked away just off the Cowgate. Even so, the incessant rain meant Janie had co-opted a squad car to take the two of them there. She had worried that Shauna Lennox would be unwilling to identify Mihailovic's body, but her old schoolmate had instead been quite enthusiastic about the idea. Now they both stood on one side of a narrow table, what was clearly a body laid out underneath a white sheet. On the other side, Cerys Powell, the mortuary assistant, waited patiently.

'You ready for this?' Janie asked, and when Lennox nodded, Cerys reached down and skilfully rolled back the sheet to reveal the dead man's head and shoulders.

Vaclav Mihailovic, if that was who this was, looked a lot more peaceful now than when Janie had first seen him in the woods south of Haddington. Someone, probably Cerys, had cleaned the dirt from his face and tidied up his hair. Eyes closed, he might have been sleeping, save for the unnatural texture of his skin and his utter stillness. Clean shaven, the faintest hint of a five o'clock shadow darkened his chin and around his mouth, and tiny holes in his earlobes showed where he had recently worn earrings or studs. Janie couldn't recall noticing them at the scene, made a mental note to follow up with Lennox about them.

'It's . . . Yes, it's definitely him.' Once more Lennox reached out for the face, real this time rather than a picture. Once more her hand hovered in the air above the cold, dead flesh before she curled her fingers into a fist and snatched it away. This time she shoved it against her mouth in an attempt to stop the cry from escaping.

'It's OK, Shauna.' Janie put her hand on Lennox's shoulder, slightly surprised when her old schoolmate leaned into what had never been intended as a hug. For long moments the three of them stood there in silence, save for the occasional sniff from Lennox. Then finally she pulled away, dabbed at her eyes with a wad of tissues.

'How did he die?' she asked in a voice that sounded like it might break at any moment.

'We don't know,' Janie said at exactly the same time as Cerys. Both stopped, looking at each other until Janie motioned for the mortuary assistant to take the lead.

'There's no obvious sign of trauma or injury. Nothing to suggest violence, certainly. Dr MacPhail will be conducting a post-mortem examination later this afternoon, so hopefully we'll have a better idea after that.'

Lennox nodded her head once, although Janie doubted the woman had taken in much of what Cerys had said. She reached her hand out towards Mihailovic's head once more, fingers just brushing the curl of the dead man's fringe before jerking away again. She turned from the body, looked to the door. Janie reached out and opened it for her as Cerys hastily rolled the white sheet back into place.

'You'll find them, whoever did this?' Lennox asked.

'We'll certainly do everything we can, but I'll be honest with you, Shauna. It's the best part of a week since anyone saw him. That's a long time for evidence to be lost.'

They walked through the waiting room and out into the mortuary's reception area. Janie glanced briefly at the door she was more used to going through, the one that led to the examination theatre and the cold store. She'd be in there soon enough. Too soon, really, although it was always nice to see Cerys.

'I'll need to talk to you again soon anyway,' she said as they stepped out into chill, damp air. The squad car that had brought them down was long gone, so both of them were going to get wet.

'Will you?' There was a vagueness about Lennox's voice and

her movements, that Janie had seen before in people who had just found themselves bereaved. It was one of the reasons why she'd not conducted a full interview with her before coming to the mortuary.

'We need to find out more about Mihailovic. Vaclav,' she corrected herself. Lennox needed to be treated as if she had been the dead man's wife. 'Anything and everything you can tell us about him can help us build a picture of who he was, and from that what might have happened to him.'

'I can give you a statement now if you want.' Lennox shrugged her arm out of her sleeve enough to look at her watch. 'They gave me the day off work, so I've nowhere to go really.'

Janie considered the day very much not off work that faced her back at the station. The start of any new investigation was always the most chaotic time, with everyone running around gathering any and all information, whether it might be useful or not, then feeding it back to both the senior investigating officer and the Holmes II computer system. Yes, she should be back in the incident room overseeing that process, but on the other hand, this was another part of that information-gathering. Beside her, Lennox was peering out from the small overhang at the entrance to the mortuary, considering the rain.

'You sure you're up to it?' Janie asked.

'Well, it's walk back to your police station, just up the road a ways, or off into town to catch the next bus to Broxburn.' Lennox held her hand out and felt the air. 'Reckon this is easing off for now, but I'd no' fancy my chances for long.'

18

'Must've been what, four years ago now? You remember Val Bowie, right?'

They had chanced the rain and managed to walk from the mortuary back to the station without getting too soaked. Now Janie sat in interview room one again, Shauna Lennox across the table from her. They had decided more coffee would probably be a mistake, but Janie had let DC Fairley sit in on the proceedings. He was taking notes with a slow but neat hand, saying nothing all the while.

'Bowie?' Janie cast her mind back to school, surprised how hard it was to remember. 'Short. Blond hair. Had a thing for one of the football lads, didn't she?'

'Aye, that's right. Johnny Peters. Trialled for Hearts but never quite made the grade. Think he's a bricky's labourer now. Val though, she works in IT, same as me. We were both at some horrible convention up Fountainbridge way. Boring as sin, it was. Don't think I'd spoken to her since we left school, but a familiar face is a familiar face, aye?'

Janie wasn't entirely sure where this was going, but knew better than to interrupt. Lennox took her silence as permission to go on.

'The both of us decided an afternoon listening to senior management going on about workflow prioritisation or some bollocks like that was a waste of our time. Snuck out of the conference centre like we was playing hooky from school again. Found ourselves a nice wee bar and had a good old gossip about things. An' that's when I first saw him.'

It took Janie a moment to catch up. 'Mihailovic?'

'Aye. Who d'ye think I was talkin' aboot?'

'Wasn't sure, to be honest. So you first met him in a bar four years ago. What was he doing there? Working?'

'No.' Lennox gave the word two syllables, the emphasis firmly on the first. 'He was there wi' a couple of mates having a drink like we was. Val hit it off wi' one of the others, right enough. Big man name of Sasha or something. I think Vash was as embarrassed by the two of them as I was. Guess that's why we got talking.'

Janie scribbled a note on her jotter pad. 'This would be the gang boss Sasha? Runs a lot of the immigrant workers on the building site.'

'Aye. Think they knew each other from home. Didn't speak much about him, mind. Don't think I ever saw him again, now I think about it.'

'But you met up with Mihailovic after that. Vaclav.' Janie tried again. 'Vash.'

'We swapped numbers, aye. Didn't think much of it at the time. Couple weeks later I was feeling a bit down though, so I sent him a text. Went back and forth like that for a while. Then we met for a drink an' . . . Well . . . One thing led to another.'

Janie was busy scribbling 'where phone?' on the notepad, so missed most of Lennox's apologetic shrug.

'So you've known him four years or so. Apart from that first meeting, did he ever introduce you to other friends?'

Lennox paused a moment before answering, but Janie didn't get the sense she was trying to hide something. More looking for the best way to explain an unusual relationship.

'I mean, I met some of the folk he shared a flat with. Couple of people from his work. Sasha that one time. Don't think they were close friends, mind. More people he could speak to in his own language, ken?'

Janie nodded as much in encouragement as understanding. 'So you were in a long-term relationship with this man. Did neither of you ever think about taking it further?'

'How d'ye mean?'

'I don't know. Moving in together. Sharing a flat.'

An expression of such deep sorrow fell across Lennox's face, Janie could almost feel a lump in her own throat.

'We talked about it, on an' off. Even looked at a few places. But every time it looked like it might happen something came up.'

'Such as?'

'Ach, it was too expensive or we couldnae get the references or . . . You know what it's like tryin' to rent in this city when you're no' loaded, aye? When you've nothin' saved for a deposit.'

Janie paused in her note-taking, looked up at Lennox sitting across the table from her. Until now she'd not really thought they had much in common aside from both having been to the same school.

'Still live wi' my folks, aye. Before you ask.' Lennox laughed mirthlessly. 'Twenty-eight years old and I'm still in my wee bedroom in Broxburn. You can imagine how pleased my da' would be if I'd brought Vash home. A foreigner, five years older'n me. Works on a building site? That'd go down really well.'

'I thought IT paid good money,' Janie said, and saw from the look Lennox gave her that it had been the wrong thing.

'No' the secretaries,' she said with surprising bitterness.

'I'm sorry. It's not really any of my business, Shauna. I'm just trying to put together a picture of . . . Vash. What kind of man he was, whether he might have had any enemies, owed money to the wrong people, that sort of thing.' Janie put her pen down and leaned back in her seat. 'What kind of plans did he have for the two of you?'

'Vash didn't have any enemies, far as I know. Everyone liked him, he was that kind of guy. If he owed anyone money, he never mentioned it to me. He sent some of his wages back home, helping with the cost of his gran's care, I think. That was another reason we couldn't really afford our own place. Why he was stuck in that shit hole up Craigmillar way.'

'OK.' Janie picked up her pen again, let it hover over the page without writing anything. It was just a prop, really. DC Fairley would get all the details. 'Let's come forward in time a bit then. If I remember rightly, the last time you saw him was quite a while back?'

Lennox pulled out her phone, but didn't really look at it. Sniffed, and rubbed an invisible tear from her eye. 'Aye. It's been a couple months since we last met up, but we spoke once a week, maybe.'

'These were fairly regular meet-ups, I take it?'

'Aye. Just after payday was always good. If we had a bit of spare cash we could maybe go somewhere and . . .' Lennox trailed off, her brain catching up with her mouth. Out of the corner of her eye, Janie saw DC Fairley's pen slow, then hover. A quick glance at him showed the start of a blush darken his freckles. How did someone so innocent in the ways of the world end up a detective constable? With a shake of her head, she turned her attention back to Lennox.

'Think back to that last meet-up. Was it any different to your previous dates? Did you talk about anything you'd not talked about before? Did Mi—Vash seem anxious or worried about anything?'

'No' really. I mean, maybe he was a bit withdrawn, but he had his moods, same as us all. I think that flat in the tower block was getting him down, ken? I mean, it'd do my nut in living like that, an' I still live wi' my parents. Think he went away determined to get out, like. Find some way to make it work. Make us work.' Lennox put the emphasis on 'us', voice starting to break as the realisation hit that there never would be an 'us' again. She studied her phone, the expression on her face suggesting she wasn't quite sure how it had appeared in her hand.

Perhaps it hadn't been such a good idea to press on with this interview so soon after dropping the bombshell news of Mihailovic's death. Janie hadn't quite gauged the depth of the relationship properly, but it was clear her old schoolmate was distracted, likely in shock. She gave Lennox a little time to regain her composure before speaking again.

'What about the last time you spoke? That was a few weeks back. Is that unusual? To not speak for that long?'

Lennox shrugged. 'Like I say, Vash could be moody sometimes, withdrawn, aye. But I wasnae expecting him to call for a couple of weeks, was I?'

'Were you not?' Janie tried to remember their earlier conversation, but some of the details were fuzzy.

'No, I told you, didn't I? He said an opportunity to earn some good money had come up. All above board, but he'd have to take time off the building site, and he'd be away for a fortnight, maybe three weeks. He was that excited about it, really. Reckoned he'd make enough we could put a deposit down on a place.'

For the briefest of moments a look of pure excited joy washed the lines from Lennox's face. The cruel reality brought them back and she hunched in on herself as if someone had kicked her in the stomach.

'Did he say what it was, this opportunity?' Janie asked, even though she already knew the answer. Nothing in life was ever that easy.

'No.' Lennox shoved her hands between her knees, bent low to the table as she shook her head slowly. 'No, he never did.'

19

Vaclav Mihailovic looked very different laid out on the examination table to how he had done the first time Janie had seen him. He was still dead, of course, but flat on his back, arms at his sides, he looked far more at peace than he had done clawing his way out of the ground. Cerys had cleaned him from head to toe, and under the harsh white light of the overhead lamps, Janie might have expected the cadaver to look pale. Instead, his skin had that same waxy yellow quality to it that she had noticed of his face when she had brought Shauna Lennox in for the identification earlier in the day. As if he had been dead weeks, not days. Or subject to the arcane preservation arts of the funeral director.

'Ah, Janie. You're here. Wonderful. We can get started then.'

She had been expecting to see Tom MacPhail in pathologist's scrubs step into the light, but the voice was not his. Although Angus Cadwallader had more or less retired a year ago, he still came in from time to time. 'Keeping his hand in', as he described it whenever he could wedge the poor taste joke into the conversation.

'Tom not here?' Janie asked, then hastily added, 'Not that it isn't always a pleasure to see you, Angus.'

'He's just getting changed. Asked if I'd help him with this one since it's so . . . odd.' Cadwallader peered at the body from a slight distance, half-moon spectacles slid to the end of his long nose.

'Surprised they didn't give this to Tony, if what I've heard so far is true.'

The click of the office door opening prevented Janie from replying, which was just as well since she wasn't quite sure what to say to that. Dr MacPhail emerged, closely followed by Cerys.

'P'nawn da,' Cadwallader said to the mortuary assistant.

'Siwmae, Angus, sut wyt ti?' Cerys replied, clearly not expecting an answer as she busied herself about the cadaver. Dr MacPhail moved into the light and began the post-mortem examination without feeling the need for any introductions.

'Subject is male, caucasian, approximately one hundred and seventy-four centimetres in height, seventy-nine kilos in weight. Exterior shows little sign of injury, no obvious lividity. Skin has an unusual texture and colour, as if it has been preserved in some manner. We'll need to take samples for testing, Cerys.'

Janie watched from a distance as the two pathologists picked over the body like scavengers on a battlefield. It took her a while to work out what was wrong, but it came to her as Cadwallader picked up one of the dead man's arms and bent it so that he could get a closer look at the hand. True, they hadn't opened up the chest cavity yet, but from the far too many post-mortem examinations she had attended in her short career as a detective, she would normally have expected there to be some noticeable stench of decay. All she could smell now was the scent of floor cleaner mixed in with the preservative formaldehyde that permeated the entire building.

'Fascinating,' Cadwallader said as he laid the hand and arm gently back down again. 'The dirt under the fingernails and abrasion on the skin of the fingers would strongly suggest an attempt to dig with his hands. But surely this man was dead long before he was buried?'

'Time of death's been a tricky one to pin down, Angus,' MacPhail said. 'Core temperature was the same as ambient when

THE REST IS DEATH

we arrived at the scene, and as you know he'd been at least partially interred. If he'd been out of the ground more than a couple of hours I'd have expected to see more damage from wild animals, even if it is almost winter. But you can see well enough, nothing's had a go at him.'

'There's very little pooling of blood, either.' Cadwallader bent close to the body again, peering at the man's flank. 'Can we turn him over, Cerys?'

Janie found herself taking a step away as the two pathologists and one assistant expertly rolled Mihailovic onto his front. Cadwallader touched the skin of the dead man's back with his gloved fingers, pressing into the flesh then releasing. Janie half expected the indentations to remain, as if the body was made of soft wax.

'Interesting.' The pathologist pointed at the spot where he had pressed his fingers. 'What do you think, Tom?'

'Well, if it wasn't for the fact he's the same temperature as the cold store, has no heartbeat and shows absolutely zero brain activity, I'd say he wasn't actually dead. He looks more like a well-made dummy than a real person. Something they might use in a film studio.'

'Agreed.' Cadwallader stepped away from the examination table and graciously let Cerys do the work of putting the cadaver onto its back once more. 'I think we need to open him up and see what's going on inside.'

Could this have been some elaborate hoax? Some joke that might have seemed funny to someone once long ago, but really wasn't any more? There was no reason this could be a film prop, even if Janie knew that those could be frighteningly realistic these days. For starters, they were prohibitively expensive. You didn't just leave them half buried in a wood somewhere. Tom MacPhail had examined the body in situ and not suspected it of being anything other than a corpse then. She trusted his judgement and skill not to get something as fundamental as that wrong. And this looked exactly like Vaclav Mihailovic. What possible reason could there be for making a life-scale, anatomically perfect model of a Serbian immigrant building-site worker?

The nugget of an idea came to her then, that this might have been the money-making project Mihailovic had mentioned to Shauna Lennox. Had he been scanned and copied for a movie? Had they launched a murder inquiry in error?

'Now that's something you don't see every day.'

Tom MacPhail's words brought her back to the present, and Janie looked up to see the cadaver opened wide. Glistening and raw, there was no doubt in her mind that this was no filmmaker's dummy.

'What is it?' she asked.

'This man was what? Thirty-two, thirty-three?' MacPhail asked.

'Thirty-two,' Janie said. 'If it really is Mihailovic. Why? Is there something wrong with him?'

Cadwallader beckoned her towards the opened-up cadaver with a single gore-smeared finger. Reluctantly, she came closer, seeing the man's insides in far more detail than she would ever care to. And yet again, there was none of the smell of decay, or even of death, that she would normally have associated with a body. Especially one that had disappeared over a week ago and had at some point been buried without any kind of coffin or even a shroud.

'What am I looking at?' she asked. 'And why doesn't he smell?'

Cadwallader glanced at MacPhail and nodded a fraction. 'Smart, this one. Didn't I always say?' He turned his attention back to Janie. 'He doesn't smell because he hasn't begun to decompose. Something seems to have killed off all the bacteria in his body or otherwise he'd have bloated at the very least. There's nothing in his stomach either, which means he was either starved or he fasted for a while before he died.'

'And how exactly did he die?' Janie asked.

Cadwallader rewarded her with a shrug. 'Well, there's the thing. We can find absolutely nothing wrong with any of his internal organs. They're all as perfect as I've ever seen. We'll have to run blood tests and toxicology, get some analysis done on his brain tissue. But I can't find anything in or on his body that would suggest an obvious cause of death. He's just dead, and perfectly preserved.'

'Could whatever did that be what killed him then? If it killed off all the bacteria on him, inside him even?'

Cadwallader gave MacPhail that appraising nod again.

'That's actually a very good hypothesis. Although I'm not entirely sure how something like that could be done,' he said.

'A massive dose of radiation, perhaps?' MacPhail asked as if such a thing were both plausible, likely, and not the least bit terrifying to contemplate.

'Radiation?' Janie took a step back, acutely aware of every nerve in her body for a moment.

'Don't worry, J.' Cerys went over to one of the storage drawers along the back wall of the examination theatre and came back with some handheld device. She fiddled with a large dial on it, then passed it back and forth over the body. It didn't click or buzz or do anything else alarming. 'Background radiation only. He's not been hiding out at Torness.'

Janie didn't know whether to be relieved or frustrated. At least irradiation would be a clue as to where Mihailovic had been, but having a complicated case to investigate was probably better than watching all her hair fall out. 'Well, if not that, then what might have caused it?' she asked.

'For the moment that will remain a mystery,' Cadwallader said. 'We'll get all the toxicology screening done, have a look at his brain. I'd like to put a few cell biopsies under the microscope too, see if whatever killed his gut flora so comprehensively had a direct effect on him at that level. To be honest though, Janie, right now this one has me rather baffled.'

'You on for that pizza later, J?'

Janie had lingered in the corridor outside the examination theatre, checking her texts and sending a few replies, in the hope that Cerys might be able to escape for a moment. The two pathologists had begun a heated discussion about obscure embalming techniques that might have led to the unusual state of preservation of Mihailovic's body, so she had made her excuses and left early. She probably didn't need to attend the post mortem at all, but a certain detective chief inspector had got her into the habit. Nothing focused the mind on a murder investigation quite so much as seeing the victim laid out on the slab. And while they still didn't have a definitive cause of death, this was beginning to look like murder to her.

'Hope I can get away from work at a half-decent hour, but aye. Reckon I'll have earned pizza and wine after the day I've had.'

'It's a date. Your place or mine?' Cerys smiled as she spoke, the words intended as a joke. So why did Janie feel the tips of her ears burn as she heard them? She was as bad as Connor Fairley sometimes.

'There's better pizza at mine. And wine, for that matter.' It was true. Cerys lived in a tiny flat in a part of Pilrig that leaned more into Haggis suppers and bottles of Buckfast. Bruntsfield was a little more cosmopolitan. 'Might as well make the most of it while we can.'

Cerys raised an eyebrow at that. 'Something up?'

Janie hadn't realised how much she needed to vent until she started telling the mortuary assistant about the notice to quit, the suddenness of it and how difficult it was to find time to look for somewhere else, let alone actually find a place she and Manda could move to.

'Couldn't have come at a worse time, really. Start of a major investigation and everything. But you don't want to hear about all that, do you?'

'Oh, I don't know.' Cerys jerked a thumb back towards the door to the examination theatre. 'Probably better than listening to those two old hens argue all day. I'd quite like to get poor Mr Mihailovic sewn back together, but it might be hours before they've made up their minds.'

'I was looking for him, you know?' Janie leaned her back against the wall as she spoke, settling in even though she knew she really should be getting back to the station and the incident room. 'His girlfriend, partner, whatever. She came to me not that long ago, worried he'd not been in touch. What are the chances control handing the case to me? Might have taken an age to identify him if it had been anyone else.'

'You're one of only two DIs in the Edinburgh team, J. Who else were they going to give it to?' Cerys settled against the opposite wall of the corridor, arms crossed and ready to give Janie a telling. It was what she needed, but they were both interrupted by the examination door as it swung open. Dr MacPhail's head popped through the gap.

'Reckon that's him ready for tidying-up now, Cerys,' he said before noticing Janie. 'We'll have a preliminary report to you this afternoon, Janie. Biopsies and toxicology will take a little longer, OK?'

Before she could answer, he'd withdrawn again, the door banging closed behind him. Cerys pushed herself from the wall, put a hand gently on Janie's arm. 'Pizza and wine, tonight. And you, me and Manda are going to sort this all out, right?'

20

McLean sat at his desk, trying to concentrate on the transcripts of the Drake Biotech security staff interviews and failing badly. A half-eaten muffin and an empty coffee cup were all that remained of a very late lunch, something he knew would get him into trouble when he finally made it home at the end of the day. That wasn't so far off either, a quick glance at the clock confirmed. Not that there was much to show for all the hours. Such was the lot of a DCI, of course. Sitting around waiting for the inspectors to bring him news of what the sergeants had organised the constables to do. There had to be a better way, surely.

A knock at the open door gave him a welcome excuse to abandon the pointless task. Detective Constable Mitchell leaned half into the room, the dark skin of her scalp shining under the overhead lights. McLean wasn't entirely sure why she shaved her head, nor whether he should ask.

'Something come up, Cass?'

'Possibly, sir. One of the Leith patrol cars reckon they might have spotted the van from the CCTV footage. Thought I'd ask you for a second opinion before we make a move on the owner.' Mitchell crossed the room to his desk and handed McLean a folder. Inside, a half-dozen A4 prints of photographs could really have been an email, although to be fair the screen on his tiny laptop computer was a bit rubbish.

'This is the CCTV footage from the night of the break-in.' Mitchell came around the desk so that she was standing on the same side as McLean's chair. Not quite in Lofty Blane's class, she was nevertheless taller than him standing and loomed over him while he was seated. McLean took the proffered sheet and pulled the desk light over, the better to make out details in the over-enlarged fuzzy image.

'And this is what the Leith patrol car saw first thing this morning.' Mitchell slid the next photograph across the desk, then followed it up with a couple more. McLean could see that they were all of similar off-white Transit vans, but then there was no shortage of them in Edinburgh or anywhere else. What gave him hope was the obvious rusty dent in the front where the driver had presumably failed to notice a street lamp or bollard. And where the steel of the roof curved down at the top to meet the windscreen on the passenger side, a distinctive arrow shape of rust or flaking paint.

'I reckon this one's the best.' Mitchell pulled out the last of the photographs from the folder and handed it over. McLean wondered why she hadn't led with that one, as it had been taken at a very similar angle to the CCTV image. Side by side there was no doubt in his mind they were the same vehicle.

'You've run the plate, I take it?'

'Aye, sir. It belongs to a freelance painter and decorator by the name of Keith Campbell. Address in Restalrig.'

'We know anything about him?' McLean looked at the now-empty folder, guessed the answer.

'The guy's squeaky clean. Not even a parking ticket as far as we can tell. Jessica's running the name through the system and we've got the Social Media team looking into him too. Should have a background file put together in an hour or so, but he's certainly not on any watch lists.'

'So it's possible he has a perfectly good reason for his van showing up on our cameras the night of the break-in.'

'Apart from the cloned plates, aye?'

'Yes, them.' McLean couldn't quite believe he'd forgotten that particular detail. Too much reading dry interview transcripts maybe. 'We'll need to bring him in for questioning about that if nothing else. Wouldn't hurt to have a wee look in the back of his van either.'

Mitchell started gathering the photographs back together, but McLean stopped her putting one of them away. All the rest had been taken from the front, which made sense given they were trying to identify a van by damage done in that area. This one showed the whole van from the side, complete with a logo and company details in such poorly painted script it couldn't have been a great advertisement for the services of a decorator.

'Any idea where he is now?'

'Patrol said he was working at an address in Joppa. New development of luxury apartments or something.' Mitchell glanced at her watch. 'Probably be knocking off soon, mind.'

'OK. Bring him and his van in both. I'd like to have a word with Mr Keith Campbell.'

McLean wasn't sure what he'd been expecting when DC Mitchell had brought him the photographs of the van, but the man sitting quietly in interview room two was not it. According to his driving licence, Keith Campbell was sixty-one. What little information the team had gleaned so far told them he was single and lived in a semi-detached ex-council house in Restalrig, from where he ran his painting and decorating business. He operated as a sole trader, filed his accounts on time and paid his taxes. All in all a model

citizen. Except that the more McLean studied him, the more convinced he was that Keith Campbell was a lie.

He looked closer to forty than sixty, for starters. True, a shaved
head hid grey hairs more effectively than any special shampoo, but
the man's complexion was far younger than his years too. Perhaps
the painting and decorating game took less of a toll on a person
than, for instance, being a detective. McLean wasn't so sure.

'He's no' happy about being brought in for questioning, sir.'

Beside him in the observation room, DC Mitchell held a
slightly thicker folder this time, nervously passing it from one
hand to the other.

'Resisting arrest?'

'More being a crabbit auld bastard, as my mother would put it.
The sergeant who brought him in got a right earful.'

'And his van?'

'In the car park. Since we've got it on CCTV with cloned
plates, we're well justified bringing it in here, whatever he tries to
say about his rights.'

'Not still got those plates on though, I take it.'

Mitchell shook her head. 'No. Registration, insurance, MOT
are all fine. As it happens, it genuinely does have a duff brake
light. Should help if he decides to make a noise about police
harassment.'

'You've had a look inside?'

'Aye. Couldn't see anything out of place, but then it's a right tip
in the back. Paint pots, ladders, toolboxes. I mean, nothing you
wouldn't expect a decorator to have. Would probably be a lot tidier
if it was a smaller van, to be honest. Most of his gear looks like it
rattles around every time he takes a corner.'

'Plenty of room for a small group of people on their way to and
from a break-in though.' McLean turned away from the screen
and opened the door. 'Let's go ask him what he's been up to these
past few days, eh?'

Campbell was inspecting his fingernails when McLean stepped into the interview room, Mitchell following close behind. His hands were surprisingly clean for someone who wielded a paintbrush all day, his clothes too. But then he might have worn an overall and gloves. He looked up swiftly at the noise, barely contained rage in his clear blue eyes as he focused on McLean. It faded swiftly as he took in the detective constable. Mitchell had that effect on people.

'Mr Campbell. Sorry to keep you waiting.'

'What the fuck is all this aboot, eh? I'd a brake light no' workin'. Why're youse lot treating me like I'm Osama bin fucking Laden?'

'You think that's why we brought you in? For a brake light?' McLean pulled out a seat and settled into it. Behind him, DC Mitchell stood at the door.

'That's what the sergeant told me, aye. You no' got anythin' better to do wi' your time?'

'Actually, I've many better things to do with my time. One of which is tracking a van with a description that fits yours very closely. Everything except its number plates, that is.'

Campbell's initial burst of anger appeared to have burned itself out, but he still had a nervous energy about him that felt like it could turn violent at any moment.

'Don't ken nuthin' aboot that. Who're youse anyways?' He jerked his chin upwards at the two detectives in a manner that didn't endear him to McLean much.

'Of course. Introductions. I'm Detective Chief Inspector McLean, and this is my colleague Detective Constable Mitchell. We're part of Edinburgh Specialist Crime's Major Investigations Team.' McLean gave the decorator an insincere smile. 'And you're Keith Everett Campbell, of number thirty-two Castlecraig Avenue in Restalrig. Is that correct?'

'Sounds about right.' Campbell fixed McLean with those hypnotic blue eyes. 'So, you going to tell me what this is really aboot?

An no' some pish aboot number plates, aye? Or am I just going tae get up and walk oot of here, since you've no' charged me with anything.'

Up until that point McLean had found the man irritating, a bit more cocky than someone being hauled into an interview room should be, his anger a little too modulated to be real. Crabbit auld bastards with no record of any brush with the law generally weren't all that up to speed on the minutiae of investigative procedure, though, so either Campbell was an avid reader of crime fiction or he wasn't quite as squeaky clean as his lack of paper trail suggested.

'A van identical to yours was caught on CCTV. First heading out of the city in the direction of Loanhead and later coming back the way. Identical, as I said before, except for the number plate.'

'You sure it was my van? Only, way I hear it, those cameras don't always pick up the plate, right? Must be more'n one Transit van in Edinburgh, aye? Thousands of them all the same.'

McLean ignored the obvious attempt to take control of the interview. It was still interesting that the man had tried all the same. Some people were like that by nature, of course. Was there something more going on here, or was he just being paranoid?

'Are you aware of a company called Drake Biotech, Mr Campbell?'

'Doesn't ring any bells.' Campbell shrugged again. 'Biotech? That's like medical stuff, aye?'

Even if he'd stopped at 'bells', McLean would have known the man was lying, but the need to embellish the lie was textbook. He knew Drake Biotech and where its research facility was based, even if he'd managed to keep his face bland at the mention of the name.

'Only, the night your van went out past Loanhead with fake plates on, there was a break-in at the Drake Biotech research labs. Big new building in the science park at Easter Bush. I imagine you've probably done some decorating work there, right?'

'Don't get much commercial work these days. I'm strictly domestic, see?'

'According to the security camera footage, a team of five people broke into the research facility via a fire door whose alarm had been deactivated. We have to assume that someone working for Drake Biotech or with security access arranged for that door to be unlocked. They might have got in, done as much damage as they wanted and left again without being noticed, only one of them decided to run out through the front door. Set off all the alarms.'

'All very interesting, Detective Chief Inspector. But I don't see what any of it has to do with me.'

Was that another tell? Most people in a stressful interview situation would not have remembered McLean's full title. Campbell's initial anger had cooled far too swiftly. Now he was altogether too calm. Not his first rodeo.

'You could fit five in your van, no worries. Two in the front with you driving, three in the back. Or were you one of the five who broke into the lab?'

'Are we done here?' Campbell made a show of looking at his watch. 'Only, I've really better things to be doing with my time than listening to this pish. If you're no' gonnae arrest me?'

McLean's smile was genuine this time. He pushed back his chair and stood up. 'Aye, I think we're done. DC Mitchell will show you back to your van.'

Surprised, it took Campbell a moment to gather his wits. By the time he'd stood and straightened his coat, Mitchell already had the door open.

'Thank you, Mr Campbell. You've been very helpful,' McLean said as the decorator walked out into the corridor. 'Just be sure and get that brake light fixed, aye?'

21

'Who the hell is Keith Everett Campbell, that's what I need to know.'

A half-hour after the decorator's van had left the police car park, McLean was back in his office, sitting at the conference table with a mug of over-brewed bitter coffee. His own fault for not bringing in any milk, but he could cope with it black. He'd probably regret drinking it so late in the afternoon when he couldn't sleep later, of course. He had the feeling there was still a lot of the day to go yet.

'We've worked up what we can at short notice, but the man's got very little on record. Basic website for his decorating business. Just a page with contact details really. He doesn't appear to have any social media accounts.'

DC Mitchell and DS Blane had joined McLean for a catch-up after the interview. Blane had a folder with far too few sheafs of paper in it and was pretending to consult it as he brought them up to speed.

'Is that so unusual? I don't either,' McLean said. The look Mitchell gave him suggested that maybe it was.

'OK,' he went on. 'Well, I'm certain he's involved in the break-in.'

'How so?' Mitchell asked. 'We didn't get anything from him at the interview, and he didn't say a word to me all the way out of the station.'

'You mean he didn't confess, Cass? He was hardly going to do that now, was he? No, he knew about Drake Biotech though. I'd lay good odds he's been in there as part of a decorating team, even if I doubt he's been a painter more than a couple of months. Then there's the way he feigned a lack of interest when I told him about how the team broke in. And for someone with no record, he seemed to know his way around a police interview well enough.'

'Aye, I thought he was just a bit cocky,' Mitchell said.

'It was more than that.' McLean glanced briefly at his phone, laid out on the tabletop beside him, its screen blank. 'I half expect to get a call in the next hour or so from someone in MI5 telling me to back off. Although now I think about it, in the past they've approached me when I'm away from the station, so it'll probably be a brown envelope under my windscreen wiper. They do love their cloaks and daggers.'

'You think Campbell's a spook?' Blane asked.

'Something like that. Maybe private sector rather than government, but it boils down to the same thing. Makes me wonder about the reason for the break-in, though. Could be the animal rights thing was just a distraction.'

Both detectives stared at him in silence for a while, their expressions a mixture of disbelief and perhaps concern. It was Blane who finally broke the awkward silence.

'So what's our next move then?'

'Well, if it was up to me I'd put everything we've found so far into a report, send it to the chief constable and get you two to go help Janie with what's obviously a much more important investigation. As it is, we'll have to keep on digging into the mystery that is Mr Campbell. If I've not been approached by the security services in the next twenty-four hours, that is.'

'What if you are? If he is under their protection somehow?'

'Well, then I'll tell that to the chief constable and she can find the best way to let Nathaniel Drake know.' McLean said the words, but knew that any such task would fall to him in the end. 'Meanwhile, we'll never get a warrant to tap his phone and I'm not wasting money on a full surveillance team. If he's what I think he is, then he'll be looking out for any of us lot following him anyway. I might be able to call in a favour though. See if I can't outsmart him.'

'What did you have in mind?' Mitchell asked.

'Best you don't know. Plausible deniability and all that. Leave it with me for now, but keep digging through the records to see if anything comes up. Maybe check his tax details go back as far as they really should. See how long his website's been up and running. That sort of thing. Even better if we can find out who his friends and associates are, but that might have to wait for now.'

The two detectives nodded their understanding. Blane shuffled his few papers into order and closed up the folder, then the two of them stood to leave.

'You going to the briefing, sir?' Mitchell asked as she gently slid her chair back under the table. It took McLean a moment to understand which briefing she meant. He checked the clock on the wall and then his watch. Still an hour left.

'Aye, I'll be there. And if Janie needs more detectives to help, that's higher priority than this, OK? Dead bodies take precedence.'

He picked up his phone once they had gone, swiped the screen to life half expecting a text or email telling him to back off. There was nothing, and he had to admit to himself that it was more a hope he would be handed an excuse to stop this waste-of-time investigation. Except that it had just got a whole lot more interesting, hadn't it?

Standing up with a minimum of creaks and groans, he went to the door and looked out into the corridor. There was no one about, but he closed the door anyway, retreating to the corner furthest from any other offices before placing the call. It answered before the second ring.

'Tony. It's no' often you're the one calling me.' Jo Dalgliesh's voice croaked like a sixty-a-day smoker, even though she'd quit years ago. Did vapes make you sound like that?

'Given how often you ring, it hardly seems necessary. I take it you're not working on anything important right now?'

'Always working on something important, Tony. But aye, it might be a quiet moment. How'd you . . .?'

'You picked up quickly, and I can hear piped musak in the background. You're in a cafe somewhere, upstairs at John Lewis, at a guess, and your phone was to hand. How am I doing?'

'OK, OK. So you're a detective chief inspector. Top marks. I take it this wasn't a social call. What is it you want?'

'It's possible you can do me a favour and get your hands on a juicy story at the same time. You interested?'

He might have felt a little guilty at passing on information to a reporter, but McLean had been used by the press enough in the past to know it could work both ways. Dalgliesh had been a thorn in his side for years, corrupting young officers and using the most underhand of methods in pursuit of stories hardly worth the ink. She'd also saved his life a couple of times now, and they'd reached a level of mutual understanding that almost bordered on friendship sometimes. Even so, he was taking a risk getting her involved. At least he had the seniority to make that call.

And yet he had taken the trouble to close his office door before phoning her, had even gone to the far side of the room to avoid being overheard. That spoke to a certain degree of guilt, surely.

Getting up from the seat at the conference table, he was halfway across the room to open the door again when his phone chirped a message. Harrison had received the initial post-mortem examination report on the dead body found out in East Lothian, and now she was forwarding it to him for comment.

Door open, he slumped in his seat and woke his laptop, the better to read what the pathologist had to say. Fifteen minutes later he was standing at the door to what had once been his office, tucked away at the back of the station. Smaller than he remembered it, or was it just that his new room was so unnecessarily large?

'Got the email, I take it?' Harrison asked as she looked up from her own computer.

'Aye, I did. Makes for interesting reading. It's not often Angus is completely stumped like that.' McLean shifted a couple of old box files onto the floor and took a seat.

'You should have heard him and Tom arguing.' Harrison turned her attention to him. 'Doesn't help us much, mind. Can't even decide whether this is a suspicious death or not.'

'A body half buried in remote woods? That's about as suspicious as it comes, Janie.'

'Aye, I know that. But how did he die? If the PM says murder, then it's easier to get the team motivated. Makes all this overtime budgeting worthwhile.' Harrison lifted an all too familiar-looking folder from a pile and then let it drop again. 'If it's just someone interfering with a dead body or failing to report a death . . .' She didn't bother finishing the sentence.

'Seems to me it's suspicious enough. And the manner of the man's death too. Scrubbed clean of all bacteria? I don't know how that's even possible, but it's certainly something that had to have been done to him, and not by accident.'

Harrison bobbed her head slightly in acceptance of this, then slumped back in her chair. His chair, although he'd not sat in it in years. She looked tired, McLean saw, but then that was hardly surprising. He remembered the long days and longer nights he'd spent in this very room immediately after being promoted to DI. He'd tell her it got better with time, but did it really?

'At least Tom and Angus are both confident whatever happened to Mihailovic isn't contagious,' she said. 'Bad enough he looked like he'd tried to dig himself out of his own grave. Imagine if the press got hold of that.'

'They sniffing around already?' McLean asked.

'The usual suspects, aye. That ghoul of a friend of yours, Jo Dalgliesh, called me a couple of hours ago. I swear if I find out who gave her my number . . .'

McLean let out a long slow breath, as much to cover his embarrassment at the mention of the reporter as anything. Dalgliesh hadn't said anything about speaking to Harrison, but then the reporter always was good at keeping things to herself if she wanted to.

'If there's one thing I've learned down the years it's that however hard you try to keep it a secret, Jo Dalgliesh will always find your number. What did she have to say for herself anyway? You think she knows?'

'No, I don't think she does. I mean, she knows we found a body, but she didn't drop any hints like she usually does. Too much to hope it stays that way for long though.'

Harrison rubbed at her eyes, and McLean could see her suppressing the yawn. Outside was almost completely dark now, the back wall of the neighbouring building cast in rough shadows by the light from other windows. Another day gone and not nearly enough done.

'You got your next steps planned then?' he asked.

'Aye. I'm putting together a team to go door to door in Mihailovic's apartment block. Not that I'm holding out much hope, mind. Going to speak to all his work colleagues, narrow down the time when he might have gone missing. It's all wrong though. I can't find any motive. Seems he was well enough liked, didn't owe anyone money. If he'd been in a fight that went too far and someone tried to hide his body to cover it up, I'd understand that. But this . . .'

Again, the detective inspector let her words trail off. McLean knew the feeling all too well. Questions begging more questions and not an answer in sight.

'I've told everyone working on the Drake Biotech break-in to help if you need the manpower,' he said. 'Reckon it's a lot more important than keeping some rich weird guy happy.'

Harrison's shoulders slumped in relief. 'Thanks. We'll probably need them. How's that going anyway?'

A ping on his phone stopped him from answering. He pulled it out, scanned the text, put it away again. 'That might be something. Not sure, but I need to go and check it out. I'll let you know as soon as I do.'

Harrison eyed him suspiciously. 'Evening briefing's in half an hour. I take it you'll no' be there?'

'Sure you'll manage without me,' he said, then turned and left the room.

22

McLean felt a tiny pang of guilt as he clumped down the stairs and out the station's back door. It was important to show support to the two new detective inspectors, and technically he was part of the command structure for the murder investigation, if that's what it actually was. But he knew Harrison would cope fine without him. There would be more briefings, and this was something he had to do now.

Emma's little electric Renault Zoe slipped silently into the evening traffic, and soon McLean was heading north across the park towards Jock's Lodge. For once the roads weren't too congested as he turned onto Restalrig Road and then down the side streets that would bring him to Castlecraig Avenue. He spotted the battered white Transit van parked outside number thirty-two easily enough, and as he drove past he could see a light on behind the frosted-glass front door. A few car lengths further, he found what he was looking for, indicated and pulled into a space on the opposite side of the road.

'Took your time, din't you?' Jo Dalgliesh opened the passenger door and slumped into the seat the moment he had clicked the button to unlock it. Swaddled in her second-skin old leather jacket, she wore the kind of woolly hat ancient aunts give children for Christmas, a heavy scarf wrapped around her neck and thick gloves on her hands. She rubbed them together all the same, then held them in the direction of the dashboard. 'Turn the heating on, won't you? It's bloody freezing out there.'

McLean did as he was told, hitting the button to heat the seats as well. The little car hummed gently, but soon began to warm. He'd lose a few miles of range for it though.

'So, what have you got for me then?' he asked.

'Patience, Tony. I can't feel my fingers right now. Amazed I was able to text you at all.' Dalgliesh finally pulled off her gloves and shoved her hands in between her legs. 'Jesus, can this thing no' go any hotter?'

'You want me to drive around a bit? Doesn't look like Mr Campbell there's going anywhere soon.'

'This car's electric, Tony. Driving it's no' going to make it warm up any quicker. Are you no' cold yourself?'

'Not really, no.' He'd had the seat heater on since getting in, and the steering wheel was heated too.

'Anyways, you're wrong about Campbell, see?' Dalgliesh nodded her head towards the house and McLean saw a silhouetted figure at the front door.

'How'd you know . . .?'

'If I told you, you'd arrest me. Best not to ask, aye?'

McLean held his tongue. He'd asked Dalgliesh if she knew anything about Campbell, knowing full well that if she didn't then she'd start to dig. What had surprised him was how quickly she'd got back in touch, telling him to meet her here.

'No' taking the van this time. Where're you going, my friend?' Dalgliesh muttered to herself as they both watched Campbell walk past his parked Transit and stand in the darkest point between two street lights. He had a phone in one hand, and it briefly glowed enough to show his face before he tapped it off and shoved it in a pocket. Moments later an elderly VW Golf pulled up alongside him. He looked swiftly from side to side, but if he saw McLean and Dalgliesh he gave no indication. A moment later he was in the car and it was pulling away again. Squinting, McLean made a mental note of the registration.

'You going to follow them or what?' Dalgliesh thumped the dashboard with one hand. Doing his best to supress a sigh, McLean thumbed the Renault into life, checked his mirror and pulled out. At least they were facing the same way.

'You knew he was going to be picked up,' he said as they slowed for the end of the road. The VW had already turned left, and McLean had to wait for another car before he could pull out to follow.

'Aye. Just don't ask me how.'

'And what were you going to do if they arrived before I did?'

'Make a note of the plate and ask a friend to run it for me.'

McLean didn't ask which friend; he was fairly sure he already knew the answer. Instead, he concentrated on following the VW without being too conspicuous about it. There had been training, half a lifetime ago, in how to tail another vehicle. But he was damned if he could remember much of it. What little he could was probably out of date by now. At least Emma's car was inconspicuous, unlike either his old Alfa or Dalgliesh's Jaguar. They would have both looked increasingly out of place as the VW took them first south through Piershill and round Duddingston, then on towards Craigmillar.

'Mixes with some of Edinburgh's great and good, does your Mr Campbell,' Dalgliesh said as the VW pulled into a parking space in front of a tenement block that looked like it was scheduled for demolition. McLean was too busy driving nonchalantly past, hoping to avoid being noticed, to pay it much heed. What he saw in a swift glance was not encouraging: graffiti-sprayed boards covered the ground-floor windows; bin bags completely blocked the short flight of stone steps that led to the front door hanging slightly ajar. Inside the car and travelling away from it, there was no way he could smell the stench of rotting garbage, piss and worse, but he wrinkled his nose at the imagined rank odour all the same.

'I thought they'd bulldozed all of these places,' he said as he guided the car into a space between a battered pick-up truck and a mini on blocks, its wheels nowhere to be seen.

'Aye, well, most of them. The developers who were going to build new houses on these plots went bust. Cooncil's still arguing over what happens next.' Dalgliesh fidgeted in her coat pocket for a moment before pulling out a slim e-cigarette. Shoved it in her mouth and chewed at the end of it for a moment before scowling at McLean. 'What? It's no' switched on, is it. Helps me think.'

'So who lives here that Campbell needs to go and see in person?'

'Search me. Something's up though. See?' Dalgliesh pointed her vape at the windscreen. Squinting through the rain-speckled glass, McLean saw Campbell come out of the front door, jog down the steps and lean to the door of the VW in conversation with the driver. After a moment's heated discussion, a second figure climbed out. Together they went back into the tenement, Campbell's colleague knocking a rubbish bag in passing. It rolled down the steps and came to a stop in the middle of the pavement.

'Reckon that's my cue.' Dalgliesh popped off her seat belt and opened her door.

'You can't go out there,' McLean said, although he didn't reach out to stop her.

'Well, you can't go out there, can you, Tony? Campbell knows what you look like, aye? Me, I'm just a scruffy auld wifey minding my own business.'

The reporter climbed out of the car with much huffing and groans, slammed the door shut and set off across the road. A billow of vape smoke enveloped her head as she passed under a street lamp. McLean found himself gripping the steering wheel and willed his fingers to relax as she stepped nimbly past the stray garbage bag. Without a pause, the reporter trotted up the steps as if she lived in the hovel of a tenement block and had every right to be there. She certainly looked the part.

He checked his watch as she disappeared through the door, beginning a nervous countdown. Not that there was much he could do if she didn't come out again. After five minutes had passed, he called in the plate on the VW. Registered to a Christine Vaughan, address in Newhaven. Five minutes later, Campbell and the driver, who he assumed was Vaughan, came out of the front door as casual as if they did it every day. As they both climbed into the car, McLean's phone buzzed a text, and when he checked he screen he saw it was from Dalgliesh.

Top floor. Might want to see this.

The VW spluttered into life, its headlights casting shadows on the nearby buildings as it made a three-point turn and drove away. McLean waited until the brake lights had disappeared around the corner at the end of the street before he climbed out of the Renault and followed Dalgliesh's route to the tenement door. His earlier assumption about the smell of the place had been, if anything, an underestimate. The narrow gap up the steps between ripped black plastic bags was slick with something that might have been rain but probably wasn't. Inside, the stench grew worse despite the window at the back of the stairwell being more broken glass than whole pane. He covered his mouth and nose with the sleeve of his jacket, careful not to touch the wobbly handrail as he climbed the stairs to the top floor.

Dalgliesh was waiting for him on the landing, her own face covered with an N95 mask. Cursing under his breath at his forgetfulness, McLean pulled his own out of his pocket and slid it on. Living with someone who was recovering from a stroke and was severely immunocompromised, he always carried masks these days. Remembering to put them on was another matter entirely.

'They came out of that flat.' Dalgliesh pointed at the left-hand of two doors leading off the top landing. It hung slightly ajar, the only light inside filtering in from the hall. 'Didn't say anything as they left, but I could tell the woman wasn't happy about something. Your man Campbell seemed calm though.'

'Christine Vaughan, if she's the person who owns the car.' McLean shoved his hand into his other pocket and produced a pair of latex gloves, snapped them on and approached the half-open door. 'I don't need to remind you not to touch anything, aye?'

Dalgliesh looked like a grandmother being taught to suck eggs, but said nothing as McLean eased through the gap and into the hall.

'Hello? Anyone home?'

No answer, so he took another step, careful where he put his feet. The hall was tiny, barely room enough for two people to stand. One door opened onto the smallest shower room McLean had ever seen, another onto a bedroom that was almost entirely taken up with a single bed. The third door opened onto a living area with a tiny kitchen at one end that probably broke a dozen health and safety rules. This room had a window looking out onto the street, an elderly television in the corner and a pair of tatty IKEA armchairs no doubt lifted from a nearby skip. Dumped on one of them was a camouflage-coloured backpack of the kind you might get in an Army Surplus store, its contents strewn around the floor and on a low Formica table.

'Presumably they came here looking for someone, but he wasn't in,' Dalgliesh said.

'That's my thinking too. It's odd though. The front door wasn't forced, so either Campbell's got a key but couldn't be bothered closing it behind him, or whoever lives here went out without bothering to lock up.'

'Well, it's no' as if there's anything worth stealing in here.'

McLean had to admit Dalgliesh had a point there. Still his attention was drawn to the backpack and its distributed contents. There were some low-grade electronics, wires with crocodile clips on both ends, a digital multimeter, something that looked like a computer circuit board wired up to some AA batteries and a tiny LED screen. He wasn't going to touch anything, probably shouldn't even be in this man's flat, but Campbell had come here soon enough after having left the police station that it was of interest. Something odd was going on here, and he was determined to find out what.

'Paul Sanderson.' Dalgliesh's voice echoed slightly, and when McLean looked around it was to see her returning from the hallway. She had a couple of envelopes in her hands, although at least she had put her gloves back on.

'What did I say about not touching anything?' he asked. The reporter ignored him, turning the first envelope over to read the address on the back.

'Junk mail, by the look of it. This one's from Greenpeace. Begging for money, I'd bet.'

'Doubt he's got any to spare, looking at this place. Remind me again why you texted me to come see it?'

'Just thought you'd want to know where those other two came.' Dalgliesh put the envelopes down on the tiny counter that was part of the kitchenette end of the living room, quite clearly not where she'd found them. 'And an excuse for me to have a nosey myself. If there's a story here I've no idea what it is, mind.'

'Beginning to think that myself.' McLean levered himself back up to standing with only a modicum of creaks and groans. 'Still, we can run the name and address through the system. See if it comes up with anything. Might call Mr Sanderson in for a wee chat tomorrow, if we can find him.'

'We done here then? Only I could do with a lift home if it's no' too much bother. Don't fancy waiting for a cab in this part of town.'

McLean let his gaze fall over the room one more time. Everything was old to the point of wearing out, not so much second-hand as third or fourth. Liberated from skips or piles left out for the binman to take. Whoever Paul Sanderson was, he clearly didn't have any money.

'Hang on a minute, Jo.' McLean shuffled carefully around the spilled contents of the backpack until he was standing close to the other chair. It faced the television, prime viewing position, and was the more comfortable-looking of the two. Or least uncomfortable would probably be a better description. The TV remote lay on the floor to the opposite side of the other chair, but it was the pair of boots in front of it that had caught his attention. Old like everything else in the room, they were at least well cared for, the leather soft with dubbin. They sat on the floor almost exactly where an average man's feet would land when they were seated in the chair, as if Sanderson had taken them off while watching telly, and then left them there when he'd gone to bed. Except that the bedroom was empty, the flat too.

Carefully lifting up the left boot, McLean peered at the underside. Mud had stuck in the tread, a little of it scattered on the threadbare carpet. Juggling his phone with one hand, he managed to snap a photograph of the sole, but he had to put the boot back down again before he could search his pockets for a small evidence bag.

'You want a hand wi' that?' Dalgliesh asked. 'Only I don't think your wee baggy's big enough.'

'I only want a bit of the dirt from the sole. That and the photo, should be able to tell where he's been recently.' McLean scraped the crumbs from the carpet into the bag and sealed it up tight.

'Only if you think you know where that might have been, aye?' Dalgliesh said. When McLean stood and turned to face her, she was staring at him with that familiar, quizzical expression on her face.

'Reckon I do. Break-in at a research place up at the Bush Estate. It's a bit beneath my pay grade, really, but, well, it's complicated.'

'Complicated?' Dagliesh echoed, fitting far more sarcasm into that one word than it could possibly hold.

'I'll tell you what I can, Jo. Since you've been such a help.' McLean shoved the bag into his pocket and stepped towards the door. 'Let's get out of here first though. Not sure I can take the stink any more.'

23

Early morning, and for once it wasn't raining as Janie parked the pool car in front of the Portakabin site office. Beside her, DC Bryant stifled a yawn and then turned the movement into an elegant stretch. Somehow Jessica always managed to look elegant, even in the worst of circumstances, but with Janie feeling as tired and frumpy as she did, it seemed particularly unfair. She'd stayed up far too late the night before, fuelled by pizza and wine and helped by Cerys and Manda as they scoured the websites of letting agents in a futile search for somewhere else to live. By the time the mortuary assistant had left with a cheery promise to keep looking, it had been hours past her bedtime. Then there had been the horribly early morning briefing to deal with, setting up the day's investigation and handing out tasks to the sergeants. Janie could have happily gone home and slept until it all went away, if only that were an option.

'OK then.' She checked her watch, took a deep breath. 'Let's see how popular we are today.'

Outside the warmth of the car, a lazy wind whipped around the half-finished buildings and straight through her coat. Janie shivered at the change in temperature and hurried to the site-office door. When she pushed it open, it was to find a small cluster of workmen surrounding the desk and filling most of the space. A chatter of voices was cut off by the sound of one she recognised.

'Quiet, all of youse. I cannae sort your problems if youse all shout at me at once.'

'Scuse me,' Janie tried, then elbowed her way through the crowd until she was at the front. Babs the site manager sat in her chair, protected from the throng by the expanse of her desk. Her blond eyebrows rose in surprise.

'Detective Inspector. I should have known. Always trouble when the polis show up unannounced.'

'Is there a problem here?' Janie half turned to take in the assembly.

'Aye, there is. Seems Sasha's no' turned up this morning, which means half our workforce isn't here either, since he's the one drives the crew van.'

What were the chances? 'That's a problem. It was him I needed to talk to most urgently. And then anyone else who worked with Vaclav Mihailovic before he disappeared.'

The site manager's frown deepened, wrinkles creasing the thick foundation on her forehead. Janie hadn't really noticed before, but Babs was considerably older than she looked at a casual glance, her blond hair showing grey at the roots.

'You found him then?'

A quick glance around at the assembled workmen suggested at least a dozen crowded into the small space. On a site this large, they'd probably be team leaders in their own rights. Anything Janie said in front of them would spread like gossip in a police station. She pointed to the door that led through to the small conference room in the adjoining Portakabin.

'Can I have a word in private?'

Babs didn't try to hide her sigh, but it was short-lived. She stood up, raised her voice to the crowd. 'Right then, youse lot. If there's work you can be doing without the rest of your crew, then get to it. Otherwise go get yourselves a coffee and be back here in half an hour, aye?'

Grumbling, the workmen all shuffled out. Not all workmen, Janie noticed. There were a couple of women in amongst them she wouldn't want to get into an argument with. Soon enough it was just her, Babs and DC Bryant.

'Bit of an improvement on the tall lad you brought in the last time,' the site manager said as she noticed the detective constable for the first time. She ran an absent-minded hand through her hair and put on the leeriest smile Janie had seen in a long time. Her voice was almost sing-song as she continued. 'What can I do for you, hen?'

Bryant didn't miss a beat, her notebook already out, pen poised. 'Full name, address and phone number of your gang boss Sasha, for starters. He was here yesterday, I take it?'

'Aye.' Babs leaned forward, revealing perhaps rather more décolletage than Janie needed to see as she tapped at the computer keyboard and played with the mouse. Behind her, a printer sprang into life and spat out a single sheet of paper, which she pulled out and handed over. 'No' sure how to pronounce his proper name, so we all just call him Sasha. He in some kind of trouble?'

Janie took the page, scanned the details and handed it to Bryant. 'We found Mihailovic. He's dead and the circumstances are very suspicious. That's why I need to talk to everyone who worked with him, and his gang boss going missing like this only makes me want to talk to him more.'

Behind her, Janie heard DC Bryant's quiet voice as she called in the details. They had agreed not to let the building site know they were coming, just in case someone decided to not be there when they arrived. Too much to think that Sasha's unexpected non-appearance was a coincidence though. With a bit of luck he hadn't fled too far yet.

'Bloody nightmare. I always thought Sasha was OK. Been

working with him five years now. More, even.' The site manager bent to her computer again, and soon the printer spat out another sheet. 'This is what we have on file for Mihailovic. I can pull together a list of names of people who might have worked with him, but like I told you the last time, he last handed in a time sheet more than three weeks ago. As far as the company's concerned, he doesn't work for us any more.'

Janie took the sheet of paper and scanned down it. The printer had done a half-decent job of reproducing Mihailovic's photograph, and the sight of that face gave her an involuntary shudder as she recalled seeing it both on the post-mortem examination table and out in the woods near Haddington.

'Sasha's the one who'd be able to tell you who worked with him too, of course.' Babs nodded at the page Janie was reading. 'We checked everyone's work visas, but Sasha was the one who organised everything for the foreign workers. Picking them up, taking them to the right site.'

A memory of their previous conversation broke through Janie's concentration as the site manager talked, but it took her a moment to put the pieces together.

'These other sites,' she said. 'You don't have one out to the east of the city, do you? Tranent, maybe. Or Haddington?'

Babs cocked her head to one side, then held up a hand and jerked one finger to indicate Janie should follow her. She pulled out a key ring as she walked to the conference-room door, unlocked it and reached inside to turn on the lights. They banged and clicked as they came to life, buzzing in the cold air.

'These are our sites across Scotland,' she said as she pointed at a map pinned to the far wall. 'And these are the Edinburgh and Lothians ones at better scale.'

Janie walked up to the wall, seeing pins in Aberdeen, Dundee, Glasgow, Edinburgh and Inverness on a map taking in the whole of Scotland. Alongside it, pins in a map of East Lothian showed their current location, a site in Craigmillar, one on the outskirts of Loanhead and one a bit further east. Leaning close, she could just make out the tiny writing beneath the blocky outline of a town. Ormiston.

'How long have you been working there?' She tapped a finger against the paper. The site manager produced a pair of spectacles from somewhere as she crossed the small room to join Janie at the maps, slid them on her nose and then peered almost as closely.

'Ormiston? Three years, maybe? Half the houses are finished and sold now.'

'And would Mihailovic have worked there? Would Sasha?'

Babs took the spectacles off, folded them and tucked them into the top of her blouse. 'Mihailovic, I'd have to check, but Sasha for sure. He was managing a team out there just a fortnight back.'

Janie leaned in closer still, peering at the lines of the roads, the shapes of the fields and the irregular green squares of woodland. At this scale the map didn't show farm names, but it was easy enough to see the spot where Bogside Farm would be, the strip of trees that formed Priory Wood. Coincidence that it was within walking distance of the new development? Well, Janie didn't really believe in coincidences now, did she.

'Anything from control on our missing Serbian yet?' Janie asked as she pulled out of the building-site entrance and slid the pool car into the morning traffic. The address Babs had given her for Sasha wasn't far, but she didn't hold up much hope the gang boss would be there.

'Nothing yet, but it's only been an hour. Patrol's outside his flat just now keeping an eye on it. No one there, by the look of things.'

'Colour me surprised. He's done a runner just like the rest of them.' Janie considered turning on the blue lights cunningly hidden in the pool car's bodywork, but they were making good enough progress really. 'Kicking myself for tipping them off we were looking for Mihailovic.'

'To be fair, J, it's not like you knew we were going to find him half buried out in the woods. We thought he'd gone home to Serbia.'

'Aye, you're right. Would've been easier to find out what happened to him if we could talk to his flatmates, mind.'

'So what are you thinking then? This man Sasha and a bunch of his work gang buried Mihailovic out in those woods. I get that. But why?'

Janie made a swift turn across oncoming traffic and into a side street, earning a little chirp from the front tyres and an angry horn from a driver she had in no way put in danger but had probably woken from their morning commute stupor. She took a moment both to slow the car and gather her thoughts before answering.

'It's a strange one. Tom – the pathologist – wasn't sure how Mihailovic died. It wasn't violent, for sure. My thinking is that he died in his bed, in that flat in the tower block most probably. You saw the place, right? That's illegal multiple occupancy and half a dozen other violations before we even start looking at the modern-slavery angle. I'd say they made the body disappear rather than draw attention to their situation. Only that just made things worse for them, didn't it.'

'And now they're all running. Or run.' Through the corner of her eye, Janie saw Bryant nod her head. 'So now we've got a suspicious death that might really just be failure to contact the authorities and illegal disposal of a body.'

'Still crimes, right enough. Just not quite as serious as murder.'

'Doesn't explain how he came to be half out of the ground like that though, does it. Fair creeped me out that.'

'You and me both, Jessica. I still get the shakes just thinking about it. And it's worse than that. He was clean. Like so squeaky clean he had no live bacteria in him at all. I don't even know how that's possible.'

'Some new drug perhaps? Or maybe he got some black-market antibiotics and they turned out to be designed for a horse rather than a man?'

Janie had to admit that was one of the better possibilities, but they turned the corner into the street where Sasha the gang boss lived before she could say so. Two squad cars were now parked outside the front door of a three-storey tenement, a uniform officer keeping a third space clear for her to park in.

'Top floor left, ma'am,' the constable said as she showed him her warrant card. 'We knocked, but there's no answer. No one in or out since we got here forty minutes ago.'

'Neighbours?'

'Retired couple downstairs. All the others are out at work, apparently.'

Janie stretched her neck and shoulders in a vain attempt to ease some of the tension that had settled on her since discovering her main suspect had gone awol. 'OK. Search warrant should be coming through any time now. Might as well have a chat with the neighbours until then.'

24

The ground-floor flat of the tenement building had a gloomy, oppressed feel to it, not helped by the thick lace curtains to the front and high wooden panelling on the walls. The couple who lived there were, as the constable had said, quite elderly. Mr and Mrs Robertson – he appeared to be profoundly deaf, while she was tiny and bent over as if the weight of the whole building bore down on her shoulders. She left her husband watching television in the living room with the sound turned right down, and took Janie and DC Bryant through to a spacious kitchen at the back. Its tall window looked out onto a drying green and more tenements beyond, the lace curtains thinner here where privacy was less of an issue. Even so, it was a dark room, made more so by the unlit bulb in the single overhead light.

'Fifty years since John and I moved in here and I don't think I've ever had a visit from a police officer before. This is a good neighbourhood, you know. A quiet neighbourhood.'

Mrs Robertson had offered them tea, and was now busying herself about the stove. Janie suppressed the urge to help the old lady, knowing from experience with her gran that it was best to wait until asked.

'I'm sure nothing bad has happened here,' she said. 'We just want to have a word with the gentleman who lives on the top floor. Do you know your neighbours well?'

'The top floor, you say? Sasha?' The old lady shook her head without turning away from the kettle and teapot. 'I wouldn't say I know him well, but we say hello whenever we see each other. He's been helpful too. Doesn't mind lifting heavy things for me, puts the bin out. He's from Serbia, I think. Belgrade. Not a country I know much about, really.'

'Has he been here long?'

'Let me see.' Mrs Robertson stared up at the cracked and stained plaster cornicing as if the answer might be written there. Not that she'd be able to read it, so high was the ceiling. 'Five years now? Maybe six? It all blurs a bit around the pandemic, don't you think?'

'I don't suppose you remember the last time you saw him?' Janie asked.

'Oh, that's easy enough. It was yesterday afternoon, about three. Unusual to see him then, he's usually at work. He headed out with a great big bag over one shoulder. You know those duffel bags, like the army use? Could have fitted a body inside it and nobody would know. He's a big lad though, is Sasha. No problem carrying something like that.'

'Did you speak to him? Did he say where he was going?'

The old lady shook her head again, poured boiling water into the teapot with an unsteady hand. 'I was on my way in with some washing off the line. Never really dries properly out there, but it's nice to give it a bit of an airing. I asked him if he was going anywhere nice, what with that big bag of his and everything. He just laughed and wished me a good afternoon. Very polite, that Sasha. He's Serbian you know. Comes from Belgrade.'

Janie risked a glance at Bryant, who had been taking notes during the conversation. The raised eyebrow was all the communication needed.

'Was . . . is he a good neighbour, then?' Janie asked as Mrs

Robertson poured too much milk into three tiny china mugs and then followed up with tea so weak it would fall over at a harsh word.

'Sasha? I've known worse. There was a young family up there for about ten years. Far too many for such a small flat, but what can you do? Started with screaming babies and ended with two boys running up and down the stairs, playing football out back. Och, the noise. It's as well John's deaf, you know. It would have driven him mad.'

'But Sasha isn't like that, then?'

'No, not at all. Oh, he comes and goes at all hours. Sometimes had company my mother wouldn't have approved of. But times change, you know. Fifty years ago you'd not have seen any foreigners in this street, and now they're everywhere. Not that there's anything wrong with foreigners, you know. I'm not one of those racialists. Sasha's a perfectly good neighbour, far as I'm concerned. Even if he is . . . you know . . . not one of us.'

Janie looked at her insipid tea, then up at Bryant again. The detective constable's pained expression no doubt mirrored her own. The buzz of the doorbell, out in the hall, offered some small hope of escape.

'Oh, I wonder who that could be?' Mrs Robertson said, not making any move to answer.

'It's probably one of my colleagues,' Janie said.

'I'll go see.' Bryant was on her feet before Janie could move.

'She's a nice young girl,' Mrs Robertson said as she lifted a shaking cup to her lips and took a tiny sip. 'Are you two a couple? I've heard that's a thing these days.'

Janie was about to explain once more that she was a detective inspector and that Bryant was her junior colleague, but the woman in question reappeared before she could say anything.

'That's the warrant sorted, J. They're just fetching out the big red key, then we can go and have a wee look upstairs.'

★ ★ ★

159

The big red key made short work of the front door to the top-floor apartment where Sasha, otherwise known as Aleksandr Jovanović, lived. Janie hung back on the landing while a couple of uniform offi-cers wearing stab vests made a quick inspection to be sure that no one was hiding inside. It didn't take them long, but she still had time to pull on a pair of latex gloves before stepping over the threshold.

The flat itself was much the same in layout as the one two stories down, only without the dark wooden panelling to the walls, the heavy lace curtains to the windows or the two elderly pensioners. The living room boasted a fine view of the tenements on the other side of the street, and beyond them a few church spires pinning the ground to the sky. Janie was fairly certain she would have been able to see the Pentland Hills in the distance if the cloud base hadn't been so low.

It was clear that Sasha worked in the building trade by the look of his furniture. The phrase 'show home' sprang to mind, and no one piece really matched either the room or any of the rest of it. Apart from a saggy leather armchair angled towards a large televi-sion, nothing appeared to be much used, either. There were no books on the shelves, no pictures on the walls. Nothing to suggest a person lived here at all.

The same was true of the one bedroom and small shower room, each kitted out with the kind of furnishing found in identi-kit housing-estate houses all over the country. Cheap and functional, Janie could imagine Sasha diverting a few workmen from whichever building site he was overseeing whenever he needed something fixed. Had Mihailovic been here? Assembled that flat-pack wardrobe? It was possible.

'Reckon he's gone for a while,' Bryant said as she pulled open drawers to reveal very little in the way of clothing. 'Took his tooth-brush and all.'

'Well, we knew he'd done a runner.' Janie checked her watch, sur-prised how much of the morning had already gone. 'If he left about three yesterday, who knows how far he might have got by now?'

'All the way to Belgrade?' Bryant was making a joke, possibly in poor taste and at the expense of the elderly lady downstairs. That there was a nugget of truth in the suggestion only made it worse.

'Not sure we're likely to find much here. If he had a computer he's taken it with him. Phone, too. There's a landline in the hall, but it's probably only there so he can get his broadband. Everyone uses mobiles these days.'

Janie wandered over to the bedroom window and looked down at the scruffy square of drying green below. A stone wall separated it from the drying green of the tenement block across the way and the neighbours either side. She wondered idly whether Sasha rented the place or owned it. Either way it was going to be empty soon, and Janie needed a place to live. There was only the one bedroom though, and the Robertsons downstairs. She didn't much fancy being asked to take someone else's bins out every week.

'You want forensics to go over the place?' Bryant asked, but before Janie could answer, her phone rang. Dragging it out of her pocket, she saw that the number on the screen was the incident room back at the station.

'Please tell me you have some good news,' she said before even waiting to hear who had made the call.

'Detective Inspector? I . . . That is . . .' The hesitant voice of DC Connor Fairley stuttered down the line.

'Aye, it's me.' Janie didn't add that it was her phone number he'd called so who else was he expecting. 'What's up, Connor?'

'I've just had a call from Border Control. The all persons we put out for . . .' DC Fairley paused a moment, no doubt psyching himself up to pronounce the name. 'Alek . . . Aleks . . . Aleksandr Jovanović? Is that right?'

'Just call him Sasha, Connor. Everyone else does.' Janie studied the patterns in the fitted carpet, fairly sure where this conversation was going. 'He's fled the country already, aye?'

'What? No. I mean, he was trying to. On a cruise ship out of Rosyth.'

Trying to. Which suggested he hadn't succeeded. 'Wait. Are you telling me they've got him in custody?'

Interview room three wasn't quite as nice as the one across the corridor where Janie had met Shauna Lennox at the start of all this. Walls painted institutional beige and no windows, it felt like somewhere to put things you wanted to forget about. It was fitted out old-style, with a table and chairs bolted to the floor, a solid ring set into the former for restraining the more violent detainees.

Not that the man sitting on the wrong side of the table had shown any signs of violence yet. Quite the opposite. For all that he was a bear of a man, Sasha the gang boss had apparently turned meek the moment he was caught trying to stow away on a cruise liner scheduled to leave Rosyth on the evening tide. Beside him, looking like a child in comparison, the duty solicitor was a tiny woman. Not so much short as small. As if she were further away than you thought. She'd eyed Janie suspiciously the moment they entered, but allowed a brief smile and a nod to DC Bryant.

'Right then, shall we get started?' Janie pulled out her own chair and sat down. Bryant remained standing by the door. 'Aleksandr Jovanović.' Janie read from the printout she had been given by the custody sergeant. 'Is that your full name?'

The big man leaned forward, cuffed hands clasped together like two enormous tattooed hams. 'Is so. Your people find it hard to pronounce, so they call me Sasha, no?'

'And do you know why you're here . . .' Janie left a deliberate pause before adding 'Sasha?'

'You don't have to answer, Mr Jovanović,' the duty solicitor said.

'I have nothing to hide,' the big man said, which seemed unlikely.

'You were trying to get onto a boat headed for Rotterdam.' Janie consulted her papers again. 'Seems you had all the correct paperwork for a cabin steward, but the shipping company has no record of employment for you. Not surprising, since the last time we met just a couple of days ago you were working on a building site as a gang boss.'

'I prefer term "site foreman",' the big man said. 'Is less, how you say? Confrontational?'

'But you decided to jack that in and run off to sea. Why would you do a thing like that, so soon after being interviewed by the police?'

'You don't have to—' the solicitor began, but her client interrupted her.

'I always want a life on open wave?' Sasha had the decency to make it a question. Beside him, his tiny solicitor winced.

'So. You're a merchant seaman as well as a building site gang— foreman. A man of many talents, it would seem.'

Across the table from her, Sasha clasped his hands together and shrugged, but he seemed to have run out of bonhomie.

'Why did you run, Sasha? Did someone tell you we'd found Vaclav Mihailovic?' She stared him in the eyes as she continued. 'Or did you go back to check he was still where you'd buried him?'

Something flickered across the big man's features then. At first, Janie thought it was anger, and braced herself for the denial. But the gang boss stayed quiet, and after a moment she realised what he was feeling was actually fear.

'You did bury him out there in the woods, didn't you.' She made it a statement rather than a question, again watching closely for any telltales before the man could claim he knew nothing. Sure enough, he shook his head slowly from side to side, eyes still down at the tabletop rather than looking at Janie. He opened his mouth to speak but was rudely interrupted by the tiny woman at his side.

'As your solicitor it is my duty to inform you that you do not have to answer these questions, Mr Jovanović,' the duty solicitor said. For all her tiny size, her voice was strong. 'You would do well not to incriminate yourself any more than is absolutely necessary.'

Sasha considered her for a moment, nodding gently as if to indicate that he understood. Then he spoke anyway.

'I not kill Vash. He was friend. We go drinking together. But he get sick. Very sudden. Shivering, fever, you know? I take him home, put him to bed. Go for doctor, but then the others call me and say he dead.'

Janie saw the look of pleading in Sasha's eyes, shiny with the beginning of tears. He was either a consummate actor, or this was the truth as he saw it. She said nothing, but gave him a slight nod of the head by way of encouragement to continue. The duty solicitor crossed her arms and glowered at her with a stare that could strip paint.

'Is big problem with dead man in flat. Much attention. Better if nobody know, you understand? And Vash, he have no family back home to take body.'

Shauna had said different, Janie knew. A gran with dementia and money sent home to help with her care, hadn't it been? She let that lie pass for now. The first part of the gang boss's excuse was far more plausible. She'd seen the place and could well imagine the trouble that would come from a dead man being found there. Nobody wanted the kind of attention reporting that to the authorities would bring, and yet more often than not, trying to avoid reporting it ended up making even more trouble.

'Guess that didn't work out, aye?'

Sasha shrugged, tried to wave his hands in an expansive 'what can you do?' gesture, but was thwarted by the cuffs.

'So you took him out to Ormiston and buried his body there. Why hide him away in the woods though? Surely you could just shove him under the foundations of one of the new houses.' Janie studied the man's face as she spoke, looking for any emotional tics and finding plenty. Sasha's eyes widened at the suggestion, the blood draining from his cheeks.

'I am not criminal,' he said, voice almost squeaky with

indignation despite the clear evidence to the contrary. Janie held her face impassive, made no reply and left a silence for him to fill.

'I help my people, no? That is all. If Vash found dead in flat, you arrest everyone. They lose jobs. No money. They sent home, but no jobs there either. No money. Why you think we here in the first place?'

'So where are they all now? Everyone in that flat's gone. You tried to run too.'

For the first time since the interview had begun, Sasha looked to his solicitor for permission to speak. She stared up at him and made a gesture that suggested he'd dug his grave already, might as well climb into it too.

'I panic,' he said. 'When you come look for Vash at work, I go see he not found. I . . .' And now the big man started to shake. For a moment Janie thought he was finally going to use those muscles he'd spent many hours in the gym and even more hundreds of pounds on steroids building. But then she remembered the scene out in the woods, the horror of it. She remembered the look on the young lad's face. Charlie Johnson had seen the body in the half-light of dawn. If Sasha had been out to look earlier, he'd have been using a torch. It had been horrifying enough in daylight.

'You didn't try to bury him again?' she asked. The big man had been staring down at the table, studying his hands and the cuffs between them as if he'd never seen them before. When he looked up, his eyes glistened with unshed tears.

'I am not brave man, Detective Inspector. I see . . . Is something evil happen to Vash. Something old and dark like my nanna tell stories to frighten me when I little boy. I run like devil himself on my tail. I tell others flee too. You lock me up now.' Sasha held his two hands out, palms up and fingers curled in a gesture of surrender even though he was already wearing cuffs. 'I safer in jail.'

25

T he outside light shone above the front door as McLean swept up the drive and parked the little Renault close to its charging point. He stared at the pale yellow lamp as he fiddled with cables and set the car up for its nightly feed, wondering why it was switched on. Normally the front of the house stood in darkness, save for the glow from the kitchen window to the side. All the rooms he and Emma actually used looked out onto the garden at the back.

It occurred to him as he stepped through the back door into the unlit utility room that the obvious reason for the light being on was that someone had come to the front door. Of the regular visitors, only Madame Rose habitually used the front entrance. McLean hadn't been expecting her to visit, but then he never really did. She just turned up. Never particularly unwelcome, but not exactly invited either.

In the kitchen, the absence of cats in front of the Aga could be read either way, but the lack of obvious signs of tea-making suggested it wasn't the medium come to make obscure prognostications. McLean gently touched the side of the kettle to be sure. It was warm, but not recently boiled. Curiouser and curiouser.

He dropped his case onto one of the kitchen chairs, then for no obvious reason tucked it under the table before heading out of the other door and into the main body of the house. Voices spilled from the part-open library door. No, just one voice, insistent and ever so slightly familiar. There was no anger in that voice, no sense of threat or danger, but it had that tone of the preacher about it. And a twang to the accent as McLean began to pick up actual words. American. He knew that voice.

'. . . Just saying, Em. With the sort of stem cell therapies we've been working on, you could be right as rain in six months. Better than you were before even—'

Nathaniel Drake stopped mid-flow as he saw McLean come into the room. He sat at one end of the sofa, close to where Emma had placed her wheelchair. So she was using that today. Never a good sign. Before McLean could say anything, Drake had sprung to his feet like a man made of rubber. He stepped carefully around the coffee table, one hand held out to shake.

'Detective Chief Inspector. They told me you lived in the neighbourhood, but I had no idea it was this gorgeous house.'

Wary, McLean took the proffered hand. Drake's grip was firm, dry and surprisingly cold.

'Mr Drake,' was all he could think of to say. He glanced around the room, half expecting to find a couple of hulking bodyguards lurking in the shadows. But as far as he could tell, Drake had come here alone. There had been no car outside, either. Had he walked?

'I just love these old houses.' Drake's enthusiasm might have been genuine, for all McLean knew. His accent made everything he said sound effusive. 'Scots Baronial, isn't it? Mid-nineteenth century?'

'I'd no idea you were an expert on Scottish architecture, Mr Drake.'

'Please, call me Nate.' Drake glanced at his wrist and what didn't look much like a watch to McLean. 'I should be going, anyway. You're just back from work. Don't want to keep you from your good lady wife.'

'I . . .' McLean started to correct the man, then realised he didn't care enough to bother. 'I'll see you to the door.'

Drake turned briefly to where Emma still sat in her wheelchair. 'Nice to meet you, Em. And think about what I said. Modern medicine can work literal miracles these days.'

'I'll think about it,' Emma said, her smile as pained as McLean might have expected it to be. He led Drake to the front door, pulled it open onto a night turned fully dark.

'Did you walk here?' he asked.

'You sound surprised, Detective Chief Inspector.' In the pale yellow wash of the outside lamp, Drake's skin looked like part-melted candle wax, but his eyes were bright, his smile full of boyish mischief.

'Well, I am, a little. A man of your net worth, wandering the streets alone?' He glanced out towards the rhododendron bushes, but saw no security men lurking behind the leaves. 'And call me Tony, please. If this isn't business.'

'It really isn't. Not here to talk shop, Tony. I was actually surprised when I found out this was your house. I saw it as I was walking by and thought I just had to go and knock, see who lived in such a wonderful building.'

McLean couldn't tell whether he was having the piss taken out of him or Drake was absolutely serious. Then again, the man had never struck him as the kind of American who understood irony the way the British did. Perhaps he was being absolutely honest.

'I'm surprised you'd be out walking alone. Don't you have bodyguards? Security?'

'In Manhattan, sure. LA it's an absolute necessity. Pain in the ass, too. That's what I like so much about Edinboro. I can walk where I want and nobody pays me a lick of notice. You have no idea how great that feels.'

'Well, I guess we're neighbours now. At least for as long as you're staying at the old Spenser place.' McLean glanced in the direction of the house, even though he wouldn't have been able to see it from where he was standing even if it hadn't been dark. 'Maybe next time I can give you the full tour. It's been a long day though, and Emma tires easily ever since . . .'

'Of course, of course.' Drake nodded, took a step away from the front door, then stopped. 'Tell her though. I mean it when I say we can help her. No reason she needs to be stuck in that chair.'

McLean started to say that she wasn't, but Drake had already turned away again, his loping stride carrying him off down the drive and into the shadows.

'Before you start, I had no idea who he was when I answered the doorbell.'

Back in the library, McLean hadn't even had time to open his mouth before Emma had begun her explanation. She didn't owe him one, he knew, but he was intrigued all the same. Crossing the room to the hidden cabinet behind one of the bookshelves, he pulled on the copy of *Whisky Galore* and swung open the door to reveal a dwindling collection of bottles. Time to pay the Scotch Malt Whisky Association a visit. Or maybe a trip to Cupar and The Bottle Shop at the weekend. If he wasn't up to his neck in some tiresome investigation.

'Dram?' He held up an empty glass to Emma, but she shook her head as he'd known full well she would. After another moment's agonising decision-making, he plucked a bottle from the shelf and glugged perhaps a bit more Ardbeg into his own glass than he'd intended, made up for it with a splash of water. He should really have had something to eat first, but seeing Nathaniel Drake in his living room had thrown him off balance.

'How's your day been then?' he asked Emma once the drinks cupboard was closed up again and he had settled into an armchair.

'You mean apart from getting an unexpected visit from the tenth richest man in the world?'

'Actually I don't think he's even in the top hundred.' McLean regretted his glib words as soon as he saw Emma's reaction to them. 'Sorry. You do know I'm investigating a break-in at his research facility out at Easter Bush, right?'

'I do, and he didn't mention it. I think it took him a while to realise whose house he had come to ogle.'

'So he used that story on you too?' McLean considered Drake's parting words. They had seemed genuine enough, however implausible the idea of someone like him wandering the streets of Edinburgh alone at night sounded. 'Maybe he really is just a fan of our vernacular architecture.'

'You can't stand him, can you, Tony.' Emma reached down and started massaging the wasted muscles in her legs as she spoke. Normally McLean would be on his feet at once to help her, but something about her words struck a nerve.

'Can't I?' he asked.

'Well, you sound like it. If I didn't know you better I'd say you'd dismissed him out of hand just because of who he is. What he is.'

'I . . .' McLean opened his mouth to complain, then swiftly closed it again. Emma was right, after all. He had allowed his prejudices to colour his attitude to Drake when in truth he knew very little about the man besides what the papers said about his net worth. He took a sip of whisky as Emma moved from one leg to the other, kneading her calves. After a moment she sat upright again, face a little flushed for a change.

'I get it, really,' she said. 'He's a billionaire, living in a house previously occupied by that horrible Saifre woman and before her the even more horrible Gavin Spenser. They're both of them people who use their money to gain influence and get away with things ordinary folk can't do. But you know what Mr Drake's first instinct was when he saw me having a bad day?' Emma double-checked the wheel locks were in place before levering herself onto her feet. 'He wanted to help. Didn't know what was wrong with me except that I answered the door in my chair, and all he could talk about was the new therapies his company were coming up with. Fixing spinal cord damage, rebuilding muscle tissue, helping the brain to heal itself after stroke damage. Cutting-edge research.'

'So he's a sucker for a pretty face.' McLean put his glass down and stood up himself, Emma took a couple of wobbly steps before leaning heavily into him for support, as he'd thought she would. So much of this was routine now, they didn't even have to ask.

'I might take offence at that, you know?'

'What?' McLean put on an offended tone of his own. 'But it's true.'

'Keep digging, Anthony McLean.' Emma pushed herself away from him, the strength coming back to her legs after too long sitting. Balance and coordination would take a little longer, McLean knew, so he stayed close as she picked a careful path to the door. But not too close; he didn't want it to seem like he expected her to fall. He followed her back through the dark house to the kitchen, noticing how she stayed close to the wall, one hand not quite touching anything but always ready should she need support. Only once she had reached the kitchen table, pulled out a chair and settled into it did she relax. Both hands on the tabletop, she let out a long slow breath.

'Tea, perhaps?' McLean filled the kettle and hefted it onto the hotplate, all too aware of his whisky waiting in the other room.

'Camomile, please. And then I might go to bed. It's late, Tony.'

The words were said without rancour, but they cut all the same. McLean had texted to say he'd be late the moment he'd known it would happen. He was all too aware that it was happening more frequently though; this was two nights in a row now. How swiftly he fell back into old, bad habits.

'I'm sorry, Em.'

'You going to tell me what's happening?'

McLean fetched a mug and the camomile teabags, set them on

the table as the kettle began to plink and roar. He should probably have put less water in it so it boiled more swiftly. Another old habit.

'Your new friend Nathaniel Drake, actually. Think we've probably found the people who broke into his lab.' As he set about making her tea, McLean told her about the CCTV footage, the van and its driver, the favour from Jo Dalgliesh. That last one got him a raised eyebrow, but Emma didn't interrupt. She'd always been a good listener, a useful sounding board, although there were things he couldn't discuss with her any more. Not since she'd quit her forensics job.

'We've got a name and address for the car driver, just need to track down the guy from the flat, get someone in the lab to analyse the mud from his boots and bring them all in for questioning. A lot of work for such a minor crime, but the high heidyins say it's got to be done.'

'And that's why you're grumpy about Mr Drake. Because you think he's leaned on someone high up and they're passing on the favour.' Emma didn't voice it as a question, and the slow nod of her head as she spoke confirmed it wasn't. But then she looked up, caught his gaze. 'Have you considered that they might be leaning on you just because of who he is? He might not have asked anyone to intervene at all.'

26

The phone call came through as he was drinking coffee and contemplating a third slice of toast. McLean grabbed the handset from the table and peered at the name that lit up the screen. He thumbed the accept icon without a moment's hesitation. Control would have texted if it wasn't important.

'McLean.' He glanced up at the clock above the door as he spoke, even though the time had been displayed on the screen of his phone along with the caller name. It was still half past six in the morning, the light through the kitchen window grey and hesitant.

'Good morning, sir. Sorry to call so early, but you put out a search for a Mr Paul Sanderson?' The control operative made it a question, even though she must have had the full details on the computer screen in front of her. McLean took a moment longer to place the name than he would have liked. The untidy top-floor tenement in Sighthill, door unlocked but nobody home.

'You've found him?' he asked.

'A body's been found, sir. Preliminary ID is that it's Sanderson, although that's still to be confirmed. Police Sergeant Kenneth Stephen is at the scene. Duty doctor and pathologist are on their way.'

'Has it been assigned to Specialist Crime yet?'

A slight pause. 'That's why I'm calling you, sir.'

Suppressing his sigh, McLean glanced up at the clock again. It was still half past six as near as didn't matter. Technically this call should have gone to the night shift team at Major Investigations if it was considered suspicious enough to warrant their attention, but he had put out an all persons lookout for Sanderson.

'OK, send me the details. I'll head over to the scene and see what I can do.'

For once the rain held off, and McLean was glad of it as he parked Emma's car at the western entrance to Craigmillar Castle Park. A couple of patrol cars had been lined up at the start of one of the many paths that crossed the wooded parkland, two uniform constables doing their best to stay warm as they directed the few hardy morning walkers away. One of them recognised him as he approached, which at least saved time.

'Morning, sir. Kenny . . . Sergeant Stephen said to keep an eye out. You want me to show you to the scene?'

McLean couldn't work out whether the desperation in the young constable's voice was from cold or boredom. No doubt a brisk walk through the trees would help him warm up and pass a little time both. Leaving his colleague to man the cordon alone wasn't that friendly though.

'It's OK. Reckon I can find it myself if you point me in the right direction.' He ducked under the tape that had been strung across the path but which would do nothing to stop anyone from walking into the woods a few dozen paces to either side.

'Aye, sir. Right you are. Follow this path to the first fork, then take the right turn. It's no' far.'

McLean nodded his thanks, stuck his hands into his coat pockets and set off through the scrubby trees. He'd only gone a short way before a lone figure came striding towards him. A little closer and he recognised the duty doctor.

'No rush, Tony. He's dead. Not going anywhere in a hurry.'

'Thanks, Phil. Good to know, I suppose.'

'Should warn you though. It's an odd one. Creeped me out a bit if I'm being honest.' The doctor gave an involuntary shudder that could have been the cold. 'Funny how they get you that way sometimes, eh?'

Without waiting for an answer the doctor hunched into his coat and set off again towards the car park. With a shrug, McLean carried on along the path through the leafless trees until he came to the fork, then took the right-hand turn as he'd been instructed. It had been a while since last he'd visited Craigmillar Castle or walked the paths through the nearby park and he had no idea what to expect of the scene until he arrived at the edge of a natural clearing and found another pair of uniform constables and more cordon tape. Beyond them a couple of forensics technicians were struggling with a tent.

'Morning, sir,' one of the constables said, lifting up the tape so McLean wouldn't have to bend too far. 'Sergeant Stephen's over at the forensic van. He's acting CSM until the rest of the team get here.'

'Thanks.' McLean wanted to use the constable's name, but found he couldn't remember it. That was the problem when you rose so far up the hierarchy, the policemen just kept on getting younger, and they all began to look the same.

It was clear that the centre of activity was a bench set at a point where two paths met in the middle of the clearing, although from where he stood he couldn't see what, if anything, was on it. He kept well away, skirting around the edge until he reached the van. It must have come in from a different direction, backing down a wider track. It must also have had a kettle, as most of the more senior uniform officers had congregated around it and were warming their hands on a variety of mugs, chatting. One of them saw him coming and broke away from the crowd. At least McLean recognised this one.

'Morning, sir.' Police Sergeant Kenneth Stephen held out his steaming mug. 'Coffee?'

'I'm fine, thanks, Kenny. You called me in specifically on this one, right?'

'Aye. Pretty sure it's the man you were looking for. Paul Sanderson?'

McLean followed the sergeant's gaze over to the point where the bench had now been covered by the forensic team's tent. Standing on the outside adjusting the fit of his white paper overalls, the pathologist Tom MacPhail was chatting to his assistant, Cerys.

'How do you know it's him?'

'Mostly the driving licence and the name on his bank cards. Of course he could be someone else entirely and he's stolen Sanderson's wallet, but the photo on the licence looks like him. Sort of.'

McLean was going to ask what Kenny meant by 'sort of' but decided it would be just as easy to see for himself.

'Grab me a set of overalls, can you? Might as well go and get acquainted with the deceased. DS Stringer should be here soon. You can bring him up to speed on who found the body and all that.'

The first thing he noticed as he stepped into the forensics tent was how much warmer it was inside than out. McLean hadn't thought the wind so bad, especially in amongst the trees, but taking it away felt a bit like opening the door on an oven.

The second thing he noticed was the smell, even through the thin paper mask he'd pulled on. Not the rot of a body left out for days to bloat and decay, nor the more pleasant scent of loam warmed by the morning sun, this was an oddly antiseptic smell. It put him in mind of the mortuary, and for a moment he wondered if either Dr MacPhail or his assistant Cerys had brought that stink of formaldehyde and embalming preservatives in on their clothes.

But then the scent changed, becoming more like sandalwood and linseed oil, like the warning of a headache.

'What is that?' The question was out before he'd seen the body, but as soon as he did, McLean was prepared to forgive the lack of any answer.

Paul Sanderson, if that truly was who this man had been in life, sat on the park bench for all the world like he was resting his legs for a moment before carrying on with his walk. Hands in his lap, cradled around something that looked like a small wooden box, his head had tilted back, staring at the sky now obscured by the forensics tent. He wore baggy cargo pants and an army surplus camouflage jacket at least two sizes too big. Indeed, the initial impression McLean had was of a child wearing a man's clothing, except that Sanderson's face was not that of a child. Creased and leathery skin puckered around sunken eyeballs, and his slightly parted, cracked lips offered a glimpse of rotten yellow teeth. A two-day fuzz of white stubble clung to his hollow cheeks, merging into ratty curls of greasy grey-black hair.

'Jesus. Looks like that Nazi guy in that old movie. You know, the Holy Grail one?' It was Cerys who broke the silence that had fallen heavily on the small group in the tent. McLean took a moment to get her reference, not thinking *Indiana Jones and the Last Crusade* was that old a film until his brain did the maths. Chances were it had come out before the mortuary assistant had even been born. She was right though, except that as far as he remembered, Walter Donovan had ended up exploding into a pile of desiccated fragments. Shrivelled like he'd been left out in the desert sun for too long, Paul Sanderson was nevertheless still whole.

'Seems to have lost his shoes, too.' Dr MacPhail had crouched down in front of the body, taking in the whole before focusing on the details. He reached a gloved hand forwards and gently lifted one foot, shone a pen torch on the sole. 'Looks like he walked a good distance barefoot.'

'There was a pair of boots in his flat.' McLean recalled the scene, made a rough calculation of distance from there to this park bench. 'Quite a walk.'

'Indeed.' MacPhail bent forward and shone his torch at the dead man's face. McLean watched in silence as the pathologist swiftly and expertly went about his job. For long minutes the only sounds in the tent were the click of the crime scene photographer's camera and the low-murmured words as MacPhail directed his assistant.

'Surprised you haven't asked me for a time of death,' he said as he finally stood up straight and took a step back from the body.

'I know you can't tell me. Not with any great accuracy. And anyway, it's like Cerys said. He looks like he's been dead a hundred years, but I know that's not possible.' McLean looked down at the body again. Despite his pose, Paul Sanderson didn't look in the least bit peaceful.

'Can we move him enough to get a look at what he's holding?' He pointed at Sanderson's hands, thin fingers interlaced to form a bony cage over whatever it was that had been so important to him.

'Reckon so,' MacPhail said. 'There's no evidence of a third party involved here. I can say that much. He sat down on that bench and died. Nobody killed him here.'

'But you don't know what he died of, and this isn't natural.' McLean waved a hand to take in Sanderson's almost mummified form.

'That depends on what you mean by natural, Tony. There are wasting diseases that could lead to him looking like this, although the state he's in I'd have thought he'd struggle to walk any distance. There's barely any muscle on him, and not an ounce of fat.'

'Could it be contagious?' McLean took an involuntary step back, felt the fabric of the tent against his shoulders. That cloying scent and the growing heat from four live bodies made the enclosed space feel suddenly less safe than the nice cold fresh wind outside.

'Doubtful in the way you mean.' MacPhail raised a gloved hand to his paper mask and adjusted it slightly. 'But we're taking precautions all the same.'

He bent down again, and his assistant was there as if she had read his mind. With surprising care, the pathologist prised Sanderson's fingers away, one by one, until he was able to move each hand far enough for Cerys to reach in and gently remove the item. McLean found that he had been holding his breath, as if expecting the dead man to put up a fight, or perhaps go full Indiana Jones and explode into a pile of dust and bone fragments. Instead, nothing dramatic happened at all.

'Here you go. Looks like some kind of trophy box or something. Not sure how it opens, mind.' Cerys passed the box over. It was surprisingly heavy in McLean's hands, as if it contained far more than its dimensions could possibly hold. Dark, polished wood, it was inlaid with some yet darker material in a pattern almost impossible to make out. He held it up to the light, turned it a little from side to side, but could make nothing much more of it than the pathologist's assistant. It was old, that much he could tell, the weight of centuries on it. An antique, certainly valuable, possibly priceless. So what was someone as penniless as Sanderson doing with it? And where the hell had he got it from?

27

'That's forensics done at the scene now, sir. Everything points to Sanderson walking to that bench himself. No sign anyone took him there.'

McLean had been sitting at his desk and enjoying a brief quiet moment to collect his thoughts. He looked up to see DS Stringer standing in the open doorway, a brown folder clutched in one hand like a shield. They always did that, the sergeants and constables who came to see him. Brought something that wasn't really for him to read so much as for them to hide behind. Was he really that terrifying? Or maybe he was overthinking things.

'Any word on when the post mortem might be?'

'First thing tomorrow was what Dr MacPhail said. He's got a busy schedule as is, and reckoned this one wasn't too urgent, given he seems to have died from some illness rather than violence.'

'It'd be nice to know what that illness is. The body didn't look like someone who walked into a secure research facility just a few days ago, even if his boots match the prints we found at the site.' McLean pushed his seat back and stood up with a minimum of huffing noises. 'Which reminds me. Have we got any further finding next of kin for a positive ID? I know he looks like Sanderson and was carrying Sanderson's wallet, but there's procedure.'

'DC Fairley's working on that at the moment.' Stringer paused in a way McLean had come to learn meant he was about to say something unhelpful.

'And . . .?'

'We've got Christine Vaughan being processed downstairs, but Campbell's done a runner.'

What surprised McLean most was that he wasn't surprised. A lot of things started to make sense in the light of that nugget of information. Shame they weren't the things he needed to make sense, but it was a start.

'Aye, thought he might. House empty and no sign it'd ever been lived in?'

Stringer looked like he was about to say 'How did you know?' but managed to stop himself before it came out. 'Van's still there, full of paint pots and ladders, but aye, the house has been stripped bare. Could've been like that all along, mind. It's not like we ever paid him a visit before.'

'I never really believed he was a painter and decorator. His hands were too clean.'

'You want us to pass his photo out to patrols?'

'Probably not worth it. He's not gone to ground because of us. He's finished his assignment and gone back to his unit.'

Stringer gave a single nod of understanding. 'Probably for the best, really. Cells are getting filled up the now. Janie brought in a suspect late last night.'

'The body out Haddington way?' McLean asked.

'Aye. Well, the gang boss who ran his team at the building site. Serbian by the name of Aleksandr Jovanović. Although everyone seems to call him Sasha. Weird that. Always thought Sasha was a girl's name.'

'Surprised they don't call him Boris, to be honest.' McLean saw the look of confusion on the detective sergeant's face. 'Jovanović is the Serbian equivalent of Johnson?'

It took a while, but slowly understanding dawned, Stringer's frown turning to a slightly pained smile.

'He'll be off to the Sheriff Court soon as we can get a slot anyways. I don't imagine he'll be going back home to Serbia for a while.'

'What's his story then?' McLean asked. He'd get the full rundown at the evening briefing, but the day had started too early and that had been a long time ago.

'He claims Mihailovic died in his sleep. They didn't want the attention telling us lot about it would bring, so they took him out to the woods near one of the building sites and buried him.'

'And Janie believes him?' McLean heard the criticism in his words after they'd already come out. 'Don't answer that. I'm sure she knows exactly what she's doing.'

'She's working with Jessica Bryant on this one, so I only know second-hand. They're prepping for a second interview before he goes off to court.'

'Going to be busy this afternoon then.' McLean glanced up at the clock. 'You got background on Vaughan yet?'

Stringer flapped his folder once, but didn't immediately make to hand it over. 'Aye, there's nothing recent, but she had a few brushes with the law when she was younger. Protest marches getting a bit out of hand, that sort of thing.'

'Protesting what?' McLean asked, although he was fairly sure he knew. This time Stringer opened the folder and started to read from what looked like a single sheet of paper inside.

'Animal rights, anti-vivisection. We've got her in with a bunch of hunt saboteurs down in the Borders ten years ago, and she was part of a group that tore up a load of experimental GM crops on a farm in East Lothian not long after that. Pleaded guilty and got off with a fine. All pretty quiet since then.'

'Suggests maybe the break-in was politically motivated.' Even as he said the words, McLean doubted they were true. Things were never that easy. 'OK, Jay. Let's get on with planning this thing. Sooner it's started, sooner we can wrap everything up and go home.'

Christine Vaughan was not exactly the eco warrior McLean had imagined. As she sat opposite him in interview room three, she brought to mind the word 'mousey'. Small, pulled in on herself, she radiated waves of 'please don't notice me, leave me alone', that might well have worked in any less focused a situation. Beside her, the duty solicitor tried his best to look interested in the proceedings, but he'd chosen the law over acting as a profession for a reason.

'You know why we've brought you here, Ms Vaughan.' McLean pitched his voice as a statement rather than a question, hoping the woman would hear the accusation in it. She looked at him, briefly, a flicker of anger on her otherwise bland features that was swiftly suppressed.

'Actually, no. I don't,' she said.

'We have reason to believe you were part of a group of people who broke into the research labs of Drake Biotech, in the science park at Easter Bush, a few nights ago. Along with Keith Campbell and Paul Sanderson.' McLean watched for the tell as he spoke each name, saw her eye twitch briefly at the first, an involuntary shudder at the second.

'I would advise you to say nothing at this point, Ms Vaughan,' the lawyer said, rather unhelpfully.

'You were also seen picking up Mr Campbell from his address in Restalrig yesterday evening. The two of you drove to another address in Craigmillar, entered a tenement flat where Mr Sanderson lives. Did you see Mr Sanderson? Speak to him?'

Vaughan had fixed her gaze firmly on the table in front of her, and with her head tilted downwards her hair obscured most of her features. Even so, McLean saw the frown that furrowed her forehead and crinkled the edges of her eyes. She tensed a little, no doubt fighting the urge to say something. She'd been trained well, although not as well as Campbell. Maybe he was the one who'd taken her through police interview technique in the first place. How long had he spent putting together his little team? And why the subterfuge when he could just as easily have gained access to the lab by pretending to be a painter? Something didn't add up.

'Here's the thing, Ms Vaughan,' McLean continued as if this was no more than a pleasant conversation. 'We know you're a supporter of animal rights. As it happens, I've a lot of sympathy for that position. But Drake Biotech don't do animal experiments, do they?'

He paused, although Vaughan declined to fill the silence. She shifted in her seat a little, raised her head just a fraction before lowering it again. A lot going on in that head. McLean pressed on.

'From what I've been able to find out about the company, their research is mostly aimed at finding therapies to increase lifespan and reverse the worst effects of ageing. Arthritis, dementia, Alzheimer's disease, that sort of thing. They use computer simulations, so-called Artificial Intelligence, and cell cultures derived from human subjects for their experimentation. No animals harmed at all.'

'Which begs the question why you think my client would be involved at all, Detective Chief Inspector,' the lawyer interrupted just a split second before Vaughan was about to say something herself. McLean cursed him inwardly, although the man was only doing his job.

'Not really. The question it begs is not whether she was involved – we know she was. No, what I want to know is why. Why break into a research lab that has nothing to do with animal abuse, smash up a load of expensive machinery and daub the walls with meaningless slogans? And why, Ms Vaughan, when you've gone to all that trouble to get in unseen, does your co-conspirator Mr Sanderson walk straight out the front door past the security guard and all the cameras?'

'It was you lot, wasn't it?' Finally Vaughan spoke, her voice low and filled with anger.

'Ms Vaughan—' the lawyer began, but she silenced him with a glance, turned that same glare on McLean. He'd seen worse, but from timid wee mouse to what stared at him now was quite the swift change.

'What'd you do? Snatch him off the streets, aye? I bet that's it.' She quivered with a rage that was as forceful as it was sudden. 'Or did you smash your way into his flat? Wouldn't have taken much. Paulie'd no' hurt a fly, but youse lot wouldn't care about that.'

McLean met the fiery gaze with studied calm. This was the response he'd been hoping to provoke, after all.

'When was the last time you saw Mr Sanderson?' he asked. 'Was he there when you and Mr Campbell visited last night?'

'You know he wasn't. You lot had got him already. Where've you taken him? He's no' well.'

'How do you mean, not well?'

There was a long pause while Vaughan's brain caught up with what her anger had given away. Where before she had managed to keep her expression almost blank, now the emotions played themselves across her features like a movie. She tensed as if readying herself for a fight, and then her shoulders slumped.

'Aye, so I was at that lab. What of it? You say they don't experiment on animals, but have you seen that bloke owns it? Nathaniel Drake? Looks like a bloody vampire, an' he's just the same as all those billionaire wankers, aye? Exploiting us ordinary folk so's they can have more money than anyone can spend in a lifetime. How's that fair?'

It wasn't a question he felt able to answer, and besides, he was the one who was supposed to be asking them. McLean let only a moment pass before continuing.

'You might not believe me, but we don't have Mr Sanderson in custody. We didn't pick him up yesterday either. You say he's not well, but was he like that before you both entered the laboratory?'

'Ms Vaughan, I must caution—' the duty solicitor began to say, but was interrupted by his client.

'If youse lot don't have him, then where the fuck is he? Walked out on us and set all those alarms off. No' right in the head. I told Keith not tae trust him.'

'We'll find him.' McLean decided the lie was worth saying. 'And if he needs medical attention he'll get it. But tell me, Ms Vaughan. Did you see Mr Sanderson take anything from the lab? Or was he just spraying graffiti on the walls and breaking things?'

Vaughan's eyes lost their focus for a moment as she thought about the question. Alongside her, the duty solicitor's face had turned thunderous.

'We weren't there tae steal stuff, ken? Just leave a wee message to that weird Yank bastard.' She shrugged. 'He might've taken a wee memento, mind. Paulie's always been a wee bit sentimental like that.'

'Ms Vaughan, I really must—' the duty solicitor tried again, but his client turned her anger on him.

'Must what? I've already said I was in there, aye? They know I was in there. No point pretending I wasnae. I fess up an' help the nice polisman here and mebbe he puts in a good word, see?'

McLean felt it best not to disabuse the woman of this notion, and before he could say anything she had turned back to him anyway.

'I don't know what Paulie got up to. He went intae a wee room off the main lab for a while. Took his bag and his cans, so I guess he was writin' love poetry on the walls, aye? Next I knew he was oot the door an' away. Then all hell broke loose wi' alarms an' stuff so we's all legged it oot the fire escape.'

'And Sanderson met up with you at Campbell's van? You all went back into the city together?'

Vaughan's eyes lost their focus again for a moment, then she shook her head slowly. 'No. He never showed. Must've walked home, the wee daftie. He wasnae answerin' his phone, but that's Paulie for youse. We was gonnae leave him be for a while, but then you lot pulled Keith in. You sure you didn't pick up Paulie an' all?'

'Well, that went in an unexpected direction.'

McLean and Stringer stood outside the incident room as Christine Vaughan was led away to the cells. The duty solicitor had finally managed to persuade his client to stop incriminating herself any further, and they had decided to call a halt to proceedings for a while.

'I reckon she's just being realistic about it. Either that or she knows who Campbell really is and reckons he'll come riding in to save her.'

Stringer raised an eyebrow. 'You still think he's a spook?' he asked, but before McLean could answer they were both interrupted by the arrival of Chief Superintendent McIntyre. She pushed through the double doors at the end of the corridor and bore down on them like a Spanish galleon in full sail.

'There you are, Tony. Do you never answer your bloody phone?'

McLean pushed himself away from the wall, tugged at the hems of his jacket. He reached into his pocket and pulled out the offending article.

'I was interviewing a suspect, Jayne. Had it on silent. Was there something you wanted?'

The wind dropped, McIntyre's short-lived ire deflating like a punctured tyre. She turned to DS Stringer first.

'You want to go get yourself a coffee, Jay. I need to speak to Tony for a while.'

As dismissals went, it was both obvious and graceful. Stringer nodded his head once, muttered a quiet 'Ma'am', and scuttled away.

'Any of these rooms empty?' the chief superintendent asked

McLean once the double doors had swung closed behind the departing detective sergeant. He indicated the end of the corridor, and they both went through into the last of the interview rooms. Bare walls and no window, its table had been removed, chairs bolted to the floor with just enough space between them that the subject of questioning could not easily do harm should they turn violent. The heavy iron ring poking up out of the carpet tiles suggested restraint was often necessary, as did the big red panic button by the door.

'What is it with you and upsetting important people?' McIntyre asked after she had taken the interrogator's chair. No other option, McLean settled into the seat opposite her. It was remarkably uncomfortable, he noticed.

'In general, or is there some specifically important person I've annoyed?'

'Is there any you've not?' The chief superintendent ran a hand through her almost entirely grey hair. 'This time it's come through the chief constable's office, but I don't think she's particularly involved. Just the messenger for someone even higher up the tree.'

McLean glanced around the sparse room. An almost square patch of one wall was a slightly different shade of institutional beige to the rest, where it had been repainted for reasons it was all too easy to guess. Unlike McIntyre's reason for wanting this conversation. Except that even as he thought it, the answer came to him. Keith Campbell.

'They want us to pretend it never happened. The break-in.'

McIntyre dipped her head in confirmation. 'More specifically, they don't want anyone charged. Nothing on record, though I'll do everything I can to make sure it doesn't reflect badly on your team.'

'Very gracious, I'm sure.' McLean heard the snark in his voice and didn't much like it. 'Sorry, Jayne. I know you're just the messenger here. It's just a bit frustrating to be told to stop looking when we've just arrested one of the culprits and they've given us a full confession.'

'I . . .' McIntyre's eyes widened. 'Oh.'

'But we can let her go with a caution, I suppose. Might want to get her checked over by a doctor first though. And get word back to the spooks at MI whatever to tell their man to do the same. They were all in close contact with Sanderson, after all.'

'Sanderson?' The chief superintendent's voice took on a slightly strangled quality as she asked the one-word question. McLean couldn't remember whether he'd told her about that morning's dead body, but she must have heard from someone, surely? Then again, her job meant mostly being in meetings on the other side of the country, so maybe she hadn't.

'Paul Sanderson. He was found this morning in Craigmillar Castle Park by a dog walker.' He leaned forward in his chair, elbows on his knees to ease the pain growing in his back as he briefed McIntyre. 'That's why we picked up Vaughan anyway. Would've done the same for Campbell except it turns out that's probably not his real name and he's disappeared back wherever he came from. It's one thing to have a vague suspicion, quite another when they visit the home of a man who turns up dead soon after.'

The chief superintendent ran her fingers through her hair again, scratched the back of her neck and let out a long sigh. 'Remind me again why I asked you to look into this break-in, Tony? You'd think I'd know better by now.'

It wasn't a question that needed an answer, so McLean didn't offer one.

'I can wrap things up if you want. Let Vaughan go. Stop looking for the other two. But we can't not investigate Sanderson's death, Jayne. You know that, right?'

McIntyre nodded slowly, stood with a creaking of joints that made McLean wince in sympathetic pain. 'Just try to keep the collateral damage to a minimum, can you?'

28

M cLean wasn't sure he'd ever forget the looks of surprise on the faces of both Christine Vaughan and the duty solicitor as the former was released and the two of them left the police station together. He'd wanted to talk to Vaughan some more, but felt that pushing her too hard might end up with a claim of harassment. He could follow things up with her later if necessary, when she'd had a chance to calm down and reflect upon her good fortune. It wasn't as if Paul Sanderson was going to get any more dead, after all. And until the results of the post mortem came through they didn't even know whether his death was suspicious or just unlucky.

Aye, right. Even he couldn't convince himself of that. There were too many coincidences at play, and McLean didn't believe in coincidences. Throw in the meddling politicians first asking him to investigate and then backing off when he actually started to find something and the whole thing had headache written all over it. Well, he'd told McIntyre that he couldn't not investigate Sanderson's death, and if that made the powers that be uncomfortable, he could learn to live with that.

Pondering his next move, McLean set off for his office, then had a change of heart. He could hardly give Harrison grief for pursuing things on her own if he always did the same himself.

Instead, he changed course for the CID room in the hope there might be a detective at a loose end he could coerce into helping.

As it happened, there was one desk occupied when he entered the room. DC Fairley shot to his feet like a naughty schoolboy the moment he saw McLean, snapped out a slightly panicked 'Sir!'

'At ease, Detective Constable.' McLean tried to make it easier on the young lad. 'It's Connor, isn't it?'

'Aye, I mean yes, sir.'

'You spare an hour or so?' He glanced at his watch, all too aware how the afternoon was getting away.

'I've a few interviews to transcribe, but they can wait, sir. What did you need?'

'Some printouts of photographs from evidence and a pool car. You reckon you can get me those?'

The detective constable nodded so vigorously McLean worried he might break his neck. He grabbed a notebook from his desk and plucked a pen from the breast pocket of his jacket. 'Which items were you after, sir? I'll get right on it.'

McLean gave Fairley the details and sent him off on his errands with an arrangement to meet in the station car park in fifteen minutes. The young man's enthusiasm was endearing, really, although no doubt it would wear a tired senior detective down after a while. Had he ever been that eager to please? It was hard to remember so far back, but he probably had been. Ah well, a couple of years in the job would soon blunt DC Fairley's keenness.

The afternoon was all but gone by the time they arrived at Drake Biotech. McLean had taken one look at the pool car the detective constable had secured, a not so old BMW with a petrol engine and flappy paddle gear change, and decided Fairley could drive it. Too long with Emma's electric Renault Zoe, he wasn't sure he'd know how to operate something so complicated.

'Here to see Professor Caine,' he said as the two of them

approached the reception desk. There were a lot more security guards around the place, McLean noticed. Stable door and horse sprang to mind.

'Do you have an appointment?' the receptionist asked. McLean was about to say that no, he didn't, and neither did he need one, but Fairley stepped in with uncharacteristic forwardness before he could speak.

'Aye, he knows we're coming. I called in to check he was here. Detective Chief Inspector McLean and DC Fairley? That's E Y. Should be on your system there.' The young detective constable pointed towards the computer screen that lit up the receptionist's face and illuminated her momentary scowl.

'Of course. One moment.' The receptionist picked up a phone and punched a single button. McLean turned his attention to Fairley.

'Good work calling ahead. I should have asked you to do that anyway, but it never hurts to take the initiative on things like that.'

The detective constable's face flushed at the praise, the tops of his cheeks darkening in a band of freckles that wouldn't have looked out of place on someone half his age. Before he could say anything, the secure door at the back of the reception area buzzed open and the man they had come to meet stepped through. Greying hair askew, he was wearing a lab coat that sported several impressive stains. His face was almost as grumpy as the receptionist's as he peered over the top of his half-moon spectacles, but he broke into a rictus smile when he saw McLean.

'Inspector. It's good to see you again. Do you have news?'

'Is there somewhere more private we can talk?' McLean gestured towards the security door, beyond which he knew there was a conference room and that spectacular central atrium. Caine looked rather surprised to be asked, but rallied swiftly.

'Of course, of course. This way.'

They followed him through the door and into the administration wing of the partially completed building. When the professor led them into the conference room, McLean saw paper plans strewn across the large table where he'd sat and talked to Caroline Wheeler a few days earlier. Caine bustled over and tidied them all away before he could see more than a few outlines of the building works.

'Sit down, sit down.' The professor looked wide-eyed around the room. 'Can I offer you coffee? Tea?'

'Thank you, but no. This shouldn't take long.' McLean pulled out a chair, indicated for Fairley to take the one next to him. 'We've had some small success with our investigation so far. Pretty much certain we've identified one of the men who broke in. The one who exited by the front door, if you recall.'

The professor drew out a chair at the head of the conference table, quite a distance away, and settled into it slowly. 'You say "pretty much certain". Can you not arrest this man? Question him? Surely with the right inducements he might be persuaded to give up his fellow criminals.'

'Alas, no, we can't. Much as I'd like to.' McLean weighed up the pros and cons of giving Caine too much detail in what was now a different ongoing investigation. His initial distrust of the man had not changed, and as he opened his mouth to ask something, McLean interrupted him.

'Can you tell me, Professor, what is it that you actually do here? Your research, that is. How does it differ from the more conventional approaches taken by other biotech labs in the field?'

Caine's mouth remained open a moment longer than was perhaps necessary as his brain caught up with this change of tack. He closed it slowly, brow furrowed as he seemed to collect his thoughts. After a short while he leaned forward, forearms resting on the table amongst his folded plans, and fixed McLean with a glare familiar to any postgraduate student who has asked an interesting question.

'What do you know of Methuselah, Inspector?'

'As in the Old Testament? Lived the best part of a thousand years? That Methuselah?'

'The same. And according to the Bible it was nine hundred and sixty-nine years, but let's not quibble. The Old Testament is full of men living far longer than the span we achieve today.'

'I didn't take you for a religious man, Professor.'

'I'm not. Although there is much of value to be found in the Bible if you can bear the mountains of rubbish it's hidden under. No, Inspector. I am not a man of faith, and I very much doubt anyone in ancient times lived for a thousand years. But there are people throughout recorded history who have lived longer than average. In simple terms you might say they were blessed with good genes, although the science is a great deal more complicated than that. The point is, they existed. And at times when medical science was either in its infancy or utterly non-existent.'

'And that's why you're so interested in archaeology, then,' McLean said, receiving a half-smile from Caine for his efforts.

'Exactly so. I've studied the past, with a special focus on those people who have outlived their natural span. I've made it my life's work to trace where they are buried, those few of them that were buried. Over the years I've collected viable samples from the remains of perhaps two dozen men and a handful of women. Detailed analysis of what DNA we've managed to recover has already yielded far better results than even I expected.'

'The clinical trials Dr Wheeler is overseeing?'

'Those, yes.' Caine nodded his head once. 'And there's Nathaniel's therapy, too. That's working remarkably well.'

'His . . .?' McLean recalled the strange drink Drake had been forcing down when they had first met, like used engine oil that should really have been changed a few thousand miles earlier. 'Oh, his rejuvenation programme.'

'A rather dismissive way to sum up decades of research and a dietary and medical regime tuned to the specific genetic code of one person,' the professor said. 'But yes, that therapy.'

McLean glanced briefly to his side, where DC Fairley had already gone through several pages of his notebook writing everything down. He'd not asked the detective constable to do that, but it kept him quiet.

'Is it not a touch unethical to experiment on your boss?' He turned his attention back to the professor as he asked the question, catching a glimpse of an expression very different to the bland, almost friendly one that Caine had been affecting beforehand.

'Mr Drake approached me, Inspector. Not the other way around. He's delighted with his progress so far. And I'd be a fool to do anything to him that might cause harm.' The professor lifted both hands towards the ceiling. 'I'd lose all this, wouldn't I?'

'Fair point,' McLean conceded. 'So you use samples of ancient remains to make your drugs, treatments, whatever? Is that what the lab's for?'

Now the professor didn't even try to hide his irritation. 'No. Have you not been listening? We sample the remains, read the code written deep within them, and use that knowledge to build new therapies from scratch. What did you think I was doing? Cooking up ancient bones into soup? I'm a scientist, Inspector, not a crank or witch doctor or whatever.'

'My apologies, Professor. I—'

'And besides, that lab isn't even finished yet. We've not used it to do anything. The drugs we use for trials are made in a facility in England.'

McLean considered asking where Nathaniel Drake's treatment was made, but that wasn't really why he'd come to see the professor.

'Thank you. I didn't mean to imply anything. I was just exploring the possibility that the people who broke into the lab might have accidentally poisoned themselves.'

'Serve them right if they did. But it couldn't happen.' Caine shook his head again, then stopped. 'This man you've identified. He's unwell? Too unwell to question?'

'You said nothing was taken from the lab,' McLean said instead of answering the professor's question.

Caine sighed, took off his spectacles and cleaned them on the corner of his lab coat. 'I told you already. We've done a full audit of the lab, Inspector. They broke equipment worth north of a hundred thousand pounds, and it's going to cost a great deal just to get the room redecorated. Cover up that ridiculous graffiti they sprayed everywhere. But no. They didn't steal anything. Is it important? Is theft a more heinous crime than mere vandalism?'

'I can assure you we take all crime seriously, but I needed to be certain. And given your links to archaeology, well . . .' McLean reached inside his jacket and pulled out the photographs he'd asked DC Fairley to print for him before they had come to the biotech lab, photographs of the inlaid wooden box that had been found clasped in the lap of Paul Sanderson, deceased. The professor took them, slid on his spectacles again and then peered over them at the images, an air of vague interest on his face.

'Eastern European, late-medieval period, possibly, though I can't be sure. I'd have to hold the thing, look at that inlay with a magnifier. It's a nice little piece. Seen something very like it in a museum in Belgrade, I think.' Caine put the sheets down with a flourish. 'I take it there's a reason you're showing me this?'

'You've never seen it before?' McLean asked.

'No.' Caine shook his head slowly, pursed his lips as if searching an encyclopaedic memory. 'Unless it's from that museum. Why?'

'The man who broke into your lab and then walked out the front door while his friends were still trashing the place. He . . .' McLean was about say Sanderson had the box with him, but he was fairly sure that Caine was lying about never having seen it before. No reason to give the professor any more information if that wasn't a two-way street. Time for a little white lie. 'We found it where he was living. It doesn't really fit with the rest of the decor, so I can only assume he had recently acquired it. We thought maybe he found it here.'

'Here?' Caine laughed, an odd sound a bit like a piglet being strangled. 'This is a biotech lab, Inspector.'

'And yet you base your work on analysis of ancient remains. So you can understand why I might make the connection, yes?'

'Well, as I said before, Inspector. This lab isn't functional yet. I've no idea where your suspect got this, but it certainly wasn't from here.'

Caine picked up the pictures again, leafed through them without looking. Gone was the genial, friendly fellow who had greeted them on their arrival; now he was all anxious nerves and agitation. As good a confirmation of his suspicions as a full confession, as far as McLean was concerned. The box had been stolen from the lab. So why didn't the professor want to admit it? And why had Sanderson stolen it at all?

29

'Come on, everyone. Let's have a bit of quiet now. Plenty to be getting through and not a lot of time.'

Janie pitched her voice above the general hubbub in the main incident room, even though the effort was almost too much for her tired bones and aching head. She and Manda had again sat up late into the night before, searching the letting agency websites for somewhere to live. Or to be more accurate, showing each other the most ridiculous apartments at rents neither of them could afford, while cursing at their landlord's son and their own ill luck. They'd stopped at the one bottle of wine between them, but on top of the stress and not enough food, it had been more than enough.

'OK. Since I've got your attention now. Let's start with the good news. Thanks to the good folk at Border Control over in Rosyth, we have our main suspect in custody. He's kicking his heels in Saughton right now, and not likely to be going anywhere else soon.'

'Is there anything left for us to do, really? If we've got him in custody?'

Janie wasn't entirely sure who had asked the question. It came from a cluster of uniform constables and admin staff towards the back of the room. A couple of detectives from one of the other major incident teams were lurking in the crowd too. They'd been drafted in to help process the mountains of information gathered at the tower block the previous day, and no doubt wanted to hang around where there was a whiff of overtime in the air.

'Questions at the end of the briefing, aye? But fair point. And it leads on to what I was going to bring up next anyway. We know who buried Mihailovic out in those woods and possibly why. What we don't yet know is what killed him. You'll have all read the PM report by now, so you know that's got the pathologists puzzled too. Right now they don't think it's anything contagious, but it's crucial we confirm that as soon as possible. Last thing we need is more bodies turning up, right?'

The muttered agreement that came from the assembled officers was less enthusiastic than Janie would have liked, but it was early in the morning and no doubt many of them felt as bad as she did.

'So, order of the day. We need to trace Mihailovic's movements from his last sighting alive up until the moment he was found dead in his bed in the fourth-floor flat in the tower block.'

Janie could almost sense the question that formed in the body of officers in front of her, answered it before it could find a mouth to speak itself.

'And yes, I know we also need to confirm that he actually did die there. I'm not just taking the word of a man who tried to do a runner as soon as he knew we wanted to talk to him. It's a starting point though, and it's the best we've got right now. So we'll be finishing up with door to doors in the tower block and speaking to everyone at the building site who worked alongside him. Find out who knew Mihailovic by name, who spoke to him more often than a casual nod in passing on the stairs. If you're not sure what you're meant to be doing, see DI Gregg.' Janie turned to her colleague. 'You anything to add, Sandy?'

'Only that the press are sniffing around this. Someone from the tower block's decided it's better to complain to the tabloids than us. They'll probably try to play some racist anti-immigrant angle, usually do. Let's not give them anything to work with, shall we? Especially the details about how the body was discovered. Last thing we need is people panicking. We've no evidence to suggest this is something contagious, so if any reporter starts asking you questions, you send them straight to me or Dan Hwei in the press office, right?'

There hadn't been time that morning for more than a cursory chat with the senior officers regarding their ongoing investigations, so it was news to Janie that the papers had picked up the story. Not surprising, perhaps, but unwelcome all the same.

'Thanks. I shouldn't need to remind you all that any unauthorised speaking to the press is a sacking offence, right? I know what they can be like, but try not to give in to them.'

The mutter of acknowledgement was even less enthusiastic this time, although Janie doubted that was out of any love of the media. Time to wrap things up and get the team to work. She was about to ask for questions before setting everyone to their tasks, when the door to the incident room pushed open. Expecting perhaps Detective Superintendent Ritchie or DCI McLean, Janie was surprised to see a young uniform constable push her way through the parting crowd.

'Detective Inspector Harrison, ma'am?' she asked, even though it was plain she knew who she was talking to. Without waiting to be answered, she held out a freshly printed sheet of paper. 'This came in just now. Thought it could wait until the briefing was done, but the duty sergeant said I should bring it straight to you.'

PC Lenzie, that was her name, Janie recalled. Alice, she thought, but wasn't quite so sure. Don Gatford was duty sergeant that morning, if she remembered it rightly. So this could be an elaborate prank on either her, the constable, or both of them. A quick glance at the paper disabused her of that notion.

'Thank you, Constable. I'll take it from here.' She folded the sheet and put it in her pocket before addressing the briefing. 'Right then, everyone, something's just come up that you all need to know but which goes absolutely no further than this room. Got that?'

The silence was more reassuring than a half-hearted round of 'aye's could ever be. All eyes were on her, but it was Sandy Gregg who asked the question.

'What's up?'

Janie took the sheet back out of her pocket, unfolded it and handed it to her fellow DI, aware how stupid it had been to put it away in the first place. In her defence, the news printed on it had come as a bit of a shock.

'There's been a break-in at the mortuary,' she said. 'Two bodies have been stolen. One of them is Vaclav Mihailovic.'

She almost collided with Detective Chief Inspector McLean, such was her rush to get out of the station and down to the mortuary. He had paused at the top of the steps right outside the back door to the station, looking up at the grey clouds as if trying to decide whether he should go back for a coat or not.

'You've heard the news then?' He moved to the side, indicated with a gentlemanly sweep of the hand that she should go first. No need to ask where she was going in such a rush she'd not even thought to grab her own coat.

'Aye. We were in the middle of our morning briefing. Surprised you weren't there, actually.'

McLean looked a little sheepish as he fell into step alongside her.

'Yes, well. I was running a little late. Thought I'd slip in towards the end and give everyone a pep talk, but the call came in about the mortuary. The missing bodies. One's your man from out Ormiston way, isn't he?'

'Vaclav Mihailovic, aye. And the other one's the park bench in Craigmillar Castle Park?'

'Paul Sanderson,' McLean confirmed. It was a while since Janie had walked any distance with him, and she had forgotten how swift a pace he set. A half a head taller than her, his stride took more effort to match than she cared to admit. Too much driving around the city, not enough exercise. And the mad hours she'd been working since her promotion didn't help either.

'They done the PM on him yet?' she asked, even though she was fairly sure she knew the answer.

McLean shook his arm to release his wristwatch from the sleeve of his tweed jacket. 'It was scheduled for about now, so I guess I would have been headed this way anyway.'

A couple of squad cars were already parked either side of the mortuary gate, an ambulance closer to the front door. The uniform constables waved the two of them through without even asking to see warrant cards, which might have been worth a reprimand if Janie only had the energy. And if she hadn't been distracted by the incongruous sight of someone being wheeled out of the mortuary rather than into it.

'Cerys.' Janie rushed forward the moment she recognised the figure lying on the gurney, given away mostly by the shock of spiky pink hair. Wrapped in a silver blanket, the mortuary assistant had an oxygen mask on, and what little Janie could see of her face was deathly pale. She stopped a half-dozen paces short of the waiting ambulance as her brain caught up with her emotions.

'Is she going to be OK?' she asked of the nearest paramedic. 'What happened?'

'Took a nasty blow to the back of the head and she's hypothermic. She's been unconscious, but she's responsive now.'

Janie took a step back, watched as her friend was loaded into the ambulance. Part of her wanted to go with Cerys to the hospital, but in truth there was nothing she could do there. Better to find out what had happened, and let the doctors do their job.

'Royal Infirmary,' the paramedic said to her as he saw the

direction of her gaze, the expression on her face. 'We'll take good care of her.'

'Thank you. I'll check in later.'

When she turned back to the mortuary entrance, McLean had disappeared. Janie found him in the staff canteen, where an ashen-faced Dr MacPhail sat at one of the tables, a mug of tea clasped between both hands. He looked up at her with a hopeful expression on his face, but she had nothing to give him.

'You up to telling us what happened, Tom?' McLean asked in that soft, low voice he always used when dealing with victims of trauma. It took a while for the pathologist to reply, and Janie filled the time with fetching coffee for her and the DCI. As she sat down, the canteen door opened and the familiar figure of Dr Cadwallader bustled in.

'Tony, Janie.' He nodded a simple greeting, then focused his attention on his colleague. 'Came as soon as I heard the news. You OK, Tom?'

'I'm fine now. Thanks, everyone.' MacPhail took a long swig of his drink and then grimaced as if it had gone cold. 'Just had the shock of my life, which for someone in our line of work's saying something, eh?'

'Take us through it from the beginning if you can?' McLean had his notebook out, Janie saw. She should probably have done that herself.

'Not much to say. I came in as usual, got myself ready to do the PM on your park bench man, Tony. I knew Cerys had done the prep work last night, so it was just a case of hauling him out of the cold store and getting stuck in. Only, she wasn't here yet, which isn't like her at all.' MacPhail reached into his pocket and pulled out his phone, a battered old device with several cracks in its screen. 'I texted her to ask if everything was OK and what time she thought she'd be here. I just assumed her bus was late or something. When I didn't get an answer, I thought I'd fetch out the body myself. Went to the cold store and pulled out the drawer. Nearly shat myself when I saw her lying there. Thought she was dead.'

Perhaps it was the late night and lack of sleep in general, or maybe the shock of seeing one of her friends in a bad way, but it took until then for Janie to understand why Cerys had been wrapped in a silver blanket. What the paramedic had meant when he'd said she was hypothermic. Despite the warm canteen room and hot mug of coffee, she shivered in horrified sympathy.

'She was in one of the cold-store drawers?'

'Aye. The one where your man Sanderson should have been. She must have come in first thing to get set up for the PM. Interrupted whoever was stealing those bodies.' MacPhail nodded once, then ran shaking fingers through his straggly hair. 'If I'd waited any longer for her to turn up, she'd probably be dead.'

30

Janie preferred her own tiny office at the back of the station, but there were times when DCI McLean's larger room at the front made life a lot easier. It had space for a long conference table, for one thing, and a coffee machine. Someone had even remembered to buy milk, although sadly they'd not thought to get some biscuits at the same time.

'OK, everyone. Shall we get started?'

As senior officer in the room, it made sense that McLean be the one in charge. Janie found it easy to fall into the role of assistant, even if hers was the most advanced of the two suspicious death investigations that had been thrown together by cruel circumstance. Everyone else at the table was either a detective sergeant or constable, and the little murmuring that had gone on before fell away to nothing.

'As I'm sure you've all heard, there was a break-in at the city mortuary sometime early this morning and two cadavers were stolen. Janie—DI Harrison and her team were already looking into the death of Vaclav Mihailovic, and I understand that investigation was quite well advanced. The other body, Paul Sanderson, was only discovered early yesterday morning, and was scheduled for post-mortem examination later today. Early indications were that he had died from some illness rather than foul play. What was the story with Mihailovic? It was strange, wasn't it?'

Mid-sip of coffee, Janie swallowed swiftly and cleared her throat. 'Well, apart from the way he looked like he'd tried to dig himself out of his own grave, he had no living bacteria either in or on his body. Dr MacPhail was going to do some further tests, but it's most definitely strange. The only thing that could possibly do that to a person would be a massive dose of very powerful antibiotics. And even then . . .'

'Enough to kill him?' McLean asked.

'That was the initial cause of death put forward, but we're waiting on toxicology results, and there should have been more damage to his insides if that's what did for him. It's possible he was self-medicating and got the dose spectacularly wrong. The whole set-up in the flat where he was living is – was – dodgy, so hardly surprising they tried to make him disappear rather than calling in the authorities. That's how I was going to write it all up, anyway. Not so sure now.'

McLean scratched at his cheek with two fingers as if he'd missed a bit shaving that morning and it was irritating him.

'OK. Well. Sanderson was found dead on a bench in Craigmillar Castle Park. He appeared to have walked from his bedsit flat, about a mile and a half away, in his bare feet. He was emaciated, I'd say he looked almost like he'd been dried out like a piece of leather, but that might just be my memory painting pictures. Pathologist reckons he died where we found him, and not from any violent action. Likely he'd been suffering from it for a while, whatever it was that killed him. That would explain his strange behaviour at Drake Biotech the other night.'

'You think he was the one walked out the front door?'

'I know he was. Got a full confession from one of the others in the group. There's a wee problem with that though. We've been told to shut that investigation down.'

The silence that fell on the room was only emphasised by the *whoop whoop* of a siren in the street outside, disappearing as quickly as it came. Janie looked at the faces of her colleagues, all showing the same disbelief.

'What?' she asked eventually.

'Best I can piece together, the break-in was a put-up job by one or other of our esteemed intelligence services. Fellow going by the name of Keith Campbell organised it all, recruited a local band of animal rights and eco warriors, fed them all a line and did whatever his bosses wanted him to do while they caused a suitable distraction. There's no confirmation of that, just speculation on my part. And Keith has already disappeared, gone back to being whoever he was before.' McLean lifted his hand to his head again, then seemed to realise what he was doing and put it back down again. 'Lucky me, I get to tell Nathaniel Drake.'

'But what about Sanderson?' DC Bryant asked. 'We can't ignore a suspicious death. Especially not when someone's nicked the body.'

'That's what I told Jayne McIntyre before the body was even stolen, and I intend to stick to my word.' McLean spread his hands out on the table, as if laying out invisible cards. 'We won't be arresting or prosecuting anyone for the break-in at Drake Biotech, but that doesn't mean we don't thoroughly investigate Sanderson's death. Especially not now someone's stolen his body. We need to find out what connects him to Mihailovic. There must be something. Work, social, maybe the animal rights angle? Anything, really. We also need to find out how someone broke into the mortuary and got away with two bodies. Forensics are already going over the scene, but I want every piece of CCTV footage from the building's security and anything in the surrounding area. Two bodies means a vehicle. Let's find that before it ends up torched in a quarry somewhere.'

'You think that likely?' DC Mitchell asked.

'More likely hidden in a garage or warehouse somewhere. That's another thing. Where would they take the bodies? What are they going to do with them? Store them? Destroy them? Why those two, anyway? Go over the pathology reports from the scenes where they were found.' McLean checked his watch. 'I'll head down to the mortuary once we're done here and have another chat with Angus and Tom, see what they remember, if anything.'

'We'll need to set up interviews with all the mortuary staff.' Janie felt something flutter in her chest at the memory of an unconscious figure being wheeled out of the building. 'I'd better check up on Cerys too.'

McLean closed up the notebook that had been on the table in front of him, and which Janie hadn't seen him write anything in. 'Right then. I think we all know what we have to do. Let's get cracking, and we can all meet up for a briefing at six.'

Janie cadged a lift to the Royal Infirmary from a squad car, knowing that it was probably not proper use of Police Scotland resources. Taking a pool car would have been worse though, and she didn't much fancy chancing the buses. She used her warrant card to get her past reception and asked a couple of helpful nurses in passing as she found her way to the ward where Cerys was being kept for observation.

Hospitals were not her favourite place, unlike DCI McLean who seemed to be on first name terms with every nurse he met. He'd spent months visiting his sick grandmother, hadn't he? That was the story she'd heard at least. Before her time, much like how the old lady in question had once been the city pathologist before Janie had even been born.

Such dark thoughts; that was why she didn't like coming to hospitals. They always brought out the worst in her because there was never a good reason to be in one. And this time it was her friend who had almost died, not some suspect or witness who needed to be interviewed.

The ward she finally arrived at was small; four beds and a window that gave a good view of the neighbouring building. It took Janie only seconds to locate Cerys, partly because the other three beds were unoccupied, and partly because she already had a visitor.

'Dr MacPhail. Tom.' She spoke without thinking, and immediately cringed at the loudness of her voice in the near-silent room. The pathologist looked up, did his best to smile as he recognised her.

'Detective Inspector Harrison.' He struggled to his feet. 'Janie.'

'How is she?' Janie glanced at the figure lying in the bed. Pale as one of the corpses she looked after at work, Cerys had sunk into her pillows and might have disappeared altogether were it not for the vivid shock of her dyed hair. Even that looked less colourful under the ward lights, as if it weren't something in a bottle that made the pink so vibrant but the woman herself. She was hooked up to a drip, a tube up her nose. Beside her bed, machines silently monitored her vital signs.

'They've got her sedated,' Dr MacPhail said, perhaps a little unnecessarily. He looked as tired as Janie felt, his hair dishevelled, salt and pepper stubble starting to show.

'For hypothermia?'

'Turns out it was a bit more serious than that. Whoever shoved her in that drawer must have hit her over the head first. She's got a nasty fracture to the skull. If I was looking for silver linings I might say that cooling her body down to fridge temperature probably helped, although maybe not cudgelling her in the first place would have been better.'

Janie moved closer to the bed, found herself reaching to take Cerys's hand, stopped. 'Cooling her down reduced the swelling on her brain?'

'Something like that, aye.'

A silence spread between the two of them then, not uncomfortable but perhaps a little awkward. In the many hours she had spent in the company of the Welsh mortuary assistant, Janie had never heard Cerys say much about her boss. And yet here he was, sitting vigil by her bedside. Was there more to their relationship than the platonic friendship and mutual respect Janie had observed? Did it matter if there was? Angus Cadwallader and his assistant Dr Sharp had been together as long as she had known either of them, so it wasn't as if there was no precedent. And it wasn't like the police either, where that sort of thing meant reorganising shift patterns and teams to avoid unnecessary complications. Not that any of the police officer relationships she had observed had ever lasted more than a few months.

'She'll be OK, right?' Janie asked, as much to divert the awkwardness her thoughts had allowed to grow.

Dr MacPhail shrugged. 'It's not really my area of expertise, living patients.' When he saw that his joke had missed the mark, he quickly spoke again. 'But the neurologist who was in earlier seemed to think things were a lot better than they could have been, given the nature of the injuries.'

'The cold store,' Janie said.

'Aye, the cold store.' Dr MacPhail looked back to Cerys. 'But maybe best we don't tell her that's where they put her, eh?'

Janie had been staring at her unconscious friend, but now she turned her attention to the pathologist. 'What? Why?' she asked before the reasons worked their way through. 'Oh. Right.'

'I mean, we can maybe tell her later. When she's fully recovered, you know? But if it was me, it'd freak me right out. Not sure I'd be able to carry on working in the mortuary at all.'

'C'n hear you, y'know.'

Janie turned her head so swiftly she felt a crack of pain spear up her neck, but Dr MacPhail was quicker still. They both crowded the bed where Cerys had opened her eyes in tiny slits.

'You're awake,' the pathologist said, which seemed a little like stating the obvious to Janie. He placed a hand briefly on the rail that formed one side of the bed, then withdrew it almost as quickly. 'I'll go find a nurse. Stay with her, Janie.' And then he hurried out of the ward.

Janie let him pass, then moved closer to the bed. She reached out as Cerys lifted one trembling hand and took it in hers.

'Cold,' Cerys said, although her hand felt very warm indeed. Her voice was little more than a croaky whisper. A far cry from the loud and cheerful Swansea accent Janie was used to.

'Don't try to speak. You've got a tube down your throat.'

Cerys opened her mouth as if to make a response to that, but closed it again quickly. She squeezed her eyes tight shut as if concentrating on something. Or maybe it was a wave of pain washing over her, as her grip grew tighter still. Janie held on until a couple of nurses arrived, Dr MacPhail not far behind them, reluctantly relinquishing her hold so that she could make room. She stood back and watched as they expertly removed the tube and checked their patient over, and it was only as the scene began to blur that she realised she'd started to cry.

31

McLean had first visited the examination theatre of the city mortuary as a teenager on one of many 'take your children to work' days with his grandmother, so it was a place he was perhaps more familiar with than most normal people. It had seen several refits and updates since then, but it was still much the same as he always remembered it, and that gave it a sense of reassuring solidity in an otherwise ever-changing world. Maybe that was why he kept coming back, as much as the job.

On this occasion, the central examination table stood empty. Its stainless-steel surface gleamed, drainage channels clear of blood and gore. Staring at the wall of cold-store cabinets, McLean shuddered at the thought of Cerys Powell trapped in one. By all accounts she'd been unconscious the whole time, but even so it was the stuff of nightmares. There'd be a backlog building soon if they didn't track down the missing bodies and whoever had taken them, those drawers filled and more in cold storage elsewhere. He recalled too another body taken from the mortuary, although that one had been dead far longer than either Mihailovic or Sanderson. A young woman who'd lain forgotten, walled up in the basement of an old mansion on the outskirts of the city. How long ago had that been? His first case as a newly promoted detective inspector? He found he couldn't remember at all.

'Reminiscing on old times?'

The voice dragged McLean back to the present. He turned to see Angus Cadwallader enter the examination theatre from the small office to one side.

'Something like that.' He looked over the pathologist's shoulder, hoping for more people. 'Tom not here?'

'He's gone to the hospital to see how Cerys is doing.'

'He'll probably see Janie then. I think she was quite upset about the whole thing. I'd not realised she and Cerys were so close.'

'The youth of today, eh?' Cadwallader tilted his head slightly at the joke, more than enough given the seriousness of the occasion.

'So, what are we to make of all this then, Angus? How did someone get in here, wheel out two bodies and away without anyone noticing? Anyone but Cerys, of course.'

'Well, you know the security systems we have here as well as anyone, Tony. Whoever came through here did so very early in the morning, when the building would have been locked down pretty tight. There's always someone here though. You never know when we might get a new patient in, after all.'

'So who was on night shift last night then?' McLean asked. 'Apart from Cerys.'

'Jill in admin is sorting you a list, and calling everyone in so you can speak to them. I take it that's why you're here?'

'Mostly, aye. DS Stringer's reviewing the CCTV footage, checking the camera angles and all that sort of thing, but I suspect they just drove up in a mortuary van and backed up to the loading doors like everyone else. It's amazing what you can get away with if you act like you're supposed to be doing it.'

'Too true.'

'Still, how they were stolen is only one part of the puzzle. I need to see if there's anything that links the two missing bodies, too. That might point to why they were taken and who by.'

'By whom, Tony.' Cadwallader did that single shake of the head again. He was trying to lighten the mood, McLean knew, but at the same time both of them were worried for the mortuary assistant. There was nothing either of them could do for her directly though.

'Of course, Angus. Correct grammar at all times. You helped Tom with the examination on Mihailovic, didn't you?'

'I did, yes. Janie came along to watch, too. Picked up that habit from you, I dare say.'

McLean ignored the subtle dig at him. 'I've read the report. You didn't come to any conclusion about cause of death?'

'It was an odd one, for sure. From the inside he looked almost like he'd been embalmed somehow. No sign of decomposition, and he'd not even been nibbled by the local fauna out in the woods where he was found. Janie had an interesting suggestion, actually.'

'She did?'

'Aye, she did. Tom and I were musing on the lack of decomposition in the body. There was no bloating in the stomach, which you'd normally expect to see. There was absolutely no living bacteria in his gut, or anywhere we swabbed him, to be honest. Janie wondered if whatever had killed it all had also killed him.'

'And might it have done?'

'Well, eventually, yes. It's the bacteria in our guts that break down our food for us. Take them away and you'd starve after a while. We're more symbiotic organisms than most people realise, you know.'

'So what might have caused that? Some kind of poison?'

Cadwallader let out a long breath through his nose. 'We did have a bit of a discussion about that. It's the most likely scenario, for sure. I don't know what would clean him out so thoroughly and not leave any traces in his bloodstream though. We've done the simple toxicology tests and come up with nothing. Still waiting on some more detailed results. His stomach was completely empty, which you might expect from some kind of lethal purging. It didn't leave us anything for analysis though.'

'Any other indicators?' McLean asked as the pathologist turned away and indicated for him to follow. They went through to the office, where Cadwallader's assistant Dr Sharp already had the post-mortem report up on the screen of her computer.

'Tracy's been going over the photographs again. There was a mark on his arm, inside the elbow. Just the one, so unlikely to be a drug habit. We thought at the time he'd maybe given blood some-time in the past six months, but it could have been a catheter for introducing something into his bloodstream, not taking it out.'

McLean dug out his spectacles and slid them onto his nose, bent close to the screen where the waxy yellow flesh of a dead body filled most of the available space. It took him a while to get the orientation right, as Dr Sharp had zoomed in so close it was hard to see what was what. Cadwallader didn't help much by jab-bing at the flat surface with a knobbly finger.

'See the crook of the elbow there? It's faint, but there's a slight dimple and paler area. Almost completely gone.'

'And that was caused by a needle?'

Cadwallader made a non-committal noise. 'Could be, but we're really speculating here, Tony.'

'Well, we've no body, so speculation's all we've got to work with at the moment, Angus. Let's run with it. Say this is what you and Tom think it is. Not necessarily giving blood, but an injection site. A catheter insertion point.' McLean waved at the screen again. 'And if whatever was injected into him is what killed off all his bacteria, then why would he do that? If we rule out recreational drugs, since there's no evidence of repeated use?'

Silence greeted the questions as all three of them struggled for answers. The pathologist puffed out his cheeks, then let the air escape through his lips in a not-quite raspberry. Dr Sharp reached for the mouse, as if zooming yet further into the image might give them more insight.

'I don't even know any recreational drugs that would cause the kind of effect we saw,' Cadwallader said. 'It's like everything in and on him that was living suddenly died. Him included. There's some very powerful antibiotics that might possibly do that, at very high doses. Stuff designed to treat horses and cattle. But like I said, we'd expect to see metabolites in the blood toxicology. Other physical signs, too.'

'Which you haven't?'

Cadwallader shrugged. 'Not in the first instance, no. Which is why it would be good to go back for a second look. Shame we can't exactly do that now.'

There was much to think about from his discussion with the pathologist. McLean left the examination theatre and headed towards the admin offices where he'd left DS Stringer to review CCTV footage from the previous night. Mihailovic's death was even more strange than Harrison had described it. Whoever had stolen the body must have been behind whatever caused that death, which begged the question, had something similar happened to Paul Sanderson? Their outward appearance couldn't have been more different, Mihailovic perfectly preserved, Sanderson withered away like he'd been left out in the sun too long. With no postmortem examination having been carried out on the second body and the only person who'd had a chance to study it closely unconscious in the hospital, it was hard to know what similarities there might have been between the two men. Except that someone had gone to great lengths to steal them both, had been prepared to kill to hide whatever secrets they held.

And then there was the wooden box Sanderson had been clutching. The box he had almost certainly taken from Drake Biotech, but which Professor Caine swore blind he'd never seen before. McLean believed that about as much as he did in God, which was to say not at all. Could that box have been the cause of Sanderson's death though? Something inside it, perhaps? And if so, how did that connect to Mihailovic? Did it connect at all, or was he just chasing shadows?

None the wiser for his musing, he stepped into the admin office to see Stringer deep in conversation with one of the secretaries. Neither of them appeared to be watching any kind of video, which didn't bode well.

'How are you getting on with the CCTV?'

Stringer startled briefly at being disturbed, but recovered himself swiftly. 'About that, sir. There's a bit of a problem.'

Of course there was. Nothing was ever simple. 'What kind of problem?' McLean asked.

'Seems there was a glitch in the system last night. There's no CCTV footage from any of the cameras in and around the building between half two and six this morning.'

'Someone deleted it?'

'No, sir. That would show up on the data log. There wasn't a power cut or surge or anything either. Everything's fine, there's just no video footage for three and a half hours. Jill here was just showing me.' Stringer nodded towards the secretary he'd been talking to. McLean recognised her as a smiling face at the reception desk from time to time, although now hers was an expression closer to anguish than joy.

'I just don't understand it at all,' she said. 'I've pulled up the camera feed dozens of times before. See, we use it when the vans arrive so's we can let them in. It's all on the network now, mind. No' like the old days when we had a stack of tapes in one of the storerooms.'

'Can you show me?'

McLean found himself fetching out his spectacles and peering at a computer screen for the second time that day as Jill brought up camera feeds on her system for him. Four small squares for four different cameras.

'This is live right now.' She gestured at clear, hi-res footage of the front door, the back entrance where bodies came in, and a couple of corridors inside, then reached for the mouse and clicked on some icons. 'This is footage from last night.'

McLean barely saw the change on the interior cameras as the screens flicked to recorded video, but the outside images turned dark around the edges and lost their colour. Nothing moved in the minute or so he stared at the screen save for a person coming out of a room and walking down the corridor. Spiky pink hair, it could only be the mortuary assistant, Cerys.

'What time's that?' He peered even closer, looking for a clock somewhere on the image. Found it at the same time as the secretary gave him the answer.

'Twelve thirty-seven. That's so like Cerys when she's on the late shift. Gets everything set up ready for when the pathologists come in the next day.'

'What room's that she's come out of?'

'That would be the canteen, I think. Most of the other assistants spend the whole shift in there, just waiting for any new bodies to arrive.'

'Could she have been going to deal with one then?' McLean asked, then realised that he'd spent at least a minute watching blank CCTV footage of the receiving entrance.

'We didn't have any come in last night. Quiet for once.'

'Can you fast forward to when it goes off?'

'Aye, bear wi' me a moment. This new system's no' like the old one.' The secretary fiddled with her keyboard and mouse, the images flickering in response.

'How long's the new system been working then?' McLean asked.

'Och, I don't know, rightly. Six months, maybe? Should really have got the hang of it by now, but apart from checking the back door when there's a collection or delivery, I've no' really needed to.'

McLean understood that well enough. How many electronic devices did he have that he'd learned how to use only as much as he needed? His phone could probably land a spacecraft on the moon, but texting and phone calls were about the only things he ever used it for. Maybe maps too, now he had to find charging points for Emma's car.

'What's that?' He jabbed a finger at the screen just as all four images displayed on it went blank. A small circle in the bottom corner of each one, he'd hardly paid it any attention until that moment. Typical it should disappear then.

'What?' the secretary asked, but tapped a couple of keys to make the video footage go backwards. As it reappeared, showing empty corridors and the slightly ethereal glow of the outdoor night-vision cameras, McLean saw the circle again. A logo – when he peered closely he saw a name and some strange swirling pattern that a designer had no doubt been paid a fortune to come up with.

'Scanlan Security Services.' He spoke the words out loud.

'Aye, they run all our security now. Private contractors. They're no' bad, really. I can get you their contact details if you want.'

'Please do. I'll need to speak to them.' McLean stared at the name as the image spooled forward again before going blank. Shouldn't the logo stay if the cameras had failed? He had to admit that he wasn't nearly technologically minded enough to know that. Luckily he knew plenty of people who were.

'Go back again, can you?' he asked. To her credit, the secretary did so without comment, then paused the playback without him even asking. McLean peered closer, concentrating on that logo. It was odd, for sure, but that wasn't what had caught his eye.

'I've seen this somewhere before recently,' he said after a while. The only problem was he couldn't remember where.

32

Scanlan Security Services occupied a nondescript warehouse and office unit in the same Loanhead business park as Police Scotland's control centre, not all that far from the haggis factory. As he drove Emma's little Renault Zoe along the familiar roads, McLean wondered whether that wasn't how he knew the logo after all. It didn't sit right though. There was something else.

'Did you manage to get through to someone senior?' he asked DS Stringer as they pulled into a parking space between two Transit vans.

'Ranald Scanlan himself.' The detective sergeant had his phone out, details on the screen. 'Although to be honest I don't know if that's the boss, his son, or an intern who just happens to share the family name. There's not much on the web about the company at all.'

'Looks quite new and shiny.' McLean peered through the windscreen at the clean building with its neat signage and spotless windows to the front. 'Let's go and see how helpful they're feeling.'

Ranald Scanlan turned out to be a middle-aged man with frameless spectacles and a dome of a bald head. He was waiting for them in reception, or possibly chatting up the secretary at the front desk.

'Come through to my office, Detective Chief Inspector,' he said once the introductions had been made, then led McLean and Stringer into the back of the building. That neither of them had been signed in or given a visitor's pass was perhaps not the best advertisement for a company specialising in office security, but the door they had to go through to get to the business side of things was protected by both a keypad and remote card reader, so that made up for it a little. McLean had seen something similar recently, and this time it clicked. He remembered where he'd seen the logo, too.

'Drake Biotech,' he said, causing Mr Scanlan to stop walking with such suddenness he might have been a robot switched off.

'What?' he asked, a little shiftily.

'Drake Biotech. The new research labs in the science park.' McLean waved a hand in what might have been the right direction. 'You run their security too?'

Scanlan squirmed in his designer suit like a little boy who really needed a wee. 'I'm not . . . That's to say, client confidentiality . . . We . . .'

'That'll be a yes then. Knew I'd seen the logo recently and I just couldn't place it. They had a break-in there not that long ago too. What are the chances of that, eh?'

Scanlan stared at McLean with eyes wide like a frightened rabbit. He swallowed once, the sharp point of his Adam's apple stretching past his collar and tie before he managed to pull himself together.

'Perhaps we could talk about this in here?' He gestured at the nearest door, then opened it onto a small conference room rather than the promised office. 'It's deeply embarrassing to the firm, I can tell you.'

'That's putting it mildly,' McLean said. 'I already have one link between these two break-ins. Now it seems Scanlan Security is another. Should I be looking more deeply into your operation here, Mr Scanlan?'

'I can assure you, Detective Chief Inspector, that really isn't necessary.' Scanlan held up both hands in the universal signal of surrender. 'We had a problem with the servers last night. A DDoS, if you know what that is.'

'Distributed Denial of Service,' Stringer said. 'Would have thought an outfit like this would have sufficiently robust systems to deal with that sort of thing.'

'Aye, well. There's robust and robust. This wasn't like anything we've ever seen before. The whole tech team were in all night dealing with it. We had to shut down a number of our remote sites to stop them from being attacked and, well . . .'

'Well?' McLean prompted, even though he knew what the answer was.

'We switched off the mortuary cameras because they weren't thought to be high priority,' Scanlan admitted. 'We had to do what you might call a little ad hoc prioritisation, yes? We monitor a few sites where night-time security isn't as important as during the day. One of the emergency team will have made the call, but I'd have done the same. I mean, who'd try to break into a mortuary?'

Scanlan's laugh was one of strangled nerves, which meant he was either a very good actor or telling the truth. It was still too much of a coincidence that they should have been forced to switch off the surveillance feed the same night someone broke in and stole a couple of bodies, which didn't say much for their client confidentiality. The attack on the company's servers had to have been coordinated with the body snatchers, which spoke to a higher level of sophistication than McLean liked to contemplate.

'Who might have known that you had the city mortuary contract?' he asked.

'I . . .' Scanlan paused, his face slack as something whirred away behind it. 'No one outside of the company should have known. Well, I mean, we don't tell the world who our clients are. Not as a matter of course, certainly. We might approach a client for a reference if we're bidding for work elsewhere, but that's all done in the strictest confidence.'

'And you haven't asked the mortuary to do that?'

'No.' Scanlan shook his head slowly. 'Not as far as I'm aware. We've not had the contract long anyway. Six months, I think?'

McLean made a scribble in his notebook, more for show than to remind himself of anything. 'What about Drake Biotech? You had that contract long? Had them give you glowing testimonials?'

The expression on Scanlan's face went from nervous and embarrassed to confused and then defensive.

'I can't—'

'Talk about your clients, I know. But I know that you run Drake Biotech's security because I've seen your logo on their camera footage and they've got those same door-entry systems as you have at reception. State of the art, it was described to me by the lead researcher there. Professor Magnus Caine. Have you met him?'

'I . . . Actually, yes. I have. Not in relation to our security contract, but there was a corporate function a few months back where he gave a fascinating talk about genetic therapies and new ways to reverse ageing. I probably only understood a quarter of it, but he was very persuasive.'

McLean couldn't help but notice the change in Scanlan's demeanour as he spoke about Professor Caine. Almost as if a light had gone on inside his head. It was more than relief at being off the subject of his company's failure though.

'If you don't mind me asking, why were you at a Drake Biotech corporate function? Do they usually have subcontractors at such things?'

'Oh, no. We're not subcontractors. Not the way you say it, anyway. It's, well . . . What I said before about client confidentiality? I guess it doesn't really apply in this case. We were bought out about two years ago. Scanlan Security Services is part of Drake Corporation now.'

McLean drove carefully out of the car park, merging with the constant traffic that flowed towards the city like blood in a vein. Had he been on his own, he might have wasted a little time going to Macsween's to buy some haggis, but then he remembered Emma wasn't such a big fan of the stuff, and there was only so much he and the cats could eat. He was not alone though. In the passenger seat, DS Stringer had been tapping something into his phone, hopefully updating the incident room with their latest findings. Now he slid the handset into his pocket.

'Well, that went in an unexpected direction.'

'You're not kidding, Jay. Looks like we've opened a right old can of worms.' McLean indicated, then turned out of the business park onto the Loanhead road. Any hope that he might be driving against the rush-hour traffic soon died as he was forced to a halt well before the lights. It was early for the heavy flow, but the roads were always busy these days.

'You think someone at Scanlan's behind all this?' the detective sergeant asked, then added, 'Whatever this actually is?'

'Well, that's the nub of it, really. What is this? We've got a break-in at the lab by animal rights activists who turn out to be a diversion for some MI5 spook doing God knows what. One of the team turns up dead in the park, looking like he's not eaten in months and shouldn't have had the strength to wield a spray can, let alone smash up a lab. I'd really like to know what he died from just in case I've got a new disease about to spread through the city, but someone breaks into the mortuary and steals his body before the pathologist can have a proper look. And whoever does that has the ability to break the servers of a sophisticated security services company to order. A company that it turns out is a fully owned subsidiary of Drake Corporation, whose labs were broken into, and am I going round in circles?'

That McLean asked this last question as he entered the round-about at the city bypass might have been cause for a poor joke, but DS Stringer didn't rise to the bait.

'Don't forget the other body,' he said, which was marginally less helpful.

'I won't, don't worry. Not that I have any clue how it fits into everything else. Or even if it's supposed to fit. Could be whoever broke into the mortuary only wanted Sanderson, took the other body to throw us off the scent.'

'Or they could have been after Mihailovic and took Sanderson to throw us off the scent.'

'Not helping, Jay.' McLean eased the car to a halt as the Burdie-house lights turned red, took the opportunity to close his eyes and squeeze the bridge of his nose to relieve some of the pressure building in his sinuses. 'Let's assume for now that they wanted both bodies, and that there's a connection between Mihailovic and Sanderson somehow. Their deaths are both strange, but on the face of it very different. Sanderson we can link to Drake Biotech's labs, but what about Mihailovic? He was a builder, might he have worked on that site at some point?'

'That's Janie's investigation.' Stringer took his phone out and started tapping at the screen. 'I can ask when we get back to the station, but what are you thinking? They both somehow got them-selves infected with something at a biotech lab that isn't even operational yet? Something that came up with different symptoms and which no one else who's been near the place has caught?'

Put like that, McLean knew it was fanciful. That was the prob-lem with having too little information, the temptation was to make connections where there were none. Or to miss them when they ought to be obvious.

'You're right, of course. But there has to be a reason they were both taken before they could be fully examined. My gut tells me there's more of a connection between them than their being in adjacent cold-storage drawers.'

'Find that link and we find our missing bodies?'

'Something like that, aye.'

They drove on in silence for a while, Stringer staring at his phone and occasionally tapping something into the screen. Only as they were approaching the big roundabout at Cameron Toll did he speak up again.

'What about that weird box Sanderson had with him? You think that's important?'

'Well, Professor Caine told me it's not his, but I'm not entirely sure I believe him.'

'Why would he have something like that in a state-of-the-art lab?'

'Looking for samples of ancient DNA, most likely. He admitted that was his thing, tracking down long-lived figures from ancient history and extracting the secrets of their longevity from their mummified remains. It sounds a bit, I don't know, science fiction to me, but he told me before I showed him the photographs of the box.'

'And then denied it was his?'

'Said he'd seen something similar in a museum in Belgrade. Reckoned it was Eastern European, probably five hundred years old.'

'Belgrade. That's Serbia, right?' Stringer said as they approached the turning that would take them to the station car park.

'Capital of, yes. Why?' McLean asked, then joined up the dots in his head. 'Oh.'

'Mihailovic was from Serbia, wasn't he? And that bloke we arrested for burying him out in the woods. I think all the other workers in his flat were from there, weren't they?'

33

Janie considered calling the station to get a lift from a passing squad car, but opted instead for a taxi from the hospital after she'd left a sleeping Cerys to the tender ministrations of the nurses. The trip across town gave her time to check in on the progress of the various different strands of their newly merged investigations, which was why she was able to redirect the taxi driver before the changed destination would have caught the early rush-hour traffic.

Three squad cars and an armoured Transit van were parked in the road outside the tower block where Vaclav Mihailovic had lived and, if Sasha was to be believed, ultimately died. That felt like overkill, even more so as she flashed her warrant card at the pair of uniform constables standing guard at the entrance. This part of the operation was supposed to have been a detective constable and some uniforms knocking on doors and showing people photographs of Paul Sanderson. Someone must have decided a more heavy-handed approach was needed, just a shame they'd not run it past her first.

'Who called in the riot squad?' she asked of DC Bryant when she tracked the detective down, huddled in the corner of the main hall, close to the back door that led out to the drying green, deep in conversation with a handful of uniform constables.

'Oh, you're here, J. Thought you'd gone to the hospital.'

'Only so much time you can spend sitting with someone who's fast asleep. She did wake up though. Doctors are keeping her in for observation, but she should make a full recovery.'

'That's good news. Could do with some, really. It all got a bit heated here, but things have calmed down now.'

Janie looked around the open space, populated almost entirely by police officers. 'No shit. What happened?'

'Fourth-floor flat. The one that was empty? Well, it's got new tenants in it already. One of them took exception to DC Fairley. Not sure what he said. You know Connor, he wouldn't hurt a fly. But one minute he's at the door asking if he can come in, next he's on the floor with blood pouring out his nose.'

'You arrest whoever hit him?' Janie asked, then realised it was the wrong question. 'He OK?'

'He'll be fine. Squinty nose might give him a bit more of a rugged look, too. As to the guy who did it, well.' Bryant glanced across the hall to where another huddle of officers stood. As she looked the same way, Janie saw that they were towering over a man who'd been forced to sit on the floor. His hands were cuffed, and his white wife-beater vest had what looked like fresh blood-stains on it. Resisting arrest, she expected. At least that's what anyone she asked would say.

'He keeps saying "No English, no English" whenever someone tries to ask him a question. That's bollocks, of course, but we're trying to track down someone who speaks Serbian and will actually talk to us anyway. I thought it best not to try and press anyone in the block to translate. They've got to live here after we're gone.'

It was good thinking, exactly the kind of thing she'd have expected from Bryant. Even so, it added another layer of complexity to what should have been a fairly simple job.

'What about the reason you came here?' Janie asked. 'Have you managed to speak to anyone who's not violently opposed to our existence?'

'Cass is working her way through the upper floors right now, but a lot of the constables had to come and deal with this nonsense.' Bryant waved towards the now-silent man. 'I called in some backup, but honestly, I wasn't expecting half the station to arrive. Must be a quiet afternoon in the city.'

Janie considered the situation. 'He was in that same flat we visited last time? Where Mihailovic used to live?'

'Aye. Didn't take them long to fill it up again by the look of things. Why? You thinking of going up there?'

'That's exactly what I'm going to do, Jessica.' Janie gestured to the two nearest uniform constables, both useful prop forwards if she was any judge. 'But don't worry. I'll take some muscle with me.'

'What about our hothead over there?' Bryant pointed at the source of all their trouble. 'You want to try and persuade him his English is just fine?'

She could try, but it would probably be a waste of time. 'He punched Connor, you say? And there were witnesses?'

'Two uniforms right there, aye. It's not as if there was any provocation either. Some folk are just born stupid, I guess.'

'OK then. Arrest him, get him back to the station and charged. If that doesn't loosen his tongue we'll just have to get a professional translator in.'

Backed up by her two new uniform constable friends, Janie might have felt reasonably safe, but she wasn't stupid. The first one, PC Jeremy Allan, stood to one side of the door while his colleague, PC Chris Mayhew, rapped hard on the thin wood with his knuckles. They were each of them a head taller than her, and half as broad again across the shoulders, so that standing between them felt a little like being stuck down a well.

'Police. Open up,' Mayhew said in a voice that would have sounded great in a TV drama, but which was perhaps unnecessarily provocative. Unsurprisingly there was no response, but when he reached out to knock again, Janie stopped him, a thought occurring to her that should have come earlier. She took a step closer to the door, tapped it more lightly.

'Nadia? Are you in there? It's Detective Inspector Harrison. Remember me? We talked before, about Vaclav Mihailovic?'

Silence followed her words, but it was a different kind of silence. The kind of silence a person made when they didn't want you to know they were listening.

'I'm sorry if my colleague upset you all earlier. He only wanted to ask you a couple of questions about a man you might have seen. Someone who might have been friends with Vaclav.'

More silence, but did it have a slightly different timbre to it? Or was Janie just talking to a door?

'Nadia, I—' But she wasn't able to finish what she had intended to say, as the lock clicked and the door opened to a narrow gap. The face that looked out past the heavy chain was undoubtedly that of the young woman, but for a moment Janie had doubts, such was the change in her. She'd plastered make-up on, but no amount of concealer was going to hide the bruising around one eye or the swollen capillaries pinking her eyeballs. Her hair was a mess, greasy as if she'd not washed it in days.

'I know nothing,' she said in a slur that suggested either lack of sleep or some kind of narcotic.

Beside Janie, PC Allan reached for the door. She stepped into his path, waved a hand to his colleague to stay back as well. The lack of reaction from Nadia didn't bode well, but Janie had to try. She took out the printed photograph of Paul Sanderson that had only been lightly photoshopped to hide the fact that he was dead.

'Do you know this man?' she asked, then when Nadia didn't

shift her focus, added, 'Nadia. Do you know this man?' in a louder voice, and shook the paper gently.

Slowly, like a glacier moving, the young woman lifted her head and peered with one eye at the photograph.

'Who is?' she asked.

'We think he might have been a friend of Vaclav. An associate, maybe.'

'Vaclav?' Nadia asked. 'Who is?'

Janie tried to catch the woman's gaze, but it was like trying to hold jelly in your fingers. Whatever she was on, they'd get nothing of any sense from her. She was folding the paper ready to put it back in her pocket when a voice from deeper inside the flat rattled out something in a harsh and guttural language she didn't understand. Nadia must have, because she flinched a moment after it had finished, again in that slow, distanced way.

'Am needed. I go now,' she said, her bloodshot gaze finally meeting Janie's as she slowly closed the door on them. It was only an instant, but there was something in that look, some desperate, pleading connection. If ever a woman needed help, it was Nadia. Janie would have to do something about that.

'You want me to break down the door, ma'am?' PC Allan asked. 'Sure me an' Chris heard screaming.'

It was tempting, Janie had to admit. But then there'd be paperwork and complaints and enquiries. And besides, it was more than a lock keeping the young woman tied to that flat, this tower block. Whoever was running the work gangs had some hold on her, most likely threats to family back home. Breaking down the door and taking her into protective custody wouldn't help them. This particular lock needed more careful unpicking than that.

'Thanks, but let's leave it for now. We can always come back later.' She turned away from the door, determined to do just that. She could only hope it wouldn't be too late.

★ ★ ★

'You got a moment, Kirsty?'

Janie stood at the half-open door to Detective Superintendent Ritchie's office, relieved to find it occupied for a change. It wasn't often she managed to catch Ritchie at the station; their senior detective was more often found over at Gartcosh working with the National Crime Agency. Rumour was that she would have switched over to the agency if DCI McLean could have been persuaded to take the promotion to her post. As if that would ever happen.

'A moment, Janie, aye. More than that . . .' Ritchie pushed her chair back from her desk and stood up, gesturing towards the conference table at the other side of the office. Unlike McLean's next door, this one was covered in neatly stacked piles of folders and other things almost certainly above Janie's pay grade and security clearance.

'How's the investigation coming along? Investigations, I should say.' The detective superintendent shook her head wearily and settled into one of the less comfortable seats.

'DCI McLean—Tony's out with Jay chasing up a possible lead. I've got Lofty going over all the CCTV footage we can find. I'd say we were getting somewhere with Mihailovic's death and burial, but his body going missing's kind of complicated things.'

'That's putting it mildly.' Ritchie tried a smile, but seemed too tired to make it stick. 'You've got the guy who buried him out in the woods, though?'

'Sasha, aye. Aleksandr Jovanović, I should say. He's on remand and not going anywhere soon, but even if I believe what he says about trying to dispose of the body, he didn't do that on his own. I'd lay good odds on most of the other men in that flat being roped in to help. That's why they all disappeared as soon as we came looking for Mihailovic. I can't help thinking there's more going on than just a gang boss and a team of itinerant building-site workers, too.'

'How do you mean?' Ritchie asked, her gaze momentarily sliding past Janie towards the clock that hung above the door.

'I'm not exactly sure. Part gut feeling, I suppose. I told you about the young woman, Nadia, right?'

'Aye, you thought there might have been some modern-slavery angle there. I've run it past the NCA team working on that. They've nothing specific, but they're going to keep an eye on it.'

'Might want to chivvy them along a bit, if that's the sort of thing you can do.' Janie told the detective superintendent about her encounter with Nadia earlier that afternoon, her surprise that the young woman was still in the flat and horror at the state she was in. 'Doesn't help that we ended up with a whole mob going into the tower block. I wanted it done quietly, minimum disruption. All we wanted to know was if anyone there recognised Sanderson. Only one of them had to take a pop at Connor.'

'DC Fairley? Why'd anyone want to hurt him?' Ritchie's nonexistent eyebrows arched at the question. 'Is he OK?'

'I only saw him for a minute or two. Looked like he was concussed. He's away to the hospital for a check-up and X-ray. Likely broken nose, so he'll be off work for a day or two. Hopefully he'll learn to duck next time.'

'And the guy who hit him?'

'Kicking his heels in the cells until we can get a translator. There were plenty of witnesses, so it's not hard to see what'll happen to him. I'm more worried about Nadia though.'

'You think she's being held there against her will?'

'She has to be. Otherwise why would she still be there? Everyone else has left, and there's a new gang of workmen in the flat, but she's still there. Cooking and cleaning for them and God knows what else.'

'That's not necessarily slavery though, J. She might be getting paid for that. Shitty wages, below minimum I'd guess, but is it so strange for a place like that? If what you tell me about the place is true and there's a couple of dozen itinerant workmen in there, coming and going at all hours too, well, it would make sense for them to have a cleaner. And if there's several of those flats in the building then there might be a bunch of them living there permanently.'

Janie had to admit that the detective superintendent had a point. She'd seen a couple of other women hanging out washing, after all. Older than Nadia but all speaking the same language, they probably had a small flat to themselves and did laundry for the building-site workers. A little bit of Serbian cooking to make them feel less homesick. But if that was the case, why had someone beaten the young woman?

'You could be right, Kirsty. I'd be much happier if you were, to be honest. It's just . . .'

'Your gut tells you different?' Ritchie managed a tired smile again. 'You sound a lot like Tony sometimes, you know?'

'Thanks, I think. You know he's right more often than not though.'

The detective superintendent nodded slowly, her gaze darting to the clock again. 'That he is. And I'll make sure the modern-slavery team hear your concerns about this Nadia. If there's an organised gang working out of that tower block, they'll find it and put an end to it.'

'Thanks,' Janie said as she pushed her chair away from the conference table and stood up. Beyond the glass window the sky was darkening to evening now, another day with far too little achieved. 'I know we're all crazy busy, but I'd not be able to live with myself if I hadn't tried to do something, you know?'

34

Darkness had fallen completely by the time McLean drove Emma's little Renault up the drive and parked it alongside the charging point. It still had plenty of range left, but he plugged it in anyway, the habit having become something of a ritual over the couple of years he'd been borrowing the car. He really should get something of his own, he knew, but when was there time to research the alternatives these days? Glancing over at the coach house, where the battered remains of his beloved old Alfa Romeo lay under a tarpaulin awaiting expensive restoration, he briefly considered the idea of getting it converted to run on batteries like the Renault. It wouldn't be the same though, and he'd long since given up any thoughts of using it for work. That was the reason it was under a tarpaulin and not ready to take him out into the hills, after all. No, he'd have to get something new and reliable. Or keep on using Emma's car. It wasn't as if she was going to be using it herself anytime soon.

Mrs McCutcheon's cat stared at him from her spot in front of the Aga when he let himself into the kitchen, a look on its face that spoke eloquently of the disappointment that there was no take-away curry. Or haggis. Cecily Slater's cat was nowhere to be seen, but that wasn't so unusual if it was dry out and there were small animals to be hunted.

Through the open door to the front of the house, he could hear the low mutter of conversation that meant Emma had a visitor. Without even needing to think about it, McLean knew who it would be. Only Madame Rose would be here at this time of the evening, and sure enough, when he stepped into the library she was sitting on the sofa, halfway through what must have been a fascinating anecdote judging by the rapt attention on Emma's face. What he hadn't been expecting was for there to be someone else there hanging on the medium's every word.

'Mr Drake. What a surprise,' was all he could think to say, since it was the truth.

Madame Rose tailed off in her story, her attention focusing on McLean with all the glare of a World War Two searchlight. 'Tony. You're home at last.'

Before she'd even finished speaking, Drake was already on his feet. As if someone had put a firecracker under his arse, wasn't that the expression? It was hard to tell what he was thinking, such was the uncanny stillness of his face, but he did his best to crank it into a smile.

'Detective Chief Inspector.' He held out his hand to shake, an oddly formal gesture given the setting. 'I do hope I'm not intruding again.'

'I don't imagine Emma would have let you in if she didn't want to, so no.' McLean took the man's hand, perhaps a little reluctantly. His skin felt cool and too dry, almost as if it were rubber rather than flesh. 'Just a social call, I take it?'

'Look at you two, squaring off like dogs.' Emma pushed herself slowly upright, so that by the time McLean made it across the room to her chair, she was already standing. The hug he gave her felt awkward with Drake watching on.

'Sorry I'm so late. It's been a day.'

'Aye, I know. You texted, remember?'

'I should probably be going,' Drake said, still standing and looking every bit as awkward as McLean felt. Only Madame Rose seemed unmoved by the whole tableau.

'So soon, Nathaniel dear?' She reached out a hand and patted the sofa cushion beside her. 'Sit down a moment and let me finish my tale. Sure Tony won't mind. Will you, Tony.'

It was a statement rather than a question, and McLean knew better than to argue with the medium. The initial shock of seeing the billionaire in his living room again had worn off now, and his detective's brain was keen to find out exactly why Drake had come round.

'Not at all.' He helped Emma back into her seat, then turned to the bookcase and the hidden drinks cabinet. He should probably have something to eat before starting on the drams, but it really had been a day. 'I'll be needing a drink though. Can I get anyone else anything?'

When he pulled the spine of the fake edition of *Whisky Galore* to trip the latch that allowed the bookcase to swing open, Drake let out a loud whoop of laughter.

'Is that for real? You have a drinks cabinet hidden in your book-shelves? Jeez, that's brilliant. I have got to get me one of those.'

It was the most animated McLean had ever seen the man, and it went some way to making him seem a bit human. When he turned to face the group, Drake had seated himself beside Madame Rose, exactly where she had instructed him to. McLean knew the power the medium had to take command of any situation if she so chose, but even so he was impressed that she had managed to work that magic on an American, let alone an American tech billionaire.

'I wouldn't be at all surprised if there wasn't one in that house of yours already. It was built much the same time as this place, and this sort of thing was all the rage then.' He reached for a bottle, thought better of it and selected a different one. 'Mind you, given who last lived there, you might want to be careful before opening it. Never know what you might find.'

'Fair point. I've heard rumours about that woman that you'd not believe. Most of the C-suite types in Silicon Valley are terrified of her.'

'Then they are wiser than I'd ever have given them credit for.' McLean held up the bottle. 'Dram?'

'Just a wee one, thank you, Tony,' Madame Rose said at the same time as Drake shook his head and added, 'Thank you, but no. I'm on a strict regime and alcohol's not part of it. Never liked the taste of liquor even when I did drink.'

'All the more for us then.' McLean poured drinks for himself and Madame Rose, having seen Emma's shake of the head and knowing that she wouldn't want any alcohol either. Her reasons were more understandable than Drake's, but he wasn't going to judge either of them.

'So, Rose,' he said as he handed her a glass. 'What was this tale you were so eager to tell us all?'

'The thing you have to remember with all the old myths and legends is that they all start off as an exaggeration of the truth.'

McLean was glad of his whisky as Madame Rose took up the threads of whatever it was she had been telling Emma and Nathaniel Drake when he had arrived home. He would have been even more glad of a hot meal first, perhaps have settled for a ham and cheese sandwich at a push, but he'd learned long ago that it paid to listen to the old medium. Especially when she was in full-on declaiming mode.

'Take the legend of King Arthur and the Knights of the Round Table, for example. All the elaborate stories of Merlin, Uther Pendragon, the fae magic and suchlike. I'm sure none of that actually happened.'

Was it his imagination or did Madame Rose wink ever so slightly at him as she said this? McLean hid his reaction behind a sip of whisky. Ardbeg, heavily peated, it brought unbidden an image of perfectly preserved bog bodies to his mind. Smooth, leathery skin, impossibly supple after thousands of years. Ageing stopped at the moment of death.

'But Arthur himself? One man uniting the warring factions in post-Roman Britain? Of course he existed. I've no doubt in his life he did great things, and then when he died the storytellers got to work.' Madame Rose paused long enough to take a sip from her own glass, breathing deep of the heady aroma. There was always a reason for her tall tales, and the fact that Professor Caine had been talking to him recently about a very similar subject wasn't lost on McLean. He'd have to puzzle out the meaning for himself, of course. Rose rarely came at a subject head on.

'It's the nature of a story to embellish, after all. The boring details are glossed over, all the focus given to the glamorous. What do they teach in creative writing classes? Conflict is everything? Or something like that.'

'But conflict isn't necessarily violence,' Emma said. 'It can be as simple as having to overcome some obstacle to get what you want, can't it?' She lifted both arms, stick thin under her baggy woollen cardigan, then let them fall back down into her lap. 'Like desperately wanting to go back to work, but not having the strength any more.'

'Very much like that, Emma my dear. But I have allowed myself to be distracted from the point I was hoping to make. The stories are exaggerated, yes, but they are based in essential truth. Your man Arthur might not have pulled thon sword from the stone, but he brought peace for a while. And it's the same with the even older tales, the men who lived long past their natural span. That's your goal, I believe, Nathaniel. Is it not?'

Drake started a little to hear his name. 'What? Oh, yes, Rose. That is my aim in life. To unravel the mystery of why we grow old and die. Modern medical science is close to answering so many of those questions, finding ways to hold back time. You talk of King

Arthur. How long was the average lifespan in those days? Thirty years? Thirty-five? We can keep people alive three times as long as that now, but what kind of life is it, hooked up to machines and needing nurses to wipe your ass for you?'

'What kind of life indeed.' Madame Rose held her glass up to the light, the cut-crystal tumbler sparkling as she turned it this way and that before bringing it back down to her lips for a sip. 'And do you think the people whose stories became legend were decrepit when they finally died? Senile, perhaps? There's a few go mad, of course. But who's to say they weren't mad to start with? You'd have to be a little mad to want to go on for ever, would you not? To live to see all your friends and family wither and die?'

If Drake understood the not so subtle dig at his character, he didn't show it. There was an earnestness about him that bordered on innocence, although McLean wasn't fool enough to think someone could amass a fortune as large as Drake's without some worldliness about him. The world knew about his fascination with eternal life, too, so it was perhaps not that big a surprise that Madame Rose was making that the focus for her story. Turning it into a morality tale was perhaps a little on the nose, but Drake didn't seem to mind. Or maybe it was just that whatever regime Professor Caine had him on, whatever treatments he had already undergone, they so rid his face of expression it was impossible to tell what was going on behind that mask.

'Of course, in the legend Arthur was taken from the battlefield and laid to rest in a cavern deep within the earth, not dead but sleeping. Ageless and ready to wake and come to Britain's aid in her time of greatest need. I suppose you might call that suspended animation, Nathaniel. Cryo-sleep, perhaps, like Walt Disney.'

'I . . . What?' Drake shook his head as if waking from an unplanned afternoon nap.

'Walt Disney. You know, Mickey Mouse and all that? There's been rumours for years that his body was frozen when he died, waiting for a time when medicine can cure him, pare back the years so that he can be young again. Have you never considered that, instead of this . . . unusual diet and exercise regime of yours? Live a full life, then trust your body to be repaired and revived?'

Slowly, the cogs began to turn in Drake's head. McLean could see the man beginning to understand. How would he react to Madame Rose's humour? Americans weren't renowned for their sense of irony, after all. Billionaire tech bros least of all.

'Ah, you almost got me there, Rose.' He barked out a laugh that reached his eyes, even if the skin on his face didn't so much as wrinkle. 'They only froze Walt's head. It's in a hi-tech storage facility under the *Pirates of the Caribbean* ride in Disneyland. Reckon it'll be a long while before science can rebuild him, but I aim to be around when it does. Whether he's still sane when they wake him up? Who knows.'

'I always thought that was an urban myth,' McLean said. 'He was cremated, wasn't he?'

This time Drake's smile brought a little animation to his face. 'Maybe they cremated a headless corpse to throw folk off the scent. I've been under the ride though. There's way more machinery than is needed to run it, and the backup power supplies are off the scale. Still . . .' He slapped his hands against his knees, using them to push himself to standing. 'I really should be getting on. If I don't check in soon, my head of security will start worrying, and we wouldn't want him breaking your front door down, now, would we?'

Later, after both Drake and Madame Rose had left, McLean took himself through to the kitchen and started to fix up that ham and cheese sandwich. A clatter at the back door was Cecily Slater's cat coming in to join Mrs McCutcheon's in front of the Aga, which meant that the weather was due to turn bad again. As they both stared at him with expressions of utter disappointment at his earlier haggis failure, it occurred to him that he had never even tried to give either of them names. Was there any point, with cats? It wasn't as if they came when they were called.

'Here you go. It's all I've got, right?' He picked a slice of ham from the packet, tore it in two and tossed it towards them. Mrs McCutcheon's cat didn't move, but Cecily Slater's pounced on the morsel as if it was a live mouse. A contented chirrup of purring overlaid the sound of mastication as she set about her treat.

'Talking to yourself's the first sign of madness, you know, Tony?'

Behind him, Emma walked slowly into the room. When he turned, she self-consciously took her hand from the door frame where she had been using it for support. Not a wheelchair day, but neither a good one.

'Aye, and the second sign's when you start answering yourself. Or maybe when the cats start talking back.'

'Madame Rose is well gone then. She's forever talking to the cats and I'm fairly sure they tell her everything that's been going on since her last visit.'

McLean had thought the same thing on many an occasion, usually without much conviction. Emma's voice, tired as it was, held little by way of levity, which made him wonder whether she didn't half believe it herself.

'Any particular reason why she popped round, or was she just getting her monthly update from her spies?'

Emma lowered herself into one of the chairs with an audible sigh of relief. 'Probably that, although you can never quite tell with Rose. She checks up on me every couple of days, even when we're not doing therapy.'

'And Drake?' McLean had wanted to ask, couldn't quite find a way of doing so that didn't sound petulant, and so decided to jump right in.

'Oh, I reckon she knew he was going to show up, yes. You know what she's like.'

'I . . .' McLean was momentarily flummoxed. 'That's not what I meant, but . . .'

'I know, but I don't think Nathaniel knew why he came round either. Poor man, I think he's basically a bit lonely. Doesn't find it easy to make friends, and he can be a bit intense too. I suspect the one is the reason for the other. That and his money, of course.'

'His money?' McLean's brain caught up with his mouth a second too late. 'Oh, right. Can't be easy knowing if someone's being nice because you're rich or because they actually want to spend time with you. It's all a bit awkward though, him dropping round like that.'

'Anthony McLean, I hope you're not impugning my reputation.' Emma put on an air of mock indignation, but it didn't last. Like everything else, it was too much effort.

'I was planning on going to see him tomorrow, actually. As part of an ongoing investigation, so I couldn't really bring it up in front of you and Rose.'

'I thought you'd been told to stop looking into the break-in.'

'Well, no, I was told not to press charges against the two suspects. That's not quite the same thing. And it's all got a lot more complicated since then, hence the late nights.'

McLean finished making his sandwich, cut it in half, and only then thought about what he was doing. 'You want one?' He offered the plate to Emma.

'No, thanks. I'm fine.'

'Have you eaten anything this evening, Em?'

For a moment he thought she was going to lie to him, but she'd never been very good at that, and she knew it.

'Maybe a couple of biscuits at teatime. I had lunch, mind.'

'Em, you're never going to get your strength back if you starve yourself.' McLean looked down at the plate and his sandwich, no longer quite as appealing as it had been a few moments earlier.

'I just . . . I don't know. I don't feel hungry even though I know I should. Food tastes of nothing. Ashes.'

Emma played with her hands, twisting them around each other as if trying to wash them without soap or water. He reached over, took them in his own. 'How long's this been going on? You were fine when we had Hattie and Meg over. That was a lovely meal.'

'I can eat just fine, Tony. It's just . . . I never seem to feel the need. And I don't much enjoy it any more.'

'Have you spoken to anyone about it?'

'I'm talking to you now, aren't I?'

'That's not what I mean, Em. Does Rose know? Dr Wheeler?'

'There's not much gets past Rose, so aye, I'd say she's guessed something's up. That's maybe why she pops by so often. I didn't want to bother Caroline though. She's that busy the whole time.'

'And she said to tell her if any new symptoms came up. You need to call her in the morning. Better yet, I'll call her and take you in myself.'

35

J anie knew she shouldn't be doing it even before she saw the
tower block over the rooftops of the nearby council houses.
Early morning, the light had a flat grey quality that promised a
cold day, the looming presence of the tower like a sleeping giant
that might wake at any moment. Low cloud almost shrouded the
top of it, but at least there was no rain. Not yet, anyway. Rain
would have made this plan even more foolish than it already was.

Through the passenger window, she saw a couple of uniform
officers sitting in a squad car parked outside the tower block. Neither of them noticed her as she passed the entrance, too busy
chatting to each other. She couldn't blame them, really. It wasn't
the most exciting of assignments. She followed the road round to
the far side of the block and pulled into the verge where the
broken-down fence gave a half-decent view of the drying green.
No sign of any activity this early in the morning, but she didn't
imagine it would be long.

On the seat beside her lay the burner phone she had bought the
night before from a little shop on South Clerk Street, close by the
bus stop she usually waited at for her ride home. It had a full charge
and she'd put a few useful numbers in the memory. Her own for
one, but also the nearest women's refuge centre and another for
the Downham Trust. Whether any of them would ever be used

was another matter. It had seemed a good idea when she'd had it, after her chat with Detective Superintendent Ritchie the evening before. Now, in the cold light of day and with nobody up and about, she was beginning to have doubts. This might all be a waste of time and money.

Pulling out her own phone, she skimmed through the morning reports. All the scant information that had come in during the night shift and a few possible leads from further CCTV analysis. As she was typing a quick reply to DS Blane, a text message came in from McLean, telling her he was taking Emma to hospital for a check-up and might be late in. Janie almost replied to ask which hospital, just in case he might be able to look in on Cerys, but movement on the other side of the fence distracted her.

The back door to the tower block had swung open, and three figures stepped out. Each held a basket full of washing. Janie recognised the two older women from before, and there between them, as if she were a young ingenue being chaperoned, was Nadia. The young woman moved stiffly, but not in the stooped manner of someone not quite in their own head. More like someone trying hard not to put too much pressure on their bruises.

As Janie watched, the women set about hanging washing on the lines. Good luck getting any of it dry in the current weather, but this was exactly what she had been hoping for. Nadia stayed close to the other two at first, but eventually the nature of their task began to spread them apart. Time to do this, if she was ever going to.

When she stepped out of the pool car and locked it, the wind whistled around her in search of all the tiny gaps in her jacket and trousers, finding too many ways in to chill her skin. Janie shoved the burner phone in one pocket, then followed the path worn in the litter-strewn grass to the point where the tower block's youth came and went at their leisure. It was a while since last she'd ducked through a tear in a wire mesh fence, but some skills you never lose.

Nadia looked up as she approached, her swollen eyes masking her expression. The beating she'd taken must have messed up her sight, as she didn't recognise Janie until the two of them were only a few paces apart.

'You?' A single word filled with both questioning and alarm. Nadia looked around to where the other two women were busy emptying their own baskets.

'Me,' Janie confirmed. 'An' I brought you something.' She pulled out the phone and swiftly dropped it into Nadia's washing basket before anyone could see. 'Use it, don't use it. Up to you. I'd very much like to chat sometime. And you never know, I might be able to help.'

She didn't wait for an answer. Head down, hands shoved into her pockets and shoulders slouched like a teenager, she scuffed the crumbly surface of the yard as she sauntered to the back door, looking for all the world like she had every reason to be there. From the corner of her eye, she saw one of the other two women look at her briefly before bending to her basket for the next pair of smalls.

Through the ground-floor lobby of the building and out the front door, Janie paused by the parked squad car and tapped on the window to get the attention of the young uniform constable in the driving seat. He started as if woken from deep sleep, face creasing in anger until he realised who it was.

'Morning, Constable,' she said as he lowered the window. 'Keeping an eye on everyone coming and going, are we?'

'Detective Inspector, ma'am. Nobody said. I should have . . .' He spluttered to get out some coherent reply while fumbling with the door handle, but she waved for him to stay put.

'It's OK. Just checking up on something. When's your shift change?'

'About half an hour. We'll wait for the relief crew though. Might be a bit late, what with the staffing cuts and all.'

The perennial complaint. Janie had a lot of sympathy for it too. Everyone being asked to do more with less, and not just the police. Was it any wonder gangs like the one Sasha Jovanović had been overseeing had such a hold on their workers?

'DC Bryant should be out here with a team by then. Finishing off the door to doors we never managed yesterday. Don't reckon there's any need for a uniform presence here after that.'

'The young laddie, Connor. He OK? Took quite a hit. Needs to learn to duck.'

'Aye. Rest of the week off work, he'll be fine. Bit of a concussion and a wee squint to his nose. Nothing serious. He'll have a shiner for a few days too, but the doctor gave him the all clear.' Janie straightened up, a click in her back not quite audible above the breeze. 'I'll pass on your advice next time I see him.'

The drive back to the station gave Janie plenty of time to reflect on how foolish she'd been, going into that tower block with no backup and nobody knowing she was there. It was barely a day since DC Fairley had been punched in the face by an angry resident, after all. Formulating the plan, she'd worked on the principle that Nadia would not even give her the time of day if she turned up with another detective, or worse, a full team in tow. Going alone had been meant to show a degree of trust, but it could have gone horribly wrong. Connor Fairley was proof of just how dangerous the job could be, and how swiftly a situation could escalate. He'd got away with a broken nose, but Janie knew all too many officers who'd had far worse.

She'd got away with it, this time. And as a DI, it was her call to make. She knew if one of her sergeants had done the same she'd tear a strip off them though. There was always the chance too that the whole exercise was a waste of time. One of the older women might find the phone and confiscate it before Nadia could use it. One of the men might see it and take the opportunity to beat her some more simply for having it. The young woman might throw the phone away to avoid that situation happening, or she might trade it for drugs or other favours. Or it might be just the lifeline she needed, and as soon as she could find herself a quiet space to be alone, she might use it to call one of the numbers in its memory. All Janie could do was wait.

And get on with the rest of the job, of course. As she pulled into the car park at the rear of the station, she saw that DCI McLean's car was parked in front of the charging point, although not actually plugged in. A quick check of the time on the dashboard clock showed that he couldn't have spent long at the hospital. Whatever it was about, she hoped Emma was OK. She'd find a way to ask, or McLean would tell her.

Inside, the usual busyness of shift change hummed around the rear lobby and the stairwell. Tired night-shift officers were heading to the canteen for their tea, or checking out on their way home. The day shift filed into the locker rooms to change into uniform, or headed to the canteen for breakfast. Janie had already been in a couple of hours earlier to pick up the pool car, but the siren call of bacon roll and coffee was hard to resist. How many hours had it been since her mug of instant and slice of toast in the flat?

A gaggle of detective constables and sergeants hogged one of the tables when she stepped into the melee that was the canteen. Lofty Blane towered over everyone, as he tended to do even when he tried not to, and so was the one to spot her first. He waved her over, but by the time she'd managed to secure both roll and mug, a number of the team had already departed.

'Is it something I said?' she asked only half in jest as she settled into one of the chairs. Opposite her, DC Mitchell gave her a strange look.

'You're the boss, J. Should be in the C-suite with all the other suits, not slumming it with the workers. Scares the wains off if you come and sit with us.'

It was meant as a joke, but there was truth in the detective constable's words too. For all that she wasn't much older than them, her seniority made Janie a figure of authority to the latest intake of plain clothes and uniform constables alike. They'd not known her as a DC herself, not like Lofty Blane and Jay Stringer. Neither had they worked with her long enough to treat her like a valued colleague. It was almost as depressing a thought as knowing she'd only a month left in her flat. Still nowhere else to live, and both Manda and she were far too busy to even start looking. If she carried on this way she'd be both homeless and spurned at work.

'You want me to take my spoils back up to my tiny wee office then?' she asked with a little less humour in her voice than she had intended. 'Ach, don't mind me. I was up far too early this morning.'

At least the bacon roll was good. Janie set about it with a hunger she'd not known was on her until the first bite. Washed down with what must have been the first mug out of a new brew of coffee, it wasn't until she was licking salty grease off her fingers and wiping them with a paper napkin that she realised everyone was watching her.

'What? I was hungry, aye?'

Mitchell shook her head, but smiled as she was doing it. Checked her watch. 'I'd better get going. Need to finish the report for the procurator fiscal on your friend Sasha.'

'Shouldn't that be Jessica's . . .' Janie started to ask, then remembered where DC Bryant was spending her morning. 'Thanks, Cass. Events rather took over.'

'Aye, I know. How is Cerys, by the way?'

'Not spoken to her today, but the doctors reckoned she'll make a full recovery. Should probably be letting her out soon. I'll check in on her later if there's time. Better if I could tell her we'd found the two bodies and whoever took them, mind.'

'The DCI got any leads on that yet? He was talking to the security firm, wasn't he?'

'Aye, it's all in the briefing notes. I think he was going to see someone at Drake Biotech today. Find out if there's any link there. We've still not found any connection between the two stolen bodies. Well, apart from them being stolen, of course.' Janie took her phone out, swiped it awake and stared at the screen as if any notifications might have come in without her feeling the buzz of the handset or hearing the overloud ting. There was nothing, of course, but as she slid it back into her pocket she had a sudden, almost dizzying sense of déjà vu.

'Expecting a call?' Mitchell asked. 'Only that's the third time you've looked at your phone since you sat down.'

'Kind of.' Janie considered telling the detective constable about what she had done. Mitchell was perhaps the most likely member of the team to understand her faulty reasoning. But before she could say any more, the phone finally started to buzz and ring. She pulled it out in a hurry, swiping the screen and lifting it to her ear before fully registering the number of the caller.

'DI Harrison?' came the voice from the other end. Not Nadia. Janie confirmed they'd got the right number, listened to the caller and their message. Across the table from her, DC Mitchell raised one slim eyebrow in question. All the other detectives and uniform officers had left by the time she ended the call, which at least made the decision easy.

'That report you're preparing for the PF. Reckon it can wait a couple of hours?'

'I guess,' Mitchell said. 'Why?'

Janie held up her phone. 'That was Saughton. Seems Sasha Jovanović is in solitary following a bit of a bust-up in the dining hall. He's asking to speak to me. Figured you might like to come along.'

36

She'd been in worse interview rooms, but somehow knowing this one was deep within the heart of His Majesty's Prison Edinburgh made the drab walls and high-up, frosted-glass window feel uniquely oppressive. Janie sat on one side of a battered Formica-topped table, DC Mitchell in the seat beside her. On the way over, she had told the detective constable about her early morning solo visit to the tower block, where even now DC Bryant and a team of uniform constables was conducting door-to-door interviews to determine whether anyone in that entire building had known Paul Sanderson. If they would admit to as much, especially after the fracas of the previous day. Mitchell's silence had been worse than any loud condemnation, waves of disapproval radiating off her like menopausal hot flushes.

Or maybe Janie was overthinking things and the detective constable had no comment on what her superior officer got up to before the shift started.

A click of the door disrupted the uncomfortable silence. Janie looked up to see Sasha Jovanović standing between two large prison officers. The former gang boss wore his prison scrubs well, although to be fair he'd not long been issued them so they'd hardly had time to become too torn or stained. He had been staring at his feet, cuffed hands held slightly ahead of him, but now he looked

252

up. His face broke into a broad smile, accentuating the growing bruise and swelling around one eye. It reminded Janie oddly of the injury Nadia sported.

'Detective Inspector Harrison. You come. Is good to see you, no?' His gaze flitted over to where Mitchell sat. 'And you have brought Detective Constable Mitchell. I am honoured.'

'Quiet, you. Sit down and shut up till you're spoken to.' One of the prison officers shoved Sasha into the waiting chair, the other hooking the gang boss's handcuffs onto the loop set into the table-top. Only when they were both sure he was secure did they turn their attention to Janie.

'More trouble than he's worth, this one. Starting fights on his first day. He'll learn soon enough.'

'Thank you, officers. I'll take it from here.'

The first man, the one who had told Jovanović to be quiet, stared at Janie with a look somewhere between disbelief and disdain. She'd met his type far too often before to be particularly bothered. No doubt he thought policing was man's work, a woman's place waiting at home with his tea ready on the table for when he got back. What must he think of DC Mitchell, not only a woman but a black woman? That he had so far not even looked at her, let alone acknowledged her presence, spoke loud enough.

'You can wait outside. We'll be quite safe,' she said, holding the officer's gaze. As she'd expected, he backed down after a few seconds. Partly the inevitable reaction of the bully when someone calls their bluff, partly the understanding somewhere deep within his hindbrain that, woman though she might be, she was also a detective inspector and could make life very difficult for him if she chose to. With a shrug, he waved his colleague to the door.

'Steve not like me,' the gang boss said once the two prison officers had left.

'To be honest, I don't much like you either.' Janie settled back into her seat, crossed her arms, and stared at the man. The more she studied his face, the more injuries she noticed. The swollen eye was bloodshot, and his nose had a squint to it that would likely match Connor Fairley's. A small bandage had been taped to one earlobe, hiding what could very well be a bite mark. 'Looks like a few of the other inmates feel the same way too.'

'Is my own people. Good Serbians who do what they are told. Only, someone tell them I am, how you say it? Stool pigeon? Grass? Informant?'

'And why would they do that?' Janie asked, although the obvious answer had already presented itself to her.

'I know too much, perhaps? They fear I will . . . what is expression? Spill beans? Sell out my comrades for kind word in the judge's ear?'

'And do you?' Janie asked. 'Know too much?'

Sasha tried to give an expansive shrug, but the cuffs made it small. 'That depends. What is in it for me if I do?'

'I think you've been watching too many detective shows on the telly. That's not how it works in real life.'

It was plain by the way his shoulders slumped at Janie's words that the gang boss knew as much. He tried to lift a hand to rub at his face, but the cuffs and short loop of chain meant he had to lean down instead, as if bowing to the two detectives.

'Let's start with a few simple questions, shall we?' Janie pulled out her phone, swiped the screen awake and searched for the right photograph before placing the handset on the table. 'Do you know this man?'

The gang boss instinctively reached for the phone, but it was too far. Once again he bowed in his seat, leaning forward for a better look at the picture.

'Who is?' he asked, the slightest shake of his head suggesting he really didn't know.

'That's what I was hoping you might be able to tell me,' Janie said. 'We think he might be . . . associated with Mihailovic. You ever see the two of them together?'

Sasha leaned forward again, his nose almost touching the table as he squinted at the photograph on the screen. It wasn't perhaps the best image of Paul Sanderson that had ever been taken, the man had been dead at the time. But it was all they could come up with at short notice.

'I never see this man before.'

Janie took her phone back, slipped it into her pocket. Still no call or text from Nadia, but it was only a few hours yet.

'OK. I guess it's possible you never saw them together. But I've been asking around about Mihailovic. Seems he was about to come into some money. And I don't mean a promotion on the building site. You know about that, don't you, Sasha.'

From the way the gang boss went very still, Janie knew she'd hit the mark. She settled back in her chair and let the silence grow, confident that Mitchell would say nothing. It lasted no more than ten or fifteen seconds, but it felt like an age to her. How much longer it must have been to the man sitting opposite, as his loyalties, fears and mental calculations played themselves out across his bruised features. When he broke, it was with a satisfying slump of the shoulders.

'Is man I know. Pay good money. Danger money. I not know what he do. I not ask. But he come look for people for job. Sometimes gone a few days, sometimes two weeks. Always they come back a bit changed, no? Quiet, maybe. Sick like hungover, but better in a week or so. He give them pills to help maybe sometime. Or medicine in bottle. They get better one month. Strong, no?' And here the gang boss tried once more to move his arms, perhaps intending to do a bicep flex, forgetting his handcuffs and the restraining loop on the table. 'And they have money. Enough to bring family here. Or pay off debts and go home.'

'And Mihailovic? You put him in touch with this man?' Janie asked.

Sasha shook his head. 'I not want, but Vash, he beg me. Need money for move out of shared flat in block. He want find place with girlfriend Shauna, you know? Vash, I say. Is not safe. But he go on and on, so I give in. He gone two weeks. Longest time. But he fine when he come back. And he have money. More money than he earn on building site in six months.'

'What happened to it? The money?' Janie asked.

Sasha did that half-shrug again. 'I not know. You ask people in flat. He have nothing on him when they call me to say he die in sleep.'

Thousands of pounds, gone just like that. If she hadn't seen the post-mortem report, known that whatever killed the man it hadn't been an obvious attack, Janie might have thought she was looking at a perfectly good motive right there. It didn't sit well though. Yes, someone had probably stolen Mihailovic's money, but even thousands of pounds in cash could take up a surprisingly small space. Almost anyone in the flat could have taken it. Apart from Nadia, they were all long gone.

'This man you know, who has these jobs that pay so well. He have a name?'

The gang boss shook his head slowly, eyes down so Janie couldn't see them. She'd known this would be his reaction, but the question had to be asked.

'How did you contact him, then?'

'I not contact him. He always contact me. A phone call. Never the same number twice, but I know voice, yes?'

Plausible, but Janie was still convinced the man was holding back the best. 'So what did you do when he contacted you? Put the word out among the gang you're in charge of? Easy money, just don't ask any questions?'

Again with the ineffectual shrug.

'You ever do it yourself?'

'I . . .' Sasha shook his head again, his early loquaciousness turned to stuttering silence now.

'So you don't know what the jobs involved. You were just the man putting desperate people in touch with someone almost certainly engaged in very illegal acts. And I imagine you got a cut, right?' Janie didn't wait for the gang boss to respond. 'Only, that makes you an accessory to any crimes committed.' She turned to DC Mitchell, who had been quietly taking notes and saying nothing all the while. 'Add that to the list, will you, Cass?'

'Already done.'

'Wait. No.' The gang boss reached out with both hands as if to physically stop the detective constable from writing down anything more. His restraints made a dull clinking noise as they held him back, and he gave up the effort, slumping into his seat again. 'But I am helping, no?'

'Has he been helping?' Janie directed the question at Mitchell.

'Not sure there's anything here we didn't already know. We knew Mihailovic was expecting to come into some money. He was going to move in with his girlfriend, wasn't he?'

Janie thought of her old schoolmate, Shauna Lennox. Another person she needed to show the photograph of Paul Sanderson to, if no one else had managed to come up with a link between the two missing dead men yet. That was going to be a fun conversation.

'That's what she said, aye. Didn't know where the money was coming from though.' She turned her attention back on Jovanović. 'But I think you do, Sasha. I think you know perfectly well who was borrowing the men on your work gang from time to time. I think you know exactly what they were being asked to do, too. And I expect your cut was a lot more than ten per cent. So. If you want the charges limited to what we've already got you in here for, and if you want me or maybe my boss to "have a word with the judge", as you put it . . .' She couldn't stop herself from making little bunny-ear quote marks with her fingers as she said the words. 'If you want us to be sympathetic, then we're going to need a lot more than "a man I know".' She did it again with the fingers, unrepentant.

Across the table from her, Sasha clasped his hands together, tried to put them in his lap as if protecting his manhood, the very essence of him. The cuffs and chain didn't allow even that much.

'I can't,' he said finally. All trace of his earlier bombast was gone. Now he sounded truly scared. 'They kill me.'

'They already tried. Got to you in here where you should be safe.' Janie leaned forward, elbows on the table. 'We can protect you, Sasha. But only if we know what we're protecting you from. Tell me who they are and we'll make sure they get nowhere near you.'

37

McLean had hoped to catch up with Janie Harrison when he arrived at the station a little later than usual, but her office was empty. True to his word, he had taken Emma to the hospital early, fully intending to stay with her until she had been seen by one of the specialists. He'd also been hoping for a chance to have a chat with Dr Wheeler about things other than Emma's slow recovery and lack of appetite, but the neurologist had not been in. When it had become clear that the wait could be several hours, Emma had insisted he leave her there and go to work. Sensible, pragmatic, it was true, but part of him wondered if she hadn't guessed at his ulterior motive anyway.

It didn't matter. He'd catch up with Dr Wheeler eventually. Meantime he needed to speak to Janie to get up to speed with the ongoing investigation.

Only as he was letting himself into the incident room did it occur to McLean that he could talk to any of the detective sergeants, or indeed DI Gregg, and get exactly the same information as he would from Harrison. Was he so set in his ways that he needed to work with her and not one of the other more than capable officers in his team?

'Morning, sir. DI Harrison's away at Saughton with DC Mitchell. If you're looking for her.'

The young detective constable, Connor Fairley, offered up the information before McLean could even ask. It might have been considered presumptuous, had he not been actually looking for her. Fairley looked like he'd been in a fight, one eye half swollen shut, the other ringed with bruising, and his nose had a kink in it that hadn't been there the last time McLean had seen him.

'What on earth happened to you?' he asked.

'This?' The detective constable pointed at his face. 'Bit of a misunderstanding. The lad who misunderstood's due an appearance in front of the Sheriff anytime now.'

There was something different about Fairley. Other than his obvious injuries. McLean couldn't quite put his finger on it, his mind being pulled in too many other directions.

'Doctor gave you the OK to come back to work, I take it?'

'Aye, sir. Fit as a fiddle. I'd be back out to the tower block with DC Bryant, but she thought it might be a bit provocative. After what happened yesterday.'

'Probably wise.' McLean looked around the room, emptier than he would have liked. 'You helping DS Blane with the CCTV footage?'

'No, sir. I've been going through the dead man's belongings. Sanderson's, that is. The other one didnae have anything with him when he was found, so I'm told.'

'Belongings? I didn't think anyone had been to his flat yet.'

'They've not, sir. I meant the things he had on him when he was found. He'd no money in his wallet, but there was a couple of cards wi' numbers on them we've been trying to trace. IT have unlocked his phone too. I've made a start cataloguing that. It's that wee box he had wi' him that's fascinating, mind.'

It struck McLean that he'd never heard the detective constable utter so many words before. That was the thing that had been bothering him. Fairley was shy to a fault, particularly for a police officer. Especially around officers senior to him, and women. And yet here he was not batting an eyelid at talking to a DCI with twenty years more experience than him. Twenty-five, maybe. The doctor might have signed him off as fit to work, but that blow to the head had surely knocked something into him. Or out.

'What about it?' he asked. 'The box, I mean. It's down in evidence, I take it?'

'Aye. I mean, no. It was. I brought it up here to gi' it a better look, see?' Fairley pointed to a table shoved up against one wall. A couple of cardboard boxes of the kind the evidence store used sat on top, the lid off one.

'Let's have a look at it then,' McLean said. For an instant almost too swift to be noticed, the detective constable stiffened. Something dark flitted across his bruised features, his hands clenched into fists and it felt almost as if the room grew colder. Then Fairley shuddered like a dog fresh out of the river. One of the overhead fluorescent tubes banged into life, bringing much needed light back to the room.

'Aye, sir. Sorry. It's over here.' The detective constable strode across the room, and by the time McLean caught up with him he had the small wooden box in his hands. Dark ebony inlay formed intricate patterns in the polished surface, almost painful to look at under the slightly stuttering artificial light.

'You work out how to open it?' McLean asked as the detective constable turned the box this way and that. Fairley startled, as if he'd been caught looking at dirty pictures on one of the office computers. As if he had forgotten McLean was even there, despite only a few seconds having passed since he picked up the object.

'I . . .' He shook his head. 'No, sir. No' even sure if it does open.'

'May I?' McLean held out his hand to take the box, but the detective constable didn't immediately hand it over. If anything, his arm seemed to move away, trying to hide his prize behind him like a toddler with his favourite toy.

'Good point. Should probably wear gloves.' He fished a pair out of his jacket pocket and snapped them on with the swift ease of someone who has done it many, many times before. Fairley hadn't bothered, of course. He was still holding the box close to his body, protective like a mother with a newborn child.

'Detective Constable?' McLean pitched his voice a little louder than necessary, his tone verging towards parade ground sergeant. Something in it finally got through to Fairley, who blinked like a man waking, shuddered again, then offered the box. When McLean took it, the detective constable's shoulders slumped a little, and he let out a long breath.

'So this is what Paul Sanderson had with him when he died.' He held the box up to the light, then carried it over to the nearest window instead. Fairley followed him like a faithful hound.

'Are you sure you're OK . . . Connor?' McLean had to dredge his memory for the man's first name. At the sound of it, the detective constable straightened a little, colour rising in his cheeks and showing off the freckles that had almost disappeared into his bruises.

'I . . . I'm no' sure, sir.' His voice sounded different, the hesitancy of earlier encounters returned. Concussion could do strange things to the brain. McLean knew that all too well.

'Maybe you should go and get yourself checked up again, aye? Take the day off to recover.'

'I . . .'

'That's an order, Detective Constable. In case I wasn't clear?'

Fairley stared for too long, not at McLean but at the box. Then he slowly managed to drag his gaze up to the DCI's face. There was something missing in those eyes; the man should never have been signed off OK to come to work. Eventually he nodded, just once.

'Aye, sir. Sorry,' he said. One last glance at the box, still nestled in McLean's latex-gloved hands, and then he turned and walked out of the room.

★ ★ ★

As McLean watched the door close behind DC Fairley, he was struck by how quiet the incident room had grown. Looking around, he half expected all the police officers and support staff to be staring at him, wide-eyed and open-mouthed, but they were all still going about the slow, methodical business of the investigation. And as he looked at each person in turn, so he began to hear the muted conversations, the clattering of fingers on keyboards, the squeak of castors on floor tiles. Bit by bit, as if he'd been under-water and only now resurfaced, the sounds of busyness came back to him.

'You OK, sir?'

It was a cruel echo of the same question he had asked the young detective constable, only when he looked around to see who had asked it, Sandy Gregg was the one with the worried expression on her face. Her gaze drifted down to the box in his hands, both eye-brows rising in perfect unison like a pair of Olympic divers on the springboard.

'Funny you should ask,' he said, and even his voice sounded a little odd. As if someone else was using it a few yards from where he was standing. 'I was just having a word with DC Fairley about this thing.' He held up the box, unsurprised when Gregg flinched away from it. 'Only, I think he's still not right after getting punched in the head yesterday, poor lad.'

'Heard about that, aye.' Gregg might not have realised it, but she had inched back a step. 'You need any help with that?' She didn't sound as if she meant it.

'No. Thanks.' McLean hefted the box again, fairly sure he could feel something shifting inside it. He turned it this way and that, fingers feeling nothing of the surface through his thin gloves. The inlay was so intricate and so expertly crafted it was completely seamless. A puzzle box indeed, but the nature of it was unimport-ant to his investigation.

'I don't think we're going to learn much from it. First time

I saw it I reckoned Sanderson had nicked it from the lab he broke into. Probably thought he could get some cash for it to buy drugs. Might even have been going to see his dealer when he went to the park, only he never made it to the meeting.'

Even as he said the words, McLean knew it was more complicated than that. Far more complicated. Why had Sanderson left his flat with no shoes on? What had actually killed him? And why had someone stolen his body before they could find that out? What had he, Christine Vaughan and Keith Campbell really been doing at Drake Biotech in the first place? Too many questions and every answer only begged more. He carried the box back to the table, slipped it into its forensics plastic bag and ziplocked it closed, then placed the whole lot into the cardboard evidence box.

'Get someone to take that back down to the evidence store, can you, Sandy? Unless someone comes forward claiming it's been stolen, we'll just have to assume it actually belonged to Sanderson. His family can fight over who gets to keep it once this whole investigation's done.'

'He doesn't have any family,' Gregg said as she picked up the lid and placed it firmly on top.

'None at all?'

'Not that we've been able to trace, no. Neighbours hardly knew him, but then that's not unusual for the kind of digs he was living in. Landlord's a company specialises in renting to benefit claimants. They want to know when they can get into the flat and gut it, by the way. I hear they've plans to knock the whole block down and build new housing on the site. Seems a bit daft, but I guess they can make more money that way.'

'It's always about making money, Sandy. Criminal or legitimate, always about making money.' McLean peeled off his latex gloves and dropped them into the nearest bin. Half expecting to be told off for using the wrong one, he glanced around the incident room again. 'You under control here?'

'Aye, pretty much. Lofty's got a team on the CCTV, Janie's away talking to the gang boss, Jovanović. Jessica Bryant's finishing up on the door to doors over at the tower block. We're putting together a file on Sanderson based on his previous, but there's not a lot we can dig up about Mihailovic.'

'Sanderson had form?' McLean couldn't immediately remember whether he'd known that before.

'It's mostly public disorder stuff, and all when he was young. Not that he was exactly old when he died, mind.'

'How old was he?' Another fact McLean should have had at his fingertips. Was he losing his touch, or just tired?

'Thirty-one. But the last thing we have on record for him was when he was nineteen.'

Thirty-one. McLean recalled the body on the bench in Craigmillar Castle Park. If he'd not been told, he'd have put the man in his late sixties. Older, even. On the other hand, he'd seen Sanderson's pigsty of a flat, knew how the man had lived a good few of those thirty-one years. Was it any surprise he looked the way he did? Was it even important?

'Tell you what. I'll take that back down to evidence.' He gestured at the cardboard box, now hiding the intricately decorated wooden puzzle box within. 'You got the chain of evidence sheet?'

'Somewhere here, aye.' Gregg shuffled through the pile of papers on the table before coming up with the relevant document. Without his spectacles, McLean could barely make out the squiggly signature of whoever had signed the boxes out of evidence. He added his own illegible squiggle on the next line anyway, then slipped the sheet of paper into the box.

'Tell Harrison I'd like a word when she gets back, will you?' he said, then hefted the box and headed out the door.

38

Time was the station had held evidence for all its ongoing investigations and much else besides. The basement had been the realm of Police Sergeant John 'Needy' Needham and he had kept the evidence stores meticulously organised. He'd also had a mental breakdown when his father had died and begun copy-cat murders in the style of one of the city's most notorious serial killers, so on balance McLean felt it was for the best that most of the evidence store was now housed in a nondescript but very secure warehouse on the outskirts of town.

What they held in the much-reduced basement storage was only evidence that might be needed in the most active of investigations, and items that had not yet been fully catalogued. It was the first stop after forensics had done with it, or sometimes an interim storage until forensics could clear a gap in their busy schedule.

No one had been all that keen to step into Needy's shoes, and so evidence was fitted into the general work rota. Even so, McLean was surprised to see Sergeant Don Gatford at the desk when he pushed open the door with his backside and shuffled into the small reception room. Partly it was because the old police sergeant was usually better at landing himself the easiest of assignments, although on reflection a few hours in the basement was quite a cushy job. Mostly it was because he was sure the man had retired a few months back.

'Present for you, Don.' McLean slid the cardboard box onto the counter that separated the actual evidence store from the rest of the station.

'Morning, sir. What have you got for me this time?' The old sergeant huffed his way out of his chair and came over to the counter. As he did so, McLean lifted the lid and pulled out the chain of evidence sheet so that the puzzle box could be signed back into the custody of the store.

'Possessions of the late Paul Sanderson, whereabouts currently unknown,' he said.

'Aye, I heard about that. Nasty business. The lassie from the mortuary, she OK?'

It didn't surprise McLean that the sergeant knew all about what had happened. He was second only to Grumpy Bob in his ability to ferret out every last nugget of gossip. His concern for Cerys Powell seemed genuine though, which was a surprise. When had desk-bound Sergeant Gatford ever had a chance to meet the pathologist's assistant? Then he remembered that Cerys was a regular at the same pub where all the hardened drinkers from this police station went after their shift was over.

'Been making new friends, have you, Don?' McLean watched a little flush of colour spread across the sergeant's cheeks, matching the red of his nose. 'Last I heard she's going to be fine. Janie . . . DI Harrison's the one to ask though. They're good friends.'

'Aye, I'd heard that.' Gatford leaned over the box, then very gently reached inside and pulled out the clear plastic evidence bag. The way he held it reminded McLean of a very posh-looking lady in tweeds he'd once seen clearing up after her dog had left a message on the Meadows. He grasped the bag between thumb and forefinger, holding it away from himself as if it were radioactive.

'Is there a problem?'

'What?' Gatford looked confused at McLean's question, then noticed what he was doing. 'Oh. Sorry, sir. Not sure what that's about.'

'You're not the first person to act strangely around that thing,' McLean said as the sergeant placed the bag down on the counter and pulled the paper form over. While Gatford struggled with his spectacles and searched for a working pen, he picked up the box, still wrapped in plastic, and had another look at it. Apart from the obvious quality of its construction, and the shifting weight inside it that suggested there must be a way to get it open, McLean could see nothing unusual about the thing. But then he was no great expert when it came to antiques and odd curios. He knew some-one who was, though.

'Hang on a minute, Don,' he said before the sergeant could scribble his name on the sheet and accept the unwanted item back into the evidence store.

'Sir?'

'Beginning to think this might be more important than it looks. Keep it signed out to me. I'm going to take it to someone who can maybe shed a little more light on it.'

There was always a parking space on the street outside the gates to the house. McLean had even seen the car previously parked in it pull out and drive away at the same time as he turned Emma's little Renault into the road. As if it had been waiting there for him to arrive, keeping the space from being taken by someone else. One of life's little mysteries, he supposed, and given the state of the city's parking, not something he was going to try too hard to unpick. Hefting the cardboard evidence-store box under one arm, he plipped the lock on the car, hurried across the road and ducked in through the gates.

The first time he had visited this house, directed to its owner by none other than Chief Superintendent Jayne McIntyre, McLean had inadvertently gone in through the back door. It wasn't until much later that he realised the houses on this part of Leith Walk had originally been built facing onto the parallel street. Years of development had split once grand merchants' houses into small apartments, the backs of many of them turned into shops like the one from which Madame Rose ran her fortune-telling trade. The occult curios and antiquarian books side of things took place in much of the rest of the still-undivided house, and since that was the reason for his visit, McLean naturally took himself to the original front door rather than the tradesman's entrance.

'Tony, how delightful to see you. And in the middle of the day too.' The medium met him at the door without his having to ring the bell, as if she had known all along the exact date and time of his arrival. Possibly before he was even born. 'Do come in. I've got the kettle on, let's have a cup of tea, shall we?'

All too aware of the protocols, McLean followed Madame Rose into the house. As they crossed the large, open hallway to the kitchen, he felt the gaze of many pairs of eyes upon him. Sure enough, when he looked up to the first- and second-floor landings, a multitude of cats stared back at him from various improbable hiding places. Her familiars all, he felt certain they kept the medium informed of everything important going on in the city, no matter how daft that might sound if he said it out loud.

'You have a puzzle for me, I suspect,' Rose said after the niceties had been dealt with and the tea poured. A large slice of cake to go along with it would not do McLean's waistline any favours, but he found it hard to care.

'How did . . .?' he began to ask, then shook away the unnecessary question. Even if he did ask, he'd only get an infuriatingly cryptic answer. Instead, he opened up the cardboard box and pulled out the bag within.

'I'd like you to give me your appraisal of this,' he said. 'It's having an odd effect on some of the people in the station.'

269

Madame Rose put her cup down in its saucer with an almost inaudible clink and stared at the wooden puzzle box for a moment. 'I'm not surprised, Tony. I felt its pull a good fifteen minutes before you arrived. Very powerful indeed. May I?'

When McLean nodded his assent, the medium reached across the table and took up the box in both hands. Even though it was still wrapped in plastic, she held it as if it might be an unexploded bomb.

'Oh, this is very old. Very old indeed. And such a wondrous piece of work.' She made to unzip the bag, then stopped. 'You say some of your officers have been acting strange around it? Do you know if any of them have opened it up?'

'I don't think so. I wasn't even sure if it could be opened. What actually is it? Do you know?'

'This?' And now Madame Rose did unzip the bag and take out the wooden cube. 'This is a puzzle box, but also a repository. A place to put something of extremely high value. Or something extremely dangerous. Or both, of course. Where on earth did you get it, Tony?'

McLean didn't answer at once, distracted by the way the medium's overlarge hands cupped the box, her chunky be-ringed fingers caressing the inlay in gently swirling motions. She kept her gaze firmly on him while she did it, as if deliberately not looking at what she was doing.

'It was in the possession of a man we found dead in Craigmillar Castle Park a couple of mornings back,' he said eventually. Aware that he should not really be discussing the details of an ongoing case with a member of the public, McLean nevertheless gave Madame Rose a full briefing on the situation, missing bodies and all.

'Ah. The poor fellow must have been overwhelmed. Much like your officers. At least those of them who are susceptible to such things. You and I are made of sterner stuff. It cannot get its teeth into our souls.'

McLean knew better than to ask, but he couldn't stop himself from raising a questioning eyebrow.

'I rather fear I know what I will find inside here.' The medium had continued to caress the outside of the box all the while, her fingertips following the inlay as if it were a maze. Now they stopped, and she looked around the room as if searching for creatures lurking in the shadows. There were some, their feline eyes fixed firmly on the kitchen table, although that might have been more to do with the cake.

'I think I have it now, and we should be safe enough in here.'

Before McLean could ask what Madame Rose meant by that, her fingers flexed slightly and something clicked. Before his eyes, gaps appeared in the surface that McLean could have sworn had not been there before. He half expected there to be a hiss of escaping air, the stench of something long since festered away to dust. Instead, he thought he heard the faintest echo of laughter, caught a scent of summer grass that dissipated before he could even be sure it was anything other than his imagination.

'Right then. Let's be a little careful, shall we?' The medium eased the plastic evidence bag under the puzzle box before gently prising it open. McLean found himself holding his breath as he leaned forward for a better look at what lay inside. He still couldn't tell how the closure worked or fitted so tightly no one had been able to see the joins, but most of his attention was on the interior anyway.

It was lined with ruched velvet the colour of darkest claret, a hollow in the centre far larger than the wizened lump of black something that it held.

'Well now. There's something you don't see every day.' Madame Rose tilted the box the better to let light pick out the details of the lump. McLean peered in but couldn't make out much in the way of detail.

'What is it?' he asked.

By way of answer, the medium placed the box carefully in the centre of the table. She stood up and crossed the room to a drawer. The shuffling noises of hands searching for something in amongst a lot of other things went on for just as long as it might have done in McLean's own kitchen before she came back to the table brandishing a set of tarnished silver sugar tongs. With a delicate touch, she eased them into the box and gently pulled the lump out, holding it up for McLean to see.

'A long time ago, that was a human heart, I think.'

Now that it had been said, McLean could see all too well the shape of the shrivelled organ, the lobes and veins picked out in leathery detail. As he peered at it, Madame Rose tilted the tongs this way and that, the better to see the whole thing. They both noticed the markings on the underside at the same time.

'What's done that?' McLean asked. 'Looks like a mouse has got into the box.'

'It's worse than that, I'm afraid.' Madame Rose lowered the shrivelled lump back into its velvet coffin. 'Whoever did this has opened the box and then closed it again. That takes an unusual degree of skill and understanding. And the marks look more regular than any animal would make. Like a scalpel or something.'

McLean reached for the box, then drew his hands away. The pieces of a different puzzle began to fall together in his mind, although the picture they formed was still frustratingly obscured.

'I think I know who's done this, and maybe even why.'

39

Her phone rang as she was parking the pool car outside the police station. Janie glanced at the screen, then at DC Mitchell sitting beside her.

'You go on in, Cass. I don't think this'll take long.'

Mitchell raised a single, pencil-thin eyebrow, but said nothing as she unclipped her seat belt. Janie tapped the answer icon as the detective constable closed the car door behind her.

'Hello?'

A silence hung at the other end of the line, although not the sound of someone having cut the call the moment it was answered. Janie waited it out, knowing how much courage it must have taken to make the call in the first place. Assuming this was who she hoped it was.

'I . . .' A woman's voice, so that was a good start.

'Nadia?' Janie tried to put as much sympathy into that one word as possible.

'Is police woman? Harrison?'

'Detective Inspector Harrison, aye. But you can call me Janie if you prefer.'

'Janie.' Nadia didn't sound convinced. 'You give me phone. Why?'

'I thought you might want to talk. Without anyone else listening in.'

'They not let me have phone. Only make call for me. One time, every week. I speak to my son so I know he OK.'

Janie let out a quiet breath, as much in relief that her instincts had been right as anything.

'We can help,' she said, although at that moment she wasn't entirely sure how. 'Get him to a safe place and you too. Text me your son's full name, where he is at the moment, who has him. Any detail you can give me, and I'll do everything I can to make him safe.'

Another long pause before Nadia spoke again. 'I not know him, the man they are showing everyone. I never see him. I think is unlikely Vash know him either.'

The change of subject took Janie by surprise. 'Sanderson. His name's Paul Sanderson. Does that sound familiar at all?'

'No. I not hear it before. I not know this man. I not think anyone know this man.'

Much as she didn't want to, Janie found herself believing the woman. Eliminating one line of enquiry was, in theory, a good thing, but it left them with too many unanswered questions all the same. There had to be a link between the two stolen bodies, she was sure of it.

'Did you know that Vaclav had done some work? Not on the building site, but something extra? He was hoping to earn enough to get away, I think. Go and make a new life with Shauna.'

At the mention of that name, Nadia gave a little gasp. Or perhaps it was a sob. 'He was so full of plans. So happy. And then he fell sick. So soon he died.'

'Do you know what the job was?' Janie asked. In the back of her mind she was formulating more questions, but she was all too aware that Nadia might hang up at any moment.

'Is not job. Not work, he say. He go to some place outside city. They take some blood, put him in room with no window, give him food, drink. He watch some TV, read paper, sleep. Two week, is like holiday only he not leave room all time. They pay him lots money. Send home with number he call if he sick.'

'Did he call the number?'

'I not know. I think not or he not die, yes? Or they come for him?'

It occurred to Janie that maybe they did come for him, once they knew where he was. Although why Sasha had taken the body to the woods if he'd been the one to put Mihailovic in touch with the people in the first place was a puzzle for which she had no answer. Maybe it wasn't them at all. Or maybe he had contacted them and they had told him to dispose of the body before it drew too much attention. So many possibilities. If only she knew who these people were, and where they had taken the bodies.

'Do you know what happened to the number? What about the money?'

'Money I not know. Sasha take maybe. Sasha take everything.'

'Sasha is in jail. He won't be taking anything from anyone for a long time.'

'I—' Nadia began to say something, then stopped. 'I go now. Will speak again.'

Before Janie could say anything else, the call was cut. Had that been the sound of voices in the background? Someone coming? Or had the knowledge of Jovanović's arrest somehow upset the woman? Janie stared at the blank screen of her phone without seeing it as her mind replayed the conversation. She needed to speak to someone in the modern slavery unit directly, not keep on going through Detective Superintendent Ritchie. What did they know about the situation playing out under their noses in the south-east of the city? Did they even know at all? There had to be a way to help, but without knowing Nadia's full name, there was little she could do. Arresting her might get her away from the men controlling her, but what would happen to her son in that situation? And there was no guarantee she'd be treated well after being arrested anyway. Chances were someone else was holding on to any papers she might have. Undocumented, she'd face the horrors of the immigration services. The hostile environment. As if treating people already here like they were vermin would stop desperate others from coming.

Janie tapped the screen of her phone to send out a group text to the team, arranging a meeting for a half-hour's time. Before she could complete the task though, a new text lit up, the ping of its arrival very loud in the quiet confines of the pool car. A message from Nadia, it wasn't the name and location of her son, but a mobile phone number. Presumably the one Mihailovic was supposed to call if he felt ill. It didn't take a genius to figure out that the extra work Sasha had been lining up for some of the men in his team was some kind of experiment. Why else take a sample of someone's blood and then have them shut away for a couple of weeks?

Still pondering the implications and staring at her phone in expectation of more messages, Janie almost walked into DI Gregg as she stepped through the back door of the station.

'Oh, sorry, Sandy. Didn't see you.'

'No bother, J. Was hoping I might bump into you anyway. The DCI was looking for you. Wants a word.'

Janie finally slipped her phone back into her pocket. 'That's handy. I need to talk to him myself.'

'You wanted to see me?'

Janie had felt the weight of her phone in her pocket all the way up the three flights of stairs to DCI McLean's office. It hadn't pinged any more messages, so she'd have to get the number Nadia had sent her to the comms team and hope they could trace it. The possibility of a breakthrough in the Mihailovic case was a tantalising one, but she knew better than to get her hopes up too high.

'Just wanted a catch-up, really.' The detective chief inspector sat at his desk, reading spectacles perched on the end of his nose and a folder open in front of him. Janie went to the conference table and fetched herself a chair. There was a small cardboard box like the ones they used in the evidence store on the tabletop, and as she turned away from it she thought she heard someone whisper something.

'Did you . . .?' she asked, but it was clear that McLean hadn't spoken, so she shook the thought away, placed the chair in front of his desk and sat down.

'Think I might have made a bit of headway,' the DCI said, even if his expression suggested otherwise. 'What have you been up to?'

Janie paused before answering, partly to gather her thoughts and partly because she was sure someone out in the corridor had started muttering in a low voice. As usual, McLean's door had been open when she'd arrived, and she'd not bothered to close it. She didn't recall seeing anyone else out there though.

'Had a bit of a breakthrough tracking Mihailovic's movements in the run-up to his death,' she said and proceeded to tell the DCI all that she'd learned from both Sasha Jovanović and Nadia. She thought about not telling him how she'd persuaded the young woman to talk, but decided in the end it was easier to lay everything out for him. If any senior officer was going to understand the occasional need to stray a bit from procedure, then it was Tony McLean.

'That's . . . a little unorthodox,' he said after a moment's hesitation. 'But your call to make, and it got results so I can't see anyone complaining.'

'What do you reckon though? Is someone running some kind of unlicensed medical trials? Something that might have led to Mihailovic's death?'

'It certainly sounds like it, even if both of your witnesses probably have their own reasons for lying.'

'Aye, I reckon Jovanović is drip-feeding me information to try and save his skin. He knows we've got him on disposal of a body, but there's no way he did that on his own. I'd be surprised if the work gangs he runs don't do a bit more than just building sites. Something to pass on to the NCA, I think. If nothing else, they've got a better budget than us for this kind of thing.'

McLean nodded his agreement at that, then took off his spectacles and snapped them closed. 'This young woman, Nadia, sounds like one for the modern slavery unit, too. They've got the cross-border connections needed to extract her son from whoever's got him. But if what she says is true, then it might well tie in with what I've found out.'

Janie watched as the DCI hauled himself out of his chair and walked across the office to the conference table. He was limping slightly, which meant the weather was about to turn bad most likely. When he reached out and pulled the top off the cardboard evidence box, the whispering came back again, almost loud enough to make out words.

'Did you say . . .? Oh.' Her question was cut short as he held up a clear plastic evidence bag, within which lay a dark wooden cube maybe fifteen centimetres on each side. 'Is that . . .?'

'This is what Paul Sanderson had clutched in his hands when he was found dead on that park bench, yes.' McLean unzipped the bag and reached inside. 'I thought he might have stolen it from the lab, but Professor Caine denied ever having seen it before. Thing is, I don't really believe him.'

Janie was so transfixed by the sight of the small object that she almost didn't catch what McLean had said. As he had pulled it from the bag, so the whispering had started up again. It reminded her of the time she and the DCI had visited Nathaniel Drake, only there was no PA muttering into her earpiece to blame this time.

'You don't?' she asked after quickly glancing at the door to see if someone was lurking outside.

'Well now, where to begin? I took this to Rose to see if she could give me any information about what it actually is.'

'Rose? Why her?'

McLean frowned at the question, still holding the box in one hand. 'It's . . . how can I put this? Would it surprise you if I said I thought it was having a strange effect on some of the officers here?'

Still hearing whispers that clearly weren't coming from anyone in the room, Janie could only shake her head slowly. 'No. Not really. How though?'

'Sandy Gregg didn't want to go anywhere near it. Don Gatford, of all people. He held the bag it was in like someone had just handed him a severed head. And DC Fairley—'

'Wait. Fairley? He's meant to be on medical leave. After he got punched in the face yesterday.'

'Is he? Well, I sent him home anyway. He'd signed this out of evidence along with the rest of Sanderson's things to see if he could find out anything from them. Not a bad idea really, but he was acting very strange. Over-eager, almost pushy.'

'That doesn't sound like Connor at all, although he's probably still got a concussion.'

'Aye, that was my thought, but I took that puzzle box to Rose for a look anyway. She spun me a tale like she always does, but she also managed to get it open, showed me what's inside.'

As he spoke these last words, McLean proffered the box to Janie for a closer look. Something about it repulsed her, and the whispering turned into a tinnitus whining in her ear like a swarm of mosquitoes. She went to bat them away, then realised what she was doing and turned the motion into a palm-out gesture of 'no, thanks'.

'And what is inside?' she asked instead.

'The mummified heart of a man who lived in what is now Eastern Europe about six hundred years ago, apparently. Someone who's supposed to have lived far longer than normal people, but who history has largely forgotten.'

Janie fought an overwhelming, irrational urge to turn and flee the room. Her own heart was racing, throat tightened, breath hard to take. What was happening to her? Still talking, McLean seemed not to have noticed her distress, which wasn't like him at all.

'And here's a thing,' he said. 'Professor Caine's been collecting artefacts just like this, using modern DNA sampling techniques to try and puzzle out why some people in ancient times lived far longer than average. That's the basis of his research and the therapies he's been developing to reverse ageing. What Nathaniel Drake's both paying for and using on himself.'

'So this . . .' Janie pointed at the box and felt her hand shaking at the effort, '. . . is almost certainly from the lab and originally came from Eastern Europe. Serbia?'

'It's certainly a coincidence, isn't it? And you know how I feel about them.'

Janie did, felt the same way about them herself, but when she opened her mouth to say so, the words wouldn't come out. All she could see was the box in McLean's hands, its intricate inlay swirling and moving in time to the whispering voices that rose up in her mind.

'Are you OK, Janie?' was the last thing she heard before everything went black.

40

'Janie? Janie? Are you OK?'

Janie's mind was a whirr of confusion as she struggled to consciousness. Somehow she was lying down, but this wasn't her bedroom and certainly not her bed. For a moment, she couldn't remember going to sleep, or indeed going home, and then the memories all came flooding back.

'Urgh. Wha . . .?' She struggled up to a sitting position, realising as she did so that she had been lying on the short sofa in DCI McLean's office. The man himself hunkered down a little distance away from her, which couldn't have been doing his hip much good.

'You passed out. Luckily I managed to catch you before you banged your head on the table.' He stood up with a creaking of joints and an ill-disguised grimace, went to the corner unit where the coffee machine lived and came back with a glass of water. Janie took it, sipped a little and swallowed.

'I . . .' She started to speak, then stopped as the bile began to rise in her throat. What the hell was happening to her?

'Take it slowly,' McLean said as he settled into one of the narrow armchairs opposite. 'Gave me quite a shock, so I imagine it's a lot worse for you.'

'What . . .' She tried the word before committing to a whole sentence. 'What the hell just happened?'

Even as she spoke, Janie remembered the puzzle box McLean had been holding, the whispers filling her head. She glanced over at the conference table and saw the cardboard evidence box with its lid securely closed.

'I put it away. Seemed to be having even more of an effect on you than on the others.'

'You think it was . . .?'

'Don't really know what to think, to be honest. You know me. I don't hold much truck with that kind of thing, the whole woowoo stuff Madame Rose spins. There's probably a perfectly rational explanation.'

Janie noted that the DCI didn't offer one. She took another swig of water, the cold liquid washing the taste of bile from her mouth and clearing her head a little. There had been the start of a migraine aura blurring the edges of her vision, but it dissolved away with each swallow. And good riddance to it, too.

'I don't hold much truck with that kind of thing either, but . . . Oof.' She put the empty glass down, rubbed at her eyes with the heels of her hands. 'I did not like being in close proximity to that box. If that's what it was.'

'Well, I put it back in its bag and packed it away. You certainly look a bit better than five minutes ago.'

Janie massaged her temples and rubbed her eyes again. She felt better than five minutes ago, too. And that damned whispering had stopped.

'It happened before,' she said.

'What, the fainting?' McLean asked.

'No, not that. Earlier. When you first got that bloody thing out, I heard voices whispering. Thought it was someone out in the corridor at first, but it wasn't coming from that direction. It was more like it was inside my head. Not nice.'

'I can imagine.'

'But I felt the same when we met Nathaniel Drake at his house.

That time I thought it was his PA being rude, but now I'm not so sure.'

McLean brought his hands up to his face, pressed fingers against his nose in a prayer-like gesture for a moment as he thought. 'Well, if my theory is right and Professor Caine is basing his miracle cure on samples taken from the heart inside that puzzle box . . .' He shook his head. 'No. There's no way you could react to the box and Drake in the same way. Could you? I can't think of anything that could have that kind of effect.'

'Nothing rational, for sure.' Janie levered herself to her feet, pleased to see that the room no longer swayed like the Aberdeen to Lerwick ferry in winter. Even so, McLean was on his feet in an instant, one hand out to steady her should she need it.

'You took the box to Rose,' she said. 'She opened it, showed you what was inside?'

'She did,' McLean said.

'Then maybe I'd better go and pay her a visit, since she's the most knowledgeable about it.' Janie looked at the evidence box on the conference table for what she hoped would be the last time. 'And maybe you could hide that away somewhere, aye?'

'Janie dear, this is a wonderful surprise. Come in, come in.'

It had been a while since Janie had last visited the eccentric medium's house on Leith Walk. True, she'd seen Madame Rose plenty of times at DCI McLean's place on the other side of town, but something had kept her from visiting her at home. Perhaps it was because she could see it becoming something of a habit if she let it. Rose was a good listener, and Janie knew the importance of having a sounding board outside of the police. Someone she could talk to in confidence and trust that what she said wouldn't become widespread gossip. Manda was a good foil too, as was Cerys, but they were too close to her work.

For all her oddness, her 'woowoo' as Janie and McLean

sometimes jokingly called it, Madame Rose was easy to like. It was just that occasionally Janie would see the medium glance at her with a look that was a little too calculating for comfort. As if Rose was measuring her up for something. Or maybe measuring her against McLean and Chief Superintendent McIntyre, both of whom had known her far longer.

'Sit yourself down while I make us a pot of tea.' The medium busied herself about the stove and cupboards after she had led Janie from the front door straight to the kitchen. The room had a warmth about it that was more than a comfortable temperature. A lived-in feel that made it easy to relax. After her earlier unexpected collapse and the threat of her first migraine in years, Janie was glad of the seat at the large, well-scrubbed table. A cake sat on a dish under a clear glass dome, two plates and some cutlery beside it that rather gave the lie to Madame Rose's earlier claim that Janie's visit was unexpected. Unless the medium always had cake waiting to be eaten, which was a possibility given her size and solid build.

Set apart from the cake stand and plates at an oddly uncomfortable distance lay a pair of tarnished silver sugar tongs. As she noticed them, so Janie too heard the faintest echo of a whisper behind her. She turned suddenly, seeing only a cat staring back at her with wary yellow eyes. When she turned back, Rose was standing directly opposite her, teapot in one over-large hand.

'Yes. I thought that might happen.' She put the teapot down, then picked up the sugar tongs and walked out of the room with them. Janie had barely registered the strangeness of the situation before she came back in again, tongless. She went straight to the sink and washed her hands like a surgeon preparing for the operating theatre.

'Can't be too careful, my dear,' Rose said as she came back to the table. She pulled out a chair close to Janie's and sat down. 'I would have sterilised those things after Tony's visit, but I needed to check. Cake?'

Janie could only watch as the medium plucked the glass cover from the cake stand and cut two extra-large slices, placing them on plates with the skill of decades' practice. Fully intending to decline, her grumbling stomach betrayed her at precisely the wrong moment. She accepted the offered plate, enough to feed her and Amanda both for a week, it seemed, and took a small bite. Only then did she realise how hungry she was, and had to resist the urge to pick up the whole piece and shove it in her face like a toddler at a birthday party.

'What's going on?' She placed the fork down on the plate with an effort of will that could conquer mountains. Madame Rose tilted her head slightly, the light catching her eyes and making them flash an unnatural green for an instant.

'You hear . . . voices?' she asked.

'Not now, but aye. Whispers mostly. Nothing I can make out, but the intonation sounds foreign? Does that make sense?'

'I would imagine you'd struggle to understand anything said by them, unless you're a student of medieval Serbo-Croatian in your spare time?'

'I . . . No.'

'They are echoes, Janie dear. The lamentations of long-dead souls, if you like.' Madame Rose made a face. 'But then you are of Tony's mind on these things, so I suppose you do not.'

'The puzzle box. The heart inside it. Whose is that?'

'Ah yes. Straight to the . . .' The medium paused, her broad face creasing into a smile at the unsaid pun. 'The box was part of a treasure trove dug up in a remote valley high in the Carpathian Mountains. I believe it was unearthed about five years ago as part of an expeditionary archaeological dig sponsored by an American billionaire of our mutual acquaintance.'

'So it is part of Nathaniel Drake's collection then.'

Madame Rose dipped her head from side to side in a gesture of uncertainty. 'Perhaps, although it's very possible he is unaware of it. He is not a serious collector, you see. Not someone in dogged pursuit of knowledge and understanding as such. More he likes the shiny things. And of course he wants to live for ever, although I can't for the life of me imagine why. It's very much overrated.'

'And the heart?' Janie asked. She knew too well how Madame Rose could go off on a tangent if you let her.

'The heart, yes. That's the really important bit. I think . . . and even I don't have all the answers sometimes, Janie dear, but I think the heart once beat in the chest of a very particular man. One who has disappeared into obscurity, but whose exploits have been the root of many myths and legends. Even his true name is lost, but he was advisor to both Vlad Dracul and his son Vlad the Impaler. Indeed, the legends speak of one man behind the thrones of that troubled region for many hundreds of years. The literature refers to him as the magus, and it's possible of course that many different men took on that title, but my reading of the matter suggests just the one.'

'But that's . . .'

'Impossible? Well, of course it is. But impossible things happen every day, Janie. No, what you should be asking yourself is why someone would be interested in the heart in the first place. It was hidden away for a reason, after all.'

'And that was?'

'Why is a heart ever torn from its body? Why must the two be separated, one burned to ashes and the other locked away in a puzzle box of fiendish design?' Madame Rose leaned forward, her elbows on the table, hands clasped together under her chin as she stared at Janie with uncomfortable intensity.

'I genuinely have no idea,' she said, much to the disappointment of the medium. She had some thoughts on the matter, mostly leaning towards the 'what a load of old bollocks' end of the spectrum, but she was also tired and needed to get back to the real world, so forcing Madame Rose to come to the point seemed the best way to proceed.

'Oh. Well. It's quite simple, really. The magus had been too powerful for too long. That's bound to make you enemies, and eventually one of them will work out a way to be rid of you. They killed him, of course, burned his body and scattered the ashes so he couldn't come back. But his soul is a more tricky thing to destroy. That, they trapped in his heart and locked away in that box.'

'So when you opened it, his soul was freed?' Janie knew it couldn't be that simple, but asked anyway.

'Heavens, no. It would take more than simply opening the box to do that, dear. And besides, I wasn't the first to open it. Someone else did that. Someone with rare skill and knowledge, too.'

'Professor Caine?'

'And now you understand.' Rose clapped her massive hands together like a delighted child.

'Well, yes and no. I mean, I get what Caine's trying to do even if it's mad. Why not try to see if there's a biological factor behind people who've lived a long life? That's reasonable enough. But there's folk live a hundred years and more today. Why not study them rather than go digging up ancient remains?'

'That, my dear, is something you'll have to take up with him. The important thing to understand is that when you hear those whispers, you're not imagining it and you're not going mad.'

41

He should have been sorting out a team to pay a visit to Drake Biotech, calling in Professor Caine and Drake himself for interview, or at the very least waiting to hear from Janie Harrison how she had got on with Madame Rose. Instead, McLean found himself driving the little Renault Zoe away from the station in the direction of the Royal Infirmary. He had even texted ahead to let Emma know he was on his way, although she hadn't responded yet.

Being alone in the car as he crawled along with the traffic at Cameron Toll at least gave him time to think without fear of being interrupted by some new request from admin or one of his team of detectives. Not that he could make much sense of the various threads of investigation that were beginning to form the suggestion of a pattern. Too many questions that still needed answers, too many moving parts. Not helped by the uncomfortable feeling of weirdness about it all.

McLean had meant it when he'd told Janie he didn't hold much truck with such things. The mystical mumbo jumbo that Rose dealt in could almost always be rationally explained if you tried hard enough. But 'almost' wasn't the same as 'always', and there had been times over the years where he'd been hard pushed to find any explanation at all. The young detective inspector's reaction to the presence of the puzzle box was something he might have been able to file away as odd but not too worrying. Perhaps she was coming down with something, or just over-worked like everyone else. DC Fairley had taken a blow to the head and really shouldn't have been back at work, so his behav-iour could be explained away too. But was that enough to have planted a subconscious dislike of the box in the minds of the rest of the team? Sandy Gregg had backed away from it, after all. And Don Gatford was usually the most down to earth of people, so his reaction had been a surprise.

No, once was unusual, twice could be a coincidence, but three, four and more times? That was harder to dismiss. And dammit, Rose was very persuasive when she went full-on clairvoyant. There would be a rational explanation, of course. The box needed to undergo a full scientific analysis, really. He felt a bit bad about leaving it in the evidence store, but on balance it was probably safest tucked away in the basement of a police station, out of sight and out of mind.

Something of her strange magic must have still been working on him all the same, as McLean found a parking space almost straight away and only a few minutes' walk from the hospital entrance. His shoulders and hair were still damp from a sudden squall of rain by the time he made it inside though. Patting his face dry with a handkerchief, he almost missed Dr Wheeler coming down the corridor towards him.

'Oh, Tony. I didn't realise you were coming in. Em took a taxi home about fifteen minutes ago. Did she not text you?'

Instinctively, McLean fetched out his phone and swiped the screen awake, even though he knew he'd not had any messages since leaving the station.

'Apparently not.' He shrugged, put the phone away. 'Ah well. Not a completely wasted journey. I was hoping I might have a word with you anyway. If you've a few minutes to spare.'

The doctor gave him a knowing look. 'Is this about Emma?'

'Not exactly, no.'

Doctor Wheeler sighed, her shoulders slumping slightly for a moment. McLean knew all too well how overworked everyone in the hospital was, senior consultants as much as any, and the doctor was overseeing far more than her roster of patients like Emma. Which was, of course, why he wanted to talk to her. She shoved her clipboard under one arm, looked around as if only then realising where she was. 'Why don't you come in here where we can have a little privacy.'

McLean followed her to a security door, which she opened with a swipe of the ID card hanging on a lanyard around her neck. There was a small consulting room beyond it, a desk, two chairs and an unprepared examination table. One wall had a couple of old posters tacked to it, depicting the central nervous and circulatory systems in rather too graphic detail. He tried not to look at them as he sat down, but Dr Wheeler moved her own chair to a position where she was flanked by the two flayed bodies.

'Since you're not concerned about Emma, I take it this is about Drake Biotech? Professor Caine?'

McLean started to protest that he was very concerned about Emma, but stopped himself before any unhelpful words came out. Dr Wheeler had always been friendly in the past; he didn't want to spoil that relationship now.

'Aye. I've spoken to him a couple of times now, but I can't really decide what to make of him. He didn't start off as a biochemist though, I understand.'

'No, although I can't exactly criticise him for that. I've hardly specialised in just the one field myself. Magnus has always been something of a dilettante, although I think he would prefer the term polymath. Or perhaps renaissance man would suit him better. He pursues knowledge like a dog after a ball, but he's easily distracted by another ball if one comes past.'

'Sounds like you don't much rate him as an academic.'

'Am I that obvious?' Wheeler reached for the clipboard that she'd placed on the table beside her, realised what she was doing and shoved both hands together into her lap. McLean didn't need a degree in psychology to read the signs. She had been on the way to something important and he was keeping her from it, taking up valuable time.

'So why work with him then?' he asked. 'More specifically, how did you end up working with him? Did you approach him or he you?'

'Oh, he came to me. I wasn't exactly looking for more work.' The doctor tilted her head towards the clipboard. 'But the proposal came with a lot of money behind it courtesy of Nathaniel Drake. These are straitened times, Tony, as I've no doubt you know. Detective chief inspectors running around doing the work of sergeants. I'm sure you'd welcome more resources.'

'As long as they didn't come with too many strings.' McLean knew from bitter experience the problems that arose when private money got into policing. 'So Professor Caine came to you with money and a plan. Do you know how long he'd been working with Drake? How they met?'

'Ah, there's a story if you want to know how easily distracted Magnus can be. He was working on an archaeological dig somewhere in Eastern Europe. Serbia, I think. He has connections there, apparently. Drake found out about what he was doing. I've no idea how or why it came across his radar, but Nathaniel's a bit like that. Always picking up new shiny things. I guess he and Magnus are peas in a pod that way.'

'This dig was the last resting place of some long-lived figure of myth, I take it?'

'Oh, so you know Magnus's theory then.' Dr Wheeler looked a little crestfallen, as if she'd been hoping to spring the news on him as a surprise.

'He told me himself. Sounds, I don't know . . .'

'Insane? That was my take the first time he told me where he was getting his samples from. But his results are impressive. Leaps and bounds ahead of everyone else in the field. Sometimes it feels a bit like magic.'

'But it's not though, is it?'

'Magic? No, of course not. Any technology sufficiently advanced beyond the understanding of a population will seem like magic, but there's always an explanation. A logical, controllable explanation.'

'And Drake is happy with this, I take it?'

Dr Wheeler laughed. 'Nathaniel? Of course. He's the one bankrolling it all. Sees it as his moon shot. He really believes he can live for ever and Magnus can make that happen. Me, I'll take the funding and move a bit more slowly. If we can find a way to reverse stroke damage or stop things like Alzheimer's developing in the first place, then I'll be happy. But Nathaniel's not looking to cure cancer so much as reprogram himself to never get it in the first place. That's the line of research he and Magnus have been pursuing, and I have to say it's not really producing the results they want. Not quickly enough, for sure.'

McLean reached into his jacket pocket and pulled out the photograph of the puzzle box. 'Have you seen this before?' he asked.

Dr Wheeler took the sheet of paper, stared at it for a while, then shook her head slowly. 'Don't think so. What is it?'

'It's a medieval puzzle box that contains a mummified human heart, part of which has been shaved off with a scalpel recently. From what we know about Professor Caine's research methods, I'd expect it to be something he'd dug up somewhere, but he denies ever having seen it.'

Dr Wheeler looked at the image again, then up at McLean. 'You think this was taken from the lab when those eco warriors broke in?'

'That's one theory, yes.'

'But that lab hasn't been commissioned yet. Nothing on that site has. It's all still being built. If Magnus was doing bio-assays on archaeological finds he'd be using the facilities here. Everything's running here until the new place is finished. It's been a nightmare accommodating it all with all the construction delays. Sooner we can move everything over the better, so that break-in was a proper nuisance.'

It was possible Caine was telling the truth about the box, of course, although McLean doubted his gut was wrong when he thought the professor was lying. He'd hoped his chat with Dr Wheeler would clarify things, but if anything the picture was even muddier now. Time to stop talking to the minions and make a nuisance of himself with the boss.

'I've stolen too much of your time already, Caroline. You've been very helpful, as ever. Thank you for that. And for keeping an eye on Emma. I'll be sure and remind her to text me next time.'

'Just try to get her to eat a bit more, can you?' Dr Wheeler was on her feet, clipboard snatched up and at the door in an instant. 'She's not doing herself any favours right now.'

McLean checked his watch. Not quite knocking-off time, if such a thing existed in senior-detective world, but not far off either. 'I'll drop by the house just now, check she got home OK.'

42

I f he cast his mind back far enough, McLean could recall a time
when the house hadn't filled him with unease. As a child, he'd
often sneaked into the gardens for the thrill of it, even if the
chances of being caught by the elderly couple who lived there were
small. And if they had caught him, they'd as likely have invited
him in for tea and biscuits as given him any grief for his tres-
passing.

Mr and Mrs Guthrie, that was their name. He'd not thought of
them in years. The old man had been a merchant banker before
that became a euphemism, and she had mostly done charity work.
They were older even than his grandmother, childless. He'd died
first, and she'd not waited long to join him, but McLean was away
at his hated boarding school by then, and past such games as sneak-
ing into the neighbours' garden.

And then somewhere along the line Gavin Spenser had bought
the house. Almost certainly because it was so close to McLean's
grandmother. He'd carried a torch for Esther Morrison since first
meeting her at university in the 1930s, but she'd never felt anything but contempt for him. McLean had a suspicion he knew
why, even if it was something he didn't like to think about too
hard. He could still see the old man, dead in his study, murdered
by his own bodyguard. Spenser had died intestate, despite being

worth a king's ransom, and the house had lain empty for a few years while lawyers got rich arguing over the corpse.

Then along had come Jane Louise Dee, apparently at ease living in the house where someone had died so violently. Or maybe not, given that she had moved out after a few months to a massive mansion east of the city. She'd still kept the house though, empty and mothballed. A place even grown-up McLean avoided if he could.

Which was why he was sitting in Emma's car, staring through the windscreen at the mostly dark facade. There were security gates to negotiate before he could gain entry, and he wasn't sure he really wanted the hassle. But mostly it was the sense of unease the place gave him, an itch at the base of his skull and a chill in his stomach.

He was being stupid, he knew. It was just a house, not defined by the people who had lived in it for little more than a tenth of its existence. Winding down the window, he reached out and pressed the intercom. Readied himself to justify his visit to some faceless security guard. Instead, the tall iron gates began to swing open in smooth silence. The only sound as he eased the car forward through the gap was the crunch of its tyres on the fresh gravel, and even that faded to nothing as he wound the window back up again.

By the time he'd reached the parking area, the front door was open, light spilling out and casting the waiting figure in silhouette. McLean hadn't realised it was so late, glanced briefly at his watch to see that it wasn't. Low dark clouds had robbed the day of its final hours and threatened a downpour soon.

'Tony, welcome.' Nathaniel Drake greeted him as he stepped into the light. 'Or is it Detective Chief Inspector? Business call or pleasure?'

'Business, I'm afraid. But Tony's fine. Just wanted a wee chat about a few things that have come to light after the break-in at the lab.'

Without the intense back light, McLean could see Drake's face now and couldn't help noticing the raised eyebrow. Not so much the raising of it, which was probably fair enough given his opening gambit. More it was the way it stayed up longer than it should have done, slowly oozing back down into place like melted ice cream. Moved more by gravity than muscle. Drake's skin had a slightly waxy, unreal quality to it McLean didn't recall noticing the last time they'd been face to face.

'Come in, why don't you? Reckon it's going to rain soon. Just as well you drove.' Drake leaned to one side so that he could look past the detective chief inspector. 'Still driving Em's car, I see. Going to have to get me one of those.'

'Really? I'd have thought you'd be chauffeured everywhere. Stretch limousine with bulletproof glass sort of thing.'

'That's just a target on your back though.' Drake waved for McLean to follow as he crossed the hall towards the study. Trying hard not to think of his last encounter with Jane Louise Dee in front of that open fireplace, thankfully not lit now, he stepped through to the room where Gavin Spenser had breathed his last.

'You OK, Tony? Look like you've seen a ghost.'

'It's nothing. Just memories.'

'That's right. You and this house go back a long way, right?' Drake walked around the large desk and flopped into his chair. That very same chair, or so it appeared, where another impossibly wealthy man had died. Nothing in the room had changed. Apart from the blood, of course. That had been cleaned up. And the heavy lamp he'd broken over the bodyguard's head was gone too.

'You could say that.' He was about to add a comment about the room being unchanged, but now he was here, he found he wanted to leave as soon as possible. Small talk be damned.

'How long have you known Professor Caine?' McLean watched

Drake's face for any visual tics as he asked the question, but there was nothing. When he answered, his skin shifted over his features like soft rubber sheeting. As if he was a state-of-the-art robot rather than a man.

'Magnus? I'd say maybe five years? Six? Why?'

'I'm just trying to get my head around why a group of animal rights activists would target your lab. It's there on your company website that you don't use animals for testing. Everything's bio-assays and in-vitro. So I was wondering if maybe it was something to do with the head of research. He has a colourful past, does he not?'

Drake laughed at that, although again McLean was struck by how unlifelike his movements were. Not quite robotic, but not human either.

'Magnus is certainly a maverick, Tony. I'll grant you that. But he's quite brilliant as long as you can keep him on track. He does tend to get a little distracted if his mind's not a hundred per cent occupied by what he's doing.'

'A bit like Sherlock Holmes, I suppose.'

Drake tilted his head to one side, a frown trying to form but not quite succeeding. 'Oh, right. Yes, I get you. I don't think Magnus would resort to opium and bad violin playing if he got bored though. And right now he's completely focused on the work we're doing at Drake Biotech.'

'So he's moved on from the archaeology completely then?'

Was that a narrowing of Drake's eyes? The man's face moved so little it was almost impossible to tell. He sat up a little straighter in his chair though, and clasped his hands together, index fingers pointing towards McLean almost like a gun as they rested on the desktop.

'What are you getting at, Detective Chief Inspector? Has Magnus done something wrong?'

'I don't think I'm qualified to say, really. The research he does is so far beyond my understanding it might as well be magic. But I've heard tell that things haven't been going as well as planned. Results not what you were hoping for.'

'Me?' Drake pointed one hand at himself, keeping the other still trained on McLean. 'Or is that a plural "you"?'

'I'm sure Professor Caine is as frustrated with progress as anyone, but you're the one who writes the cheques. You're the one chasing a dream of living for ever.'

Something shifted in Drake's posture then, a relaxing of muscles McLean hadn't noticed were tensed. That was the problem with the man, he was difficult to read physically.

'And Magnus is attacking that problem with his usual unconventional methods, but I can assure you he's not doing anything illegal. He's not trying to cut corners just because I'm impatient for results. Ours isn't that kind of relationship.'

'What is it, then? You leave him to his own devices?'

Drake made an expansive gesture with both hands. 'I keep an eye on things, make sure the money's being spent wisely, but like you say, most of the science is beyond my understanding too. I just go by the results we've had so far.'

'So you're not unhappy with progress then?'

'I didn't say that, no. You've seen the lab, right? It's what? Two years behind schedule? More maybe? That's hurting my bottom line, for sure, but it's not Magnus's fault. And what he has done so far is pretty good. I'm fitter and healthier than I've felt in ages. All down to Magnus.'

McLean might have said that Drake didn't exactly look fit and healthy, more freakish and unnatural, but diplomacy had always been one of his better skills. Instead, he took the now slightly crumpled sheet of paper from his jacket pocket, unfolded it and passed it across the desk.

'Do you recognise this?'

Drake picked up the page, tilted it to the light, craned his neck to peer more closely than a man with perfect, rejuvenated eyesight should have needed to, then put the picture back down.

'Come with me,' he said.

McLean followed Drake out of the study, through parts of the old house that he'd not seen in maybe forty years or more, but which looked almost unchanged from when Mr and Mrs Guthrie had lived there. For a man worth something close to the gross domestic product of a small South American nation, Drake had very little by way of either security or staff, but McLean noticed a couple of dark-suited men loitering in the hallway, and at least one cleaner as they climbed the stairs to the first floor.

'I've always had a fascination for ancient history,' the tech billionaire said as he opened a door and gestured for McLean to enter. 'That's how I met Magnus, on an archaeological dig in Eastern Europe.'

The room they entered was large, its ceiling high and with the ornate cornicing that was such a signature of Edinburgh houses of its vintage. Three large windows on the far wall looked out onto the gardens McLean had once snuck through as a boy, and beyond them the tree-filled narrow gorge of the Hermitage of Braid. Arranged around the rest of the room, on shelves and in display cabinets, was an array of stuff that would have made Madame Rose go weak at the knees.

'I'd heard you were something of a collector. This is very impressive.' McLean crossed the room to where a full Japanese samurai outfit glowered at the world as if it still contained the warrior within.

'Oh, this is just a small part of it. The stuff that was already in the UK. I've a warehouse just outside San Francisco where most of it's kept. But I wanted you to have a look at these.' Drake led McLean to the far corner, where a display cabinet housed several wooden objects on individual shelves. He took one out and handed over what turned out to be a small wooden box, inlaid in the same intricate pattern as the puzzle box. Unlike that, this one had a clearly defined lid, and opened at McLean's touch to reveal an empty interior.

'From the tomb of an adviser to the Dracul family,' Drake said. 'Or at least that's what Magnus told me. That's where we met. I'd read an article about his research and how the rest of the scientific community thought he was either nuts, a fraud or both. Decided I just had to meet him.'

McLean turned the box over in his hands, marvelling at the skill of the work that had gone into it. The pieces should really be in a museum, not tucked out of sight in a rich man's house, but he kept that opinion to himself.

'They're very similar to the box in the photo I showed you. The expert I consulted about that reckoned it was from that part of the world and that time in history too. It would fit right in with these ones. You sure you've never seen it before?'

Drake took the box back when McLean offered it, placed it in the cabinet and closed the door before answering. 'I think I'd remember something like that, yeah. Where'd you find it?'

'I can't really say right now. Part of an ongoing investigation. I thought it might have come from the research lab, but Professor Caine is sure he's never seen it either.'

Something that might have been a frown passed over Drake's features, although it was hard to tell. 'Why would it be there?' he asked.

'It contains a mummified heart. I thought perhaps the professor was using it for his experiments.'

'But that lab's not functional yet. There's no work going on there even if Magnus did have it.' Drake looked around as if searching for the picture. McLean fished it out of his pocket and handed it to him. 'A heart, huh? No, if he had that he'd have told me.'

'And yet it's almost certainly from the same tomb. What are the chances of it turning up here, in Edinburgh, when these other pieces are so close by?'

Drake looked from picture to display cabinet and back again, several times, shaking his head more and more. Finally he stopped, handed the page back.

'I really can't help you there, Tony. Genuinely the first time I've seen that piece. Would love to add it to the collection if I could. Far as I know, that tomb had been raided before, at least twice. It's possible that box was taken one of those times. How it ended up in Scotland, I've no idea.'

It took him rather longer to extract himself from Nathaniel Drake's company than he would have liked, enduring both a tour of the house and a very nice cup of tea before McLean could leave. The first at least helped to erase the uneasiness he felt about the place; whatever bad vibes Gavin Spenser and Mrs Saifre had left on the place, Drake was doing a fine job in erasing them. The second he would have declined, had it not been for the certain knowledge that news of his visit would make its way back to the chief constable and first minister before the end of the day. All of which meant that by the time he piloted the little electric Renault out through the security gates, the evening briefing at the station was long over and the day-shift detectives would likely all have gone home.

The short drive to his own house didn't give much time for reflection on what he had learned from his talk with the billionaire. McLean had shown the photograph of the puzzle box to three people now, all of whom had denied seeing it before. Of those three he was fairly certain Dr Wheeler was telling the truth, or at least what she thought was the truth. Drake was more difficult to read, but also he had shown McLean his collection of similar artefacts without hesitation. There wasn't much reason for him to do that if he was trying to pretend he'd never seen the piece in the picture, unless he was trying for some elaborate double bluff.

Which left Professor Caine, who had already lied about a great many things. As he pulled up in front of the coach house doors and turned off the car, McLean made up his mind. In the morning they'd bring the professor in to the station, sit him down in an interview room, and sweat some truth out of him. A man had died clinging on to that box like it was his most dear possession, and then that same man's body had been stolen from the mortuary. If that didn't warrant a little inconvenience for the professor, McLean didn't know what did. And if Caine complained to his boss about that, then so be it.

43

It was still mostly dark when Janie arrived at the station that morning, the dawn light swallowed by low cloud. Puddles lay across the car park like scattered gems, little rainbows of oil glistening the surface of those nearest the armoured Transit vans. Someone in maintenance wasn't doing their job properly, it seemed. Overworked and understaffed like the rest of them, she reckoned.

Inside, the station was at its quietest, the time she liked the best. She grabbed a coffee from the vending machine on the ground floor, then climbed the stairs to the incident room. Half expecting to find at least a couple of the night shift asleep in their chairs, she was pleasantly surprised by the cheery smile DC Bryant gave her.

'You're in early, J. Couldn't sleep? Or do you just love this place so much you can't bear to stay away?'

She hadn't slept much, Janie had to admit. Between the worries about her imminent eviction and the talk she'd had with Madame Rose, her mind had been too much of a turmoil for her to drop off. It didn't help that her flatmate was away on some training junket for a few days either. Janie had a simple rule of never drinking when she was alone, which meant the half-bottle of Chardonnay that might have helped in the short term had instead remained in the fridge. It was probably for the best.

'You know me, Jessica. Glutton for punishment.' She glanced

around the room, not much in the way of activity to see. 'Anything interesting come up while I was away?'

'Not really. We've tracked down a bit more CCTV to go over, but that's Lofty's gig and he's not in yet.' Bryant leaned against the nearest desk and ran a hand through her hair, somehow managing to still look fresh despite having worked through the night. Janie wished she knew what the secret was, she could have done with some of it herself.

'Did you see that old wooden box the DCI had out of evidence yesterday?' she asked.

'The one they found with the dead body out in the park? Aye. Creepy thing. Made my skin all itchy just being in the same room as it. Why'd you ask?'

'Just something I wanted to check. Wasn't sure whether to go up to his office for it or back down to the basement.'

'It's back in evidence now. I saw Lofty taking it down there after the briefing last night.' Bryant stretched and yawned expansively, as if only then remembering she'd been on duty ever since then.

'You can knock off a wee bit early if you want, Jessica.' Janie checked her watch. 'I'll no' tell your line manager.'

'I'm fine, J. But thanks. Still some reports to get squared away before the morning crowd arrive.'

Janie left the detective constable to her work, set off towards the basement and the evidence store. She heard whispers as she stepped off the stairs into the rear atrium of the station, but it turned out to be a couple of uniform constables having a chat in the corridor to the locker rooms. Pretending not to have noticed them, she took the next flight down. The quiet deepened the further she went, only the slight squeak of her soles on the linoleum floor to break the silence. As she approached the door through to the store, it occurred to her that this early there might not be anyone there. Evidence might need to be logged at any time of night or day, but like everywhere else in the station, staffing was a problem.

It didn't look good as she entered the reception room. The metal shuttering had been pulled down over the counter where items were signed in and out. Janie could make out a line of brightness underneath it though, and in the crack beneath the door alongside. Either someone was in there catching forty winks, or they locked up the night before without checking the lights. She raised her hand and rapped gently on the door.

'Anyone in?'

As she spoke the words, Janie realised that she still hadn't heard any whispering. The only noise was the sound of chair legs scraping and low muttering that had the distinct edge of curses to it. On instinct, she took a step back from the door, as if expecting it to fly open. Instead, the clattering of chain against metal heralded the rise of the shutter, like dawn come to the basement world. Only when it was fully open did the man behind it lean forward, gnarly old hands on the counter, and peer out like a bear rudely awakened from hibernation.

'Have you any idea what time . . .? Oh, morning, Detective Inspector. Sorry about all that. I was just—'

'Doing an important audit of the most recent additions to the store, Don?' Janie offered.

'Something like that, aye.' Sergeant Gatford rubbed sleep from the corner of one eye and stifled a yawn. 'Got to be careful with the evidence, right enough. Sacred duty and all that. Now, since you're not carrying anything with you, I suspect you're after something. What can I get you this fine morning?'

Janie leaned her elbows on the counter, stared past the sergeant to the rows of shelving and endless steel cabinets arrayed behind him. She still couldn't hear any whispering, and while she was glad of it, she was also a little worried.

'I don't want to check anything out. Just have a wee look-see. That box we found on the dead man in the . . . What?' Janie's question died in the face of Sergeant Gatford's expression.

'You've already got it, haven't you?' he said.

'The puzzle box? No. I don't think so. I was just up in the incident room and it's no' there.'

'But . . .' Gatford reached for his clipboard, a fresh chain of evidence sheet at the front of it. He flipped it out of the way to reveal the sheet beneath, already filled out. 'You sent the young lad down for it already, didn't you?'

Janie pulled the clipboard towards her, taking in the information swiftly. Sure enough, the puzzle box had been signed out of evidence late the previous night, only a few hours after DS Blane had handed it back in. No wonder Sergeant Gatford was annoyed at the team, but also no wonder Janie couldn't hear any whispering. Although she had been hoping she wouldn't anyway.

She checked her watch, checked the time on the sheet again. Could it have been up in the incident room when she'd gone in there earlier? No, she'd have seen it even if it wasn't trying to fill her head with nonsense. And DC Bryant would have told her too. Another glance at the sheet, the name printed beside the scrawled signature. Detective Constable Connor Fairley was supposed to be on medical leave. So what was he doing checking evidence out of the store?

And where on earth were he and the puzzle box now?

'He's not answering his phone, and he's no' at his mum's.'

Janie stood in the middle of a rather busier incident room. An hour had passed since she'd discovered the puzzle box missing, and the mystery of its disappearance was only getting deeper. No one had seen DC Fairley come in or leave, which was causing the duty sergeant a great deal of embarrassment. Even now a couple of constables were going through the station's own CCTV to pin down exactly when the young lad had gone, and hopefully in which direction.

'Wait. He still stays with his mum?' The question was out before Janie had time to think it through. Given that she was about to be evicted from her flat, and still hadn't found anywhere else to go, it wasn't perhaps all that surprising that Connor should still be living at home. She might end up in her old bedroom in Broxburn if she wasn't lucky.

'Have you seen what rents are like these days?' Bryant replied, then added, 'Sorry, J. Course you have. That was insensitive of me.'

'No bother. Did she say when she last saw him? His mum, that is?'

'Aye, says he went out about eight last night. Told her he was on the night shift. She gave me a bit of an earful about that actually.' Bryant rubbed at the side of her head as if it still stung. 'Thought we should be going easy on him, what with being injured in the line of duty and all that.'

'Did you tell her he was meant to be on medical leave?'

'Aye, no. Thought it would maybe worry her even more. You know what mums can be like.'

Janie did, although it had been a while since last she'd spoken to hers. Time to try a different tack.

'Has he got an airwave set? Can we track him on that?'

Bryant shook her head. 'Aye, he has an airwave set. We all do. No, we can't track him on it cos it's in his desk drawer in the CID room. He didn't even lock it.'

'OK. Get on to the phone company and see if they can triangulate him from his mobile.' Janie paused before adding, 'Unless that's in his desk drawer too?'

'No. Reckon he's still got it with him, but it's just going to voicemail every time I try. Might be switched off.'

Janie was about to suggest that it might be because he was lying face down in a ditch somewhere, but was interrupted by the incident-room door swinging open to reveal DCI McLean and Chief Superintendent McIntyre. They had clearly been in heated conversation all the way from wherever they had met, the end of it spilling out across the suddenly silent room.

'What were you thinking, bringing something like that in here in the first place?'

'Be reasonable, Jayne. It's evidence. What else was I supposed to do with it? Ask Rose to lock it up in her basement?'

'I . . .' But whatever the chief superintendent's suggestion was going to be, she kept it to herself as the realisation that they had arrived at their destination dawned on the both of them. McIntyre straightened her jacket, gaze sweeping the room until she spotted Janie.

'Please tell me this is all some terrible joke and both DC Fairley and the evidence he took from the stores have been found?'

At least she made it a question at the end, Janie supposed. 'Nothing yet, sorry. We only found out what he'd done an hour ago. He signed the box out of evidence at half ten last night, but nobody we've spoken to even saw him here except Sergeant Gatford.'

'How can . . .?' the chief superintendent began to ask, but then dismissed the question with a single shake of the head. 'What are you doing to find him?'

'Well, as far as we can tell he came and left on foot. That's not to say he didn't get a taxi or hop on a bus, but none of the pool cars are unaccounted for.' Janie ran through the rest of the actions they were taking, swiftly because there weren't many.

'OK, so where he's taken it is still unknown. How about why he took it? Was he planning on selling it? Has he got debts he can't pay? Or might someone have approached him about it, offered him a wad of cash to steal it from evidence?'

'If that was what he was doing, he'd hardly sign it out in his own name, would he?' McLean asked.

'I don't think he'd do something like this for money,' DC Bryant chimed in. 'Connor's about as straight as they come. It'd be sweet if it wasn't a little annoying sometimes.'

'So why did he do this then?' McIntyre asked.

'Maybe someone's threatened him?' Janie said. 'Only, what with? This is career-ending behaviour.'

'He was acting quite strangely yesterday,' McLean said. 'Thought it was concussion from him being punched. Told him to take some time off. I should really have followed that up and checked how he was doing.'

Janie opened her mouth to protest that it was her responsibility, but she was cut off by the chief superintendent.

'Let's not go apportioning blame until the problem's solved, shall we? At least until young Connor's been found. Is everyone here?' McIntyre cast her gaze around the room as if she were a primary school teacher doing a head count. 'More or less. Why don't we have a quick briefing. Tony, what were your actions for the day?'

Janie watched the detective chief inspector gather his thoughts, but before he could share them with everyone else in the room, the door burst open and a uniform constable hurried in. By the look on her face, something terrible had happened. As she began to tell them, phones began buzzing in pockets and on tables. Janie felt her own handset buzz in her jacket.

'It's the detective constable. Connor. There's been an incident.' Everyone besides Janie, McLean and Chief Superintendent McIntyre was looking at their phones, not paying any heed to the flustered constable.

'Take your time, Kayleigh. What's happened and where?'

'Connor, ma'am. DC Fairley. They say he broke into that research lab out at Easter Bush. Beat up two of the security guards.'

Janie was lost for words, as, it would seem, was the chief superintendent. It was left to McLean to ask the obvious question.

'Is he still there?'

The constable looked at him as if he was mad to ask. How could he not already know? 'Aye, sir. He's no' going anywhere. He's deid.'

44

'Caine's not at his home, and that snooty PA has just told me that Mr Drake is out and cannot be contacted, whatever that's supposed to mean.'

McLean watched through the corner of his eye as DI Harrison ended the latest of a number of calls she had made since they had left the station, headed south. She didn't put the handset away, but instead fidgeted with it as she stared ahead. Preoccupied, frustrated, shocked. They both were.

'Could be Drake's at the lab, or maybe the hospital?'

'I've got Jessica on to tracking them both down. She was night shift, should really be going home for a kip, but I don't think any of us are going to get much sleep for a while.'

'Any more information about what's happened to Connor?'

'Not a lot. Only that he turned up at the lab, waved his warrant card at the security guards and then attacked them both when they tried to stop him going into the building. One's still unconscious and the other's not making much sense. Says that Connor knocked him out too, and when he came round he found, well . . . Guess we'll find out.'

Rain spattered the windscreen as McLean turned off the main road and into the parking area in front of Drake Biotech's new labs. Wet, the building took on an even more sinister aura. Its glass frontage was streaked with tears, or was that just his sense of foreboding? A couple of squad cars had already arrived, constables rolling out tape to establish a cordon around the car park. That seemed a little daft to him, given how large the building site was and how many other entrances there must be.

'Going to have to get more officers in if we want to seal this place up tight. Shut down any building work and put a list together of everyone who's here.'

He'd spoken the words towards the view in front of the car, but when he turned it was to see Harrison already out the open door, her desperate hurry evident in her every move. McLean unclipped his seat belt in a more leisurely manner, clambered out of the driver's seat, locked up and took a path around the puddles. An ambulance stood silent a few metres from the front door, its lights still spinning in a lazy arc. Inside, a paramedic crouched beside the seated form of a security guard, one hand holding a bandage to his forehead. Blood seeped through the white gauze, and the guard had that faraway stare of someone in deep shock.

'Who's in charge?' he asked of the first constable he found. A young lad out of Mortonhall station, if memory served. PC Jesmond, wasn't it? Keith?

'Sergeant Stephen was first at the scene, sir, along with PC Inchly. They're away at the building site offices just now.'

McLean didn't know Police Constable Inchly, but Kenny Stephen was a reliable man to have in charge of securing a crime scene. 'OK. That's good. Me and DI Harrison are going to have a look at the . . .' He paused, somehow unable to say 'body'. Jesmond nodded in understanding.

'He's in the lab up that way.' He pointed towards the corridor McLean knew led to the lab that had been broken into. Of course that was where he was. Where else would he be?

'Thanks. Don't let anyone else into the building except for the duty doctor and pathologist, OK? Names and contact details of anyone who was already here.'

The constable nodded his understanding as McLean set off towards the lab. He found Harrison already at the door, bent down and examining the entry code keypad. It looked like it had been melted, charred wires poking out of a mess of plastic that gave off a foul chemical reek.

'What the hell could have done that?' Harrison asked, not waiting for an answer before pushing through the unlocked door. Her urgency was perhaps understandable, although McLean knew it was also misplaced. Speed was no longer of the essence here. It was too late for that. Still, he lengthened his stride to keep up as the detective inspector crossed the lab to the door at the other end. The room had been tidied since the last time he'd been there, the benches all neatly organised, expensive machinery humming away quietly to itself. Even the graffiti had been painted over. Only the area near the door was disturbed, the keypad for the entry system destroyed in a manner similar to the first one. Another pair of uniform officers stood a little further away from the closed door than might be expected of a team guarding a crime scene.

'Sir, ma'am,' the older of the two said. Police Sergeant Barney Clifford was an old hand and as steady as they came. The expression on his face told McLean everything he needed to know.

'He's in there?' He nodded towards the door. 'You been inside, Barney?'

'Aye, sir. Only for a moment, but we had to check he was . . .' Sergeant Clifford swallowed hard, his Adam's apple tight in his neck. 'Closed the door an' no one else's been in since.'

McLean nodded. 'Thanks. You keep an eye out for the doctor, aye? We'll have a wee look, see what's going on.'

PS Clifford almost deflated with relief, the tension flooding out of him as he tapped the young constable on the shoulder. 'Come on, son. Let's leave the detectives to their job, aye?'

The two of them picked a path through the laboratory to the far door as McLean turned his attention back to Harrison. She was tense enough for the both of them, no doubt steeling herself for what was to come, but she'd had the forethought to put gloves on and pull a mask over her face. He took a little time to do the same, not looking forward to what lay on the other side of the door. The worst part of the job, it pained him that this wasn't the first time he'd lost a colleague in the line of duty.

'OK, let's get this done.' He reached for the handle, half expecting to receive a shock of static electricity from it. Grasped it tight, took a deep breath and pulled open the door.

McLean had only recently seen the body of Paul Sanderson on the park bench in Craigmillar Castle Park, so he thought he might have been prepared for the sight in front of him now. It wasn't the same though, seeing someone you had known, worked alongside, spoken to not so long ago, and now dead. There was the added knowledge that Connor Fairley had been young, too. Barely a year out of uniform and just getting the hang of plain clothes work. This sort of thing shouldn't happen to anyone, but it really shouldn't have happened to him.

The young detective constable sat slumped against the far wall, legs splayed out towards the door, hands to either side of him, palms up. He wore a suit, the kind he always turned up for work in, but it was frayed at the arms and torn across the front as if he'd been fighting some monstrous beast. As he stepped closer, McLean saw that Fairley's fingernails were ripped and dirty, but there was no blood on his fingers. The soles of his boots were caked with mud, some on the floor in little shapes where it had dried up and fallen from the chunky treads.

'What the hell happened to you, lad?' McLean pressed his mask closer to his face, even though he was fairly certain whatever it had been was not contagious. Not in any physical way at least. Careful not to disturb the body, he crouched a few feet away and took in Connor Fairley's face. What was the last thing the young man had seen? Was it still there, burned on the back of his eyes like they used to believe of old? Whatever it was, it must have been dreadful.

'Poor sod.' Across the other side of the body, Harrison had also lowered herself into a crouch. She reached a hand towards Fairley's wide staring eyes, but stopped herself from touching them closed before McLean could remind her not to disturb the scene any more than was necessary. 'I'm going to have to break the news to his mum.'

'I can do that, if you want,' McLean said. 'I'd imagine Jayne would probably offer, too.'

'Thanks, but no. It's my responsibility. He was my responsibility. Christ, what could have done this to him? He was fine just a couple of days ago. A concussion from a punch to the face doesn't do this.'

McLean looked to what Harrison was indicating, noticed for the first time how stick-thin Fairley's arms were, the material of his jacket hanging off them, his shoulders like a cheap wire coat hanger. The more he took in, the more it felt like the detective constable had picked out clothes for a man two sizes bigger than him. Or he had shrunk. His close-cropped red hair seemed longer, too, as if his scalp had shrivelled away from it. The freckles that marred the tops of his cheeks had darkened even further until they looked like war paint or some strange ethnic tattoo. The illumination in the room wasn't good, but Fairley's skin looked strange too, and it took McLean a while to realise where he'd seen something like it before. It wasn't like Sanderson's skin, which had gone leathery like buckskin or chamois; this was more of a soft rubber covering stretched taut over the detective constable's cheekbones and nose. Like the way Nathaniel Drake had looked, only more extreme. More dead.

'I think we should probably get out of here. Leave him for forensics and the pathologist to deal with.' McLean put his hands on his knees and levered himself upright with a grunt. As he backed towards the door, he took in the rest of the room again, not much changed from the first time he'd seen it. Little more than a large storage cupboard, really, it had no windows, a narrow ventilation grille high up near the far corner. The walls were smooth white, a bit like marker board, but with only a slight sheen to them. A few containers had been piled up at the far end, and that single table stood empty in the middle directly under one of the dim ceiling lights. Almost like an altar.

As the thought crossed his mind, McLean looked back at the dead detective constable one last time. He'd been expecting something similar to Sanderson's body, perhaps even looking for ways they were the same, but there were differences too. Fairley had collapsed into the position he now occupied, whereas Sanderson had sat down so carefully he'd remained that way even in death. Sanderson's hands had been in his lap, gripped tight around the puzzle box that must surely be the reason for both of these deaths, even if he didn't want to think too hard about how that could be. Fairley's hands . . .

'He doesn't have it. The box. Why did neither of us notice that when we first came in?' It was almost as if he had forgotten it existed. As if something had blanked it from his mind.

'What was that?' Harrison asked, her voice echoing slightly, and more distant than McLean was expecting. He looked up from Connor Fairley's horrified, dead face to see that she had moved to the far side of the room, close to the narrow vent. She held one hand raised to the wall, fingers not quite touching the surface as they traced invisible lines.

'What are you doing?'

'There's something here.' Harrison turned her head slightly from side to side, as if trying to get a better line of sight at something, or maybe pinpoint a sound so quiet McLean couldn't hear it from where he stood. Maybe he wouldn't even hear it if he was right beside her.

'We should leave, Janie. You know how much it upsets your flatmate if you contaminate her nice clean crime scene.'

'Manda's away the now. It'll be someone else I'm pissing off. But you're right, only . . .' Harrison didn't finish the sentence, cocking her head again as if hearing something.

'What is it?' McLean asked.

'Whispers,' Harrison said, and pointed at the wall. 'Coming from that way.'

45

Connor Fairley was dead. Janie couldn't quite get her head around that. Only a couple of days ago he'd been walking about, talking, enjoying a laugh with DS Blane as they reviewed CCTV footage, getting punched in the face by an irate Serbian.

And now he was dead.

Somehow, even staring at his body, it didn't quite sink in. Perhaps it was because he looked . . . wrong. Detective Constable Fairley had been twenty-two years old, a few months shy of his twenty-third birthday. And yet the body lying slumped against the wall of this small, airless room could have been twice that age. Older. Oh, it was Connor, there was no doubt in Janie's mind about that. But somehow the change in him stopped her from being able to process his loss beyond the immediate ramifications. His mother would need to be told, and that fell to her. There would have to be an inquiry, and that meant spending quality time with Professional Standards. She had failed him, and that was her fault.

DCI McLean was his usual calm self, quietly taking in all the details without touching anything. Janie had almost closed Fairley's eyes, but managed to stop herself. Even if his stare was the most unsettling thing about his corpse. What had he seen as he breathed his last? What had been going through his mind?

The whispers, when they came, were almost a relief. With them came the memory of why they had been looking for the detective constable, what he had taken. The mystery of how she could have forgotten the puzzle box until that moment was one Janie could compartmentalise and lock away for later consideration. Now, she knew that it had to be close even if Fairley didn't have it with him.

She stood up, straining her ears the better to hear. As if the hushed, muttering voices weren't simply in her head but coming from a particular direction. On the other side of the dead detective constable, McLean was saying something, but she didn't catch it. Instead some sense that wasn't hearing directed her to the far end of the small room, where a narrow grille circulated fresh air. A few metal cases had been shoved up against the wall, and for a moment she wondered if the puzzle box might be inside one of them. But those whispers suggested greater distance, though she couldn't say how she knew that. Almost as if they were coming from inside the walls.

'Janie. You OK?'

A hand on her shoulder made her almost jump out of her skin. With that contact, the whispers faded, her other senses coming back to her. Janie looked up at McLean's concerned face, then past him to where Connor Fairley's body lay slumped against the wall. He was still dead. It wasn't all a dream.

'Sorry. I thought I heard something. Like there was someone behind this wall.' She reached out her hand and touched the surface. Warm like sunburned skin, it had a slightly rubberised feel to it that made her deeply uncomfortable. Like the two of them were standing inside some giant sex toy.

'Aye, you said. Whispers. We still need to go. Duty doctor and pathologist will be here soon, forensics with them. Let them deal with poor Connor here, and we can try to work out what happened to him. Bring whoever did this to justice.'

'Whoever . . .?' Janie was momentarily distracted by the whispers, louder now. She shook her head to try and rid herself of them. 'Aye, right. Need to bring your pal Drake in for questioning. That chief scientist of his too.'

McLean held up his mobile phone. 'No signal in here. This room must be shielded somehow. I wonder what they were using it for.'

'Storing that bloody box. Isn't it obvious?'

As soon as she said it out loud, Janie knew it was true, even if she couldn't quite make the logical steps to come to that conclusion. Maybe because there was no logic, and Madame Rose was right. She still felt a bit of a fool for saying it in front of McLean, the arch sceptic. Only the look he gave her wasn't one of concern for her sanity or ridicule at her foolishness. It was worry for them both.

'I fear you might be right, and I think I might know why.' He took her arm, gently pulling her away from the corner of the small room and back towards the half-closed door. Janie was surprised at how reluctant her feet were to let him. She had to struggle to walk, the whispers digging into her brain, cajoling her, begging her to stay. Was this what had happened to Connor? Had he spent too much time in close proximity to that damned puzzle box and gone mad? Had the voices persuaded him to take it from evidence and walk all the way here? No, that was daft, surely. Wasn't it?

When she finally managed to get her feet working, stepping out into the lab was like emerging from a sauna and plunging through broken ice. Janie almost yelped in pain, managed to turn it into a cough that had the two uniform officers backing off in alarm. She couldn't blame them if they'd seen poor Connor lying in the store.

'Let's just close that for now, shall we?' McLean released her arm and pulled the door until it was not quite shut. As he did so, Janie felt the whispers fade away almost to nothing. They were still there though, insistent like midges on a spring evening beside a Highland lochan.

'It's here somewhere. Not far at all,' she said before realising nobody had asked her the question. The two uniforms looked at each other, a pair of raised eyebrows between them. McLean's face was a more concerned frown.

'The puzzle box,' she explained, as if they were all idiots. 'It's here, in this building. Connor brought it here. Probably walked all the way from the evidence store, the poor wee soul. But he carried it all the way, knocked out two security guards and somehow forced his way into that room because of it. That's what killed him, don't you see?'

Judging by their looks, none of them did. Janie wasn't quite sure how she did either, for that matter. It was true all the same. And the box, or that wizened nugget of a heart inside it, was the crux of whatever all this was. It needed to be found, and it needed to be destroyed. Only then would anyone be safe.

Janie strode out of the laboratory, uncaring as to whether DCI McLean or either of the two uniform officers were following her. Damn the clairvoyant and her illogical woowoo, but she was right. There was a thing that needed doing, and no time to argue the case with anyone.

'You. I need your security pass now,' she said to the still-conscious guard when she arrived back at reception. He was standing close by the entrance doors as his companion was wheeled out to the ambulance, eyes still glazed with something beyond concussion.

'I . . . What?' Janie was pleasantly surprised to see him unloop the card hanging from a lanyard around his neck and pass it to her at the same time as he asked the question.

'Are there any parts of the building this doesn't give you access to?' She held up the card in his line of vision, impatient at how slow he was. Could he not sense the urgency? The need for action?

'Ah'm no' sure. Bob there was the one wi' all the clearance.' The security guard waved a hand in the direction of the ambulance like an unenthusiastic king waving at his subjects. Janie shoved the security pass into her pocket and hurried out through the still-open doors.

'Hold up a moment,' she called to the paramedic as he was about to swing the ambulance doors closed. He gave her a puzzled frown, but did as asked. She hauled herself into the narrow space, where the unconscious Bob lay on his gurney, strapped down and with an oxygen mask fixed over his head. His eyes were closed, clearly still out for the count, and there was no sign of a lanyard or security card. Of course, the paramedic would have removed it while making sure his airway was clear.

'What did you do with his card?' she asked as she jumped down from the ambulance. The paramedic looked at her with a quizzical expression on his face, but she saw how his hand went unbidden to one of his pockets. 'Hand it over, aye?' she added.

He pulled out the card and lanyard, but didn't immediately give them to her. 'There's protocols. I'm no' sure . . .'

'There's a dead detective constable in there, and that passkey is going to help me find the person who killed him.' Janie pulled out her warrant card, held it up for the hapless man to see. 'If you're worried about protocols, tell them Detective Inspector Harrison took it from you.'

As he was digesting the information, Janie snatched the lanyard from his fingers and marched back into the building. It was only then that she noticed DCI McLean watching her, the slightest of smiles on his face.

'Nicely played,' he said before she could berate him. 'What's your plan now?'

'I'm going to use this to get into the building and search it until I find that box.' Janie tapped the security card against the back of her hand. 'And then I'm going to arrest whoever I find with it.'

'Sounds good to me. Where do we start?'

Janie opened her mouth to answer, then closed it again when she realised she didn't know. Standing there in the reception foyer, she could no longer hear the whispering. The memory of it felt more like imagination than reality, too. Whatever strange energy had propelled her from the horrible storage room had seeped away. Now she was left with two electronic security passes and a growing sense of embarrassment at how she had taken them.

'The whole place is built around a central refectory and breakout area,' McLean said after what must have been an awkward pause. 'Maybe we should start there?'

Janie looked past the reception area to the corridor leading to the lab where they had found Connor Fairley. She had gone straight there on arriving at the building, led by McLean, who had been there before. Now she stopped to consider the layout, she realised how little about Drake Biotech's research facility she knew.

'Just how big is this place?' she asked.

They went back along the corridor, past the laboratory where the two uniform officers had decided to stand guard outside now. Neither said anything as they passed, but Sergeant Clifford nodded, his face sombre. A dozen paces further along, a set of locked doors yielded to the magic touch of Bob's security pass. McLean held the door open for her like a gentleman, and Janie stepped through into a jungle.

'Bloody hell. I thought this was a research lab, not some James Bond evil villain's lair.'

The central area of the building formed a huge glass-roofed atrium, with a shallow carp pond in the middle and tropical foliage everywhere. Across the water from where they stood, tables and chairs filled a space that could have been mistaken for an outdoor cafe, were it not for the utter lack of customers.

'I came here with Professor Caine the first time. It's quite impressive, really. When they finish the place, this is where all the scientists are meant to mingle, drink coffee and come up with bold new ideas.' McLean followed a path through tall bamboo shoots to a Japanese-style bridge that arched over the pool. As Janie walked a little behind him, she began to see how the place fitted together, with other paths leading to similar security doors that presumably opened onto other laboratory and office wings. Looking up, she saw grey clouds and a smear of rain, but on a good day the view must be spectacular. From the right spot you could probably see the Pentland Hills and the Hillend artificial ski slopes. If they ever got the labs finished, it would be a great place to take a break from work, chat with your colleagues and brainstorm new ideas.

'Strange that they should finish this place first, before there's any researchers here to use it. Why do you suppose they did it that way?' she asked, but before McLean could answer, the noise of a door opening echoed through the foliage. Janie spun around, trying to locate where it had come from. Not the door they had entered by, for sure. It had to be one of the other, unfinished wings.

And then the whispers came on again, only this time they weren't quiet. They filled her head like a swarm of angry wasps. Unbalanced, she put a hand out to steady herself, but the table was suddenly at an angle, her legs buckling, the world once more spinning into black.

46

'W hy do you suppose they did it that way?'

McLean heard Harrison's question but had no time to parse it before a noise on the far side of the atrium distracted them both. He felt something pass over him, like a gust of warm, stale air from a long-sealed room, and then a clattering of upturned table brought him to his senses just in time to catch the detective inspector before she collapsed to the floor. Lowering her down gently, he felt for a pulse and found it strong. Under closed lids, her eyes flicked as if she was trying to read something in a hurry, and she was as limp as a rag doll.

'Janie?' He couldn't stop himself from asking the question, even though he knew full well she was in no fit state to answer him. At least he'd managed to stop her from bashing her head open on one of the tables, or falling into the pond and drowning.

Crouched down beside the unconscious detective inspector, McLean heard the footsteps hurrying along one of the paths towards him. He looked over the top of the nearest table, searching the gloom through the leaves to see who was coming. It could have been another police officer, or even one of the security team, but he was somehow not surprised when Professor Caine hurried over the narrow bridge. Ready to accost the man, he stopped when he saw the vacant look on Caine's face, and what he was carrying. Gripped tightly between two hands and held away from his body as if it were pulling him, the puzzle box almost glowed. And was that a sound coming from it? Like tinnitus, or the distant screaming of gulls.

So intent was he on completing his task, the professor failed to notice two detectives lurking in amongst the tables, and hurried off towards a different door. McLean took one look at Harrison, lying on her back between two chairs. She was breathing steadily, eyes still flickering away under closed lids. She'd wake soon, he was sure, and while it would perhaps be best if he was there to help her, he really needed to follow the professor and see what the hell he was getting up to. Pulling a cushion from the nearest seat, he slid it under her head.

'I'll be back soon. Don't worry,' he said, to no response.

Through a gap in the bamboo shoots, he saw a rectangle of light appear on the far wall, then extinguish as if someone had opened a door and gone through. McLean wasn't quite sure why he was trying to be stealthy as he took the path to the edge of the atrium and worked his way around. He'd taken out his phone to call in some backup, but much like the storage room where poor Connor Fairley had breathed his last, there was no signal. Something must have been jamming it. Most likely a security measure to prevent the easy theft of research secrets, although it seemed odd to have such a system up and running when there was no actual research to steal.

A swipe of the pass Janie had given him turned the red LED lights on the door lock to green. He pushed through into a short, brightly lit corridor that ended with a pair of stainless-steel elevator doors. No screen to indicate floors, there was only another security card reader to summon the lift. McLean was reaching to do so when he noticed the entrance to a stairwell off to one side and swiped that door open instead. Beyond, steps led only down into a gloom punctuated by low-wattage lights that cast more shadow than illumination.

'Down it is, then.' He checked his phone once more, but there was still no signal. The chances of that changing as he descended into the earth were slim to nothing, so he put the handset away and concentrated on the steps. Far enough down to be well below the level of the carp pond in the central atrium, they ended at another set of security doors. Unlike those in the main body of the building, these had reinforced glass windows set into them, revealing a long corridor beyond. McLean swiped the security guard's pass and went through.

The quality of the air changed, noticeably cooler as he walked along what was more of a concrete-lined tunnel than a corridor. He tried to think what direction it was taking him, but the turns made from the front entrance lobby to this place made that all but impossible. Was this sprawling underground complex part of the original plans? He couldn't imagine something like that getting past the council easily, but then again, Nathaniel Drake had the ear of the first minister. And a lot of money.

The tunnel ended at yet another security door. Peering through, he saw a wider corridor beyond, one wall lined with what looked like glass. When he swiped the security card against the reader, there was a noticeable delay before the red turned to green and the lock clicked to allow him through. Once on the other side, he saw that the glass wall separated the corridor from a series of what looked like small rooms, each equipped with a narrow cot bed, table and single chair. Across from each bed, a flat screen was set into the wall, and a narrow door revealed a toilet with presumably some kind of washing facilities out of view. Something Harrison had told him came to McLean's mind then, the story told her by the young woman Nadia about how Vaclav Mihailovic had been able to make some extra cash, no questions asked. These small rooms were designed to house human test subjects, and for days rather than hours. The only thing he couldn't work out was how a person could get inside. The glass frontage was seamless, and aside from the narrow entrance to each room's toilet, there appeared to be no other doors.

'The whole wall lifts up into the ceiling, in case you're wondering. Each cell is hermetically sealed, has its own air, water and drainage. State-of-the-art bio-containment facility. It's eye-wateringly expensive and the main reason this site's years late being finished.'

McLean whirled around to see who had spoken, even though he'd recognised the accent from the first couple of words. Professor Caine had put down the box somewhere and now held a gun in one hand. The sight of it was so incongruous, it took McLean a while to understand what he was looking at and the danger it represented.

'It's real. You can trust me on that.' The professor waggled the gun like they do in the movies, but it remained pointed largely in McLean's direction. He stood close enough that he could hardly miss, far enough that rushing him wasn't likely to prove much of a success. Playing for time was the best option, although it occurred to McLean that nobody actually knew where he was. Except Caine, of course.

'Your boss know you're down here?' he asked. 'He even know there is a down here?'

The professor shrugged, then gestured with his free hand for McLean to head towards the doors at the far end of the corridor to where he had come in. 'He's in here already. Why don't you ask him?'

If Harrison had thought the buildings that made up Drake Biotech's research labs were like a Bond villain's lair, then the room into which Professor Caine forced McLean confirmed it. There was something of the hewn-out cavern about the place that reminded him of the underground complex at Gilmerton Cove. How many years ago was it they'd found that poor journalist's body down there? Too many to count. This space was a little larger, but much of the bare rock was hidden behind grey concrete or painted steel. Two glass-fronted cells were set into the far wall, although these were smaller than the ones outside. Inside one of them, looking rather lost and forlorn, sat Nathaniel Drake.

'He can't hear you, in case you were wondering,' Caine said. 'Can't see out either. These containment cells are state of the art.'

'What are you doing with him?' McLean approached the glass slowly, but the man on the other side made no sign of having noticed him. He sat on a low bench much like those found in the holding cells at the police station, elbows on his knees and head in his hands.

'He came to me last night, you know. Mouthing off about a picture you'd showed him. So in many ways this is your fault, McLean. Well, yours and those animal rights idiots. It's no matter though, we're ready now.'

'We?' McLean asked as he turned away from the glass. Somehow he didn't think the professor was including Drake in that collective.

'We,' Caine confirmed, but didn't elucidate, merely gestured with the gun towards the centre of the room. Lit by a bank of moveable overhead lights, it was dominated by a sophisticated-looking operating table. To one side stood something that was halfway between an industrial robot and a horror movie director's wet dream, all spindly mechanical arms and shiny steel blades. Beside it stood a stainless-steel trolley, on top of which lay the puzzle box. As he took a step towards it all, McLean saw that the polished concrete floor around the edge of the room gave way to a circle of darkest black in the middle. Operating table, killer robot from Venus and box were all inside that circle.

'I'm guessing you didn't dig this all out yourself,' he said.

'No shortage of strong workmen with little by way of curiosity if you know where to find them and have the money to spend.

And anyway, the land around here's riddled with caverns like this one. People have been digging in the ground for millennia in these parts. Coal, silver, gold, who really knows? Maybe they just didn't much like the sun.'

'And all to find the secret to eternal life?'

'Oh, I have that already. Only it's not what you think.' Caine waved the gun again, a little too casually for McLean's liking, indicating that he should hurry up. He found himself tensing as he crossed the line from concrete to whatever the black surface was, and yet there was no sudden shock, or alarms going off, or laser beams forming an inescapable cage around him. Nothing. As he approached the steel trolley and the box sitting on top of it, the air felt maybe a tiny bit warmer, but he might have been imagining it. Or it might have been the lights overhead.

'On the ground and cuff yourself to the operating table,' Caine said.

'With what?' McLean held his hands out empty. He couldn't remember the last time he'd had a pair of handcuffs in his pocket.

'You police always have cuffs, don't you? It's part of the uniform.'

'You may not have noticed this, Professor, but I'm not in uniform. I'm also a detective chief inspector. We're more the generals directing things than the soldiers doing the actual fighting, if you get my meaning.'

Caine glowered at him, eyes narrowed for a moment as he thought. Then he waggled the gun again, motioning McLean towards the glass-fronted cells. Drake still sat in one, oblivious to the world outside. The glass pane that formed the front of the other one rose on silent motors as the professor tapped at a screen on the console.

'Inside. And don't piss me off any more. These cells are hermetically sealed biohazard containment units. You wouldn't want me to forget to switch on the air supply, would you?'

'What's in this for you, Caine?' McLean asked as he stepped over the small gap in the floor where the glass had seated. 'You can't hope to get away with it.'

'Trying to talk me out of it, are you? Expecting me to fall on your mercy?' As the glass slid into place, the professor's voice almost completely disappeared until he tapped at the console again. It came back louder, but from a different direction, piped through a speaker in the ceiling of the small cell. It was a little disorienting, like a television with the picture slightly out of sync with the sound.

'. . . too late for that, I'm afraid. But don't worry. You'll see soon enough, and you'll come round to his way of thinking, too.'

'His?' McLean's breath misted the glass slightly as he spoke. He hadn't realised he was standing so close to it, took a step back. 'You mean Drake?'

Caine shook his head. 'Poor old Nate. He has no idea what he's got himself into. The forces he's playing with. He thinks immortality is a science problem. Something you can solve by throwing money at it. They're all like that, the rich. So narrow-minded, so focused on one thing they can't see the world around them. Tell me, Inspector. Is that the sort of person you would want to live for ever?'

McLean knew a rhetorical question when he heard one, so decided to let the professor answer it for himself. There was something not quite right about the man, beyond the whole gun and glass-walled cell thing. He had that gleam in his eye McLean had noticed the first time they had met, an enthusiasm for his work that didn't so much border on the pathological as dive straight in and wallow like a happy piglet.

'No, Nate has a purpose to serve, and he'll serve it well enough.' Caine put the gun down on the console, its barrel still pointing in McLean's direction. 'Given what's going on upstairs, we should probably get started. He's waited long enough, and fed well now.'

McLean didn't get the impression the professor was talking

about Drake feeding well. He was going to ask who 'He' was, but the look of deep longing Caine gave the puzzle box was something of a hint. Like an addict watching his spoon as it warmed over a flame.

'Do you honestly think that will work?' he asked, as the professor stepped into the black-floored area and approached the box with all the reverence of a priest at his altar. When he placed his hands to either side of it, the top popped open much the same way it had in Madame Rose's kitchen. Caine reached in and took the shrivelled heart out, holding it on one open palm.

'Not the way I imagined, no.' He frowned as he peered closely at the heart. 'Not by putting pieces of this priceless relic through those machines upstairs. Oh, such hubris. I thought I could unravel its secrets through chemistry and physics when those sciences are nothing but the bastard children of the knowledge that created this.'

'So that's what this is,' McLean said. 'You're just another charlatan feeding a rich man's ego and milking him for his money. Story as old as time.'

Caine stared at him with those mad eyes for a moment, his head cocked slightly as if he was trying to hear something over the jumbling mess of noises inside his skull. When he straightened up, he gave McLean a smile that was not the least bit reassuring, then crossed the room to the console and tapped a button.

'Hermetically sealed. It'll be interesting to see how long the air inside there lasts. Goodbye, Inspector.'

The last thing McLean saw was the professor as he twisted a dial on the console. For a moment nothing happened, and then the glass in front of him turned from clear to opaque to solid. A second later the lights went out, and he was left in utter, silent black.

47

'**W**ake up, child. It's time to go.'
Janie heard the words as a whisper, deep in the darkness and as insistent as an elbow in the ribs. She bristled at the word 'child', and then wondered who might call her that. Not her mother, for certain. In her addled memory it had sounded more like Madame Rose. With a groan, she rolled onto her side and opened her eyes.

She was lying on a polished concrete floor somewhere poorly lit, warm and humid. Nearby she could hear the sound of water trickling, as if there were a waterfall or a broken pipe. A pond. A narrow bridge like the ones she'd seen in photographs of Japanese gardens.

'Ugh. Wha—?' She tried to sit up, clanged her head on the underside of the table and swore. The pain brought memories with it, and she took a moment to let them get themselves in the right order as she massaged what was surely going to be a sore bump on her skull soon.

Looking down where she'd been lying, she saw one of the cushions had been taken from the nearest chair and put under her head as a pillow. How like the detective chief inspector to be that considerate, and yet still go off leaving her alone. She pulled out her phone, checked it for messages before noticing there was no signal. The time on the screen showed she'd been unconscious for no more than ten minutes, but it still seemed odd nobody had come looking for her. Where had McLean gone if not for help?

About to head back the way she had come, Janie realised that she wasn't entirely sure now which of the doors was the right one. The central atrium had a symmetry to it that had no doubt been pleasing to the architect, but it meant that all the doors out of it looked identical. She was fairly sure she'd crossed the bridge to get to where she'd collapsed, and set off in that direction, but as she moved, so the whispers started up again. And this time they seemed to be coming from one of the doors at the other side of the room.

'I don't believe in all this mystical mumbo jumbo,' she said to herself, without as much conviction as she would have liked. She crossed to the door anyway, found that it hadn't quite closed itself properly when the last person had used it, whoever that might have been.

Beyond, a short corridor led to an elevator, with a single stairwell door alongside it. Like the one she had just come through, this one too hadn't fully shut itself after whoever had last used it. That seemed too much of a coincidence for it not to have been intentional, and the only person she could think of who might have left a trail was the DCI.

The stairs led only down, eventually opening up onto a wide corridor that seemed hewn from the rock. On one side, glass opened onto a series of small rooms, each kitted out like a tiny bedsit. These were almost certainly what Vaclav Mihailovic had described to Nadia, where the poor fellow had been brought for whatever illegal medical trials had been carried out on him. Whatever procedure it was that had ultimately killed him. Janie felt little satisfaction in having unpicked that particular puzzle. The ramifications were far-reaching, complicated, and likely to piss off a great many very powerful people. She began to understand why McLean felt the way he did about politicians.

Voices spilled through the door at the far end of the corridor. Janie paused a couple of paces away from it to listen in, unwilling to move closer lest she be spotted through the narrow reinforced-glass window set into the upper half of the fake-wood veneer. Although the insistent whispering in her head made it hard to hear what was being said, she recognised Drake's American accent straight away.

'. . . lost your mind, Magnus? What the hell are you getting up to here? This place isn't finished yet. We're not licensed for trials.'

'There you go with your talk of licences. So shackled by the petty bureaucrats. I thought you had more vision, Nate. More drive. Don't you want to live for ever? Conquer disease and death?'

'You know I do, Magnus. So why did you lock me up in one of the bio-containment cells for hours? And why in God's name are you pointing a gun at me?'

Without realising she had moved, Janie found herself right up close to the door. She pressed her ear to it, angling her face to catch a partial glimpse of the room beyond. All she could see was the centre, where an area of floor appeared to have been painted black, with a table in the centre with something set on it. She couldn't see what, as Nathaniel Drake stood at the edge of the black floor, blocking the view. It looked a bit like an operating theatre, but one designed by an insane architect who had watched too many dystopian SF movies.

'Let's just say I've started to doubt your commitment to the cause, Nate. Chummying up to that bloody policeman? Telling him everything.'

Walking as he talked, Professor Caine appeared in Janie's limited field of view. She hadn't met the man before; he'd been interviewed as part of DCI McLean's investigation, but she'd only seen the transcripts. If someone had asked her to describe what a generic professor looked like, then this would have been it. Except that the adjective 'mad' might have been appended to the noun.

Thinning grey hair all awry, he looked as if he'd been sleeping in his crumpled tweed jacket and baggy trousers, and he was indeed holding a gun in one hand.

'Is there someone . . .?' As if feeling her gaze through the glass, he began to turn. No doubt sensing his moment, Drake made a lunge for the professor, one hand reaching for the gun. With a sharp crack that sounded like a bone snapping, it went off and Drake jerked back, dropped to his knees, one hand pressed to the other arm as blood began to seep through his fingers onto the floor.

'What the actual fuck, Caine?' The shock in the man's eyes and the whiteness of his face made him look more human than Janie thought she had ever seen him. There was betrayal and bewilderment in that expression too. There was an expression, which was a distinct improvement.

'It's just a flesh wound. You'll heal quick enough once he's back to his full strength. Now be quiet. I'm sure there was someone outside.' The professor turned to the door. Janie stepped back, her eyes taking in the almost total lack of places to hide between her and the far-distant elevator and stairs. There was one other door opposite the wall of glass, its security light already glowing green, unlocked. She hurried over, pulled it open and slipped inside, easing it closed as Caine's shadow fell on the glass she'd been looking through moments earlier.

Holding her breath, she listened as the professor stepped out into the corridor, made a huffing sound, then went back to whatever he had planned to do with Drake. So intent was she on listening for any indication that she'd been discovered, she didn't at first take in what the room she had entered held. Lit only by the faint glow coming in through a small window in the door, she saw the familiar shape of a mortuary examination table under a bank of adjustable lights, something corpse-shaped lying under a sheet atop it. Almost impossible to make out on the other side of the room, a bank of small doors must be a cold store for cadavers. What the hell were they doing down here that needed postmortem facilities? It didn't take a genius to guess.

Moving slowly to avoid making any sound, Janie inched away from the door and across to the examination table. Most definitely a dead body, she eased the corner of the sheet up to see who it might be. Vaclav Mihailovic stared up at her with that same horrified expression she remembered from the woods near Ormiston. She dropped the sheet down again with a shudder. At least she knew now who had stolen the bodies, knew who had almost killed her friend. Time to get out of here, call in the firearms team and get this whole building swept. But where the hell was McLean?

She was turning away from the table and its grim occupant, eyes now attuned to the darkness, when without warning all the lights blazed into life. Blinded by the sudden brightness, Janie could only half see the shape standing at the far corner of the room.

'Well now. What have we here? Another little sneak thief in my parlour.'

The voice was enough for her to know that it was the professor. Stupid of her not to think that there might be a second way into this examination theatre, accessed from the larger room. As she blinked and squinted, one hand shading her face, details began to resolve. First and foremost the gun pointed directly at her. Without quite knowing why, Janie put her hands up, and as her vision began to clear further, she saw a glint of smile on the professor's face. He took one step further into the room, leaving the doorway clear, and indicated for her to go through.

'What is this place?' Janie's question was out before she remembered the man she was asking had a gun aimed at her back and had already shot at least one person today. The victim was there, not more than ten feet from her, sitting on the floor, blood soaked through the arm of his jacket and going sticky on the polished concrete.

'Detective Inspector Harrison, this is a surprise.' Nathaniel Drake grimaced, the pain bringing something like animation to his previously lifeless features. It suited him better than the faux-youthful look he'd clearly wasted a lot of money on.

'Are you OK?' She looked briefly around at the professor before going over to check.

'I think it's what they call a flesh wound in the movies. Normally the hero shrugs it off and gets the bad guy in the end, but this hurts like a bitch and my arm's useless.'

'You really need to get that cleaned and stitched up. What the hell's going on here, Mr Drake? What is this place?'

Drake's head turned away from Janie's and she followed his gaze as it swept over the room. Past the complicated-looking operating table and robotic surgeon, the puzzle box sat on top of a small stainless-steel trolley. Its lid was open, and that was when Janie realised that the whispers had gone silent. As if all those voices, all those souls, were holding their collective breath in anticipation of something.

'This was supposed to be the most secure lab. Both biologically speaking and from an industrial espionage point of view.' Drake shuffled around on his backside to get a better view, winced at the motion. 'Seems Magnus has made a few changes to the place since I was last down here. It's not supposed to be operational yet. Hasn't had approval from your Home Office for one thing.'

'Aye, but what is it?' Janie glanced down at the floor where Drake's blood had pooled. It was close to, but not touching the black paint. Or was it paint at all? It put her in mind of something else entirely. As she reached tentative fingers towards it, the whispers started up in what was clearly alarm. She snapped her hand away with such speed and ferocity Janie wondered if it was of her own volition.

'This is the intersection between cutting-edge science and what I suspect lesser intellects would call magic.'

Professor Caine stood inside the ring of darker floor, his face lit by the overhead lights in a manner that made him look like a cartoon mad scientist.

'Magic?' Janie stood slowly, all too aware of the gun still pointing at her. 'Is that what you did to Vaclav Mihailovic? Magic him to death? And what about Paul Sanderson too? You cast a spell on him because he stole your wee box there?'

Caine walked over to the trolley table and placed the gun down beside the puzzle box.

'Was that his name?' he asked. 'Poor fool had no idea what he was dealing with.'

'And what exactly was that?' Janie asked. In the back of her mind she figured talking was better than getting shot at, and the longer she kept the professor occupied, the more chance there was of someone coming looking for her. But where the hell was McLean?

'It's a container, my dear. That's the simple answer. But it has some very interesting properties. Took me a very long time to work out exactly what it was doing, but the inlay is impregnated with . . .' The professor paused a moment, as if looking for the right word. 'Spores isn't quite right, although that's part of it, I suppose. There's an almost undetectable viral load coming off the surface.'

'Viral?' Janie took an involuntary step back, almost treading on Nathaniel Drake. 'Is it . . .'

'Contagious?' Caine picked up the box gently and ran his fingers over the surface. 'Oh, very. But not everyone is susceptible to the . . .' Again that pause. His lectures must have been excruciating. 'Well, let's just say most people feel nothing in the presence of the box. Some react, and that reaction varies. It's to do with genetics, yes, but something much more subtle than those idiots playing with CRISPR understand.'

'So Mihailovic and Sanderson both reacted?' Janie glanced

towards the door as she asked, but there was still no sign of any rescue. 'Is that why you wanted their bodies back? So you could carry on studying them?'

The professor dipped his head once. 'Top marks, Inspector. There's still much to be gleaned from their remains. Of course, if that idiot Jovanović had done as he was told and brought the first body here rather than burying him out in the wilds, then I'd not have needed to go to such drastic ends to retrieve it. Then again, I'd not have known about the second man – Sanderson, did you say his name was? So I suppose it all worked out fine in the end.'

'What are you going on about, Magnus?' Drake struggled to stand up, his hand slipping in his own blood. 'What the hell have you been doing here? We're not even open yet.'

'Oh Nate, you are such a gullible fool sometimes. It amazes me that you somehow managed to amass so much money.' Caine put his hand into the box and brought it out again, something small clutched in his fingers. 'All this time you thought I was working for you, and really you were working for me. Me and my master.'

'Is it just me?' Drake winced as turned towards Janie. 'Or does he sound like he's gone mad?'

'You tell me, Mr Drake. You're the one who employed him. Paid for all this.'

'Enough. It's time. You will come to me now.'

There was something different about the professor's voice, as if it was inside Janie's head rather than coming to her through her ears. Had she not already been surrounded by the whispers, it would likely have been overpowering. Even with them she felt her muscles tightening to obey the command. Beside her, Nathaniel Drake clearly had no such help as he struggled to his feet with a groan. His face had taken on that waxy, lifeless quality again, and here under the bright artificial light it put her in mind of Vaclav Mihailovic.

'Don't listen to him.' She reached out and grabbed at Drake's

good arm, but the billionaire shrugged her off without even looking, stepped over the line from polished concrete to darkest
black . . . earth?

It was only as she watched Drake's foot touch the matt surface
that Janie understood what it was. Not paint at all, but purest black
soil compacted so hard it might turn to coal in a million years or
so. How deep did it go? How much of it was there? She'd read the
book, seen the film. There was no doubt where it was from and
what it was for. But what was the purpose of this whole mad
charade?

48

'You will come to me now.'

Again the professor's words felt like they were deep inside Janie's head. As if she was standing in the middle of a field in a raging storm, the wind tugging her limbs to make her walk towards the foreign soil. She fought it, took a step back, then another. The whispers formed a wall in her head, a shield against whatever it was the professor was doing to her, and with the growing distance so his pull on her faded.

'How...? You've been breathing this air more than long enough to succumb. Unless... No matter.' Caine shook away whatever thought had been occupying his head, took one step to the table and picked up the gun. Janie saw the intent in his mad eyes as he began to level it at her. Without waiting for confirmation, she dived to one side, hit the floor and rolled behind a console desk. The gun boomed this time, no closed door to muffle its roar. Once, twice, three times. She felt the impact of the bullets in the thin metal pedestal, saw three holes appear far too close to her head. Something sparked and fizzed inside, brought the acrid smell of burning electrics to her nostrils.

'Are you still alive, little mouse?' Caine's voice had taken on a sing-song quality now, all vestiges of sanity gone. Janie risked a glance around the edge of the pedestal, ducked quickly back as another shot ripped a chunk of floor away and sprayed chips of concrete over her jacket. Two more shots came close enough to make her yelp.

'Not coming out? It's no matter. I have everything I need here. You can watch if you want.'

Janie took out her phone, switched it into camera mode and poked the corner out past the pedestal, pinching and zooming to see what the professor was up to before daring to put her head in the line of fire. Caine had his back to her, the gun lying on the table beside the puzzle box. As she watched, he helped an unresisting Drake up onto the operating bed, and pushed the robotic machinery out of the way.

'You have to stop this. Before it's too late.'

The thought was her own, surely, so why did it sound like someone else's voice? A voice she almost recognised? What had the professor been pumping into the air? Janie twisted around awkwardly, but before she'd even taken in the rest of the operating theatre and the observation booth overlooking it, she knew that there would be no one there.

Using the console as a shield as much as she could, she rose slowly, first into a crouch and then almost fully standing. Caine ignored her, busy with a pair of surgical scissors cutting away at Drake's jacket and T-shirt underneath. In moments, the billionaire was stripped to the waist, the ugly welt of his bullet wound a puckered mess on one arm that he seemed to have entirely forgotten now. Indeed, he appeared to have forgotten everything, his eyes vacantly staring at the ceiling, head relaxed into the pillow at the raised end of the bed.

'Not long now, master. Almost done.' The professor spoke as if someone else was there with him as he laid out things on the small steel table alongside the puzzle box. She cast around, looking for anything that might serve as a weapon, but there was nothing to hand. Save for the console and the equipment within the dark-floored area, the room was clinically bare. Hardly surprising, given what it was, but frustrating all the same.

And then she looked down at the console itself. Slightly incongruous in the room, it looked like something you might use to control CCTV cameras, only more sophisticated. One screen was dead, a bullet hole through it, but two others showed feed from cameras. On one of them, a dejected-looking DCI McLean sat on a narrow cot bed in a tiny room, his hands together, arms resting on his thighs as he stared at the far wall. Icons along the bottom of the screen seemed to control audio and video-recording functions, temperature and humidity controls and various other things Janie couldn't immediately decipher. He had to be in one of the test-subject holding cells nearby. Perhaps she could unlock it, let him out. But which icon? If she got it wrong, what might happen?

Almost unbidden, her hand reached out, one finger tapping at a single icon. Instantly the figure on the bed reacted, first looking around, then standing up as light began to spill through a growing gap at the base of one wall. Looking up, Janie saw a slice of the shiny black glass opposite her rise. Stooping low the quicker to escape his prison, McLean stumbled out into the room.

'Watch out!' she screamed as the professor grabbed the gun from the table beside him and raised it at the DCI. To his credit, McLean's reactions were swift. He rolled to one side as the gun roared, deafening in the small room. A crack appeared in the glass behind him where his head had been. Ducking low, as if that gave him any cover at all, the DCI shuffled around the edge of the room until he was out of the professor's line of sight.

Not that Caine was paying attention any more. Instead, he had turned back to the prone Nathaniel Drake. He started to mutter words that sounded foreign and painful to Janie's ears. As he lifted both hands up to the ceiling, she saw something glint in the powerful arc lamps, the distinctive shape of a surgeon's scalpel. Before Janie could react, Caine had bent down again and cut a deep line across Drake's bare chest, right above where his heart lay. There was no way he was getting through ribs with that tiny knife, but it should still have hurt. And yet Drake didn't even flinch as his blood welled in the wound and began to run in little rivulets down his side and into his navel.

'You have to stop this, Janie.' The voice in her head spoke again, and it sounded very much like Madame Rose. Prompted by the words, and something else besides, Janie stepped away from the console and towards the area of blackened floor at the centre of the room. Was it her addled brain, or was something strange happening to it where Drake's blood had dripped from the operating table, the surface blistered and bubbling like burned skin? The air around him and the professor shimmered with a heat haze, though Janie felt no warmth on her face. Quite the opposite, a bone-deep chill had settled on the room, misting her breath. Those first few steps faltered the closer she came, muscles locked as if she, too, was freezing solid. Across the room, McLean stood equally helpless, the apparent effort of trying to move etched across his face.

As she watched on, Professor Caine raised his hands once more, the scalpel gone, replaced by the tiny nugget of desiccated heart. With a cry of what sounded like triumph, he brought both hands down onto the wound, pressing hard as if that would force the old, dead thing into the still-living flesh. Drake bucked and convulsed, let out a great bellow of pain like a wounded bear. The sound of it broke whatever spell had been holding Janie in place, the whispers in her head turned into something like a battle cry that urged her on even though she had no idea what she could do. The pent-up energy of straining against her invisible bonds launched her forward, into the glimmering light and onto the dark, hard-packed earth of another land, another time.

Everything slowed to a crawl, as if someone had hit the pause button and only Janie was still working in real time. The air about her glowed, little sparks flashing into being and fizzing out of existence like some really bad acid trip. She'd never taken drugs, never been interested in them, but this was exactly how she imagined it would be.

Ahead of her, not more than a couple of strides away, Professor Caine leaned both hands hard into the wound in Nathaniel Drake's chest as he tried to force the long-dead heart of another man into a space already occupied by a living, beating one. There was a perverse logic to it, she supposed. If all that is left of the monster is its heart, then how better to revive it than put that heart in another body? And if that other body happened to be filthy rich and influential, so much the better.

But it was madness, surely? That wizened relic of times long past was nothing more than dried-up sinew and muscle. Drake was more likely to get a nasty infection from it than eternal life as the vessel of some malign spirit. If he didn't first bleed to death from that deep cut to his chest.

And yet she was right beside the professor now, and he was barely moving. Drake's face had taken on that frozen, unreal quality again, only this time stuck in a grimace of agony. And beyond the circle delineated by the dirt-black floor, Detective Chief Inspector McLean stood stock still, off balance and with one hand reaching towards her. His expression was a mixture of bewilderment and concern. Not something so unusual, really, but it was strange to see it fixed there all the same.

'There is no time, Janie. You have to do this now.'

The voice was like Madame Rose, but different. There was an urgency in her tone that Janie couldn't mistake, an immediacy. She knew what she needed to do, too, even if she wasn't quite sure how. Reaching out, she gently prised the professor's fingers away. The cut in Drake's chest was deep and raw, the white of ribs showing through flesh and blood. Where everything else moved slowly if at all, the tiny ball of dried-up heart shivered and thrummed as it tried to work its way deeper. Not quite beating yet, but not far off. With delicate fingers and not a little disgust, she reached into the wound and grasped it.

The shock should have been enough to kill. Not just a physical thing, it washed through her mind on a tide of anger, resentment and disbelief. Something so vast she was but a gnat, as insignificant as a midge to a majestic stag. A different voice, male and dripping with arrogance, roared through her brain so loud Janie thought she might pass out.

'How dare—?'

And then the whispers were around her, at her back and sides. An army of voices, all tiny, all quiet, but like the midges they were legion. They swarmed over the presence that had been so large in her mind she hadn't understood it as a presence at all. She felt the shrivelled heart of the beast in her fingers, stuck hard into the wound as if anchored to Drake's ribs, forcing them aside in its need to go deeper. The whispers all around her like armour, like a shield, lending her strength, she pulled with all her might.

The scream brought everything back to normal speed with a snap. Janie fell backwards, one hand bloody and numb. Drake spasmed as if someone had put a thousand volts through his skull, then slumped onto the table. Before she could even register what was happening, Professor Caine was on her, hands around her throat. Mad eyes wide, veins bulging in forehead and neck, spittle frothing his lips as he snarled an inhuman wail. He was strong, too strong for her, still dazed and overwhelmed, still trying to process what had just happened. All she could do was try to fend him off, first with her good hand, fingers going for those eyes, then with the numb, lifeless hand whose fingers still held . . .

Gasping for breath as his grip tightened around her throat, Janie squeezed the professor's cheeks to force his jaws apart. For an instant she saw rotten teeth, smelled a stench far worse than the uncollected garbage bags that oozed bin juice around the doors of the student tenements. With the last of her strength she brought up her numb hand and shoved the blood-smeared mummified heart into Caine's mouth.

The effect was instant. The professor's grip on her loosened, letting Janie breathe. He reached for his own face, began clawing at it with bloodied fingers, pulling down his eyelids and twisting his lips into a grimace. As she rolled onto her side and then all fours, all she could hear was a choking, gagging sound as he tried to dislodge the lump from his throat. It seemed to go on for a long time, the sound progressively weaker as Caine sank first to his knees, then keeled over completely. She watched in fascinated horror as something seemed to bulge under the skin in his neck, work its way down past his collar and disappear.

'You OK, Janie?'

The voice was so quiet, so distant, she didn't at first understand who was speaking. Then Janie felt a hand on her shoulder, looked up to see McLean crouched down beside her. He had the professor's gun in one hand, holding it as if it were a grenade with the pin out. She was anything but OK, her mind racing as it tried both to process what had just happened and bury it so deep she never need worry about it again. Her whole body ached as if she'd been fifteen rounds in the boxing ring, and her right hand hung limp and lifeless by her side. Seeing it, blood-caked fingers crooked against the floor, it was almost as if it belonged to someone else entirely.

'Caine?' she croaked, looking round to where the professor lay on his back, mouth agape. His wide-open eyes stared up into the glare of the lights, unblinking. Had she killed him?

McLean shook his head, which wasn't quite as informative as he maybe thought it was. Janie was too tired to ask again, barely had the energy to take his free hand and let him pull her to her feet. Nearby, the still form of Nathaniel Drake lay on the operating table, one arm across his belly, the other fallen away, slack fingers pointing to the dark floor. With her head clearing, that felt less threatening, although it was still clearly made from some different material to the polished concrete throughout the rest of the complex. The marks left by Drake's blood were little whorls and craters, as if it had been acid rather than haemoglobin that ran through his veins. Given the therapies he'd been undergoing, that wasn't actually as far-fetched as it sounded.

As if hearing her thoughts, Drake began to stir. His fingers twitched, flexed and then he let out a low groan of pain.

'Don't try to sit up,' Janie said as she approached the operating table. The gash in his chest was raw, his movement setting off fresh bleeding. She looked around for something to staunch it, found gauze and bandages in a drawer close by. 'Here, rest your hand on this. Keep pressure on it until we can get a paramedic down here.'

Eyes unfocused, Drake stared around like a drunk man until he finally managed to hold steady on Janie. 'What happened? Professor Caine, he shot . . . I . . .'

'Rest, Mr Drake. Help's on its way.' Janie cast a glance back at McLean, who merely held up his phone, screen facing towards her, and shrugged. No signal, of course. Someone would have to go and fetch help, and disable all the security doors along the way too.

As if sensing she was about to step away, Drake reached up with one weak hand, barely managing to grasp her arm. His voice was little more than a whisper.

'Am I . . .? Am I dying?'

There was such pathos in his voice, Janie almost laughed. She took his hand and laid it gently down on his bare, blood-stained chest.

'Don't worry, Mr Drake. You won't live for ever, but you'll surely make it to the end of the day.'

49

S tepping outside, McLean felt like he had been holding his breath for hours and could finally let it go. The scene in front of the research centre was a chaos of squad cars, ambulances and even a few police motorbikes. It felt like he had been underground for a lifetime, and yet the sky was brighter than when he had first arrived at the lab, the clouds beginning to break up. When he checked his watch, he was surprised to find that it was barely noon. Less than an hour since he'd seen the body of poor DC Fairley, which would at least explain why nobody had come looking for him and Harrison after they had gone to search the building.

'What the hell happened?'

McLean looked up to see Chief Superintendent McIntyre. Of course an incident like this would bring her out, although the uncharitable part of his mind said it was on account of Nathaniel Drake being injured rather than the death of Detective Constable Fairley. That it spoke at all showed him how tired he was, how rattled by the events of the past couple of hours.

'Jayne.'

'Is he still here?'

McLean didn't bother to ask who McIntyre meant. He let out a sigh he'd not known was still hiding inside him.

'Drake's gone to hospital. I sent DC Bryant with him, since

he's unlikely to charm her into letting him get away. Not that I think he's a flight risk, particularly. Even if any of this were his doing, he's rich enough to lawyer his way out of trouble, and being pals with the first minister helps too.'

'You're a terrible cynic, Tony McLean. You know that?' McIntyre's gaze took in the front of the building, the assembled police cars and forensics vans. 'But you're not wrong. This is going to bite us hard if Drake pulls his money out of the city. This was meant to be the start of a bold new era.'

'I wouldn't blame him if he did, but it might not be a complete loss.' McLean waved a hand at the building. 'This wasn't his doing, but it was his fault. Depends how well he takes acknowledging that. If he tries to blame us, then there's not a lot I can do about that. I've met the man a couple of times though, and he's not what I was expecting. Might be he learns his lesson and starts over.'

'We can but hope.'

'Aye, about that.' McLean turned away from the building, faced the chief superintendent. He didn't need to say any more for her to understand the change of subject.

'DC Fairley. Connor. He's . . .?' McIntyre appeared unable to quite finish the question.

'I'm afraid so. They've taken him to the mortuary already. I don't envy Angus his job there.'

McLean had spoken briefly to his old friend the pathologist. It wasn't the first time Cadwallader's patient had been a police officer, but Fairley was almost certainly the youngest. His loss was going to hit the team hard.

'How's Janie holding up?' McIntyre asked, as if reading his thoughts.

'She's around here, somewhere.' McLean raised his head and scanned the crowd. With the unsynchronised whirling of blue squad car lights, it was hard to make out individuals in the mess of people coming and going. Harrison helped by appearing out of the throng headed their way.

'Good God, Janie. What happened to you? Are you all right?' McIntyre asked.

'This?' Harrison lifted up her hand, streaked in blood. It was all over her jacket and blouse too, flaking off her neck. 'It's not mine.'

'Is that meant to make me feel better?' McIntyre looked from McLean to Harrison and then back again. He'd seen that look of hers before, knew she was blaming him for this. Whatever this was.

'It's mostly Nathaniel Drake's,' Harrison said, as if wearing the blood of a billionaire was the most normal thing in the world. 'I'll get cleaned up soon as I can, but there's a crime scene to organise first. Then I suppose I'd better go and see Connor Fairley's mum.'

'You'll do no such thing, Janie.' McIntyre stepped forward and took Harrison firmly by the arm. 'You're coming with me. We're taking you home.'

'But . . .' Harrison began to protest, her eyes bright with adrenaline. McLean was just thinking that any moment she was going to crash when it actually happened. Fortunately for Harrison, McIntyre saw it coming too, her grip firm enough to stop the young detective inspector from collapsing.

'Here, let me help you,' he said as he took Harrison's other arm and together they steered her to the waiting car. A look of horror passed over the face of the uniformed driver as he saw the state of his new passenger, but he rallied swiftly. In moments they had a still-protesting Harrison in the back seat, McIntyre settling in beside her.

'I've already had Connor's old sergeant go and speak to his mother,' she said more to McLean than the detective inspector. 'We can pay her a visit tomorrow, when this is all dealt with and we've a few more answers for her.'

'It should have been me broke the news,' Harrison said in a

quiet voice, almost as if she was trying to convince herself as much as anyone else.

'There shouldn't have been any news to break,' McLean said, then immediately regretted it. They were both tired, probably in varying degrees of shock. He should be handing over the scene to someone else, but instead he gently closed the car door and watched as it drove off. Then he turned to the building where everything had started, and headed back inside.

They brought the professor out on a gurney as McLean was contemplating how to get Emma's little Renault out of the car park, boxed in as it was by squad cars and forensics vans. That the gurney was being wheeled towards the last remaining ambulance gave the DCI a little hope, but it was dashed when he saw the white sheet drawn all the way over the body. Odd they'd not put him in a bodybag.

'Didn't make it then?' he asked one of the paramedics as they stopped at the back of the ambulance. The young man gave him a strange look before answering.

'It's an odd one, sir. Could've sworn we had a heartbeat when we arrived down in . . .' He paused a moment. 'Down there.'

'A heartbeat?' McLean considered the white sheet and whether he wanted to lift it enough to see the professor's face one last time. Decided on balance he'd rather not.

'Aye, sir. Only, it was weird. Weak, you know? But in the wrong place, too. Almost like it was in his stomach, not, you know, where a heart's meant to be.'

McLean pictured the scene as best he could, although down in the basement lab he'd been cowering for his life and the operating table had obscured most of the view. Caine had been trying to choke DI Harrison, but Janie had fought back, forced the professor's mouth open and . . . What? Everything had changed at that moment, hadn't it? He found he couldn't easily remember at all.

'I'm sure you did everything you could,' he said to the worried-looking paramedic. 'Not your fault this one didn't make it.'

The paramedic didn't look all that reassured, but he nodded once all the same. McLean stood to one side as the body was loaded into the ambulance and watched it drive slowly away.

He still wasn't going to get his own car out any time soon, so he went back into the building, retracing his route to the underground lair. It had begun to fill up now with forensic technicians in white paper overalls, although quite what they were hoping to find, McLean wasn't sure. He wasn't going to question them all the same, even pulled on his own set of overalls when asked to.

'Hell of a place this,' one of the technicians said as he stepped back into the large central operating theatre. 'Like some kind of movie set, aye?'

That it took him so long to recognise Manda Parsons was good reason for McLean to excuse himself from the scene and go home. He had one last task to perform before he could do that though. Or two now, he realised.

'Oh, hi Manda. Thought you were away on some training do.'

'I was. Got back early and had every intention of spending the day at home. While I've still got a home to stay at. Only there was a call about trouble here in the science park and I just knew you'd be at the centre of it.'

'Well, I'm glad you came. It's a right bloody mess. Mind you, I'm not sure what you hope to find down here. I mean, I was here, I saw everything that happened. Janie too.'

A look of concern creased the forensic technician's face. 'She still here? She looked in a right state when I saw her earlier.'

'Jayne McIntyre's taken her home. Might be an idea if you could delegate whatever it is you're doing here and maybe go give her some moral support. She was a lot closer to what went down here. Two people have died, and that's shaken her up more than she'll admit.'

'That sounds like J.' Parsons pulled the paper hood down, her dirty blonde hair tumbling out in long curls. 'We're only really getting set up in here. Could take us days to process the whole place. I'll ask Steve to take over and head home. For however much longer we can call it that.'

'Aye, I heard. If there's anything I can do to help, you just need to ask. Got a couple of spare rooms if you're in a bind.'

'Thanks, Tony. Hope it won't come to that, mind. I've some places lined up for us to go and see, but this city's not cheap to live in any more.' With a single shake of the head, she wandered off in search of Steve, although how anyone could tell who was who when they were all wearing identical white suits, McLean couldn't say.

Apart from the removal of Drake, Caine and Janie Harrison, the room wasn't much different to how it had been before. Hardly surprising since it was only a couple of hours since he'd made it back upstairs and called it in. Everything was where it had been, the remote console still full of holes, the gun still resting on the stainless-steel trolley alongside the open puzzle box, the dark square of floor pocked and speckled with Nathaniel Drake's blood. For the first time, McLean wondered what the whole place had been intended for, with its hermetically sealed isolation cells and fully kitted-out post-mortem wing as well as all this.

Questions they might have put to Caine, had he survived, and that wasn't the only problem his death created. Professional Standards would be all over this by the end of the day, which meant at best Harrison would be on administrative leave until they'd done their digging. Well, he'd do what he could to keep them off her back, as would McIntyre and Ritchie. Meanwhile there was a different matter he needed to attend to. A question needing an answer. McLean scanned the floor around the operating table, both inside and out of that strange dark area. Aside from the scant evidence of Harrison's struggle with the professor, there was nothing. Treading as lightly as he could, he peered under the table and trolley, found the scalpel lying in a pool of congealed blood, but nothing else anywhere.

'Looking for something, sir?'

McLean almost brained himself on the underside of the operating table as he straightened up to see a young man in full white forensic overalls staring down at him. Steve, no doubt.

'Have you swept this place yet? Bagged anything up?' As he asked the question, McLean's gaze fell to the puzzle box and gun, more or less answering his question for him.

'Not yet, no. We'll mark it all for photographs and a scene plan first. Unless . . .' The question went unasked, but McLean knew the hope behind it. Unless none of this was necessary really, and they could all pack up and go home. If it had been up to him he would have said yes. The chances of anyone other than Professor Caine being held to account for what had happened here were slim, and he was past being charged for his crimes. A lot of politicians and senior police officers would be happiest if that was as far as it went.

'Probably best if it all gets sealed up for now. We already know who did this. The how and the why can wait.'

As he spoke, McLean moved across to the small steel table, looked down at the gun and the puzzle box. Up close, the former looked heavy, likely Eastern European, he'd guess, although he was no expert on firearms. The latter sat with its lid open, vibrant red velvet lining empty. Aware that he was being watched, he picked it up, expecting at the very least a sharp intake of breath, but Steve the forensic technician said nothing.

The box didn't feel particularly strange or special, but then it never had to him. Its odd effects had only happened to others. He turned it upside down, tapped the bottom gently and watched as a tiny bit of dust fluttered out onto the tabletop.

'Maybe bag this and the gun and get them to evidence,' he said as he placed the box back as close to where it had been as he could manage. 'Everything else will still be here tomorrow.'

50

For all that it could be dangerous, police work was seldom fatal. In her short career as a police officer, Janie had been spared the trauma of having to attend too many funerals. The previous services she'd attended had been for old sergeants who'd dropped dead of a heart attack the week after retiring, that sort of thing. Today's gathering was very different.

Connor Fairley hadn't been a police officer long, and had been plain clothes little more than a year. In many ways that made his death so much the worse. A career and a life cut cruelly short. He'd borne the brunt of being the newbie on the team with a stoicism that suggested he might have made a good detective, had he been given the chance. Fate, and Professor Magnus Caine, had robbed him of that.

He'd obviously been liked, given the turnout. Best dress uniforms, a eulogy from the chief superintendent, and a guard of honour to take the coffin from the church to the waiting hearse, then on to a plot at Liberton cemetery where his father already lay. Janie had found out far more about Connor Fairley since he'd died than she'd ever known while working alongside him. No doubt she would find out even more as the inquiry into his death rumbled on.

'That was a good service, for all that I wish it had never had to happen.' Chief Superintendent McIntyre cut a path through the crowd towards Janie. Dressed in full uniform, she was an imposing, intimidating figure, junior officers scattering out of her way.

'Your eulogy was nice. But aye, it shouldn't have happened at all. Whole thing's a . . .' Janie tailed off, unsure quite how to end the sentence without swearing, which felt wrong standing outside a church.

'How's administrative leave suiting you?' McIntyre asked, which only made her want to curse more.

'Frustrating, unnecessary, annoying. There's so much work to do and we're tied up looking for someone to blame when we all know who it was. Best way to honour Connor's memory would be to make sure it never happens again.'

'You're not wrong, but the procedure needs to be followed at least for this. You've a promising career ahead of you, Janie. Don't want this as a black mark.'

'Is it not already?'

'No. At least, not if I have any say in the matter.'

Janie stared across the heads of the crowd towards the waiting hearse. 'They're saying he had an aneurism. Slow-acting. Affected his behaviour for twenty-four hours or so before he died. Probably to do with being punched in the head at the tower block.'

'That's what they're saying, aye,' McIntyre confirmed. 'Post mortem showed localised brain damage, poor soul.'

'It's bollocks though, isn't it.' Janie only realised what she had said and to whom after the words came out, tried to make it better by adding 'ma'am'.

'I know. But this way nobody's getting the blame of it, least of all Connor himself. It's the best we can do.'

Janie kept her gaze on the distance as the hearse pulled away. She didn't want to say anything she might regret later, and there was an awful lot she wanted to say.

'How's the hunt for a new flat coming along?' McIntyre asked, helpfully changing the subject.

'How did you . . .?' Janie began to ask, but then realised she worked for Police Scotland, where gossip was like the air they all breathed.

'We can help, if necessary. We don't have police housing any more, but the principle's still the same. Can't have senior detectives too worried about where they're going to sleep to do their jobs properly.'

'Thanks, but I think we're going to be OK. One positive of being on administrative leave is I've had a bit more time to search. Manda's come up with some options too, and it's possible Cerys might join us. It opens up a whole load more options if we're looking for a three-bed place, even if the rents are mental.'

'We had it easy, my generation,' McIntyre said. 'Oh, it didn't feel that way at the time, but I managed to put down a deposit on a place when I was still a sergeant. Even after mortgage and bills I still had plenty of money left at the end of the month. I don't know how you all cope now.'

'Aye, well. Maybe if I win the lottery I can get a place of my own. It's either that or marry a billionaire, and I don't much fancy the only one I know.'

The chief superintendent smiled at that, but it faded away quickly enough. A subject they were both trying to avoid.

'How is Cerys, by the way?' she asked instead.

'Oh, she's fine. It'll take more than a bang on the head to slow her down. I think she's as frustrated being on medical as I am on admin. Neither of us take to idleness well. I guess helping us look for a flat keeps her busy until the doctors give her the OK.'

'I'm glad to hear it. Would be nice if we could track down who did that to her, but I suspect they've long since fled the country.'

'Serbia would be my guess. That seems to be the crowd Professor Caine worked with most closely. He has family there, I'm told. Had, I should say.'

McIntyre merely nodded at that. Caine's post mortem had

revealed his cause of death to be a heart attack. His own heart. In the place where it was supposed to be. There had been no sign of any obstruction in his throat or recently ingested contents in his stomach. Janie hadn't been able to attend the examination, of course, being on administrative leave and at the constant beck and call of Professional Standards. Tom MacPhail had emailed her the report anyway, and Cerys had given her the full rundown too.

'I've no need or particular desire to go to the wake,' the chief superintendent said after the silence had drawn on a little longer than was comfortable.

'I was thinking much the same, except that I should probably show face, say something to Connor's mum.'

'There'll be constables and sergeants there aplenty. You'd only cramp their style now you're a DI.' McIntyre began walking towards the road where a car waited to take her back to the station. Or like as not across the country to yet another meeting of the top brass. Not quite knowing why, Janie fell into step alongside her, stopping only when they reached the car and the driver opened the rear passenger door for the chief superintendent to climb in. A plastic carrier bag with the Waitrose logo printed on its sides lay somewhat incongruously in the footwell. McIntyre leaned in and fetched it out, holding it for Janie to take.

'There is something that needs to be done, and it would probably be best if you were the one to do it. I'd ask Tony, but you know what he's like. Perhaps not strictly proper procedure, though I can make it an order if you want.'

The back entrance to the house was a lot less grand than the front. Janie had always wondered at the tiny shops on this stretch of Leith Walk, built out from what must once have been gardens of the larger houses behind. The door she picked was half glass, with a faded sign in it that read 'Fortunes Told, Tarots Read, Occult Curios' in an elegant cursive script. When she tried the handle, it resisted for a moment before letting her in, as if she had been scanned by some invisible force and found to be an acceptable visitor. Beyond, a narrow corridor sandwiched between the shops on either side ended at a steep set of stairs that took her to the first floor.

'Not often you use the tradesman's entrance, Janie dear.' Madame Rose greeted her in a drab reception room immediately off the top of the stairs.

'It seemed appropriate this time, since I'm sort of here on police business.' Janie hefted the bag she had carried across town, direct from Connor Fairley's funeral and no chain of evidence forms to sign. Madame Rose tilted her head ever so slightly, nodded once.

'I see,' she said. 'Come through to my office.'

The room beyond reception was unlike any office Janie had ever been in, but then Rose was unlike any other person she had ever met, too. An antique desk sat in one corner, its top heaped with old books, strange artefacts and even a few rolled parchments. Nothing so mundane as a computer or tablet. The walls were lined with dark wooden shelves, heaped with more books, curios and things for which she had no name. At least three pairs of eyes stared down from the shadows, cats as black as the night regarding her with indifference. 'Cluttered' would be a good word for the place, only the centre clear of decades, maybe centuries, of stuff. And right in the middle of a faded Persian rug, a table with two chairs opposite one another held something decidedly crystal-ball shaped, hidden under a pearl-white silk sheet.

'Chief . . .' Janie started, then remembered there was history between the two of them. 'Jayne McIntyre asked me to bring you this. She thought it would be safer in your keeping than tucked away on a shelf in evidence.'

'Its power is mostly gone, but she's probably right.' Madame Rose took the offering from Janie's unresisting grip and placed it on the table before pulling out the puzzle box, still in a clear plastic evidence bag. The lid was closed, but opened easily when the medium had unwrapped everything and flipped it with a single finger. The join between lid and box was clear to see now, unlike before when it had somehow merged seamlessly into the patterned inlay. Janie peered inside, seeing only dark red velvet lining.

'It killed him. Professor Caine,' she said. 'After I . . .' The memory of forcing that hard little nugget into the professor's mouth, the look of utter horror on his face as he realised what she had done, the way it had somehow slithered down his throat. Janie was almost over-whelmed by it all, until she felt a warm hand on her own.

'You can let it all go now, Janie.' Madame Rose guided her to one of the two chairs, sat her down before taking the one opposite. She let her arms rest either side of the covered-up crystal ball, as if preparing herself for a reading.

'Let what go, though? What happened? What were those whispers I could hear? What happened to poor Connor Fairley? They're away burying him right now.'

Janie could hear the panic growing in her voice, stopped talking and made a conscious effort to calm herself. Madame Rose gave her a few moments before beginning to explain.

'They're laying young Connor to rest alongside his father, I understand. Poor man died when Connor was young, the cancer got him. The thing you need to know about Jim Fairley is that his father was an immigrant. Came to Edinburgh from a remote village in what is now Moldova. Don Gatford probably doesn't know it, but he has Eastern European blood in his veins, albeit very dilute. Paul Sanderson likewise, on his mother's side as it happens. And of course, Vaclav Mihailovic was born and raised in Belgrade. No doubt the professor would call it genetics or something equally complicated, but it all comes down to blood in the end. None of theirs was com-patible with . . .' The medium gestured towards the now-empty box. '. . . not even Caine himself. Being close to it was enough to kill poor Connor; imagine what having it actually inside you might do.'

A deep shudder ran up Janie's spine, the short hairs on the back of her neck bristling as if someone had blown chill air on her bare skin. There was a sort of logic to Rose's explanation, but only if you discounted reason and science. It didn't explain how she had been affected by the box herself, either. As far as she was aware her family tree was rooted firmly in Scottish soil. But then she had reacted differently to it compared to the detective constable, or any of the others exposed.

'I know you're sceptical, Janie. I understand,' Rose said, perhaps taking her silence as an invitation to continue. 'I'll do my best to explain what I can anyway. The heart, the magus, wanted to be reborn. That was ever part of his quest for eternal life, after all. Even with the best of medical science, a body begins to fail eventually. So he would seek out a new one, compatible with his own, and transfer his animus to it.'

'Animus?' Janie asked, the question out before she could stop herself.

'What some would call the soul, the life force, the essence of the man he had first been. All that, and the knowledge gleaned from lifetimes, were trapped inside that shrivelled lump of a heart, festering and fading away to nothing. Until Professor Caine came along, of course. To revive the magus, he needed a suitable body. He was first and foremost a man of science, so he set about finding a compatible subject using that tool. DNA analysis, studying bloodlines, genetic therapies.'

'The clinical trials?'

'Were a means of screening for potential subjects. Any who showed promise could be exposed to the puzzle box and the heart within, over a few hours, a few days, even a few weeks.'

'Mihailovic,' Janie said.

'Exactly. And Professor Caine had close ties with the city's Serbian community too. He is – was – half Serbian himself.'

McIntyre had told Janie as much after the funeral, but it surprised her that Rose knew.

'But what about Nathaniel Drake? He's American. Does he have Serbian ancestors too?'

'Not as far as I can find out, no. But he would have made the perfect host. Obscenely rich, hugely influential, who wouldn't want to be him? And of course it's public knowledge that he's been looking for a way to cheat death for years now. So the good professor began using his science and the knowledge gleaned from all the many test subjects he'd inflicted the box upon to start changing his employer at the genetic level.'

'Is that even possible?'

'I deal in what you would consider magic, Janie dear, not science. Anything is possible. You only have to look at photographs of Mr Drake over the past couple of years to see how much he has changed physically. There are gene therapies that can treat any number of ailments nowadays. Instructions carried into the body on the backs of modified viruses. It takes time to change a person at that level though. Or at least I would imagine so.'

Janie was going to protest that the reason for his change was his weird life-extending obsession and the lifestyle that went with it, but much of that had been under the direction of Professor Magnus Caine. She rubbed at her face with both hands. 'So that's why I heard whispering the first time I met him then. I thought it was his PA making calls while we were talking, but it was a reaction to the gene therapy he was undergoing. Like he was giving off weird pheromones or something.'

'I'd call it magic, myself, but you can always pretend it doesn't exist, I suppose. Like Tony does.' Madame Rose's smile had a little too much knowing in it for Janie's liking. The medium picked up the puzzle box and put it away in its bags, then stood up, indicating for Janie to do the same. 'Let's get this somewhere safe, eh? Then we can both go and have a nice cup of tea.'

51

The knock came as McLean was hefting the kettle onto the hotplate, someone at the back door. When he went through the boot room to see who it was, the figure waiting to be invited in was unexpected.

'Mr Drake?'

'Detective Chief Inspector. I hope you don't mind me dropping round like this.' The billionaire had one arm in a sling, that side of his coat hanging limp. He raised the other hand, from which swung a bottle-sized paper bag. 'I don't drink, and I know nothing about whisky except that you Scots get very annoyed when we spell it with an e. They tell me this is good stuff though.'

'That's very kind of you, but—'

'Oh, I know. You can't accept gifts that might be thought bribes and all that. Go ahead and declare it if you want, or whatever it is you have to do. It's only a bottle of whisky.'

McLean inclined his head at that, accepted the bag when Drake handed it to him. 'Thank you. I've just put the kettle on, was making a pot of tea, if you drink that?'

'Tea? Why not. I do love your quaint British customs.'

Through in the kitchen the kettle was pumping steam into the air. McLean bade Drake take a seat, and then went about the ceremony of preparing tea.

'How's Em?' the billionaire asked.

'Good as she can be. She's away at physiotherapy this evening, then off to see Madame Rose about something. Sure she told me what, but I guess I wasn't listening.'

'Ah, the redoubtable Madame Rose. You keep strange company, McLean, but she's quite fascinating. I hope I'll have a chance to speak to her again soon.'

'You could always pay her a visit. I'm sure she'd be more than happy to tell your fortune.'

Drake laughed, lines wrinkling around his eyes. His face was more animated than the first time they had met. He looked older, too. Or perhaps not older so much as less fake.

'I think I've had enough of the mystic mumbo jumbo for now, thanks.' The laughter faded away.

'They tell me Magnus died of a heart attack. Is that true?'

McLean nodded as he poured tea into two mugs, offered Drake milk and sugar which he declined.

'Aye, that's what the post-mortem report said, and I spoke to the pathologist too. There were also some mitigating factors I didn't quite understand. Seems the professor hadn't been following proper lab protocols.' He shook his head, suppressed an ironic smile. 'But we already know he wasn't following proper lab protocols, don't we. The lab hadn't been licensed for use, for one thing, and he was using a gang of Serbian immigrants to do most of his dirty work.'

McLean didn't add that they had one of those immigrants in custody and were sweating a lot of useful information out of him. Drake might know, of course. That was the problem with billionaires; their money gave them access to otherwise privileged information.

'I feel such an idiot, the way he fooled me for all those years. Gave him a blank cheque book and this is how he repaid me.' Drake lifted his hand towards the point on his chest where the incision had been made.

'How is it?' McLean asked, tilting his head in the same direction.

'Damned sore.' Drake took his hand away, flexing his fingers as he did so. 'And I'm going to have a nasty scar. But I'm alive, and I have you to thank for that. Hence . . .' He nodded at the paper bag sitting on the table.

'It's DI Harrison you should be thanking, not me. She's the one stopped Caine from cutting your heart out or whatever it was he was trying to do.'

Drake's face turned sober at the recollection. 'Truth be told, the whole series of events is a bit of a blur. I remember going to the lab to confront him about the box after you showed me that photograph, but that's about all until I woke up in the hospital best part of a day later. But I do remember Harrison standing over me with those lights behind her making it look like she had a halo, so yeah, I get that I owe her my life. And I know I can't give her anything for it neither. Bottle of whisky's too cheap for what she did for me anyway. I have done something though, made a few calls. She'll never know and I'll never tell. Let's leave it at that, yeah?'

Despite all his reservations, McLean found it hard to dislike Drake. There was no subterfuge about him, no hidden agenda, or at least none he'd been able to detect. Yes, the man wanted to live forever young, but he was quite upfront about it. He could have used his wealth and influence to make the events of the past weeks go away; could have got on his private jet and flown back to America, never to be seen in Scotland again. Instead he'd stayed in Edinburgh, been as helpful as he could, as shocked as the rest of them at what Professor Caine had been doing without his knowledge. And it genuinely did seem to be without his knowledge. He'd trusted Caine, fallen for the professor's wild claims and promising early results. Naive rather than corrupt, was McLean's assessment of Nathaniel Drake. And Emma liked him too, which, as far as McLean was concerned, meant a lot.

'On the subject of knowing things,' he said. 'Probably lose my job for saying this, but the break-in that started it all off? That was a put-up job. I'm not sure exactly which agency, some government department that wants to know everything you're getting up to in that lab of yours. They put something into your network. Virus, trojan, search me. I know less about computers than those two cats.' McLean nodded his head towards the Aga, where two round bundles of fur were pretending not to listen in on the conversation.

'I've some pretty good skills in that department, you know?' Drake raised one stiff arm and took a sip of tea. Whether the grimace was pain from his wound or he'd been lying about liking such 'quaint British customs', McLean couldn't tell. 'First thing we did after the break-in was scan the entire system. Didn't find anything obvious, but there's code that can be slipped into legitimate software that won't wake itself up before a given time. That shit's almost impossible to detect unless you know exactly what you're looking for.'

'Well, it's there. Count on it.'

'If it is, it's not going to find anything.' Drake smiled, his unnaturally straight and brilliant white teeth gleaming in the evening sunlight through the window. 'I'm going to have the whole system ripped out. Physically disconnect all the servers and replace the whole lot. That'll be expensive, let me tell you, but the whole site's been compromised both by what Magnus did with it and your lot going in heavy-handed after. Guess I'll have to make it back by charging your government extra for the first proper treatment to come out of the place.'

'You're keeping it going? Still trying to cure death?'

'Might have my sights aimed a little lower than that.' Drake raised his mug again. 'For now. I've asked Caroline Wheeler if she'll run the place for me.'

'She's a good choice,' McLean said. 'Deserves a break, too. The NHS's loss is your gain.'

'Oh, I reckon she'll still put in shifts up at the hospital now and then. She takes her patient care very seriously, does Caroline.'

'Well, she's patched up me and Emma both in the past. Looked after my grandmother before she died, too. I can't see her trying to take your heart any time soon.'

He'd meant it as a joke, but something in Drake's expression suggested McLean's words had hit closer to home than he'd intended. Or perhaps, like the wounds in his chest and arm, the memory was still too raw for such dark humour.

'Thank you, McLean. For letting me know about the break-in and everything else.'

'Please, call me Tony. McLean sounds like I'm back in school being shouted at by the headmaster.'

That brought a smile at least. 'Tony, then.' Drake lifted his mug in salute, took a sip, grimaced a little. 'This really is very good tea.'

Mortonhall Crematorium held many memories, few of them happy. The urn containing the ashes of McLean's grandparents was in the garden of remembrance there, alongside another urn allegedly holding the last remains of his parents. Not much left of them after the plane crash that had killed them a few months after his fourth birthday, he'd always been a little sceptical about their ashes. It was a focus for remembering them, he supposed, although in truth he could recall very little about them at all. Certainly hadn't been to pay his respects in far too long.

Not many people had turned out to mark the cremation of Professor Magnus Caine, either. A couple of dozen elderly friends and relatives, former colleagues perhaps, McLean couldn't be sure. He was probably the youngest in the chapel apart from the staff.

He slipped out before the service had finished, using his warrant card to gain access to the furnace room. The business of death wasn't something he would normally care too much about, but a part of him needed to see the body committed to the flames. To be certain it was gone, and with it any last vestiges of whatever had been in that puzzle box. Not that he believed in any of that stuff, but it never hurt to make sure.

The mortuary workers treated him as if he were a grieving relative, doing their best to make the clinical job of pushing the coffin into the cremator as dignified as possible. McLean didn't care. Chuck the man on an open fire and scatter his ashes into fast-flowing water. He'd been responsible for at least three deaths, probably many more. And one of those had been a fine young man at the start of a promising career. All for nothing. For the promise of eternal youth he had ended actual youth. What a waste.

Coming out of the furnace room back into the light, McLean understood how Orpheus must have felt emerging from the underworld. A sense of relief mixed with disappointment. Had he been expecting more closure? Some great sign that evil had finally been vanquished? Too much time spent in the company of Madame Rose, he was losing his sceptical edge.

A familiar figure stood by the entrance to the chapel as he made his way to the car park. Harrison was with two other women of a similar age McLean didn't recognise. All three wore black, although to be fair, Harrison dressed that way for work most days.

'Didn't expect to see you here, Janie,' he said as he approached them. Closer up, he found he did recognise one of the women, from photographs attached to various investigation reports. Nadia Petrović, a woman with an interesting and chequered past, currently helping out the modern slavery investigation unit.

'Could say much the same thing, s—Tony.' Harrison corrected herself at the last moment, as she always did. 'What brings you to this cheerful place?'

'They're just now cremating Magnus Caine. I wanted to make sure, you know?' Now that he voiced it out loud, his unnamed anxiety sounded even more daft. To her credit, Harrison didn't mock him for it. Quite the opposite.

'Was that today? I wish I'd known. I'd have come earlier.'

'Caine. He was the one who . . .?' The third woman in the group left the question hanging.

'Aye, he was the one started this all.' Harrison seemed to remember herself. 'Sorry, Tony, this is Shauna Lennox, and I think you know Nadia. Shauna, Nadia, this is my boss, Detective Chief Inspector McLean.'

Of the two women, McLean might have expected the trafficked asylum seeker to be the most suspicious of a senior police officer, but it was the other one, Lennox, who flinched. He offered her what he hoped was a reassuring smile, but it didn't seem to make her any more relaxed.

'So you're here for . . .?' he tried.

'Vaclav Mihailovic,' Harrison said. 'Strange to be cremating both men on the same day, but then maybe not.'

'Well, they've finished with Caine. I made a nuisance of myself and made sure nothing was left to chance. I don't think we need worry about him any more.'

Harrison gave an involuntary shudder, which might have been down to the winter cold settling in, but probably wasn't.

'Found a new place to live,' she said by way of changing the subject. 'Not far from the old one, actually. It's three beds, so Cerys is moving in with us. Cheaper than the old place, if you can believe that?'

McLean recalled his visit from Nathaniel Drake, the absurdly expensive bottle of whisky the billionaire had given him and his words about wanting to thank Harrison too. What were the chances the owner of her new place turned out to be some holding company of a holding company, all the way back to the man whose life she had undoubtedly saved? Well, he wasn't going to say anything.

'That's great news, Janie. Although the three of you together in one flat sounds like a sitcom waiting to be written.'

'Aye, well. We'll see. It's no bad thing I'm still on leave or we'd maybe have missed the place. Going to need the time off to shift everything, too.'

McLean doubted anyone else would have been given the opportunity to rent this mysterious new flat, but there was no need to say so. 'Well, if you need any help, give us a shout. I'm sure I can find someone to lift heavy things for you.'

'Thanks, Tony. I appreciate it.' Harrison looked past him towards the chapel entrance. 'Think that's us now. We'd better get moving.'

McLean stepped aside to let the three women past, watched as they entered the chapel. Glancing up at the tall chimney that rose from the far end, he half expected to see sinister black smoke belching into the grey winter sky as the last few scraps of Professor Magnus Caine were burned away. But there was nothing, of course. Why should there be?

With a shrug of the shoulders, he turned and walked away.

52

S he doesn't like to leave her home too often, certainly not to
travel so far as this. Things happen when she's not there to
keep an eye on them, and it's always a pain sorting them out afterwards. Mind you, things happen when she is there, too, so maybe
she just likes to complain.

It's a nice spot here, even if the winter air is bitter cold. There's
snow on the ground and clinging to the steep sides of the mountains that surround this place like a wall. The forest is heavy with
it, trees with their branches weighed down to the ground. Even
the path she trod to this place was a struggle, though worth it for
the utter quiet and stillness all around.

'Well now, I suppose we had better get this done,' she says to
nobody. The air takes her words and turns them into steam as she
shuffles the pack from her back. Little weight to it, the snow barely
sinks at all as she places it carefully down.

Inside, the box still nestles in its clear plastic bag, courtesy
of Police Scotland. She shucks off the thick, fur-lined gloves,
blows on her fingers at the chill that aches her bones, then
removes her prize from its packaging, opens the lid and holds it
up to the sky.

How long she stands there, she cannot tell. There is a procedure to these things, a ritual, if you like, although in this case she

really doesn't. If anyone were near to observe, it would seem that nothing happens, and yet she knows better. She can feel the change, gentle at first, but slowly building to a crescendo as something coalesces out of nothing. Like mosquitoes improbably swarming in the depths of winter, a darkness begins to form above the open box. And with it comes a buzzing, whining sound that only she can hear. She and any dogs unfortunate enough to be nearby. She is confident there are none, for they would surely bark and whine as the pressure of that sound builds, chase their tails or cower at the feet of their masters.

Why does she think of dogs now? She isn't really sure. It matters not, for this ritual, this ceremony is almost at an end. She can feel the box grow heavier in her hand, both physically and as a spiritual thing. Dark and ominous, it fights her, tries to test her will, but she is more than equal to this task. Not her first rodeo, as that strange American would doubtless say.

When the end comes it is almost an anticlimax. The swarm squeezes down into a hard nugget of black that drops into the box with a satisfying thump. With a simple flick, the lid is closed, no gap visible on the intricately carved inlay of its once more shiny surface. She runs expert fingers over the lines, making sure there is no mistake this time. No way out for the spirit trapped within. She can feel it in there, sense its rage and impotence both. Good. This is the way it has to be.

She places the box on the top of the low mound that sits in the very centre of this clearing. Heavier now, it sinks slowly into the snow, and then on through the earth and deep into the ground. She waits, listening with senses far more delicate than hearing as the box sinks deeper, deeper, until finally it comes to a rest. There is no mark of where it has passed, save for a little scuffing on the surface. The next snowfall will cover that swiftly enough.

'Good,' she says, as she pulls on her gloves once more, stoops to pick up the now empty pack and sling it over her shoulder. Without a backward glance, Madame Rose crunches her way out of the clearing along the path she made coming in. That didn't take as long as she feared it would. With luck she can be home in time for a nice cup of tea.

Acknowledgements

If you're looking for someone to blame for what you've just read, that's my name on the cover and I accept full responsibility. Having said which, many wonderful people have worked tirelessly to curb the worst of my excesses and encourage me to always do better. First among them are the team at Wildfire Books. They should all be credited on the next page, but a special thanks to Alex Clarke, Jack Butler and Areen Ali. And to Jill Cole for the excellent copy editing.

It's no secret that I am a huge fan of audiobooks – the only way I could read even a fraction of the books I would like to while still tending to the farm. All fourteen of these books have been brought to life magnificently by Ian Hanmore. Thank you, Ian, for your patience as much as your great skill.

Thanks also to my agent, the tireless Juliet Mushens, and all the team at Mushens Entertainment – Liza DeBlock, Rachel Neely, Kiya Evans, Alba Arnau Prado, Catriona Fida and Emma Dawson (and not forgetting Den and Seth!). You're the best!

Thank you to the booksellers, the librarians, the festival organisers and volunteers who make the literary world work. And thank you, too, if you've read this book and not thrown it at the wall in disgust. Whether you bought it with your own money, were given it as a gift, borrowed it from a library or had it thrust upon you by a stranger, I don't mind. That you have read it is enough, and I thank you for that. Without readers, I'd probably still carry on writing, but it wouldn't be half as much fun.

And finally, although perhaps most importantly, a huge thank you to my partner Barbara, whose surname I stole for my errant detective over thirty years ago. Someone has to mind the farm while I'm away in my fictional world, and she does it without complaint.

Credits note

With thanks to everyone who worked on the publication of *The Rest is Death*:

Editorial
Alex Clarke
Jack Butler
Areen Ali

Copyeditor
Jill Cole

Proofreader
Sarah Bance

Audio
Ellie Wheeldon

Production
Inka Melson

Design
Patrick Insole

Marketing
Katrina Smedley

Publicity
Federica Trogu

Sales
Rebecca Bader
Rebecca Swales
Jess Harvey
Eleanor Wood

Contracts
Helen Windrath

Finance
Will Blight